OPERATION
ARGUS

Maskirovka:
Are You Ready for the Truth?

WILLY MITCHELL

OPERATION ARGUS
MASKIROVKA: ARE YOU READY FOR THE TRUTH?

iUniverse books may be ordered through booksellers or by contacting:

iUniverse
1663 Liberty Drive
Bloomington, IN 47403
www.iuniverse.com
1-800-Authors (1-800-288-4677)

ISBN: 978-1-5320-4769-5 (sc)
ISBN: 978-1-5320-4771-8 (hc)
ISBN: 978-1-5320-4770-1 (e)

Library of Congress Control Number: 2018904898

Print information available on the last page.

2nd Edition

iUniverse rev. date: 11/27/2019

For those soldiers who manage to lead lives beyond the atrocities.
For those loved ones who cope with the trauma of
life, war, poverty, sickness, and homelessness.

We are the Pilgrims, master; we shall go
Always a little further: it may be
Beyond the last blue mountain barred with snow,
Across that angry or that glimmering sea,
White on a throne or guarded in a cave
There lives a prophet who can understand
Why men were born: but surely, we are brave,
Who make the Golden Journey to Samarkand.
—James Elroy Flecker, "The Golden Journey to Samarkand"

CONTENTS

Part IV Who Dares

Part V Journey to Samarkand

ACKNOWLEDGMENTS

THANKS TO ALL THOSE WHOSE stories inspired this book, including everyone who has sacrificed for liberty, freedom, good, and right. Although this is a novel, it is based on true events. In most cases, the names have been changed to protect the innocent, the dirty, the rotten, the good, and the pure.

You know who you are.

WWW.WILLYMITCHELL.COM

PART I

CONVERGENCE

PROLOGUE

Willy Mitchell

AS A CHILD GROWING UP in Paisley on the outskirts of Glasgow, Scotland, I was often in bars with my father, my uncles, and my cousins and extended family. There were no options for us then—no Boy Scouts, summer houses, or school camps. The only option was for family to look after their own, and that often included hanging out in bars from an early age, watching the elders getting hammered for the most part, often followed by them hammering each other or someone else, and usually Uncle Tommy was at the center.

Now, there is a difference between a bar, a pub, and an inn. An inn has rooms, a pub has food, and a bar is for drinking only—the local workingman's club, snooker or pool hall, or, in my case, my aunty Agnes's house. She turned her living room into a bar to make some extra cash, and the other kids and I would sit on the sofa watching television while the elders of the clans enjoyed a drink.

Violence was a common occurrence—the MacKay's versus the Mcleoud's, the union versus the nonunion, the Catholics versus the Protestants, Celtic versus Rangers. It didn't really matter too much, as the excuse for violence levitated above the reasoning for violence itself.

As kids, we were bundled in the corner with our Irn Bru soda, watching the action kick off and watching our role models, some harder than others, make their point.

As a young man, thankfully I made it to relatively safe ground, away from Glasgow for a while, to the Black Watch, the famous Scottish Regiment of the British Army. I learned how to kill people while my friends back in Paisley learned how to kill themselves and each other. Some of the highest heroin, crack, and other deathly drug addiction levels in the United Kingdom, if not the Western world, took care of that.

Whether one remained or escaped was a major influence on life expectancy and prison evasion for those folks growing up in the wrong parts of Glasgow. Growing up in Glasgow and Scotland has always been tough, and for those who left, many were the soldiers of choice on the front line of the British Army for the past three hundred years for a reason.

Violent times continued. After years of working in shipyards on the Clyde, I continued the family tradition and spent a lot of time in drinking holes around Glasgow and on my travels around the world.

The one thing I learned is that you can always meet someone of interest in a bar, or at least you can listen to an interesting tale or two. I have discovered and heard many over the years, some stories taller than others.

The story I am about to tell you is true. I was there.

It was a typical cold Scottish night in November, which is to say the weather was unfit for man and beast. I sat in the Rhu Inn in Shandon by Gareloch, taking a pint of Belhaven Best Bitter and a wee nip of Talisker Whisky[1], minding my own business. Opened in 1648, the Rhu Inn had been around for a while—and so had the furnishings, the carpet, and everything else in it. The old white building with black signs bearing the name was tattered from age and Scottish winters past. Inside was much the same, with its dark lighting, smell of stale

---

[1] All references to the spirit, Whisky is in the Scottish spelling given the origin of the amber nectar. Whisky was given an added 'e' for the same spirit distilled outside of Scotland including Irish, American and Japanese Whiskey by way of example.

beer and whisky, and the landlords grateful for customers still willing to spend their money there.

Gareloch, home to Her Majesty's Naval Base Faslane, one of the three nuclear submarine bases in Scotland protecting the shores of the United Kingdom, was the focus of an eclectic group of people, including submariners, mariners, protestors, security folks, contractors, and me—a by-now career shipbuilding steward, running the local union to make sure they did what they were told. I despised the job, and like my grandfather, I also despised the union, but unlike Willie, I played the game and kept my job.

The time passed pleasantly enough. The drink imparted that familiar warm glow. I glanced up at the sound of new arrivals. My curiosity grew by the moment. There was something different about the men. They arrived in pairs, until within fifteen minutes there were eight of them grouped together—Englishmen, Sassenachs, a derogatory Scottish term for English folks dating back to the War for Scottish Independence as far back as the thirteenth century. These were not shipyard workers. They nestled around the end of the bar and quietly ordered Belhaven beers.

I noticed that while they were obviously together, they remained in pairs or in threes. Yet they seemed to share in a larger collective conversation, a common whole, a bond that glued them into a cohesive unit as they flittered comment and banter between them, jumping from one apparent conversation to another. It was like watching a group of worker bees, apparently individuals yet finely tuned to one another with invisible connections.

One of the men, wearing a black leather sports coat, black jeans, and black eight-lace boots, with a heavy mop of dark hair on his head and a strong Southwest English accent, was the comedian, cracking jokes, sharing sarcasm. He was heavyset, maybe five ten, with broad shoulders and a belly laugh, apparently named Dinger.

Tom was the wiry one, with long blond hair to the shoulders. He was boyishly good-looking with the sparkly blue eyes of a modern-day Peter Pan and mischievousness written all over him. Wearing a checkered shirt hanging outside his worn blue jeans, and a pair of desert boots, he flirted with the barmaid and offered to buy her a drink. As she blushed in return, he asked her what she was doing after work that evening, making her blush even more.

Big Mal, as his nickname suggested, was a big man. Six feet five, built like a prop forward, a rugby player, he was a man of few words, but when he did speak, it was with a distinctive New Zealand accent, a Kiwi. An oversize canvas jacket covered the strength of the giant as he sipped his beer, patiently and quietly listening to the banter around him and assessing the patrons of the Rhu Inn, including me.

Red and Mitch were keen, attentive, and the quietest of the quiet bunch as they stood in the corner, always watchful and listening to all the conversations, occasionally having a dig at one of the crew or picking up on something that was said. They were the leaders of the group.

It seemed that the group was winding down like a performer winds down after getting off the stage—or like a football team that's just walked off the pitch after a cup final. As the drinks kept coming, the men all relaxed. I have always found it fascinating what watching and listening, especially in a bar, can reveal to the careful observer. Mac, with his mop of blond hair and youthful looks, his plain T-shirt and nice-looking jeans and shoes, was the smartest of all. Don't ask me how I knew this. I just did. The man looked like he had just come out of a photo shoot for a Marks & Spencer's discount clothing commercial.

On the other hand, Les was different. He wasn't as polished as Mac was. Apparently, Les wasn't his real name, as his last name was Dawson, after the then-famous British comedian Les Dawson. The group all found that funny and laughed. "Cheers, Les!" They raised their glasses and ordered another round of drinks.

One of the men, a guy called Vince, was a real character. He had dark curly hair and a moustache that you were more likely to see in an old porn movie. He was wearing desert boots and a blue-checkered shirt that hung over his jeans. I glanced over at Tom and compared their uniforms and apparent need for uniformity despite being in civilian dress. It gradually dawned on me that these men must have been soldiers—and tough ones at that. They carried themselves with an air of confidence, a sort of military swagger.

Vince was the last of the group to walk into the Rhu, arms widened beside him as though he were a gunslinger walking into a contest, or a bodybuilder with biceps too big for his arms, or, as Tom pointed out, possibly an employee at Allied Carpets who spent the day carrying rolls of carpet around, one under each arm. The group chuckled. Vince ignored them, ordered his beer, and stood alone. I could tell by his body language and expression that Allied Carpets was his nickname and one he despised. Vince was clearly the loner of the group.

I stepped out for a smoke in the chilly rain, taking shelter under the overhanging rafters at the rear of the pub. I made a call and smoked two fags. In the short time I was out there, the soldiers were in the process of reordering their next round. As I walked in, I could feel eight sets of eyes on me. Not a stare, not a glance, something different, something I had never experienced at that level of intensity before, something I would later understand to be termed as *being clocked*. They looked me over in their different ways, past my eyes and into my soul. I must have passed muster because they returned to their conversations.

Throughout that evening, I caught closely guarded snippets of *oil refineries, selection, Grangemouth, Belfast, the clock tower, Hereford, sticky carpets, Gonzo, a squadron sergeant major, boss, the Toms, the hangar, the Regiment.*

Several beers later, with only the nine of us left in the bar, the barmaid busy cleaning up and waiting for last orders, the old clock behind the bar showed 10:30 p.m. Les suddenly announced that he was taking bets of £100 each, saying he'd sneak onto the deck of one of the nuclear submarines at the nearby Faslane by dawn the next day. Wallets came out, and rolls of £20 notes appeared, along with sniggers and laughter that Les had apparently laid down the dare—apparently not the first time. The last time, he got RTU'd (returned to unit) and had to do selection for a second time to return.

Big Mal folded up the notes, grabbed a rubber band from behind the bar, wrapped up the wad neatly, and shoved it in the inside jacket pocket of his oversize coat and smiled at Les. "See you in the morning, Les!" he said.

Wager accepted, Les went off into the darkness on foot, and the rest of the group jumped into their mini fleet of Range Rovers and sped away into the dark. I watched them leave and then went home to my caravan and my Fray Bentos dinner.

The local TV news the next morning confirmed that an intruder had indeed made it onto one of the submarines. I watched the grainy footage of a man who looked a lot like Les speeding away under armed guard. Later, I found out that that was Les Dawson's last misdemeanor in the Regiment. The prankster was quickly relieved of his queen's shilling after a short stint in Colchester Military Prison. He never did see his £700 of winnings.

A few months later, I saw the news footage of an ill-fated Special Forces reconnaissance mission in Iraq on the BBC news. I immediately recognized many of those men I had encountered in the Rhu Inn.

Their call sign was Bravo2Zero.

I
SANCTUARY

San Francisco, California, United
States, October 2016, Day 1

ON LANE NINE OF THE shooting range, Mitch stood in a traditional boxer stance. His feet were positioned almost square but not quite. They were offset as if he was in a boxing ring, his left foot forward, his right foot slightly back. It was an orthodox right-hander's stance. Mitch's right arm was thrust out straight, and his left hand supported the main grip of the right holding the Browning 9 mm. He looked down the barrel. He was absolutely focused on the target downrange.

At six feet tall with broad boxer's shoulders, Mitch cut an imposing figure. Although he was no longer in the military, he carried himself like the warrior he once was. He was at the range to keep his marksmanship skills up to snuff even if he was a sure shot without regular practice. He let out a breath, slowed his heart rate, and went into the zone as he squeezed off multiple shots in rapid succession, each set of two rounds in perfect double-tap execution.

Bang! Bang! Bang! Bang!

He grinned when he saw the rounds pierce the target in a neat cluster around the X in the middle and the 10/10 scoring.

Mitch found solace at the shooting range. The world faded away, and all that mattered was the gun. He would head down to the range every week, not that he needed to practice that regularly—he was as accomplished as one could be with his weapon of choice—but it was more like a habit, something he believed he needed to do, as important as his daily run, his push-ups, his weights. These were the trainings of a former professional soldier that were hard to break. Mitch kept these rituals and disciplines in place.

He loaded his final magazine of the day, moved the target to its farthest distance, and let the entire contents loose one after another in rapid fire, all falling in the 9/10 zone of the B-27 target. "Nice," Mitch muttered to himself. He packed his Browning in its case along with the ten spare clips and zipped up the smart leather bag.

Mitch grabbed the old broom from the corner, swept his shells, disposed of his target, turned the lane light off, and headed to the exit. He shut the range door behind him before opening the opposite door back into the gun shop on the other side, removing his cans, no longer needed to protect his ears, at least for today.

Mitch stepped outside into the bright sunshine, noting that it was ten o'clock. He would head for a coffee and then on to see some of his boys at his boxing club in the Mission District, although, strictly speaking, it was not his boxing club at all. He had no ownership, no employment there, and no official role, but he went there each week as a ritual, another habit, a force of duty not dissimilar from going to see his boys, his soldiers, regularly, keeping in touch, encouraging, coaxing, coaching. Mitch was a natural leader, and men followed his lead gladly, sometimes all the way to war and unfortunately sometimes all the way to their graves.

That sat heavy with Mitch. Very heavy. A responsibility that was never really spelled out to him anywhere in his training. Death by proxy was difficult to cope with and internalize—having a hand in a soul losing its life, maybe as a direct result of one man's orders. It was worse to look in hindsight and identify the things that could have been done but weren't in the heat of the moment—often deadly moments. At his age, he'd lost the zeal of his youth. There were too many ghosts from the past that accompanied him as he went about his days.

Mitch had learned to box when he was a kid, eleven years old, growing up in a farming community in a rural town in the United Kingdom. His father was in business, so the family was reasonably well off. Some of the kids were envious about that, and Mitch was bullied. His strength of character, his genes, and his boxing helped put a stop to that over time, and as he progressed through the ranks, he added rugby to his repertoire. By the time he joined the army at the age of seventeen and a half, he was a well-accomplished athlete and fighter. Serving with the Blues and Royals, he reached the Army Boxing Final, played rugby for the Blues and Royals, then 29 Commando Regiment, 9 Parachute Squadron, and 22 Special Air Service.

His boys at the boxing club were mainly of Hispanic, South American origin and had their own reasons to turn to boxing, including, like Mitch, being bullied and needing to learn how to stick up for themselves, but also, the bling and fame associated with boxers like Floyd "the Money" Mayweather and Manny Pacquiao appealed to these young migrant kids. It was a way to get them, their parents, and their brothers, sisters, aunts, and cousins on the map in the United States of America, the land of their hopes and dreams.

Mitch would give them support, encouragement, and tips, and they all appreciated and respected him for it. As he headed across San Francisco on the number 14 bus, he remembered some of his own boxing exploits.

Later, he would head to the Marines Memorial Club for lunch at Leathernecks with Bella, his twenty-four-year-old daughter. Then he had arranged to meet with his old mate Paul at the Dubliner for a pint and to catch up.

Bella was the love of Mitch's life, the child of his first true love. He'd met Angela when he was only twenty-four, serving in the elite Special Air Service at Stirling Lines in Hereford, England. Angela, a first-generation American of Sicilian origin, was a stunning beauty. She'd stolen his heart within minutes of their first meeting all those years ago. Bella and her mother both lived in the marital home, across the Golden Gate, just ten miles away, but sometimes it seemed like they were a million miles apart from Mitch, who'd moved out of the house to live at the Veterans' Retreat in the Presidio. He'd separated from Angela for many reasons. One of them was he liked the order at the retreat, the tradition, the routine. He felt at home with his thoughts there. His many demons were less intrusive, though always lurking in the shadows of his darkest thoughts. The separation also reduced the risks for Angela and Bella. The threat of danger was never far from him, and he didn't want to expose the two women he loved to the horrors he'd seen, the horrors he could see if the wrong people showed up on his doorstep.

For a moment, Mitch felt the wave of terror and rage that had swept over him on the day he found out that Bella had been kidnapped. He took a deep breath, forcing the darkness back into its den as the bus weaved through traffic on Van Ness Avenue and passed the big Goodwill charity store, then proceeded on to the long drag up Mission Street.

Mitch and Paul had served in the Regiment together, 22 Special Air Service, and shortly after getting out, Mitch, Angela, and Bella moved to Angela's homeland in Northern California, followed by Paul, Betsy, and the girls. They lived in the same neighborhood, and the girls went to school with each other and grew up together as Mitch and Paul plied their trade as civilian contractors, not paid soldiers anymore. The money was a lot better out of uniform.

More and more, recently, Paul had been working closely with the CIA, FBI, and other clandestine, three-letter agencies from both sides of the Atlantic. Mitch didn't know what, but he instinctively knew that it was on something big. Of course, Paul couldn't say what he was doing. Mitch understood. That was just the way it had to be.

Mitch got off the number 14 at Mission and 26th Street and headed toward Valencia to the Chavez Gymnasium. Once in the front door, he grabbed a bottle of water and went toward the activity in the big hall behind.

"Morning, Mr. Mitch." The janitor smiled as he walked through.

"Morning, Benjamin," Mitch said with a warm smile and a pat on the back.

Mitch had been going there for a while; he knew all the staff, and they all knew him. He knew all the boys, and they all knew him. This was Mitch's gym after all.

As he walked into the former church hall with its wooden floor, the boxing ring was in the middle, and to either side were punching bags, weights, medicine balls, skipping ropes, and the familiar figure of Pat Durkin, Fighting Irish Pat Durkin, the San Franciscan boxer who won the hearts of his city after his victory over an all-star boxing legend at the height of his career.

That was a long time ago and many fights since. Pat had continued his attempt to make a living from pugilism over the years, but the punches received versus dollars far outweighed any advantages. Pat had struggled and fought with alcoholism and homelessness until landing the job as head coach for the Chavez Boys' Club.

That was four years ago now. Pat had cleaned his act up and gotten an apartment around the corner from the gym. He was off the bottle, straight and narrow, getting his kicks and living vicariously through his boys in the ring.

Mitch had been a big sponsor and coach to Pat. Pat turned to see Mitch and smiled. "Morning, boss."

"Morning, Pat. How's you today?"

"Top of the world, Mitch, top of the world." It was Pat's usual response.

The two boxers in the ring were sparring with passion. Pat coached, "One-two, one-two, one-two, hook. One-two, one-two, one-two, cross."

"He's looking good," Mitch said, referring to Miguel, the taller and slenderer of the two boys in the ring.

"I think he's nearly ready for the finals next week."

"He sure looks ready. Are they fighting those boys from San Jose?" Mitch asked.

'Yeah. They're a tough bunch."

"Well, good luck. If anyone can make it happen, it'll be you."

"We'll see," Pat said with a shy smile and raised his hand in return to give Mitch a high five.

"I'm going to do the rounds and head out for lunch, so I'll catch you later."

Pat laughed and shot Mitch a friendly smile. "Pop in and see Sanchez. See if you can help him with that jab of his. He's cloth eared when I tell him!"

Mitch said, "I sure will!"

As Mitch was leaving the gym, he let the good feelings he had about his relationship with Pat push away the darkness he'd momentarily felt on the bus. They were like an older and younger brother. Like an officer and a soldier, like a leader and a disciple. Mitch had invested in Pat, and Pat would never let Mitch down in a pinch. Mitch's cell rang as he stepped out onto the sidewalk, and he saw it was Bella.

"Hey, Bella, what's up?" he asked.

Bella sounded upset, and Mitch tensed up. He listened intently to his daughter and ended the call.

"Fuck!" Mitch punched the air. "Fuck! Fuck! Fuck!"

He stood there on the street, not believing what he'd just heard but somehow knowing it was true.

2
BUCK SHOOT

Andes Mountains, Southeast Chile, October 2016, Day 2

THE SUN SLOWLY EDGED UP beyond the ridge, revealing the presence of a deer in the increasing light of early dawn. The animal moved nimbly on the rocky terrain, at home in its element. Mac watched the buck, knowing that his Arctic-issue white coveralls made him almost invisible to the animal. Lying prone in the snow on the opposite ridge at sixteen thousand feet above sea level, Mac observed his prey. He was almost ready for the shot, though not quite yet. It was freezing at that elevation, but Mac didn't care. He'd driven four hours through the dark of predawn from his adopted hometown of Santiago, hiked and cross-country skied up the mountain pass into the valley with the help of night-vision goggles, and staked out his hunting stand.

As he watched the deer forage for what little vegetation grew at that height, his mind wandered back to his days in the Scottish Highlands. They were good days, mostly. Good days come and go, he knew. If there was one thing in life that was a constant, it was change.

He smiled. The deer was moving now.

The South Andean deer is a beautiful animal, he thought.

Mac lifted his binoculars to take a better look. The distinctive black mask surrounded the forehead and extended down the face, ending in the white throat. Mac estimated that the deer weighed about 190 pounds. Up this high on the bluffs, he was expecting a female, where they were safest. Bucks usually preferred periglacial grassland.

Mac's tripod was set up and ready. His heart raced. Barely breathing, Mac waited to take the shot. Having studied his quarry for weeks, he had chosen his elevated position with the sun behind him. The South Andean buck finally stepped out fully exposed. It instinctively faced in the direction of the seeker, expecting a cougar, the South Andean deer's only natural predator. The sky was a brilliant blue as the sun cast morning rays over the rocky height, illuminating the buck's position. A perfect shot!

Mac, a trained sniper, took a deep breath and then a second. He knew he had to slow his breathing and his heart rate just before squeezing the shot. The slightest deviation or the slightest movement could cost him his prize.

Suddenly, everything changed. A moment before, the dawn was quiet, even serene, before the telltale sound of an avalanche echoed through the mountain pass, spooking the deer. Snow and rock slid down a steep slope in the distance, rumbling at an ominously low frequency. Waves of snow swirled into the air. As Mac watched, he was fully aware of the awesome power of nature, so awesome in fact that the strongest of warriors were puny in comparison. Then all went quiet again.

There was a vibration on his right leg as the Thuraya satellite phone burst to life. Mac patted his coveralls in search of his phone. He pulled it out of his waist pocket and focused on the screen. No caller ID was displayed. "What is it?" Mac snapped. He calmed down when he recognized the voice of his old friend. Then he tensed up, feeling a knot in his stomach, a tightening of his throat. The message from his friend was short. There was no need for lengthy details, at least not yet.

"I'll be there," Mac said and ended the call.

His mind whirling, he tried to process the news. He'd been through tough situations before, but this one was unexpected, totally out of the blue. Having reached his saturation point working in Iraq, Afghanistan,

Nigeria, and other troubled and dangerous places in the world for the Special Air Service Regiment, a highly selective, volunteer, special forces of elite soldiers, Mac had hung up his SAS boots and become a private contractor—very lucrative, very dangerous. After a particularly scary moment in Iraq, Mac decided that he had played with Lady Luck too long, and now it was time to give it a rest.

Just a year earlier, he had done just that and decided to follow his dreams, take it easy, and settle down. He was an accomplished carpenter as a child, at school, and growing up, so he set up his woodworking shop in Santiago, Chile, to make furniture pieces for Chile's wealthy. Mac followed the Highland passions and traditions learned in Scotland as a child from his cousins, his uncles, and his father. Carpentry, fishing, and hunting deer were some of those activities.

Mac jumped out of his tight hideout, dusted himself off, and packed his tripod, his prized Nikon D5 camera, and the zoom lens into the protective case. Mac's experiences hadn't dulled his boyish looks. His blue eyes stood out, and his blond mop had grown into an unruly collection atop his head. Ronnie Kray bone-framed glasses sat on the bridge of his nose as he packed up his gear.

Everything went into his backpack. After gathering the rest of his equipment, his Snowy Owl sleeping bag, and his rucksack, Mac tidied up his camouflage site on the frozen mountain as if he had never been there. Old habits die hard. Next, Mac stepped into his *Lang Lauf* cross-country skis. Before gliding off, he reached into his backpack for a bite of salami. In his breast pocket, he located his flask with the Scottish thistle engraving and took a slug of his favorite Liddlesdale whisky.

As he pushed off down the slope, Mac took one last look at where the Andean deer had been a few moments ago, shook his head again, and scoffed, "Unbelievable!" It would be a four-hour trek back to his Land Rover before the drive home to Santiago. He was anxious to get back. He had travel plans to make. When he got off the mountain, he quickly loaded the Land Rover and began the drive home, during which he booked his flights through the travel concierge he had used for years. Safe, discreet. Peggy knew him, and he knew Peggy, although they had never met. Peggy liked to keep it that way with her clientele, as she dispatched dangerous men to mostly dangerous places around the world. Some were repeat customers, and some she would never hear of again. Mac was one of her longer-standing customers, and she was always there for him; no matter what time or where in the world, he always knew that he was in the safe hands of Peggy, the ultimate travel adviser. Tickets, hotels, planes, trains, automobiles, even travel documents, of whatever nature, and welcome packs when he arrived in country.

Peggy was not just a travel adviser but an arranger of sorts.

He had set up his woodworking shop from scratch and assembled a team of local craftsman to help him make furniture that he hoped would one day adorn the homes of the rich and famous in Santiago. In the meantime, getting a customer base was enough for him as the fledgling business grew to meet his aspirations and replace the level of income he was used to in his previous career, after the Regiment.

As Mac approached his woodshop, he recognized the two beat-up flatbed utility vehicles seemingly abandoned right outside the front. He knew who they belonged to. He reached into the back and pulled out a leather case around two and a half feet in length. He unzipped it and pulled out his Mossberg 590, M590 pump-action shotgun. Then he got out of the Land Rover and went stealthily into his shop.

The M590 was a handy weapon of choice in close-quarter situations. If used correctly, it could disable situations without the need to eliminate, although it was more than capable of taking care of the latter if required.

As he slipped into the woodshop, he could see the three thugs from the local Mano Negro gang, the leader brandishing a machete as he talked to Mac's men in menacing tones. When Mac arrived in Chile, he had taken time to go to the local language school and brush up on his Spanish, but in circumstances like these, he liked to play dumb and used his translator, George, his foreman, to help him out.

Mac moved a little closer, unnoticed until he pumped the Mossberg 590 and a cartridge slid into the breach.

"What's going on here, George?" Mac called over, with the Mossberg in his right hand pointed in the direction of the three visitors.

They stared at Mac and the shotgun in disgust and contempt.

"Mr. Mac, these dogs are asking where this month's payment is."

"Tell them same place as last month's—there isn't one."

George translated Mac's response. It was followed by a flurry of shouting in a string of Spanish that was so fast Mac had difficulty keeping up.

"Mr. Mac, he says that he has been sent by his bosses, and they are losing patience. Unless you comply, they will burn this tinderbox down when you are sleeping in your bed."

"Is that right, Pablo?" Mac said in the thug's home language, staring deep into his eyes until Pablo could see his own soul and looked away, losing the stare down.

Mac continued in Spanish, "Listen, my friend, you don't want to mess around here. Understand? You really don't. You go and tell your boss that I am a fair man and want to live in peace, but I will not be intimidated by you fuckers."

Mac went on with a menacing smile. "Now, as it happens, a close friend is the head of the Santiago prison system, and if you go anywhere near to stepping on my property again, or interfere with my business, I will make sure that every single Mano Negro member behind bars will take twice as long to get released. Understood?" The three thugs looked at each other, unsure how to respond.

"Secondly, if you harm any of my people or my property ..." Mac let his words hang. The long moment stretched on. The thugs looked increasingly worried. "As I was saying, every time you fuck with me, I'll take out three of your guys."

Mac moved closer to the thugs, shotgun at the ready. "Thirdly, you can tell your boss, Senor Romero Pablo, that if he doesn't like this arrangement, then I will gladly come visit him at his Villa Piedra Rojas and deliver the fucking news personally. Understood?"

"My boss won't like that," the biggest thug said. "You get your ass blown off if you do any of the shit you say you will."

Mac smiled and shook his head. "I believe you think what you say is true. Trust me. You don't want to find out. Look. I am a reasonable man. I want no trouble, but believe you me, if you want trouble, you are picking on the wrong man."

With that, Mac moved toward his storage cabinet with a stock of his prized possessions. Reaching in, he pulled out one of his most prized, a presentation box containing a rare bottle of Mac's favorite Liddlesdale whisky.

"Now, please send my very best regards to Senor Pablo and give him this personal gift from me. I understand that he has a liking for the finer things in life, and there is not a finer Scotch Whisky on the planet than this. You can also tell him that we would be delighted to make him a beautiful centerpiece for the new entrance he just built at his villa, complimentary, free of charge as a gesture of goodwill."

Mac wasn't sure if the peace offering would work, but he figured it was worth a try. Although he was an old soldier fully capable of waging war, he was also of a mind to avoid violence if possible. Mac then handed each of the three a less rare bottle of the Liddlesdale and bid them farewell, situation diffused, tails between their legs, humiliated but without really realizing it. Mac was a hard man, as hard as could be, but he also knew how to win wars and not just battles. He had learned this level of diplomacy in trouble spots around the world, and it worked equally as well in Chile.

Mac said goodbye to his boys and headed to his home on the outskirts of Santiago, next to the little church with its bell and "Ave Maria" every day at noon. He loved his new life in Chile—his wife and his retirement from the world of security contracting, although he did miss that sometimes.

Arriving home, Milou, his Yorkshire terrier cross, was waiting for him, sniffing the scent of the country deer terrain. The spunky, fearless little dog adored the outdoors and would have enjoyed going on any adventure.

Milou had been named after the wire fox terrier in the classic comic strip *The Adventures of Tintin*. Mac's childhood and adult hero, Tintin, was a young boy reporter who chased villains and conquered evil, no matter how complex and sinister. Milou was the original name of Tintin's trusty dog that got changed to Snowy as the comic book stories spread beyond Belgium and France to worldwide popularity. Milou was the trusty canine companion of Tintin. Together, the young reporter and Milou always won the day.

Mac was a bit of a Tintin himself, or perhaps the incarnation of Captain Haddock, along with the Thompson Twins and Professor Calculus, one of Tintin's companions. Captain Haddock was a sailor, a mariner, a cynic, a sceptic, and a worldwide adventurer with a love for helping solve crimes but a bigger love for naval rum and whisky!

Mac was one of the two. Tintin or Haddock. Either way, Mac had his share of adventures that had taken him around the world, and he had seen more than he ever wanted to. Mac's love of rum and whisky helped with that.

Mac entered the house to find his wife, Carmen, waiting for him near the front door.

"A successful shoot?" she asked, smiling and kissing him on the lips.

Mac shook his head. "Missed the damned shot. Avalanche," he said.

"Too bad. I know how much you wanted to get it."

"Yeah, I know," Mac said, fighting off the pang of sadness that struck him. "I've got a trip to take. To the States."

Carmen raised an eyebrow. "Really?"

Mac told her what was up while he packed his backpack.

Carmen was the perfect complement to the French/Belgium tone of Tintin and his adventures. Like the author of the *Adventures of Tintin*, Herge, Carmen had heavy French influences in her history. Her father had been a professor in Santiago during the times of the Chilean dictator Pinochet. He fled to Moscow, then to Paris, then to settle down the family—Carmen and her brother and sister—in the French colony of Algeria in North Africa. Carmen attended L'Ecole Française and was fluent in the language by the time she and her family returned to Chile in the 1990s, when it was safe to do so.

She possessed that mystical beauty of an intellectual, a proud Chilean woman but with French influence, not a singer, but if she were, then she would surely be the Little Sparrow, or Edith Piaf herself. Small, slight, yet powerful and passionate. Dark hair, almost black, deep brown eyes, and a pout that any Parisian woman would be extremely proud of.

Carmen was stylish, free, fun, and happy but always with the serious undercurrent of someone who had seen more than she deserved. She was the power and tower of strength standing behind Mac, no matter the challenge. Carmen would always be there for Mac, her family, and of course, as a passionate patriot, her country, Chile.

After Mac finished packing, he took a quick shower and shaved. He checked his watch and saw he had to get going if he was going to catch his flight. Carmen walked him to the door.

"I will see that the boys in the shop don't play too much hooky," she said, taking both his hands in hers.

"No need. They'll be fine."

"Just the same. I'll look in on them."

"We had some visitors from our friendly shakedown artists. Ran 'em off, but if they give you any trouble, you know who to call."

Mac was pleased that Carmen took this latest news in stride.

"Don't worry, darling," she said. "You know I don't scare easily."

Mac laughed. "Don't I ever!"

Mac kissed Carmen goodbye, got into his Land Rover, and headed to Santiago International for his flight to San Francisco. As he drove, he hit speed dial on his cell.

"I'm on my way."

3
LEGIONNAIRE

Equatorial Guinea, West Africa, October 2016, Day 2

BOB STOOD IN THE LOCAL government offices in central Malabo located on the island of Bioko in the Bay of Biafra in the oil-rich and corrupt country. As its capital, Malabo was a monument to a storied past and a harbinger of a beleaguered future. The building where Bob was waiting served as an excellent example. The once grand and imposing structure with its intricate Spanish architecture looked old and weary. Discolored moldings hung by a miracle above arched doors and shuttered windows. The white walls were green with mold, but they still hinted at the once luxurious past.

Bob had been waiting all morning to see the big man. A few pleasantries, a display of cash, and he should have his permit to remain on the island. He wasn't even sure that he wanted it, but this was an insurance policy just in case he had to come back. It was a simple transaction. Bob should have been on his way hours ago. As it turned out, Bob had ample time to study the neglected, decaying, and dying building. All things wither with time. Bob knew that. Beyond boredom, he watched and listened to the buzz of the fan that only seemed to circulate the unidentified odor that hung in the air.

What is that stink anyway? Bob wondered. *Did the big man shit himself or what?*

It was not the hottest time of the year in Malabo, but then again it was always hot and smelly there. The hotter it got the smellier it got. Today was a hot thirty-one degrees Celsius, eighty-eight degrees Fahrenheit, and particularly humid even for there. Bob reminded himself of yet another reason why he hated this hellhole.

A wandering rooster's crow sliced through the stillness just outside the big man's office window. It had been the first action in hours, and Bob chuckled at how interesting the event seemed. *How pathetic*, he poked fun at himself. Then, out the office window beyond the rooster, Bob saw him arrive. The building burst into life. He watched the big black man with his fat, sweat-drenched face through the open office door. Red-and-gold braids hung limp off his shoulders. His wet armpits had sweat-stained the shirt that pulled tightly around his belly, threatening to pop a button. He plopped his girth into his desk chair, releasing a swooshing sound as he landed. Immediately, his minions assembled before him to receive his various orders of sputtered syllables and grunts in the local dialect.

The rooster walked up to the open office door and proudly crowed again. Momentarily, the big man paused, looking anxious until the shrill, squawking tune ended. When the creature fell silent, he resumed his tirade.

Bob sighed. "What a fucking joke!" He wanted to be somewhere else, but hey, *That's Africa, baby!*

At length, the big man, Boss Baraga, granted Bob an audience.

"You look hot," he said, wiping sweat from his face.

Bob nodded, not wanting to promote conversation. The big man was clearly harried.

"Well, you go get cool then," he said, waving Bob away as he handed him his permit. "That is if you can find a place."

Bob smiled. "Many thanks for this," he said. "I love it here."

The big man growled, "Oh, bullshit. Get on out of here before I change my mind."

Bob readily complied. He left the building and headed out across town toward the British Gas and Pipeline Corporation (BGPC) compound. A stark compound at the edge of the city, it was made of concrete and surrounded by barbed wire, and at the center was a mistral of buildings looking more like bomb shelters than corporate offices.

Standing at six feet three, Bob was a big man—tall, athletic, muscular, and harsh. His cropped brown hair in a crew-cut style had remained the same since he joined the British Army twenty years ago, and after the Regiment, to take up security gigs around the globe. This latest gig in Equatorial Guinea was tiresome. Apart from his security detail and his right-hand man, Malik, he was alone, a lone wolf fighting many packs of hyenas. He had had enough of Equatorial Guinea and was ready for his next gig. *Maybe today is that day,* he thought.

He walked across the sunbaked compound to the main headquarters with sweat dripping. He stood in the conference room of the headquarters of the BGPC offices perusing his audience, wearing black boots, black pants, and a dark gray shirt, his clean-shaved face showing the single scar down the side of his cheek that he picked up in a bar in Dar Es Salam, Tanzania, many years ago. His deep brown eyes looked in the eyes of his guests before him.

Seated in folding chairs lined up across the meeting table from Bob, his audience consisted of six of the corporation's local Equatorial Guinea senior executives, all West African descent. They stared back at Bob dispassionately as Bob began his presentation. Behind the seated members was Hamza Malik and six of Bob's armed detail. Dressed in their corporate security uniforms with the distinctive BGPC badge on their chests, each had pistols strapped to their waist in addition to donning a Heckler & Koch Machine Pistol, MP5, strapped around their shoulders but cradled in both arms, ready for anything, if needed.

Bob was familiar with the MP5, his automatic weapon of choice and one he had grown up with—hence its selection for his security team. There wasn't a trick that Bob didn't know about using this versatile firearm to its optimum.

Bob started describing to the group his findings from an investigation into various breaches of the pipeline and the redirecting of many millions of gallons of oil and, more importantly, dollars, that disappeared into the African black market. Not only did this make some very rich beneficiaries of such activities but most importantly, fueling and funding illegal, and in some cases, terrorism.

Corruption in Equatorial Guinea was a way of life for many of the country's elite, where the gross domestic product per capita was over $32,000, yet most of the population survive on less than a dollar a day. Corruption was engrained into the society from the president, his family, extended family, politicians, and industry leaders. The war against corruption was a never-ending story. As Bob had come to realize, this probably would never be truly eradicated, but he was making his best efforts to do so.

"So, you see, gentlemen, because of this scam, BGPC has lost an estimated $200 million in revenues over just the past twelve months alone, a situation that we simply cannot allow." The audience looked at each other with enthusiastic nods and shakes of the head in agreement to this obvious statement about the corporation they all represented.

Bob's audience that afternoon, despite the heat and humidity, were all wearing suits and ties, and expensive suits and ties at that. The collection of dark gray, brown, and blue suits were all imports, probably from London, probably Savile Row, Bob decided. Probably more than $5,000 each, ten times what Bob had ever spent on a suit.

In addition to despising the country, he had grown to despise these people. Wearing their suits like some sort of status symbol, sweating their balls off for the pleasure. Strutting around in garments that would take the average and impoverished Equatorial Guinean fifteen years to buy. Corruption sickened Bob as he saw the contrast between starving children and fat cats with complexes dripping with opulence and gold.

That was why he was enjoying his presentation.

"Last month, I was in London, and I ran into a retired colonel, Benedicto Monabang, whom some of you may know." Although this was a statement, Bob looked around his audience knowingly, nodding as he slowly paced back and forth. No one dared look at each other but kept their eyes on Bob, some nodding, some feigning unfamiliarity.

"Last year, Monabang turned up in London, just retired, with $200 million in cash. He opened up a UK bank account, purchased a $20 million property in Kensington, joined the Royal Automobile Club, got himself a Rolls Royce, and does his grocery shopping at fricking Harrods!" The audience was now shaking their heads in feigned disbelief and disgust, while Bob knew for a fact that most of the audience aspired to a similar career progression.

"Now the thing is, what our friend Colonel Monabang didn't know was that under the UK's Anti-Terrorism Crime and Security Act, funds suspected of financing terrorist activities can be frozen." Bob shrugged. "Oh, it's a fairly straightforward process to have those funds frozen, and last week, that's exactly what we did." The audience nodded with apparent approval.

Bob continued, "But, my friends, it's kind of interesting how even a hardened military veteran like the colonel can get talking when his precious loot is no longer accessible. He now must go to Tesco's instead of Harrods. His five wives can't buy their daily dose of diamonds or even put fricking petrol in that big fricking Roller of his."

Such a grim picture had the audience looking at each other with worried expressions.

"Yes, gentlemen, Monabang did a deal with us to at least preserve part of his loot in exchange for giving us some names." Two in the audience scraped their chairs back, then stood up in protest. Bob's security detail sprang to life. "Yes, gentlemen, your names." Bob stopped pacing to stare them all down.

"How dare you!" gasped one of the senior executives.

"Of what in heaven's name do you speak?" huffed another of the audience.

One just sat there repeating, "No, no, no. no. You are making big mistake, Mr. Bob."

"We don't have to listen to this!" declared the fourth objector as he sprang from his folding chair.

One of Bob's armed detail merely stepped in front of the protester, and the executive sat back down.

Bob motioned for everyone to quieten down, for the executives seemed to all be talking at once.

"Listen, gentlemen," Bob stated over the cross conversations. "The good news is that I have a deal for all of you." The room fell silent and motionless. "Give us back $150 million of what you have stolen, and I will release you."

"What do you mean release us?" scoffed the most senior executive who had not spoken yet. "We are in Malabo, the capital of *my* country and *not* yours!" he bellowed.

Bob smiled and replied calmly, "That is very true, Mr. Kinsasha, but you see these men here?" Bob gestured to his armed security detail. "These are six of my finest. If you don't agree to this deal, right now, then there is a helicopter on the roof, as I speak, that will take you to Her Majesty s ship, HMS *Flawless*, which is currently in international waters just off the coast, ready to take you back to the United Kingdom for investigations into funding Boko Harem and ISIS."

Bob took a step backward and sat on the conference table with a cynical expression. He continued softly, "Now, I am sure that there is no truth in that rumor, but, gentlemen, you know how long those investigations can take, and you know how other skeletons have a habit of turning up." Bob winked as his senior executives slumped back into their folding chairs before him.

Bob was pleased to take them out one by one. However, while he might have been winning the battle on this particular day, it was a hard slog, as with every one he eliminated, another two would replace them—younger, brighter, smarter. Bob was a pariah to the corruptive elements that abounded in Equatorial Guinea. He was straight to the point and incorruptible, though some had tried. He was a hard man, a harsh man, a man that meant business and had no qualms with eliminating people who got in his way.

Although Bob had no family to speak of, no wife and no children that he knew of, he enjoyed the occasional lady of the night in his swanky apartment. Life in Equatorial Guinea wasn't easy for anyone, especially Bob.

After they realized that corruption wouldn't work, they sent thugs in place of business folks bearing gifts, and Bob quickly dispatched these attempts one by one until this escalated from thugs to beat him up to attempted assassinations by amateurs, escalating to former freedom fighters taking on the task and the potential riches to most recently what appeared to be a contracted, professional assassination attempt on his life.

Previous attempts had been somewhat juvenile, but this latest attempt by a former French Foreign Legion soldier of Algerian descent had gotten Bob more worried than he had been for a while. This wouldn't be the last. Bob knew that.

Bob was well connected in this relatively small enclave on the west coast of Africa and got alerts daily of any persons of interest arriving in the city. In Africa, and especially in Equatorial Guinea, every day was a power struggle. There was always someone trying to do over someone else, make a power grab, eliminate someone for their own better good, and to that end, these alerts were more like tipoffs, and that was the way Bob took them.

Six months earlier, the report came through over the fax, a photo of a tan man, looking somewhat Arabic, athletic, and weathered, like he had been around a bit. The ex–French Foreign Legion corporal, maybe thirty at most, had been out just twelve months and was now a private security contractor, with little work coming his way over the past twelve months. He lived in the Nineteenth Arrondissement, Paris, with his sister, who was a waitress and a single mother with two kids, five and seven. Born in Paris to Algerian parents, life beyond the French Foreign Legion wasn't that rosy. More recently, Hamza Malik had let it be known that his services were also available as an eliminator.

Now, although hiring an assassin isn't as easy as going to the Yellow Pages and looking one up or going to Yelp and getting a star rating, it often surprised Bob how predictable and stupid people could be in this part of the world. He looked at Hamza Malik's profile, and as odd as it seemed, Bob kind of felt sorry for him. He thought about that for a long moment and concluded that he empathized with the young man.

What the hell are you supposed to do when you leave the army and a fighting force? Work in fucking Safeway, packing bags? Bob thought.

The next fax to come through was a copy of his check-in that morning at the Sofitel. Passport, credit card, check-in, all in the name of Hamza Malik. Bob now felt sorry for the guy, quite clearly out of his depth. Bob headed down to the Plaza Independencia to go and check him out. Before he left, he checked in with the accountant and checked on the balance of his slush fund—his annual BGPC budget for greasing wheels and getting things done. Bob always found it ironic that he would use company funds to bribe people in his fight on corruption. There must have been some circular reference there somewhere, but Bob deliberately tried not to think about it too much.

He spotted his man walking out the front door of reception onto the street, facing the green of the Plaza Independencia and the cathedral, St. Isabel's, then turning right across the road and onto the path leading to Restaurante Nautico on the Bay of Santa Isabel.

Malik, about six feet tall, slim, athletic, and wiry, navigated himself across the road toward the restaurant and took a seat at a table in the bar. The waitress brought him a menu, and Bob took a seat at Malik's table. Malik looked up and seemed shocked and confused.

"I hope you don't mind if I join you," Bob said.

Malik remained silent.

"If you know what's good for you, you'll keep both hands on the table," Bob said.

Malik still wasn't talking, but he kept both hands on the table.

"How much did they offer you?" Bob asked in French.

"Not enough, by the looks of it," Malik answered.

"I'd say you got that one right," Bob said. "Now this can go one of two ways. How do you want it to go? Hard or easy?"

"I'm listening."

"Believe it or not, I've got an offer for you," Bob said. "It's a good one. At least it beats the alternative that's in store for you if you say no."

Malik raised an eyebrow. "Go on," he said.

"Here's the deal. I'm due to leave the country tomorrow night for three weeks, and I want you to stage an assassination. I will make the

28

necessary arrangements with the local press confirming a shooting and that I'm missing, out of action. You pick up your million euros for the hit on me."

"Wait, how did you know that?" asked Malik. "How do you know any of this?"

"This is Africa, baby. When I get back, the transaction will be complete. You confirm to me that you have your money, and I will bust the ass of your employer, sending them 'Go to jail, direct to jail, bypassing Go,' as Mr. Waddington would say.

"That will give you enough to buy Famoush, your sister's apartment in Paris, a permanent home for your nephews, Sami and Hakim. Give them security and a permanent place for you to stay whilst in Paris."

Malik just stared at Bob, speechless.

"Then, in addition and in thanks for your good services, I will cash you a check for a further 500,000 euros for helping me with this endeavor and capturing the perpetrators."

Bob paused, letting Malik take it all in.

"Then finally, I could do with a good assistant and a succession plan to leave BGPC at some point, and I could do with a strong right-hand man. I have an employment contract in my pocket for deputy security operations officer at British Gas and Pipeline Corporation, starting in eight weeks' time at a starting salary of $400,000 plus bonus, apartment, flights, medical, dental, pension—fully loaded. What do you think?"

"Why would you do this for me?"

"Because I can see a good man, a good soldier, sitting in front of me. I know you've never carried out a hit before. Isn't that right?"

Malik nodded. He sighed. "Frankly, I don't know what I was thinking."

"Neither do I," Bob said. "You would've ended up getting your skinny ass shot off."

"Not without a fight," Malik said.

"I have no doubt," Bob said. "So, do we have a deal?"

"Do I have a choice?"

"We all have choices. The hard part is making the right ones."

Malik smiled, held up his glass, and nodded. "Yeah," he said, "you bet we got a deal!"

Bob was a ruthless man, uncompromising, yet always looking to do a deal. This wasn't a weakness; this was a strength. Bob's role in the past was one of exterminator. By the time he got involved, it was usually too late to do a deal. Nowadays, he would think through an acceptable compromise, no negotiations. It was either accepted or, if not, would result in plan B, where the opposition always lost. No in-between. No "I'll arm wrestle you for it." No "Can I sleep on it?" No pussyfooting around. Do a deal if there was one to be done—or die. No middle ground. What was the point? It wasted time that usually ended up with a conflict at some later point. Better to get things done and dusted, bury the hatchet, decisive action. That was Bob's way. He just wondered if the corrupt corporate officers seated before him in the conference room would see fit to make the right choice, just as Malik had all those months ago.

With the amount of dirty oil money flowing around Malabo, Bob knew that there would be more to come, and this was his final swan song in Equatorial Guinea. If he could get the assholes in the room to pay back the $150 million, they'd stolen from the company, they could keep the rest, and to hell with it. Or at least they could think they could keep the rest. Bob suppressed a grin.

Boy, do these chumps have something coming! he thought.

As soon as they paid up, which should be within the hour, they'd be quickly hauled off on the chopper to the HMS *Flawless* for a not so comfortable trip to the UK. There they'd be grilled for intel. Bob was wise enough to know that the reality was that they would be held for a few days, squeezed for any further information they could glean, then probably shipped back to Malabo in first class. Back to the remaining millions in their bank accounts. Back to the same old dirty games. But Bob took solace in the fact that they'd never step on the property of the British Gas and Pipeline Corporation again.

Bob fully expected the scumbags to see reason. It was in their best interests to do so. He took further solace in the certainty that when the funds were returned to the company, he'd receive an email from the chairman of BGPC congratulating him on a successful operation, an operation that had taken Bob over eighteen months to pull off. Lord Stephenson would thank him for a job well done, and he would promptly remit the 3 percent collector's fee, making Bob a very rich man indeed. He hadn't worked out what to do next, but that could come later. Frankly, he didn't give a rat's ass at the moment. And as for Malik, he'd finally get to be the new boss. His position would be secure, or as secure as was possible in the unpredictable corporate world.

Bob's satellite phone vibrated. He recognized the number and texted, "Call you in five."

"Excuse me, gentlemen. I will give you a few moments to consider my more than generous offer," he said to the worried-looking executives.

Bob turned to the whiteboard on wheels and flipped it to the opposite side, revealing some writing not seen previously. "On that whiteboard is the bank account details I want the money wired to within the next hour. I am not interested in the rest of your assets. I am good with that. You can keep those. If I don't see that $150 million in the account in one hour, by 5:00 p.m., my friends, you will be taking a cruise courtesy of Queen Elizabeth II on Her Majesty's ship *Flawless* back to London to see your mate Monabang and my mates at Scotland Yard!" Bob eyed each executive one by one. "Understood?"

"We understand," Mr. Kinsasha said. As the senior guy in the room, his word held sway. Bob was pleased.

"Good," Bob said. "I thought you would."

Bob walked down the corridor to his office and called the number of his friend in California. The news was bad. Real bad. And so completely out of left field. Bob listened until his friend finished speaking.

"Yeah, I'll be there. I'm on my way now," he said.

4

THE GAME COCK

Hereford, United Kingdom, October 2016, Day 2

IT WAS A TYPICAL WORKDAY. On Sam's way to the office that morning from his farmstead between Ross-on-Wye and Hereford, England, he passed the spiritual home of the Special Air Service (SAS), Stirling Lines, established shortly after World War II by the Regiment founder in chief, David Stirling.

This was a nostalgic place for Sam. As a young soldier twenty years earlier, Sam had been in awe when visiting the home of the Special Forces unit of the British Army. Now, each time he drove by, Sam remembered the sweat, the tears, and the camaraderie but also the deep responsibility and sometimes sadness associated with the job. As a soldier, there was no higher responsibility and commitment than what you gave in the Special Air Service. Each member of the team knew, in absolute terms, that they could rely upon each other. There were no doubts, no gray areas, no questions, just the certainty behind the unit that led to its ultimate success.

Long shut down, demolished, and now a housing estate, Stirling Lines no longer existed, and even the last remnant of those days gone by, the SAS watering hole, the Game Cock, had unceremoniously been converted into a Tesco convenience store.

Passing by with thoughts gone by and friends lost but not forgotten, Sam drove to his new military camp outside of Hereford, the new home of the Special Air Service, Credenhill. This would be his last year, with retirement just around the corner. Sam always found it funny that they called it retirement. After twenty-two years of service, at forty-two years old, as fit as a fiddle, what the hell was he going to do for the rest of his life? Follow others into security consulting? What did trained killers do when they retired? This question always left him scratching his head. He had a few months to work out the answer.

As he arrived at the barracks, he settled into his daily routine. It was all mostly administrative at this point. Boring, in fact. But sometimes boring was okay. It beat getting shot at, though Sam missed the danger and excitement upon occasion, as did many other soldiers that he knew.

Part of his routine included making his rounds. When Sam got to the cookhouse, he walked right on in, straight to the master chef's office, and said, "Morning, Woody."

"Morning, Sam," Woody said with a smile.

A moment later, Woody handed Sam a plate of bacon sandwiches and a glass of grapefruit juice. Sam thanked him and started to eat his breakfast. Sam and Woody had been friends for a long time, and although attached personnel to the Regiment, strictly speaking were restricted to three-year tours of duty, Woody had been around since being a young corporal, and that was nearly twelve years ago now. Sam and Woody had been all over together, with a lot of time spent in trouble spots in various places in the world. As a regimental sergeant major, Sam was the most senior noncommissioned officer in the unit. When he finished eating, he walked down the modernized new corridor to his office suite.

Sam was reminded once again of the more basic, temporary feel of the previous headquarters above the quadrangle at Stirling Lines and the poster of the gangly freedom fighter armed to the teeth; it still made him chuckle today as he thought of it. The poster asked, "What do you call this man with a .50-caliber machine gun, rocket launcher, Kalashnikov, eight grenades, a machine pistol MP5, a Glock, five hundred rounds, and a machete?" The answer: "Mate." Maybe Sam would get hold of a copy of the poster and put it back up, in pride of place. "That would make the boys laugh," Sam muttered to himself.

Sam found himself reminiscing more and more lately, largely due to his pending retirement. For a moment, a ripple of panic seized Sam. He wondered what the hell he and his wife, Emily, would do when he retired. He had been wondering about that a lot lately, and the anxiety was starting to get to him. Being a soldier was his identity. He wasn't sure giving it up was such a great idea.

On the side of his desk sat a stack of papers to go through—review, make decisions, accept, reject, and make recommendations. Paperwork. When he finished with that, he oversaw some routine disciplinary action involving junior troops, and then he proceeded to the daily security briefing.

Operations in Syria continued to go from bad to worse, with the bombings between the Syrian government and Russia, USA, UK, and allies, plus ISIS and Western-backed rebel forces—Syria was a complete mess, and Sam didn't like the fact that some of his troops were caught up in it. Sam shared his opinion again to get them the hell out of there—a losing argument when against the opposition of number 10 Downing Street. A few ranks above Sam's pay grade.

Despite all the press and propaganda, they all knew that the underlying issue in Syria was the same as it was for Crimea and even the Russian enclave of Kaliningrad. This was about Russia's desire to gain and maintain all-year-round ports and avoid the reliance on their traditional ports that were frozen for the winter, somewhat hamstringing the Russian naval capability. To Sam, this just demonstrated the Russians' paranoia.

Various terror plots had been defused in the past few months—hotbeds in various London boroughs, Birmingham, Manchester, Leicester, Bradford, and Leeds. Good work by MI5, MI6, Scotland Yard, And Metro Police, and splendid work by A Squadron. Requests came for more SAS support across these metro areas.

"We are already stretched thin enough as we are, gents. You have pretty much the entire resources of A Squadron tied up. Unless I step up selection or lower the bar, I don't have any immediate answers," said Sam. "Unless we pull in the boys from 23?" Sam added, looking around the room for approval.

The 23 Special Air Service was a part-time volunteer force comprised of civilians. The volunteers were like those in the US Army Reserves, weekend warriors as they were sometimes called. They went about their daily lives in whatever occupation they worked in, and they trained in the SAS on the side. In Sam's view, this wasn't an ideal situation.

Indeed, the unit had recently lost three soldiers in Helmand Province, Afghanistan, and morale was low with family men being questioned by their wives and their families on whether their part-time playing soldiers was the right thing for them. That was a difficult conversation for a part-time volunteer to have with their loved ones. It was not a conversation Sam had ever had to have as a full-time professional soldier with no other options open to him. Maybe one day he would be a teacher like his father.

It was going to be a tough retention time for the 23, but a stint supporting covert counterterrorism supporting A Squadron might be a viable solution. Better than Afghanistan for sure.

This wasn't the first time Sam had raised this. The reality was that he had already ramped up selection by some extra five hundred candidates a year, but without lowering the bar, that would only add another fifty trained SAS soldiers to their ranks a year, nowhere near enough for the task they were discussing here.

Still no decision on that. It seemed ironic that MI5, MI6 and Scotland Yard had asked the same question regularly for the past twelve months, yet nobody had decided how to fix it.

Sounds like they're getting desperate and might fix it soon, Sam thought.

Next was their support of the US Drug Enforcement Agency, DEA, and Federal Bureau of Investigation, FBI, in Mexico, Colombia, the jungles of Belize, Brazil, and various parts of Central and South America. That was getting pretty heated out there too, especially with the cartels and the overt violence in Mexico. Sam had a small team of trainers and advisers out there. Small team, high risks.

G Squadron and the Mountain Troop had been busy keeping an eye on Sam's old friend, the Man at the Kremlin, along with intelligence on his expanded activities on the Russian borders in Scandinavia, specifically with air activity, sea, submarine, and boots on the ground. G had been busy with the Special Boat Service boys who were the naval equivalent of the SAS, Navy, Air Force, and NATO. "Great job, Harry and the boys," congratulated Sam. "Keep an eye on those Ruskies." Sam winked.

The tall, young intelligence officer, as though he was in a White House press conference, closed his portfolio in front of him dramatically, looked at the audience, and demanded, "Questions?" When there were none, he concluded, "That ends todays briefing, gentlemen. Thank you."

Sam headed over to lunch at the sergeants' mess with his old pal Harry, squadron sergeant major of G Squadron. They had grown up with each other, literally. They had been on the same selection seventeen years earlier. Both senior squadron sergeant majors when the top job came up, Sam was convinced that Harry would get it, but like the gentleman he was, Harry during his interview, he stepped to the side and was quoted as saying, "Sam is the right man for the job and the right man for the Regiment. For that reason, I am standing down and will be a willing supporter, champion, colleague, and friend to our new sergeant major." To get that kind of endorsement meant a lot to the 22 Special Air Service Regiment, and Sam was duly appointed.

"How real is this staffing problem?" asked Sam

"Yeah, well, it's all about budgets really," Harry said.

"What do you mean?"

"They keep applying pressure on number 10 to increase their budgets. They barely do, and even if they do, they take it from somewhere else, robbing Peter to pay Paul. So, they push in all directions and see us as being an easier target to get funding and boots on the ground."

"Who are they fucking kidding?" Sam retorted. "If only they knew the backlog of capital requisitions. I'm trying to support growing operations around the world with 30 percent more activity and 10 percent less funding than I had three years ago. There's only so far you can push, and with old equipment and not enough kits and support funds, then we start losing men, and that's simply not acceptable—not on my watch, Harry."

Harry nodded in agreement.

"Instead of the government funding, they're fucking wasting money on charities like the left-handed, black, dyslexic, Catholic women's church choir of Ghana. They should be funding the fucking things that are going to actually protect this country and its people."

Sam nodded. They had had this conversation many times before.

Sam and Harry both agreed that these were interesting times indeed.

They walked into to the sergeants' mess and sat down at their usual table, one with a place for each of the twelve most senior noncommissioned officers for when they were on base. It was a long-standing tradition, but nowadays, half the spaces were empty anyway, as the younger guys' preference was to do even more training at lunchtime, skipping food and having an energy bar instead. In addition, with a lot of commitments around the world, today it was just Sam and Harry. Things had changed a lot since the days when the table would be at least half-full most days. Sam missed those days.

Maybe it really is time for me to hang up my boots, he thought, realizing his mood was becoming morose. *But is at the end of the year too soon?*

Sam's closest pals, Mitch, Jimmy, Badger, Mac, and Bob had all retired. Sam was the last one remaining. It had been a good run, but it was time for the new to take over from the old. Sam was weary, no longer in day-to-day operations but relegated, promoted, to the pen-pushing job that he had today. He was ready to tend to his land, raise some sheep, spend time at home, maybe take up painting, write a book, and take the helm of some charity for the homeless or something.

There were yet more meetings after lunch. When he got through his last meeting of yet another tedious day, Sam knew that only he and Harry would go out for a pint. That was so unlike the days gone by when the group would go for a beer together. They would laugh, tease, and share things only brothers in arms could share. Now, the rest of the team typically headed out for even more intense training. Although training was extremely important to all SAS soldiers past and present, the old guard always made time for a pint, or two, or even three.

The rest of the day passed slowly. There was no excitement in it, at least not for Sam. Except that the Regiment rugby team got back into the Army Rugby Football Union final. The last time the Regiment had made the final was ten years previously, and Sam remembered it well. Mitch, Ryan, Bob, and he were at a military stadium, a sports complex in Aldershot, England. There was a big crowd for an army match. Sam remembered that Mitch broke his rib halfway through the second half but continued playing with no complaining. Dusty O'Hare played a brilliant fullback game, and Kiwi Ken, the Maori Monster, six feet seven inches and built like a brick shit house was almost impossible to stop. Unfortunately, they lost that day 24–18. It was a close game, but 3-Para were just recklessly aggressive and difficult to control. Sam and his teammates had a bunch of beers afterward to lessen the pain.

As they were wrapping up the last meeting of the day, Wills, the youngest squadron leader in the unit, piped up unexpectedly. "Hey, Sam, I heard it's your birthday. Fancy a couple of pints down at the Spread Eagle on the way home?"

Sam's eyes brightened for times long gone. "Absolutely! Sounds good," Sam said.

Maybe the day is looking up after all, he thought as they headed down to one of his favorite pubs in Hereford.

On the way, it occurred to Sam that it wasn't the first time he had forgotten his birthday over the years. The task at hand was always greater than those personal considerations. The Regiment was everything. He was turning just forty-two, yet he felt old. That was an uncomfortable feeling but maybe just a sign that this business was for young men.

Sam had a couple of Old Speckled Hens with the team. The gathering was convivial, almost like the old days. Suddenly, Sam felt his cell phone vibrate. He checked the screen, then answered the call. The pub was relatively quiet, so he could hear without going outside. He listened to his friend, the cheer of the moment immediately vanishing.

"Okay," he said, his voice heavy with sadness, "I'll be there. I'm on my way."

"What's that about?" Wills asked.

"Nothing good," Sam said. "Nothing good at all."

5

HOOKERS, FLANKERS, AND PROPS

Kettering, United Kingdom, October 2016, Day 2

RYAN RECEIVED THE BALL IN the center of the park. His rugby team, Kettering, was halfway through the second half of the game, a challenge against the team's archrivals from the Loughborough Rugby Football Club. He instinctively looked for his teammates, hoping to offload the pass to keep the ball alive and develop second- and third-phase possession. He wanted Kettering to get closer to the line and score. At this point in the game, a penalty or a try would help get them nearer to winning.

Pushing forward, he made his run, but a big bruiser of a guy with cauliflower ears protruding from a white, blood-stained headband blocked him. Ryan passed back to the left wing. Kettering was down five points. It had been a tough one so far. Battered and bruised, Ryan and his team were determined to make this important game a win. Together, united, committed.

This was a game full of local rivalry. Friendly but intense. Physical and bruising. After all, this was the game of rugby. Grassroots rugby and an immense amount of club pride as these teams pushed their limits week in week out to compete in this glorious, tough game that produced friendships and connections like no other on the planet. The closeness of the teammates in often extreme and always tough conditions was akin to the brethren created between soldiers in combat. The smell of *Ralgex* (a muscle spray), sweaty bodies, mud, the leather of the boots, it was all the sweet and sour fragrance of sheer determination.

Sally, Ryan's wife, watched the action from the sidelines, grimacing as two players from the opposing team hit her husband hard. The force of the impact knocked Ryan to the ground. He quickly got back on his feet and in the game. Sally went to all his games. She enjoyed the atmosphere of it all and loved the social life. Rugby was as much a part of her life as it was for her husband.

One of the two mobile phones in Sally's pocket rang. She took one out and looked at the screen. Number withheld. She pressed the green button on the screen.

"Hello, Ryan's phone," she said in her thick Northamptonshire accent.

Silence. Then a voice on the other end. She strained to hear over the cheering crowd.

"Let me speak to Ryan," the voice said.

"Who is this?" she asked.

"Just let me speak to him, okay?"

"He's not here right now, luv. He's playing rugby."

"Oh," the voice said. There was a moment of silence.

"You still there?"

"Yeah."

"Who is this?"

"Just have Ryan call me when he's finished."

A bit peeved at the brusque attitude, Sally said she'd give Ryan the message. The caller hung up.

Sally forgot about the call in the heat of the moment. Her husband, a veteran flanker, captain, and coach of the team, scored a try to win the game. The crowd went crazy. She stood, screaming Ryan's name.

After the game, Sally and some of the spectators accompanied both teams to the Kettering RFU Club House. The first order of business was for the teams to hit the showers. The next was to eat, numb their wounds and bruised bodies, and celebrate the beautiful game of rugby with a few beers. Sally grinned as the ritual unfolded as it always did. There was the smell of shepherd's pie and pickled red cabbage, the usual meal served after matches. She watched the boys line up for their hearty post-match meal and the rush to the bar for beers to wash down the food. Seeing that the food was going fast, Sally set a plate aside for Ryan, who hadn't yet come out of the shower room. As captain of the team, he no doubt was hosing things off and putting things in order before relaxing. All in all, the day had been a good one. She felt happy to be alive, happy to be with her husband.

When Ryan came out, he hurried to her. "Did you see that play?" he asked. "What a play!"

Sally laughed as he swept her up in his arms and kissed her. His passion was obvious, and she wondered if they'd get lucky that night. She kissed him back.

"It was brilliant!" she said. "Just brilliant!"

"God, I'm famished! I could eat a horse!" he said.

Ryan sat down at the table and began eating. Sally got up to get him a beer.

"Here you go," she said, putting the pint down next to the plate. "Drink up. You deserve it!"

Ryan thanked her and took a big swig. He kept eating, his eyes focused on the food in front of him.

"Love, you had a call on your cell during the game. He said it was important and that you would know who to call in an emergency. I told him you were playing and that you would call back."

"He give you his name?"

"No, he didn't. And I thought that was a little strange."

Ryan nodded, his face suddenly grim. A pang of worry crept into Sally's mood.

Ryan didn't like the sound of the mystery caller. He had received messages like that many times, and it always meant trouble. He knew exactly who to call, but he'd put if off for now. Ryan had business to take care of first.

Ryan sat down next to his father, who was digging into his shepherd's pie. Mr. William (Billy) Brooks was a legend at the club, and he was a hero in Ryan's eyes.

"That was a great match, son. Great comeback," Billy said between bites.

"Sure was, Dad. The boys played out of their skins."

"Bobby Wainwright had a great game at fullback."

"Yeah, he did. He's trialing for the county next week. I think he might make it all the way."

"What? To the England team?"

"Maybe. I think he has all it takes."

"He has plenty of time. He's still a young lad," Billy said, taking a long swallow of his beer.

Ryan let his father eat. He looked around the room and saw Sally watching him intently. He suddenly felt a sense of foreboding, that something wasn't right. His mother's illness was part of it, but there was something more. His soldier's instinct said there was.

"How's Mum?" Ryan asked.

"Ah, she is okay, better than she was last week, but you know, son, she's so weak after the chemo."

"I know, Dad. How are you holding up?"

"It's tough, son. Seeing the love of your life, your only love, drifting away. It's tough."

Sadness gripped Ryan. He pushed it away.

"I can't imagine what it's like for you; it's bad enough being her son. Tell her I'll be around tomorrow to put a smile on her face. Or, you could come around to our place for Sunday roast and yorky puds?" Ryan said with a smile and a pat on the back.

"Great thought. You know we're both suckers for roast beef and yorkshire pudding, but I think she's just too weak. Pop around before dinner and come and see her. Bring her some flowers. She likes her flowers."

"Will do, Dad.

"It's time to do the presentations." Ryan confirmed what they both already knew, a convenient way of moving on from the painful subject.

Billy left after the presentations, and Ryan joined the others for some revelry, though the call wasn't forgotten. He went up to Sally at the bar and kissed her gently on the cheek. She was the most beautiful woman he'd ever seen with her blonde hair, blue eyes, and cute ski jump nose. Ryan loved her buxom chest with plenty of cleavage on display and her skin-tight jeans and very attractive derriere. She was a good, down-to-earth girl, and now at forty, she still turned a lot of heads.

The crowd eventually thinned out. The locals headed to the usual pub crawl that would start at the Cherry Tree and end at the Rising Sun, probably around midnight and probably with the usual suspects being the last men and women standing.

Ryan and Sally followed them but didn't make it as far as the Rising Sun. On the way to the Cherry Tree, Ryan received a text message on his phone, and as Sally headed into the bar, Ryan made the call. He listened intently for a minute and then replied, "I'll call you and let you know."

He went into the bar to find Sally flirting with a couple of the team and vice versa. Ryan kind of liked that; he got a bit of a kick of others ogling his wife, and he also knew that it turned Sally on, as she had often talked about it explicitly in moments of passion. They went home a little tipsy and clearly more than a little horny and retired to the bedroom.

The next morning, both a little fuzzy from the day and night before, Sally followed him into their bedroom where he had already begun to pack his backpack.

"What do you mean you need to go on a trip? I need a change of scenery too. Take me with you," Sally began as she dropped down on their bed.

"I can't. You know that."

"Where are you going? When did this come up?"

"To the States. I got a call last night. It's important." Ryan zipped the backpack shut.

"I can't believe this has something to do with work. We had such a great night last night, don't you think?" She winked.

After leaving the SAS, Ryan had set up a small computer business out of London.

"Is there someone else, Ryan? What about you and I going on a vacation? How long will you be gone? When will you be back? You know my friend Gabby always suspected that you have another woman hidden away."

All ready to head for the airport, Ryan set the bag down and took his wife in his arms. "You know me better than that. Tell Gabby not all guys are like her husband. I know a great woman when I see one. There's no room in my life for an affair." He kissed Sally then added, "I would never jeopardize what we have together."

Sally smiled softly.

With his bag in one hand and a coat slung over his other arm, Ryan called over his shoulder as he hurried down the hall, "Let's plan a vacation as soon as I get back. Be thinking about where we might go. I'll call you after I land. I love you, sweetheart. Give my love to Emily, why don't you!"

Out on the driveway, Ryan deposited his backpack in the back seat of his work van and then sat for a moment before driving off.

"I'm on my way," he said softly but clearly into his cell phone.

6
OASIS

Bangkok, Thailand, October 2016, Day 2

JIMMY WAS IN THE MIDDLE of yet another party at his little hotel just a block from Patpong night market in Bangkok, Thailand. Jimmy had purchased the hotel with his Thai wife, Jenni, on the deeds a few years previously, and that night he had his usual entourage of scantily clad, beautiful Thai women competing for attention. Seductive music swirled out from the lobby to the poolside where they lounged. Most sipped mai tais, champagne, or an exotic cocktail.

Jimmy was in his element. Growing up in a hotel, enjoying a party, a tipple, and loving women. "What more could a man want?" he asked himself frequently.

He had hung up his boots upon leaving the SAS and traveled around for a year or so. He discovered Bangkok and met Jenni. They purchased the hotel from an old German guy who had owned it for years, gave it a touch of paint, and upgraded the bedrooms, pool, and bar. They got a string of local and international DJs to build up a roster that became the envy of Southeast Asia and attracted a young, international crowd of tourists as the must-go-to place when passing through Bangkok.

It was a cool place with international sounds and beats and a fair share of Thailand's beautiful people and an influx of Europeans who wanted to taste the hip side of Bangkok—without the blatant seediness but with plenty of naughtiness available. This was about as upmarket as Bangkok got, at least within three blocks of the infamous Patpong area.

The night was in full swing, the music pumping and a lengthy line outside for people to get into the bar. Jimmy had introduced a cover charge two years ago, much against the advice from Jenni and others, and although it took off slowly, nowadays, almost every night of the week, there were long lines that fattened Jimmy's pocket by $30 for each guest and seemed to make the exclusivity even more of a draw.

With the average wage for skilled workers in Thailand being just $200 a month, $30 was a lot of money. Jimmy didn't want to attract limited budgets. He wanted to attract unlimited budgets, and the introduction of rare delicacies helped that, with Cristal Champagne at $250 a pop and his range of vodkas starting at $200 a bottle up to $1,000. Jimmy was attracting an international crowd and some interesting characters.

Jimmy was on the top of the world. He had purchased the place for a song, and Jenni's friends, family, and contacts did the upgrades at local pricing, and although it looked a little tatty during daylight hours when they were closed, at nighttime it became an oasis for international visitors to sample some of the local delights, and each other if they so wished.

The place was buzzing!

The hotel had twenty bedrooms, and these were available for the night or by the hour, on demand. The hourly rate was lucrative for Jimmy, hence the inclusion of many temptations as he could find to get the Russians, Americans, British, and Germans to put their hands deep into their pockets and pay the $500 hourly fee for the most beautiful women in Bangkok, sipping their Cristal and having an experience of their lives.

He had hidden cameras recording every square inch of the property, with specific focus in the bedrooms. The footage went straight to the iron cloud and would be in storage forever. This was

Jimmy's insurance policy as he saw more and more of the rich, famous, and well healed coming through the Oasis, capturing every snort of cocaine, every intimate embrace, and every twosome, threesome, and moresome in the bedrooms.

The rooms were also available for visitors. These guests typically were couples carried away in the heady atmosphere of international beats, too much expensive vodka, and copious amounts of cocaine. Jimmy controlled the substances allowed in the hotel, and he allowed only two dealers to control the supply—marijuana, cocaine, and Es only. Nothing else crossed the threshold. The dealers, in turn for their lucrative concession, policed the venue for him and coughed up a sweet 20 percent slice of all transactions in return for the chance to earn boatloads of money from the customers.

Life was good, and the night was good when he saw a man he recognized with a white suit walking toward him with an envelope in his hand.

"Good evening, Charlie," Jimmy said, shooting the gent a welcoming smile. "What brings you to the Oasis this evening?"

Charlie smiled in return and said hello as well. "Uh, let me get right to the point, Mr. Jenkins. The US embassy received a message for you, and given its urgent nature, we thought I should bring it to you right away."

This sounded like a feeble excuse to Jimmy. He figured old Charlie was there for carnal reasons, not to deliver a message. Still, Jimmy was curious.

Why would the embassy go through this much trouble? he wondered.

Jimmy took the envelope. "Thanks," he said. "Make yourself at home, Charlie. Like you always do."

Charlie laughed and slapped Jimmy on the back. "You're a real pal, you know that?"

Jimmy nodded but said nothing. He made his way directly to his private office to open the envelope. His happy mood vanished as he read the short message. He made a call, listened, and said, "Okay, I'll be there. I'll be on my way in the morning."

Jimmy seldom let anything get to him. The news and the

unexpected summons was no exception. He went back to the club, Jenni, and his entourage. He glanced at the thick threads of cocaine lined up on a mirror in front of the executive lounge.

Why not. Fuck it! Jimmy thought. He fished a hundred-dollar bill from his wallet, rolled the bill into a tube, and did a fat line. Then he did another one. And another. The euphoric high hit him immediately. He suddenly felt great. Grand, in fact. He knew from long experience that it was the drugs, that the news he'd received bothered him more than he cared to admit. He did another line and tried to forget, just for the moment. He didn't even care if Jenni got upset with him. He'd been a coke freak when they'd first met, but he'd been off the snow for more than a year. He knew she'd be worried about why he was tasting the North Pole again after such a long hiatus.

Jimmy sighed, knowing he'd better not overindulge. He made his way to Jenni and gave her a gentle kiss on the lips. Holding both her shoulders, his arms outstretched so he could better see her beautiful face, he said, "Just got some news."

"What kind of news?" she asked, the concern clear in her voice.

"The bad kind. I gotta catch a plane to California ASAP."

"Are you sure?" Jenni asked.

"As sure as shit, honey," he said. "Sorry. But you're gonna have to hold down the fort while I'm gone."

"What's this all about? Why do you have to go back? You know the States don't agree with you."

"Can't really say more than that I have to go, Jenni."

Jimmy pulled her in close. She leaned her head against his chest. He stroked her hair, fighting back the emotional turmoil he felt whirling around inside him like a cyclonic vortex.

"Okay, Jimmy," she said. "Okay. I look after fort, like you say."

"There's my girl," he said. "Now I gotta go."

"Okay," she said. "You go. I stay. I here for you. I here for you always, Jimmy."

"I know," he said and made his way toward the nearby luxury apartment he shared with Jenni. Once there, he'd retrieve his trusty go-bag, a backpack he'd kept ready knowing that someday, one day, he'd need it in a hurry. It looked like that day had come.

As he neared the exit, he saw Uri Bokov, the local Russian Mafia boss. The prick was seated at his usual table. Baltic beauties and bodyguards surrounded him. Jimmy nodded and kept going.

Jimmy despised Uri and all that he stood for. The lout was loud and brash, had no sense of style, and his passion for young boys made Jimmy sick to his stomach. Jimmy wouldn't allow rent boys at the Oasis; Uri would find those elsewhere. He was, however, a good customer and frequented the Oasis two or three times a week, dropping $2,000 to $5,000 each visit.

Jimmy continued his exit and spotted Charlie, in his white Embassy suit, heading into one of the bedrooms with the two Thai beauties. Jimmy stopped at the front desk and said, "Make sure room number eighteen gets a complimentary stay from me, as long as he wants, and Mr. Bokov gets a complimentary bottle of Stolichnaya Red Label."

"Yes, Mr. Jimmy," the pretty receptionist said.

"And make sure the cameras are on."

"Yes, Mr. Jimmy."

Jimmy hit the street. The night air was warm, and the hustle of the streets remained just as frenetic as it had been earlier in the evening. He headed to the business district and was soon in his apartment. High security, air-conditioned, views of the city—he could be in New York, never mind in this Southeast Asian country with parts verging on the third world.

Jimmy did another line of cocaine and felt the pleasant jolt of the drug. The white powder kept the demons away—or almost did. For a second, he thought of his first wife, how he'd mistreated her, how she'd run off with his only son. The pain was still acute even after all the years that had passed.

He retrieved his go-bag, made sure it was packed with all the items he would need for the trip, and then called his usual car service to take him to the airport. On the way, he made a call on his cell. The recipient of the call half a world away picked up.

"Yeah? That you, Jimmy?"

"Yeah, it's me. Just thought I'd let you know I got an earlier flight. I'm on my way right now."

Silence. Perhaps it was a satellite delay.

"What time you get in?"

Jimmy told him.

"Perfect! The others will arrive all about the same time. Go figure that. A big convergence, eh? A coincidence?"

"I don't believe in coincidences," Jimmy said. He was getting a bad feeling about all of this. For some reason, his instincts told him there was more to the story than he'd been told. For some reason, he felt that danger lingered just over the horizon. He'd felt this before, and he knew it meant trouble. Big trouble.

"Neither do I. Call when you get in. I'll probably be there to meet you guys as you come in. If not, I'll let you know what's what. Okay?"

"Roger that," Jimmy said and ended the call.

As the armored limo weaved through the traffic, Jimmy gazed out the rear passenger window. The city glowed in white lights. There was life everywhere, but there was also death. He shivered, feeling as though a cold darkness had joined him in the adjacent seat.

Get a grip, mate, he thought. *Just get a bloody grip.*

PART II

FUNERAL

7

BROWN FUCKING
BREAD ... DEAD

San Francisco, California, United
States, October 2016, Day 4

MITCH SMILED AT THE REACTION of his friends when they saw
the Range Rover parked next to his own ride, a Ford Explorer fitted
with armor and bulletproof glass, in the shadows of the parking lot at
San Francisco International Airport. Their reunion had just begun,
the five friends flying in from all over the world. Mitch wished the
gathering was not occurring because of Paul's unexpected death, but
it was still great to see his former mates from the SAS. He took some
comfort in their presence, and he was sure they all felt the same way.
Paul's death was suspicious, to say the least. He looked forward to
getting feedback from all his SAS buddies. Maybe there was something
they could do that the authorities could not.

"Where did you get this baby from?" Mac asked with a grin. He
patted the hood of the vehicle.

"Ah, Mac, you know, may the Regiment always be with you!"
Mitch laughed.

"Yeah ... the force. Like the force, right?" Jimmy said.

"Something like that," Mitch said. "But I think you've been watching too many old movies."

All the men laughed.

The black Range Rover was no ordinary rental car. The extra grab handles and jump plates on the back and the runner plates down the side indicated that this was a trusty old pursuit and special ops vehicle used for quick entry and faster exits. It was obvious by the weight when opening the doors that there were steel plates within.

"So," Bob said, "cough it up. What's one of these monsters doing in the States?"

Mitch explained that a couple of years ago, he had been working with a group of US three-letter agencies interested in sharing techniques and equipment. As part of that sharing, the Americans decided that they wanted to test-drive a fully kitted-out SAS Range Rover. And they wanted to test it under fire. A call to the CEO of Land Rover was enough for them to oblige and kit a Rangey out to full SAS specifications.

The luxury, performance, and capability of the vehicle was taken to a new level. Specifications for a standard SAS Rangey included a built-in, full-armor package, supercharged engine, adjusted suspension, and additional running plates for external passengers and quick exit if needed. The Special Air Service and its relatives had valuable assets and friends placed around the world, and this Range Rover was just one of them. After the joint live-fire exercise, the Rangey went into storage. As soon as Mitch knew his five mates were on their way, he contacted his man at the White House and signed the Rangey out. It was as good as new with only two thousand miles on the clock.

"Can we keep it?" Ryan asked.

"You never know. They might forget who they signed it out to," Mitch said. He hit the key fob to unlock his vehicle. He popped the trunk. "Come take a gander," he said, nodding toward several boxes.

"What's this, mate?" Mac asked, picking up one of the boxes. He opened the lid and whistled. "You expecting trouble?"

Mitch nodded. "I think we better be safe than sorry is all."

The other men crowded around.

"Jeez, Mitch! You shittin' me?" Jimmy asked.

"Each box has a Browning nine-mill. No serial number. All untraceable."

"We're going to a funeral, not a firefight, mate," Bob said.

"We're going to a funeral for a guy who shouldn't be dead," Mitch said. "There's a care package in the trunk of the Rangey for you three," he said, nodding to Mac, Bob, and Jimmy. "You can unwrap 'em on your way to the hotel. Just in case we get company on the way."

"What the hell is going on?" Ryan asked. "I didn't fly all this way to put a bull's-eye on my ass."

"You got one on it anyway," Mac said. "Looks like we all do."

"Yeah, it sure does," Bob said. "And that sucks. Just fuckin' sucks."

"Oh stop it ladies. Let's move on and get on."

"Mitch … you got some explaining to do," Jimmy said.

They all laughed.

"Yeah, I suppose I do," Mitch said. "Come on, boys. We got thirteen miles to make before we hit downtown. It's two o'clock already. Traffic is going to be a bitch."

As they left the parking garage, Mitch noticed a gangly man with high cheekbones and hazel eyes. Something about the guy put him on alert. It was the way he seemed to be watching them from a nearby parking space as he leaned on his black SUV. He was wearing black pants, a black polo shirt, and a dark gray trench coat. Mitch focused on the road, keeping a fair distance from the Rangey, which Sam was driving with Bob and Ryan as passengers. Jimmy and Mac were with Mitch in the Explorer.

On the face of it, they were just attending the funeral of a friend. However, Paul's death suggested foul play couldn't be ruled out. Mitch wasn't just being paranoid. Bella had been kidnapped. Other SAS operatives had been killed or had died by strange accidents. They all had worked in operations that ultimately took out terrorists of different denominations, drug cartels, governments, and organized crime outfits like the New York mafia and the IRA. Mitch knew he was right to be cautious and diligent as they went about their lives and their businesses.

As Mitch drove, he thought about what he knew about Paul, other than that he was supposedly up to something big for the CIA as a private contractor. An apparent heart attack by the pool was unlikely, as he was a fit man and just forty-nine. Because of his apparently important work with the intelligence services, a postmortem was immediately arranged. It looked like an assassination. Some sort of lethal injection. The medical examiner found a suspicious red dot behind Paul's left ear. The blood work results had been rushed, and a preliminary tox screen revealed some odd results nobody could yet explain.

Mac, who was seated in the front passenger seat, stared straight ahead, scarcely glancing over at Mitch. Mitch looked in the rearview mirror. Jimmy was staring out the rear left passenger window, almost zombielike. None of them spoke for a long time.

Jet lag, Mitch thought. *Sadness. Rage. Probably a combination of everything. A real perfect storm.*

"I fucking hate funerals," Jimmy said.

"Based on the encrypted email you sent all of us yesterday after you called, it sounds like the fucking Russians to me," Mac said to Mitch. "The bastards. I hate the bloody Ruskies."

"You and me both," Jimmy said.

"Ditto," Mitch said, keeping his eyes on the road.

"What was he working on?" Mac asked.

"We don't know, but we do know that it was important enough to get buried deep inside the CIA and away from the eyes of the White House," Mitch said. "I have contacts at the White House, and they didn't know a thing about Paul. My source at Langley wanted to go dark. Told me about the ME finding an injection mark behind Paul's left ear and about the weird blood work on the QT."

"That's nice," Mac said, the sarcasm obvious in his voice.

"Better than nothing. Least we got a lead to investigate. My little friend at Langley also shared that Paul's mission had something to do with elections."

"The US elections?" Jimmy asked, incredulous.

"Much wider than that, I think. Deep Throat was vague. Didn't go into any detail at all. You could tell whatever it was Paul was working on was big, important, maybe very important," Mitch said.

Mitch turned onto Howard Street. He checked the rearview mirror. Sam, Ryan, and Bob were right on their tail in the Rangey. He'd been keeping an eye out for possible surveillance vehicles, but none were apparent, which didn't mean they weren't there. The Intercontinental Hotel, where Peggy had booked them six adjacent rooms, was coming up on the right.

"I was supposed to be meeting him the night he died," Mitch continued. "Pretty sure he had something big to tell me."

"Well the poor fucker is brown bread … dead now. Proper brown bread."

"Yeah, thanks for that Jimmy. Thanks!" Mac said.

"You always did have a way with words, mate," Mitch said.

"Thanks!" Jimmy said.

"I didn't mean that as a compliment you stupid fucker."

"Oh."

Mac laughed.

Then they all laughed, but Mitch sensed the tension in the car and the sadness. He pulled into the garage and parked. The guys in the Rangey found a spot a couple places down. Mitch glanced at his watch and saw it was about four o'clock, just a little after. They unloaded their bags and headed to reception and checked in.

Before they went to their respective rooms, Mitch said, "Let's meet at five, and we can head out for a bite to eat. Meet you in the bar?"

Everyone agreed.

"Let's not make it a long night," Mitch said. "We've got to be at the chapel tomorrow morning at nine forty-five."

Mitch's friends nodded. They were all silent on the elevator, which didn't surprise Mitch in the least. He had a lot on his mind too.

At just before five o'clock, Mitch headed down to the hotel bar, wondering if his friends were already there. They weren't. He took a seat at the corner of the square bar. As always, he made sure he had a good vantage point, providing him with a view back to the big, wooden paneled partition with the restaurant behind, window to the street on his right, reception straight ahead, and elevators to the left.

The bartender came over, and Mitch ordered an Anchor Steam. The bartender got him his beer. He took a big swig. He remembered the first time he had spoken to Paul in a bar while they were off duty. Mitch had heard that distinctive northern English dialect. Having lived in Newcastle for a while, Mitch could decipher and converse in the dialect. They had been in sync thereafter. Occasionally, he and Paul would engage in deliberately using the dialect, knowing few could understand them. Now these shared happy memories with Paul felt bittersweet. He recalled that when they first moved to San Francisco, no one could understand a word Paul said, and Mitch would translate for him. Mitch laughed to himself at the memory.

As he was about to take another sip of his beer, Mitch's friend, the general manager of the hotel, strolled up to him. He'd known Peter Moeller for years and was happy to see him.

"Guten Tag meine freunde," Peter said with a big smile and a big handshake.

"Hey, Peter," Mitch said and took a sip of his beer.

Originally from Dortmund, Peter was a good guy and a generous host.

"Wie viel kostet dieser Hund im Fenster?" Mitch asked in their usual banter. He knew a bit of German and had asked his friend, "How much is that doggy in the window?" It was an old joke between them. They both laughed, and Peter slapped Mitch on the shoulder as old friends do. Mitch thanked him for arranging the room upgrades for the team.

"No problem," Peter said. "Any time. Any time at all. Enjoy your stay." With that, Peter went about the business of running a fine hotel, leaving Mitch to brood over recent events. The team showed up one by one, some looking tired from jet lag. They ordered drinks and chatted quietly together. Mitch was pleased that, despite not seeing each other for years in some cases, it was just like old times.

Mitch knew the men considered him and Sam the leaders. He knew they also shared the impression that Jimmy was the joker. Bob was big and almost always serious. Ryan was a very big but gentle giant. And Mac? Well, Mac was just Mac, and he was the most eccentric of the group. The woodworker, the sniper, the hunter. Mitch suggested that they take a short walk to the Chieftain for a beer and pub supper. That certainly suited Jimmy and Bob, who didn't get the chance too often to eat good, hearty pub grub.

As they arrived at the Chieftain, Mitch noticed two men at the bar. They were deep in conversation. One was Pat O'Malley, son-in-law of the local Irish Mafia boss, a guy named Tommy Boyle. He spoke to the other man in whispers, no doubt discussing their criminal dealings, their empire, and Tommy Boyle.

As Mitch and his friends walked in, the two looked around and sipped their beers. They finished their beers and got up to leave. As they passed the group of SAS mates, O'Malley said to them in his deep Irish brogue, "Welcome to San Francisco, boys."

To Mitch, O'Malley was the stereotypical Irish thug. He looked the part with his mop of red hair, sparkling blue eyes, and a complexion reddened from too much booze.

"Who the fuck was that?" asked Jimmy.

"Nobody," Mitch said.

"Sure looked like somebody to me," Mac said.

"He's just a member of a local Irish syndicate. Provos, the successors of the old IRA with more bark than bite," Mitch said. "Guys are tough, but their former iteration was deadly, as you all so well know."

"How does he know you?" Jimmy asked.

"Long story. The Provos have been active in San Francisco for quite a while now. No worries, at least as far as I know. Maybe I'll tell you the story sometime," Mitch said. "Come on, guys, let's sit down. I'm starved," Mitch said.

Mitch knew exactly who Patrick O'Malley was. He knew his father-in-law very well from days gone by. He knew his wife from when she was a foul-mouthed teenager. They were scum then, and not much had changed today.

The Chieftain was a San Franciscan take on an Irish pub, with dark corners, wooden seating, and a stone floor. Harp, Guinness, and whiskies adorned the bar, with plenty of local favorites, Anchor Steam, Sierra Nevada, Laganitas beers, and a full range of spirits. Flat-screen TVs behind the bar and in the corners played Monster Truck games, a replay of a Manchester United vs. Liverpool game from the English Premier League, and some Ultimate Fight Club action.

Mitch assessed the clientele, noting that there were about twenty people in the bar—young, latest-generation beatniks hanging out, talking about technology, the next social media thing, texting, instant messaging, more obsessed with their phones than the conversations and the people around them.

Within a matter of seconds, the risk assessment proved low, and the six made themselves comfortable in the dark corner, with a leather bench seat on one side of the wooden table and wooden school-type chairs on the other side and at each end.

The barmaid came out with some menus, and Jimmy admired the twenty-something's curves. She wore flat shoes, jeans, and a black, skin-tight top revealing just the right amount of cleavage from her young, athletic body. With her distinctive Southern Irish accent, Ryan made the guess that she was from Cork. They ordered two all-day breakfasts, fish and chips, cottage pie, a roast beef sandwich, and Irish stew. Six pints of the local brew, Anchor Steam, and they were all set.

Upon asking, it proved that Ryan was spot-on. The man of few words had nailed the accent to not only the right province but the right Irish town. Hats off!

They sat in a silence that Mitch recognized from days gone by, wanting to enjoy their meal, replenish, recharge, and have time to reflect. Food was an important part of a soldier's life, especially if they were not sure where and when the next meal was coming from. Although they had grown to love composite rations, often, in the field, these were eaten cold, straight out of the tin, not having the time or inclination to break a stove. Having a square meal in front of you, hot and tasty, was a moment to savor and cherish.

As Jimmy was finishing off his plate, Mitch further briefed the group on what he knew about Paul, what he was working on, and the limited postmortem results. He'd only covered the very basics in the encrypted email he'd sent to his friends shortly after he'd called to tell them that Paul was dead.

"I'll know more once I have met with Paul's man at the CIA. You know. The source at Langley I mentioned. I have a call out for him and will be meeting him soon to get the full skinny on the situation—if he's willing to give me more information than he has already."

Mac said, "Heart attack, my ass. Paul was in better shape than I am."

"Yeah, it sounds fishy to me too, based on your email," Bob said.

The others agreed.

"You know," Mac said, "it sounds like the Russians are in this up to their necks. You remember the Litvinenko incident?"

They all nodded. Who could forget that?

The incident involved a guy named Alexander Litvinenko, a former Russian FSB secret service agent specializing in organized crime. He'd clashed with the Russian regime on numerous occasions. In 1998, along with others, he'd accused his superiors of ordering the assassination of the Russian tycoon and oligarch, Boris Berezovsky. Litvinenko was arrested for exceeding the authority of his position, acquitted, rearrested, and then acquitted again before moving to London with his family. He was granted asylum in the UK, where he worked as a journalist, a writer, and a consultant to the British Intelligence Services.

While in London, he wrote two books, which included accusations against the Russian secret services for staging bombings and other terrorist acts that eventually brought Vladimir Putin at the Kremlin to power. He also accused the Man at the Kremlin of ordering the assassination of Russian journalist Anna Politkovska.

On November 1, 2006, Litvinenko suddenly fell ill and was hospitalized, where it was established that he was the victim of radioactive poisoning, specifically from polonium-210. Litvinenko was dead three weeks later.

A British murder investigation pointed to members of Russia's Federal Protective Service as being the culprits and attempted extradition of the suspects, which Russia denied on the basis that extraditions were contrary to the Russian constitution. Later investigations seemed to prove the Russian government's involvement and the alleged dark links between Russia's political leadership and the criminal underworld.

"If Paul was nipping at the heels of the Kremlin, it's no surprise that he might wake up dead one day," Jimmy said.

"That injection mark is mighty suspicious," Ryan said. "I don't like this one bit."

"That's why I called you guys, apart from wanting you to know what happened to Paul so you could be here for his funeral. As I said, I'm hoping my contact at Langley can give us more."

"Well, I hope the gadger'll give it up," Ryan said. "I'm dying of curiosity."

"Bad choice of words," Bob said, his face serious.

"Sorry about that."

"No worries," Jimmy said.

They had another couple of beers and topped off the somber yet convivial evening with a round of Liddlesdale whisky.

Mitch stood and held his shot glass raised high in his right hand. "To absent friends!" he said.

"To Paul," Mac said.

"To all our good mates," Bob said.

"To the living," Jimmy said.

"To the brave! Living and dead!" Sam said.

"To us!" Ryan said.

Mitch felt a burst of pride as he clinked glasses with his friends, his dear long-term friends, friends he knew would put their lives on the line for each other without giving personal danger and risk a second thought. He only hoped none of them would have to risk their lives in the present circumstances, but deep down in his heart, he knew that there was more to Paul's death than met the eye. He sensed danger. It was palpable.

Early the next morning, Mitch met the team in the hotel restaurant for a quick breakfast. Then the team drove to the chapel, where they would pay homage to Paul and give their respects to his family. With Sam driving the Range Rover, and Mitch the Ford Explorer, the six headed north through San Francisco, down past the Embarcadero, with a view of the bay, and on by the ferry landing. As Mitch passed the Port of San Francisco Building on the right, he glanced over and paid his respects to Jack. His father-in-law, now long gone, had a memorial to his name in the building. The memorial was dedicated to Jack, the captain of the fishing vessel *Jack Junior*, so named after his eldest son, and to Jack's crew. The boat went down under suspicious circumstances. The story was that a Russian freighter ran the vessel down, but there was more to the case than that. Everyone knew it. They just couldn't prove it.

Perhaps it's the day. Our sad duty, he thought and pushed Jack out of his mind. He had enough ghosts to deal with today.

And yet the ghosts remained stubborn. They came to him as he, Mac, and Jimmy drove on in silence, each lost in thought. Mitch got into the zone behind the wheel, as if he was on autopilot, and, he figured, he actually was. He let the memories from his past in service of the SAS crowd in.

Mitch and eleven of his teammates were in a Westland Wessex HU-5 helicopter hedgehopping, in the absence of any hedges, across the snow-covered tundra in northern Norway heading toward their individual drop-off points at the extremes of the Norwegian border, one at a time. Their drop-off points were approximately a mile apart from each other, and they were to continue their lonesome journeys on skis to their designated positions and the coordinates issued in the briefing room that morning.

Mitch sat on the right-hand side of the Wessex, attached to the fuselage for safety. A tap on his right shoulder and a shout, "You're on, Mitch," was the signal Mitch had been waiting for as he was scanning the barren surface below.

With his full arctic camouflage whites over his survival gear, backpack full of equipment designed to make his arctic stay as comfortable as possible, his skis strapped to the back of his backpack, and his SA80 strapped to his chest, he was ready to go. He found his feet on the ledge below him, grabbed the rope until he got the tension, slipped the carabiner free from the safety line, and then started to abseil backward until he was at a forty-five-degree angle as the Wessex hovered above the snow, creating a micro blizzard below.

With his gloved left hand holding the rope above and his right hand below and behind, he released the brake on the rope with his right hand while at the same time pushing out with his legs and jumping backward in a controlled abseil to the ground. He landed, hunkered down on one knee, and gave the hand signal to let the dispatcher in the Wessex know all was well. The dispatcher returned the gesture, and the helicopter turned west and then banked farther north to drop the next soldier. The drop maneuver took only seconds. It would be barely noticeable on a radar screen, even if they were being watched.

The covert op had its roots in a long tradition of arctic military incursions. A most notable one involved an elite group of the Norwegian resistance fighters in World War II, now known as the heroes of Telemark. The brave men and women were tasked with sneaking into a heavy water plant to set off explosives to stop the Nazis' attempts to develop an atom bomb. The group disappeared into the arctic mountains a good distance from the plant in Norway and assembled. Surviving for weeks on skis, in snow holes, and sheltering in shepherds' hideouts, they traveled the roughest terrain, did their stealth mission, and managed to escape to tell the tale. Mitch's mission was inspired by the heroic deeds of the heroes of Telemark.

Twelve soldiers from G Squadron, Mountain Troop, were deployed on a three-day surveillance mission along a 126-mile stretch of the Norwegian-Russian border in the arctic wilderness. Their mission was to report any movement of the Russian military. Each soldier was all alone with just a backpack and a pair of skis. Everywhere was white. Snow covered the terrain, and even the insulated outer layer of clothing was white to camouflage his presence. Around the clock, the wind howled. There was no one to talk to, nothing to distract the mind. Sometimes the wind whipping around sounded like voices, like ghosts whispering. Given the proximity of the Russians, radio silence prevailed.

Mitch skied the five miles to his designated coordinates and went about digging his snow hole. He took off his backpack and skis, then recovered his digging tool, like an oversize Frisbee or mini surfboard with a blade at the front and serrated edges on the side.

Choosing a slope with a good vantage point across the Norwegian-Russian border, Mitch checked with his ski pole that there was sufficient depth of snow and worked the cutting tool to carve out packed snow blocks and create a cavity the size of his sleeping mat. He used the blocks to build the front wall and shaft to climb up and into the snow hole. He would create a window block that he could remove or plug appropriately, negating the need for him to leave the shelter once built. After about twenty minutes, his snow hole was built. He completed the finishing touches by throwing some fresh snow over the blocks he had just built and camouflaging his new home for the next three days.

Mitch was relieved to climb into the finished snow hole and out of the blistering wind. He laid down his sleeping mat and sleeping bag, pulled in his backpack, and got organized. Laying the SA80 on top of his sleeping bag, he then reached for his backpack and pulled out the small burner. He proceeded to boil some of the arctic snow as he nibbled on a slice or two of dried salami, made his coffee, and opened a pack of compo biscuits. Mitch popped the window as he drank and ate, looking out over the border to see what he could see. He felt at home, surprisingly comfortable, satisfied with his choice and snow-hole-building skills. He sent a signal from his satellite phone to confirm that he was in place.

There was plenty of time to think. Mitch was a thinker and, unlike many, enjoyed the solitude, the wilderness, the barren land, even the snowstorm whipping around him. This was the closest he could get to Mother Earth and something that Mitch had grown up with as long as he could remember, even as a boy growing up in the Lake District and practically living in the dales, glens, and fells of northern England, just below the Scottish Borders, close to his ancestral home.

As a child, Mitch practically lived in the countryside of the Lake District, and he remembered well the stag he found one day while with his loyal dog, Scruffy Murphy, a Patterdale terrier with a black, wiry coat and white beard and chest. They had come across a stag that had been snared by a big, ugly badger trap with its iron teeth and bite of a tiger. The stag looked like it had been there for some time, with a broken leg and bones popping out of its slender yet muscular leg, lying in a sheep enclosure behind a triad of dry-stone walls.

Scruffy Murphy found the stag and attracted Mitch's attention to the secluded enclosure. As Mitch arrived, it was obvious that the stag was in a serious state. Mitch knelt beside the stag's head, grabbed his water bottle, and gave the deer a drink. The stag looked him in the eyes, deeply, into his soul—a usually highly secretive, nervous, and paranoid creature, trusting and appreciating this loving and caring touch. As Mitch let the animal drink, he tried to figure out what to do next, but soon he saw the life gently and slowly fade away. Mitch actually dug a shallow grave for the stag, feeling that there was some sort of magical connection between the animal and him, wanting to give the respect that he felt was due.

Suddenly, Mitch lurched awake, realizing in seconds that he'd been dreaming, that he was in a snow hole on a vital mission. He'd seen the stag above him, tapping his foot on his chest, clawing gently at his shoulder, his face, backed by the bright, baby-blue arctic sky and the wind howling the snow around like some sort of vision. Mitch sat bolt upright, sweating in these arctic conditions, and looked around his snow hole. *What's the danger?* he thought.

The window had blown out, and the wind and snow howled around his enclosure so strongly that it threatened to compromise the wall of snow bricks at the front of the hole. Mitch grabbed the block and forced it into the aperture, rubbing snow and ice on the inside to create a seal and levering the snow tool on an angle to maintain the counterforce against the fierce wind.

Snow hole secure, he slipped down into the storm to look at its external structure and the camouflage, still standing and still holding up. In almost whiteout conditions, Mitch found this a surreal experience—until he caught a glimpse and the sound of a Russian convoy of armored vehicles passing right underneath him, less than thirty meters from the entrance of his snow hole.

Mitch, confident that they had no clue of his presence, grabbed his camera, took shots, and made notes and observations about the serious equipment in this short convoy of around twenty vehicles.

After the convoy had long disappeared into the blizzard, Mitch returned to his shelter, boiled some more snow, and made a cup of tea with a nip of whisky from his secret supply. He thought about his companion, the stag, and the image of him standing above, silhouetted by the blue sky, nudging Mitch with his hoof, warning him, waking him up from his dreams and protecting him.

Eventually, the third day came around, with some sightings of Russian military maneuvers on the other side of the border, arctic tracked vehicles, two SS1s or Scunner surface-to-surface missile launchers and what appeared to be drilling equipment. Mitch took notes and photographs before heading back deep into Norwegian territory. They wouldn't know the full picture until all the pieces of the jigsaw were pulled together and the picture complete—additional proof points from intel, satellite, intercepted communications, leaks from the other side, and patterns of activity and movement. Mitch was just a small cog in the total machine, but he and his friends were at the most dangerous edge of the equation.

Mitch and Mac converged about a mile out from the rendezvous point. They exchanged warm but brief greetings and continued on together. They were the fourth and fifth men back to their vehicles. Relieved, the men sat huddled between the two Hagglund halftrack vehicles, by the stove, waiting for the entire group to return. A burner was set up. They drank tea and ate compo rations—tinned rations such as sausages, bacon rolls, pilchards, biscuits, steak and onion, fruit pudding, apple pudding, and compo fruit drops. Most people would think this to be horrible food, but the soldiers grew to love it. It was comfort food to them. Supplements of salami and Tabasco sauce were also a part of the soldier's ritual.

The Hagglund halftrack all-terrain vehicles could practically go anywhere. The drive train was in front, a box where the pilot would sit, with the trailers behind for storage, supplies, and troops with covered canvas overhead. It was a reasonably comfortable ride back to the E6 toward civilization and then the Chinook helicopter to pick them all up. Vehicles, supplies, and equipment would go back to their temporary headquarters in Grotli farther south.

After waiting three hours, the soldiers grew concerned that the last soldier, Paul, might be in some sort of trouble. The men of the SAS would never leave anyone behind. They waited.

Out of the white, Mitch thought he saw something moving. But no, everything was white again. It was like being blind, so the imagination could fool you. Then he saw another movement in the same direction. Sure enough, the last man, dressed in the white snowsuit, came in after four hours; it was Paul. Paul had a big heart and was a fighter, as dependable and reliable as they come. They could always rely on Paul to come home with the goods. In fact, they could all rely upon each other. Implicitly. Absolutely.

A slight smile crossed Mitch's lips, remembering the gratitude that washed over him as they climbed inside the halftrack heading out. How easy it had been to joke once they were all safe.

"What took you so long, Paul? Did you have a sleep in, in that snow hole of yours?" Mitch asked.

"No, mate! Just out for a walkabout."

Mitch laughed and shook his head.

The team in the troop carrier all had a laugh, and they sang songs on the two-hour journey back to the Chinook helicopter and on to the lodge in the small village of Grotli, with open fires, hearty food, a couple of whiskies, and a game of cards.

"What are you grinning at?" Mac asked, bringing Mitch back to the present.

"Just remembering that time when Paul was last in," Mitch said. "Remember? On that three-day jaunt along the Norwegian-Russian border?"

"Which one?"

"You know."

"Yeah." Mac laughed. "How could I forget?"

"How could any of us forget?" Jimmy asked. "That Paul … he was a real righteous guy."

"That he was," Mitch said. "That he was."

8
GOODBYE

San Francisco, California, United States, October 2016, Day 5

AFTER THE FUNERAL SERVICE, BELLA'S mother drove the short distance to the cemetery. She turned into the cemetery entrance at Mt. Olivet. Bella admired the ornate, iron gates pulled wide open. The grounds beyond were richly designed with small, colorful bushes and flower beds, not just lawns between the large eucalyptus trees and redwoods. She was glad there was plenty of shade for this Indian summer, October day, which was already warming up.

"A nice day to lay Paul to rest," Angela said.

"Yeah, it could've been torrential rain. Like earlier in the week," Bella said.

"And that would have made an already very sad day utterly miserable. It was a nice service. All things considered."

Bella remained silent. She thought back on Paul's relationship with her dad and mom. Angela had known Paul for years. They had first met in Hereford when she first hooked up with Mitch. Paul and Mitch had gone on many trips together, spent a lot of time in Northern Ireland, and when Mitch and Angela eventually moved back to her hometown of San Francisco, Paul and his family followed a year later after visiting a couple of times and falling in love with the city. They had both lived in West Portal, a district of the city close to Nineteenth Avenue, Golden Gate Park, Ocean Beach, and the San Francisco Zoo, for a year and then slowly progressed north. Marin County was an escape from the fog of the city, a place to raise families across the Golden Gate Bridge. They both bought early in the Tiburon City. They stretched themselves back then, but all these years later, they had made good investments and were both sitting on nice, big houses overlooking the bay and on top of a nice piece of real estate equity. As her godfather, Bella had grown up with Paul's two daughters, Francesca and Emma. It was as if they were sisters and vice versa. Such a kind caring man. He had dropped dead so suddenly.

It goes to show how fragile life is, Bella thought as she gazed out of the window of Angela's black Audi Q8.

Bella didn't want to go to the funeral. It wasn't that she didn't love Paul and Betsy, Paul's wife, nor was it that she didn't deeply love Francesca and Emma. She did. She simply hated funerals. She despised the sadness, the self-torture, the grief. She would prefer to be at a distance, with their memories in her mind as she maybe slept in and then went to lunch with her best friends, Ashley and Chris. Maybe she would see a movie or catch up with her friend Nikita in London. She could have and would have raised a glass in memory at exactly the right moment. That right moment today was scheduled for 10:15 a.m. after all the rituals, the last post, and the interment to the ground, forever dead.

Bella had taken the opportunity to take her sabbatical, having received the news at the weekend. She worked hard and had a big job for a start-up, Executive Outcomes based in San Francisco, aggregating international risk data, analyzing it, and selling their risk analysis to large corporations to protect their investments and make global expansion decisions based upon that advice.

Their platform was kind of like a credit score for international risk taking in information from every single country, news channel, social media, poll, and election on the planet. It was put into one big database, and their secret source of predictive algorithms and artificial intelligence were in the process of learning so that these indicators could become more reliable predictors of what and where were safe to bet on.

When these algorithms were fully educated, the power of the platform would become invaluable, and the founders of that which she was employee number fourteen for would swell their bank balances as a result. It was a well-paid job for a reasonably funded start-up, and the upside for Bella was potentially huge, but the work was long and stressful at times. She hadn't taken time off since she started there two years ago at the age of twenty-two, jumping into the fray straight out of university. She deserved some time off, and the company management was happy to give her space, especially because of the death of her godfather.

Bella needed to recharge her batteries, take some time for herself to come back with renewed vigor. She would report back for duty in January, but she had some big decisions to make between now and then. She had just under three months to breathe freely and stretch her wings, just to see where she might go next. She had recently applied for a position at the CIA, and she had a good shot at joining the agency as one of its youngest analysts.

The entire time she had eaten breakfast earlier that morning, between bites of scrambled eggs her mother had prepared, Bella bemoaned the fact that adults chose what they did and didn't do, and going to Paul's funeral was certainly not on her list of things that she wanted to do that day. Her mother pointed out that she had to go, out of respect and out of support to Paul's wife, Betsy, and the girls who had become so close that they were referred to as cousins.

"Yes, but I didn't go to Uncle Luis's funeral last year."

"Your father and I gave you a pass on that one."

"Yeah, I know. I know. I had to be solid for my interview at Langley."

"That's right. But you're off from work now. There's no excuse not to go. Frankly, Bella, I think you're being selfish."

Bella hadn't said anything to refute Angela's assertion. Her mom was right. She was being selfish.

Angela guided the car into the big, empty parking lot.

"Oh, great," Bella said, looking over at her mom. "And now it's hurry up and wait."

"Grow up, Bella," Angela said.

"Mama! That's not fair."

Bella inwardly groaned. She had so much on her mind. Returning to work in three months would feel as if she had not left.

Maybe I won't go back after all, she thought. *Maybe I'll become a spook! In the meantime, maybe I'll head down to Chile and Antarctica. Maybe Dad can come with! And what about Machu Picchu in Peru?*

Bella's grandmother, Nonny, was from Peru. They had always talked about going to see her, but it never happened. Maybe she would head Down Under to see her friend Charlotte who had emigrated to Sydney with her blond-haired, blue-eyed surfer boy, or maybe head over to London to see Nikita and her old Oxford classmates.

Angela parked the car.

"And, Mama, please don't embarrass me by talking about me as if I were five years old: 'Lady Magdalen College, dual citizenship, double major in history and philosophy.' No one wants to hear any of that. They feel obliged to smile and pretend to be impressed. It is so embarrassing!"

Angela countered, "You mean I can't tell them you're joining the CIA Academy in the new year either?" She smiled knowingly.

"Mama! That's not written in stone. You know that. I have choices to make. My choices."

"Life is full of choices."

"Yeah, I know. My life is mine. It's personal, and I don't want all to know what I'm up to. Despite that, I'm not really supposed to tell anyone about Langley anyway, even if that is what I decide to do!"

Angela giggled as they ran through the familiar script. "So ... I can't tell them about your volunteering?"

"Talk about your own life, Mama."

"Aw, I'm so proud of you. It's so much fun to tell others how wonderful you are!"

"See, this is one of the many reasons why I didn't want to come."

"Oh, I thought it was because you didn't want to hang out with a bunch of old soldiers."

Bella almost smiled but caught herself. These men were more than mere soldiers. And they weren't old. Her dad was the oldest one, and he was only fifty, for heaven's sake!

Bella got out of the car and closed the door with a little too much force. She glanced toward the entrance of the parking and saw a black Range Rover and the familiar black Ford Explorer coming around the curve.

"Here's Dad!" Bella said.

She and her dad were close. Really close. She always liked spending time with him, except at funerals. That she could live without.

"Speaking of which, here comes the boys in blue," Bella joked as the two vehicles pulled up next to them in the parking.

Doors opened. The men got out.

"Don't joke, Bella. These are proud soldiers, not to be scoffed at," Angela, who had come around to the passenger side of the Audi, said in a whisper.

"A decade or two out of time for me," Bella muttered.

"And look at them. Powerful, strong men," Angela said, her voice even lower. "SAS. The envy of the world. The best of the best soldiers."

"Shall I sing the national anthem?" Bella retorted.

"No, keep your sarcasm to yourself, and I'll keep my bragging about you to myself. How does that work?"

"Works for me."

"Fine," Angela said. "Have it your way."

At breakfast, Bella had noticed that her mother had gone on a shopping trip in preparation for the funeral, and unlike the unflattering, all-black, usual funeral suit that she had worn for as long as Bella could remember, Angela looked fashionably glamorous in her new outfit, showing enough leg without being disrespectful and sufficient cleavage to catch a second look from any red-blooded male.

"Mama. You look very nice today. Did I notice that you're wearing stockings today? Dressing up for anyone in particular?" she had said between bites.

"Don't be so ridiculous, Bella."

"Busted." Bella had winked at her mom and continued to polish off her breakfast.

"There's my Bella!" Mitch said, striding over to her and giving her a hug.

Bella hugged Mitch back and said, "Hi, Dad."

She looked at Mitch's friends. The faces were familiar, the usual men who showed up for these private moments, comrades from the military, men who had fought alongside her father. Each man, all wearing ties out of respect, gave Bella and Angela a curt nod. No big, happy smiles today. Bella had no doubt that on this sad occasion, they would send off a respected soldier to the great beyond and then reflect on those they had lost before Paul when circumstances had not allowed a ceremony, or often a body to bury in the ground.

The soldiers all stood silently by the cars, almost as if they were on a parade ground standing at attention. Bella turned back to the entrance and saw more cars coming, relieved that the internment ceremony was going to start soon. One of the vehicles was the hearse.

"Hi, Angela," Mitch said, and he gave her a peck on the cheek.

"Hi, Mitch. Sad day."

"Yeah, it sure is," he said. "I know you know these guys. Sorry we were a little late for the service and couldn't sit with you."

"No problem," Angela said.

"Bella," he said, turning to her, "I know you don't know these guys, or at least not all of them. They're a sort of globe-trotting lot, you know. Hard to pin down in one place. Let me introduce you."

"I'd like that," Bella said.

Mitch did just that. Each man shook Bella's hand. Their handshakes were firm but not the finger-mashing kind. She thought that was interesting.

These guys obviously don't have to prove their masculinity, she thought, smiling at each one as they gave her their names.

Mitch turned to his friends. "Come on, boys." he said. "We have one last thing we can do for Paul today. And that's carry him home."

Bella watched as they went to the hearse. The coffin was unloaded.

Her dad and his friends, serving as pallbearers, hefted the coffin and proceeded to the gravesite. Bella and the rest of the attendees followed. To her, her dad was larger than life, a true hero, even a superman. Walking slowly with his friends as he carried the coffin bearing the body of her godfather, he looked somber but no less strong.

As a child, her mother and Bella had always mocked her father for carrying a backpack everywhere, fully loaded, always—torch, compass, water-purifying tablets, waterproof matches, mini first aid kit, length of rope, Swiss Army knife, snare, hand fishing line and hooks, insulated sleeping sack, Kendal mint cake for energy, portable stove. Everything needed in case of an emergency.

They also teased him for wearing desert boots instead of sandals when going on a trip, or taking his jacket with him, even in ninety degrees sunshine. Working out the exits before settling in any room. Bella had remembered going to a British American Business Council luncheon with her mother and father at the Fairmont Hotel in San Francisco, and with nearly one thousand people in the room and a gallery balcony above, her father refused to sit anywhere but adjacent to one of only eight emergency exits in the overcrowded room.

She remembered in London how her father had flatly refused to take his family on the Underground but stuck to above-the-ground means of transport, his constant diligence anywhere they went, positioning themselves facing the entrance and exit ways in restaurants, never backs to the door.

Even as a child, her father had taught her the importance of being diligent, one sure foot in front of the other, the basics of field craft signals used in the military for silent communication, and their famous code call that would allow them to connect with each other at a distance, reminiscent of a nonexistent bird of the jungle.

Her father had instilled in her to not be a risk taker but a risk manager; be aware of it, understand it, analyze it, and take measured risks accordingly. Bella surmised that was how her father had survived in his trials and tribulations along the way.

The pallbearers reached the gravesite. They gently placed the coffin on a carpet of Astroturf. The pallbearers stood back from the coffin as Bella stood behind her mom, who had taken a seat on one the few folding chairs lined up to the right side of the grave. Betsy sank into the chair next to her mom. Bella stifled a sob. Betsy looked so sad, as if she was about to break down. Bella couldn't imagine losing a husband, much less one as good as Paul was.

In keeping with Eastern Orthodox tradition, Mac opened the top of the coffin, allowing all to see Paul for one last time. Bella felt tears trickle down her cheeks as she watched her mom take Betsy by the arm and guide her to the coffin. Betsy's sobs carried in the warm air. Birds chirped. The sky shone a brilliant blue. All around them was life, the promise of new things, the lure of adventure, and yet there was Paul, his spirit and soul gone.

Bella wiped the tears away. She looked past the coffin and noticed that one of her dad's friends quietly positioned himself uphill from the gravesite while another remained equidistant to the far-right side. Both scanned everywhere except the gravesite. The remaining men stood shoulder to shoulder, still and solid, along the left side of the coffin.

How odd, she thought. *It's as if they're standing guard.*

Now alert to the fact that something was off, Bella looked around more carefully. Then she saw him. Far past the road where the vehicles were parked, a tall, gangly man dressed in all black with a dark gray trench coat leaned close to a large tree among the gravestones. He was clearly watching. She did not see any other cars and wondered how he suddenly appeared. Over the line of ex-military men on the opposite side of the coffin, quite a way from the road, was another man dressed in a suit. He was wearing sunglasses and smoking a cigarette.

Did those two come together? Who were they? Were they keeping an eye on the proceedings? Why?

Bella dismissed her thoughts as maybe just a piece of pre-CIA paranoia or a result of her father's teachings—be ever diligent, observant, and ever conscious about her surroundings and any potential dangers they may contain. Bella had worked out long ago that her father was not the same as her friends' fathers. He didn't work in a bank or local store. Although he traveled, he was not a traveling businessman.

Angela wrapped an arm around Paul's widow and murmured a few kind words. Bella regretted her comments as she silently watched the men across from her. She had to admit they could not be described negatively. The former soldiers were more capable of handling an emergency than anyone she knew, or indeed had heard of, not even in the movies, not even the gorgeous Jason Bourne. She was safe in their presence. There was a rugged masculinity in each of their appearances. Their confident demeanors were earned in brave deeds. No doubt it was men like these and others who had worked with her father. She chided herself for her careless remarks to her mother. These men were heroes. Bella looked at the men and realized why perhaps her mom had dressed just a bit sexily for a funeral. The men were hot in their own middle-aged way.

After the women sat back in their seats, the men individually walked up to bid their comrade a final farewell. Each man's relationship with Paul was unique.

Bella watched Mitch slowly approach the body. Was it sadness she saw in his scar-worn face? She could only imagine what Paul had meant to him.

Mitch gently placed a palm on Paul's chest and leaned close to each side of Paul's face.

Was the gesture a kiss on each cheek? Bella had never seen her dad look so vulnerable.

The minister assumed the lead at the head of the coffin. He launched into his brief sermon designed to make the attendees consider the bigger scheme of things. When the service ended, each soldier spoke to the widow before heading back to the parked vehicles. Their good wishes and sympathy began a fresh wave of grief. Wracked with emotional pain, one of the soldiers had to gently guide Betsy back to the SUV.

Wordlessly, Angela took Mitch's arm. They walked back down the sloping lawn to the parking lot. Bella walked slightly behind them.

"Are you okay, Dad?" Bella asked when they reached the Ford Explorer. Her father's friends stood a respectful distance away, letting them talk in private.

Mitch studied his feet, unable to meet Angela's and Bella's eyes. "Paul was a dear friend."

His grief hurt her heart. "I know, Dad."

Angela hugged him. "We should really go. People are waiting to follow us back to Paul's house."

Mitch nodded; his face now stoic, emotionless, hard somehow. In a way, the swift change in him scared Bella.

9

THE GATHERING

Tiburon, California, United States, October 2016, Day 5

ANGELA PARKED HER AUDI IN Betsy's driveway, noting that the widow and her two daughters had already arrived. The rest of the procession was following close behind, though there had been a slight delay due to traffic. Angela knew the roads and had taken a shortcut. She and Bella went into the house and began setting up for the reception. Betsy put a brave face on the entire ordeal, and Angela admired her for her courage, wondering how she'd react if Mitch had been the one who died.

As they put the food out, Angela couldn't help but notice how grown up Bella looked. She was no longer a little girl but a full-grown woman of great beauty. At five ten, Bella was tall by most standards. She was slender and sexily athletic with a golden-brown mane of hair. Her hazel eyes revealed a sharp intellect. Angela was proud that her daughter had inherited many of her own good looks, reflecting her Sicilian heritage, and those of her Scottish father as well. Bella was determined, fearless, brave, bold, courageous, sharp witted, and funny. She looked great in her black dress, black leather boots, and short black jacket with pearls. She was neither a girly girl nor a tomboy. And she always dressed in such a way that she would never be vulnerable, which was why she preferred flats to heels. That was another behavior she had learned from Mitch—to always be prepared for every eventuality, like having to run at a moment's notice.

Angela knew they both missed having Mitch living with them. Ever since he'd moved into the Veterans' Retreat, ever since he'd seemed to care more about the veterans than he did about them, there was a distance between him and her but not between him and Bella. A tinge of sadness unrelated to Paul's death seized her. So much had gone wrong in her life.

"You okay, Mama?" Bella asked. "Why are you staring at me?"

"I was just thinking how beautiful you are."

"We don't have time for this!" Bella said, the irritation clear in her voice.

"I know. I know."

They went back to work.

About fifteen minutes later, Angela heard car doors slamming and the sound of voices, most of them male. She rushed to the door and saw the black Range Rover. Sam, Bob, and Ryan got out. Mitch's Explorer was parked behind the Rover, and Mitch, Mac, and Jimmy joined them.

As Angela watched her husband's friends walk toward the house, toughened soldiers to a man, perhaps it was the funeral or the memories that cast her back to the fateful events of 1986. Like her sadness about Mitch, these earlier memories suddenly flashed through her mind. Was her father's death aboard his fishing boat an accident, or was it something more sinister? Was it retribution? Her lawyer had obtained a settlement from the owners of the Russian freighter, but the outcome provided no clarity as to what really happened. She shook the thoughts off. The pain of the present was enough for her to deal with. She put on her best face to greet the guests, her eyes darting to Jimmy as he walked up to the front door with his mates.

"Come in! All of you!" she said, embracing each soldier as she gestured toward the foyer with her left hand. "Come on! Don't let the flies in!"

Angela's heart raced as she saw Jimmy at the back of the line, patiently waiting.

"Jimmy!" she said.

Jimmy stepped forward.

"Angela," he said, moving close. "It's been too long."

She moved close to him, rubbed up hard and close to give him a feel of her breasts without being obvious about it. "Yes," she whispered, "it's been too long."

She kissed him on the lips, letting the kiss linger, though not long enough to attract attention. She was delighted to feel Jimmy stiffen as she pressed against her in a long embrace. She'd had a crush on Jimmy for more than twenty years. Sure, she ended up with Mitch, but Jimmy was something else, an itch she hadn't scratched, an itch she knew she'd never scratch because she was loyal to Mitch, even though they had been separated for more than a year.

Or was she loyal to him? Suddenly, she wasn't so sure.

Mitch made his way to one of the guest rooms upstairs. He had to just get away from everyone, at least for a little while. He lay down on top of the bed, folded his hands behind his head, and listlessly looked out the window. The bright red-and-orange foliage of a maple tree obscured the sun, save for a smattering of light that played off the ceiling when the gentle breeze moved the leaves.

It had all been long ago, those times with Paul, those times when he'd first met Angela. It had been less long ago since they'd separated, he and Angela. And, by extension, he and Bella. It was all for the best, he knew, but that didn't mean it wasn't hard on him.

Since moving to San Francisco, Mitch had got involved in the Veterans' Retreat in the Presidio, at first volunteering, supporting the homeless and the dysfunctional, often lonesome former soldiers. His efforts, energy, and enthusiasm to be there in support quickly led to an invitation to their board, and Mitch became a permanent fixture, eventually leaving the marital home, moving in to a neat, tidy, comfortable, and very regimented one-bedroom apartment at the Veterans' Home.

Back at the marital home with Angela and Bella, he left most everything behind apart from the contents of his trusty hold-all—a couple of pairs of jeans, polo shirts, a half-dozen of his favorite handmade Japanese socks, wash bag, laundry bag, and his trusty 9 mm Browning.

Mitch popped back home regularly, religiously for Sunday roast and occasionally to pick up some papers, a suit, his mail. He liked the structure of the Veterans' Retreat, and he liked the silent camaraderie. Unusual to most, it was Mitch's penance, his feeling of great responsibility, accountability for his life, regrets, good times, bad times, his wins and his losses.

The Veterans' Retreat was a place of solitude among friends, a way that he could give back, a place where he found comfort in the escape from—and facing—his inner demons.

Mitch met Angela for the first time in Hereford at the Starting Gate pub. He was with Jimmy that night, on one of the rare occasions they were at home. Angela was young, beautiful, and brown eyed, with beautiful, long brown hair, a clutch bag wrapped around her chest in a Parisian way—petite, smiles, adorable. Angela was standoffish, originally coming from San Francisco, now living with a host family in a rural town, Tenbury Wells, and reluctantly accepted a date with Mitch. They went to see a movie in Hereford, *Meet the Parents*, then for dinner and drinks. Mitch was busy on trips, and Angela was progressing in her equestrian career. They were married within a year of meeting.

Angela had changed. Although still beautiful, she had lost the bubbles she had when they first met all those years ago. She had seen a lot, endured a lot, been through the journey with Mitch—the silence, the upset, the arguments behind closed doors, the torment and moods caused by the pressures of his life, their life together. But they had an unbreakable connection, the emotional scars of the ups and downs, the travels, the adventures, and the deep love and respect that they had grown over all these years together.

The reception was pleasant enough, given the circumstances, but Sam was in no mood to draw the thing out. Like his five friends, he had much on his mind, aside from the feelings of grief that came with the death of any loved one. Thus, the men bade Betsy and the girls a sad farewell. Mitch said he'd stay behind to help the ladies clean up.

"You sure?" Mac asked. "We can all pitch in. More hands make the work go faster."

"No worries," Mitch said. "You guys head on out. I'll catch you first thing in the a.m."

Sam smiled, looking from Angela, who looked incredible, back to Mitch. "You sure you don't want to get a room?" he asked.

"Sam!" Angela squealed. "You're bad."

"Not as bad as you," Sam said.

"You guys are gross," Bella said.

"Yeah. Gross," Jimmy said, his grin as big as a barn.

"Come on, guys," Sam said. "Let's blow this Popsicle stand. Mitch, we'll see you first thing, mate. Right?"

Mitch saluted. "Aye, aye, Captain."

"Eat shit and die," Sam said.

"Back at ya!" Mitch said, and slapped Sam on the back.

They all briefly hugged, and then Sam and the others left Paul's house. On the way back to the city, Sam figured they all needed to talk. Of that he was certain. Just before he boarded his flight, he learned from a source at Interpol that their mutual pal had died of a heart attack in Tangier, an old mate by the name of Badger Bell. He'd emailed his team and then got on the plane.

While the local authorities didn't deem the death suspicious, Sam did. Like Paul, Badger was in fit health. Sam didn't believe in coincidences, and he was sure that his fellow team members didn't either. Mitch seemed to take the news in stride, but Sam could tell it hit him hard. It seemed that Mitch needed some distance, some way to process the added data to an already confusing data mix.

Sam drove into the city in silence, lost in his thoughts. He knew that Bob and Ryan needed to think as well, needed the silence to process the new information. Another friend dead. Another friend gone. It was getting to be a bit much. Sam didn't know what was going on, but he was determined to find out. Soon they reached Durty Nelly's, the Irish bar Mitch had suggested that they stop at for a nightcap.

"Well, looks like we've arrived, mates!" Sam said. "And no worse for the wear, eh?"

"Speak for yourself," Bob said.

"You do nothing but complain," Sam said. "Sometimes you sound like an old woman."

"Tell me about it," Ryan said.

"Oh, go fuck yourselves," Bob said. "The both of you."

"You wish," Sam said, glancing over his shoulder. He could swear that someone was watching them, that someone was on their tail. "Let's go in. I'm parched," Sam said, and they all went into the bar. Sam and Mac pretended to be watching the games as they stood close and kept an eye on the far corner booth. Three patrons were just finishing up their drinks and got up to pay the tab. Sam and Mac easily slid in their places. Once the others sat down and they ordered a round, the conversation shifted to Badger's mysterious death.

"I don't like it," Mac said, sipping his beer. "Two heart attacks in the unit so close together? Like hell in a hand basket. It just ain't happening."

"I don't like coincidences," Jimmy said.

"Neither do I," Mac said.

"None of us do," Bob said.

"I swear to God it's the Ruskies," Mac said. "I feel it in my goddamned bones."

"So, what do we do now?" Ryan asked. He lifted his pint. "Except have a few more of these. To Paul," he said, raising his glass.

"To Paul," Sam said.

They all raised their glasses. "To Paul. The old bugger," Mac said. "And to Badger."

"To Paul and Badger," the group said together.

They each took a long swallow, and then they all went silent. Sam listened to the noise of the bar and somehow felt lonely. He wanted to be back in England. Back with the boys. Back with the idea of retiring and living a dull life. Somehow, he didn't think that was going to happen.

After a while, Sam began to get tired. He could tell his mates were too. It had been an emotional day. The news of Badger's death made things even worse. They called it a night and headed back down the block to the Rangey. Suddenly, a late-model black Jeep Grand Cherokee flew around the corner and stopped in the street, obstructing their path. The driver's window was down. He glared at Sam and his friends.

Shit, Sam thought. *Is this how it all ends?* He started to go for his pistol.

The driver winked at them. No words were necessary. The threat was understated but clear: "Welcome to San Francisco, boys." The Grand Cherokee was gone, fading into the darkened street. The moment was over.

"What the fuck! That was the fucker who was at the funeral today!" Bob said.

"I knew I recognized the fucker today," Jimmy said.

"Tommy fucking Boyle," Ryan said.

"What the fuck?" Bob said.

"I think it was Boyle too," Sam said. "But I also think there were two other parties at the funeral, and maybe they're on us right now as well."

Jimmy shook his head and sighed. "You going to tell us what's what?"

"Already have. As much as I know from Interpol," Sam said. "I just think we gotta watch our asses extra close. Something's not right, and we gotta find out what."

"I'll drink to that," Jimmy said.

"Why is that not a surprise," Mac said.

10
MEMORIES

Tiburon, California, United States, October 2016, Day 5

ANGELA FELT THE EFFECTS OF the wine. Her earlier encounter with Jimmy and the cool night air coupled with the french lace rubbing on her delicate and sensitive nipples, the garters around her upper thighs, and the heightened sense of sexuality she had experienced throughout the day from putting on her new outfit that morning to the embrace from Jimmy. Angela knew she didn't want to go to bed alone again.

The wine had made her braver, and over the past hour, she had been sharing her cleavage with Mitch, bending over while cleaning the kitchen, loading the dishes, and giving all the signals that she knew how. She knew Mitch well enough that he was taking the bait, and she figured one last session of flirting would do the trick.

"Fancy a nightcap at the Farm Shop?" she asked, putting on that smile that Mitch knew all too well.

"Sure, why not. It's a chilly night after all," he responded. Angela jumped into Mitch's Explorer with the luxury cream leather seats. She hitched up her skirt, almost showing the tops of her suspenders. Despite their almost lifelong relationship, the atmosphere in the car was electric. "How was Jimmy?" Mitch cut to the chase.

"Oh, he was fine. You know Jimmy," she responded, crossing her legs the other way.

"You remember that night in Las Vegas with Jimmy, right?" Mitch asked as he put the car into drive and pulled away from the curb.

"When you two tried to get me into a threesome? Of course, I do. How could I forget? I live to regret the day," she said.

"What, that it happened?" Mitch asked.

"No—that it didn't!" replied Angela with a wink.

They remained silent for a long moment, and then they exchanged frivolous small talk until Mitch parked in front of the Farm Shop. Mitch went around to the passenger door to open it and let Angela slide out and adjust her skirt. Angela recognized this as a sign she was going to have her way that evening. She smiled smugly as they walked into the bar.

Inside the bar, Mitch did his usual sweep. In fact, he was more on edge than usual after Sam clued him and the rest of the boys in on Badger's death. Both Paul and Badger had died the same way on the same day. That, Mitch was sure, could be no coincidence.

"I'm going to hit the ladies' room," Angela said.

"Sure thing," Mitch said. "I'll get us a table."

Angela merged with the crowd. Mitch watched her go, his eyes fixed on her tight pencil dress, her long legs, the sway of her hips. He wondered why he'd left her in the first place, but, then again, he wondered about a lot of things lately. And the answers never seemed to come.

"Good evening, Julio," he said as he shook the hand of the familiar bartender from Guatemala.

"Hello, Mr. Mitch. The usual?"

"No, let's get a bottle of bubbly," Mitch responded.

"No problem, Mr. Mitch. Special night?"

"Maybe." Mitch smiled back at Julio.

Mitch looked around at the Farm Shop midweek crowd. It was eight o'clock, and the kids and families were long gone, leaving the balance of the wealthy, the beautiful, and often horny Marin divorcees looking for their next catch, with the usual group of single men looking for their next conquest in a ready-made Marin mansion.

Angela came back to the bar, having made herself more comfortable. Her blouse was unbuttoned one further notch, her breasts pushed up, showing her french lace, black bra, and attractive cleavage. With her thick brown hair, hazel eyes, cute little body, and beautiful face, she had been a catch when Mitch met her, and he thought she was probably a catch for the MILF hunters that frequented the Farm Shop today.

He took solace in the fact that he knew their connections were much deeper and that Angela and Mitch were meant exclusively for each other, unless by mutual consent. He knew that it almost happened that night in Las Vegas all those years ago with Jimmy, and although Mitch knew Angela wanted to, as did Mitch and certainly Jimmy, she just couldn't bring herself to do it. It was something she had high on her list of sexual regrets that she didn't have too much time to rectify. Angela was dressed similarly tonight as she was that night in Las Vegas with Jimmy.

"Bubbly?" Angela smiled at Mitch as she rubbed his inner thigh and made sure that he couldn't avoid a glimpse of her ample cleavage and french lace. She bent forward and whispered into his ear, "It's lovely to be with you tonight. I hope we can make it last all night." Mitch looked at Angela with his deep, sad eyes, full of love for his wife, his companion, his friend, and his rock. Maybe tonight his lover too, just like it used to be.

"You look incredible tonight, Angela."

'You don't look too bad yourself, big guy." They kissed. Angela whispered again, "William, let's go home. To bed!" She used Mitch's Sunday name.

Mitch felt a moment of elation. He leaned over and kissed Angela gently on the lips. "I think that's a terrific idea," he said.

The rest of the evening was a dream for Mitch. He so needed the warmth, the passion, the togetherness he always felt with his wife, estranged as they may have been now. She gasped when he told her of Badger's mysterious and suspicious heart attack. She held him close and told him not to worry, that everything would be okay. And for a short time, he believed her.

As they lay together in those moments following sexual satisfaction, Mitch heard the buzz of his phone, and a call came through from Sam. It was just after two in the morning. Sam was operating on UK time.

"What's up, Sam?" Mitch asked. This could not be good news at this time. Sam switched the phone to speaker mode so that Mac, who was with Sam at the Intercontinental, could hear.

"Mitch, where the hell have you been? We've been trying to get hold of you. We've been worried."

"Sorry, boys. I got caught up with something." He glanced over to Angela and her voluptuous body pleading for more.

Mitch listened as Sam told him what happened with Tommy Boyle.

"What? The Tommy Boyle!" exclaimed Mitch. "I thought he was out of the fuckin' picture."

"Evidently not," Sam said. "Saw him with my own eyes."

"Shit," Mitch said, letting out a sigh. "As if we don't have enough on our plates."

"So true," Sam said. "So fuckin' true."

Sam went on to brief Mitch of his suggested next steps. Thirty minutes later, Mitch hung up the phone and lay back next to Angela. As he slowly caressed her back and her beautiful olive skin, his mind went back to Northern Ireland and the first time he met Tommy Boyle.

Belfast, Northern Ireland, 1988

His first SAS operations assignment, Mitch was laid on his bed in the Big Green Barn, an aircraft hangar at Belfast International Airport, Aldergrove, a nondescript building and nothing to look at from the outside, but inside it had the resident security, surveillance, intelligence, and killing force of the 22 Special Air Service in Northern Ireland and was tackling the threat of the Provisional Irish Republican Army.

The hangar stood on the periphery of RAF Aldergrove adjacent to Belfast International Airport. From first and second glimpse, it was just another aviation hangar, but behind the big green doors, it was a small village, an operations center, a base for surveillance and action.

A collection of prefabricated buildings were inside, the operations room and training rooms were to the left, the cookhouse on the right, with the bar behind a firing range, and in the middle, a collection of porta-cabins that housed the thirty-soldier population of this elite unit.

An array of vehicles—Range Rovers, Land Rovers, pursuit cars, motorcycles, and boats—was lined up in neat rows in various allocated zones within the hangar—all fully loaded, fully fueled, and ready to go at a moment's notice.

The tannoy cracked, and it was a call to go and pick up an operator from a shopping mall in West Belfast—a seemingly innocent, low-profile, low-risk request.

It was around ten in the morning with blue skies and sunshine as Mitch headed out in the Special Forces pursuit car. He pulled into the mall carpark and confirmed with the ops room that he arrived on time. They explained that there had been an incident and that Mitch should sit tight.

The thing is, sitting tight on your own becomes a bit conspicuous the longer you do it. It starts to stand out like a sore thumb, with a sense of growing paranoia, as what could be innocent observations of passersby are easily construed as being clocked.

Mitch called the ops room from the car radio and was told to continue his holding pattern.

He headed into the mall to grab a coffee and sat at a cafe, positioned strategically to get an unobstructed view of his surroundings. He grabbed a newspaper, read it from front to back, started doing the crossword, and grabbed another coffee to go. After about an hour, he headed to a pay phone and called in. Same story—incident in East Belfast, no sign of the operator, hang tight.

Now there is only so much browsing one can do in a shopping mall, and after another hour of hanging around and increasing stares from shoppers, paranoia was rising by the minute.

There were plenty of stories of people getting kidnapped, never to be seen again, at least alive. It seemed to Mitch that the more time went by, the profile of the shoppers seemed to be changing. Less and less mums and kids, grandparents, pensioners, and more and more men, menacing stares. *Who are you? What are you doing here?*

Mitch went outside for a smoke, and it seemed that there were a bunch of black cabs cutting around that he hadn't noticed earlier. Given that the black cab brigade had been implicated in many of these disappearances, including the recent incident with Corporals David Howe and Derek Wood, Mitch's paranoia increased. His only level of comfort was his trusty Browning 9 mm strapped to the chest and the two spare clips of rounds in his pocket.

A couple of guys approached Mitch, and his pulse rate went from high to a level that accelerated his adrenaline to new heights. In a deep Northern Irish, grating, menacing, drawl, "Have you got a light?" one of the men asked to Mitch's relief, but they gave him that look. The type of searching look, trying to get a glimpse of his soul, see the fear in his eyes, check him out. Mitch obliged and gave them both a light, confidently, not showing his nerves, bright and breezy. Mitch noticed one of them had MUFC tattooed on their wrist.

Mitch said, "Are you watching the game later?"

"Which game is that?" they asked together.

"Man United vs. Liverpool" Mitch responded, pointing to the tattoo on one of their wrists.

"Don't think so. We have a lot to do today," said one and winked menacingly.

"Thanks. See *you* later," the other said, and they both trotted off.

Mitch headed to the car and approached it from the rear, getting the right angle so that he could see the five-light warning system. Fuck! All five lights were on! Fuck! Fuck! Fuck!

He headed back to the mall, more stares, more black cabs. He could see the two he had just given a light to window-shopping in ToysRUs of all places. He found another pay phone.

"Hey, John, I need to get the fuck out of here. I have five lights, no operator, and I'm attracting an uncomfortable level of attention."

"We're still dealing with the incident in the east. The pursuit team is tied up out there, and we don't have anyone available to pick you up," came the response.

"What the fuck! How long do you think?"

"We don't know, could be at least a couple of hours. Can you get a ride to the City Center?"

Are you fucking serious? Mitch thought. *Want me to hail a black cab and ask them to take me to that Big Green Barn at the airport? End up like Woods and Howe?* Mitch knew they were referring to the nearby train station, but that had its risks too.

Now, Mitch knew full well the sometimes-questionable accuracy of the five-light alarm system. It was a big risk to take, but at this point, weighing his options, he realized that hanging out at the mall wasn't sensible. Could he get to a train station maybe? Should he call a yellow cab from a safe part of town? Maybe, but it could take forty-five minutes to get here. Should he stop some random black taxi? Definitely not.

Mitch headed back to his car. All five lights were still on. He dropped his newspaper as subtly as he could to get to the ground and check the undercarriage to look for any additional baggage of the magnetic kind. Looked clean. Wheel arches, clear. No sign of break-in and entry. Nothing seemed suspicious apart from the five lights. Decision made. Take the risk and drive out of there. After all, it could have been a little kid playing around, a shopping cart bumping the car, a malfunction of the alarm. An IED was a possibility but, as Mitch assessed, a lower probability than getting into a firefight or worse.

Mitch held his breath as he put his key into the door and turned the barrel, heard the unclick, no blast to follow. He grabbed the handle and pulled, opening the door—no blast. He slid the key into the ignition, and the engine whirred into life, no blast. Engaged into gear, rolled away, gave it a quick burst of acceleration, no blast. "Thank fuck!"

As Mitch rounded the car park in a loop to get on the exit lane, he passed the mall one last time, and the same two men were out front having a smoke. Seemed they had their own light after all, and the one with the MUFC tattoo feigned a casual salute and winked with a big toothless smile. *Fuck!* That was one of the scariest mornings of Mitch's life.

Mitch decided to have a mosey around town to see what was going on. He called into the ops room and let them know he was out of the mall and was heading into Belfast. He took a route around the Divis Flats, Falls Road, and Shankhill Road.

As Mitch was heading back to the city to get on his route home, he was at traffic lights and next to him spotted the distinctive figure of Baldy Quinn. Quinn's photo was in an impressive position on the ops room wall, and he held the honor of being one of the IRA's youngest, most prolific killers and most wanted. Mitch called the ops room and confirmed positive identification. They advised Mitch to keep a distance, observe with caution *but do not engage.* Intel was plotting something and didn't want to blow their inside cover and the operation.

Mitch kept his distance as instructed and followed him at two to three cars' length. He bobbed and weaved—highway, back street, circles. He was either making sure he wasn't being followed or had already worked out Mitch was behind him.

After about thirty minutes, Mitch gracefully took a turn back to his route and headed to the Big Green Barn.

Mitch got back safely and went to the ops room. He debriefed them with the gallery of the most dangerous men and women of the Irish Republican Army looking down upon him. The mugshots of Tommy Boyle and Baldy Quinn stared at him.

As he left the ops room and headed for a beer, he turned and looked at Boyle and Quinn. "Until next time, gentleman," he said quietly.

Mitch woke up with a start and sweat pouring down his brow. *Tommy fucking Boyle,* Mitch thought. He looked around him, looked down, and felt the sensation of Angela's lips working their magic and getting him ready for round two. Or was it three?

Mitch was happy to oblige, and Angela very receptive. This time she wanted to fantasize about her missed opportunity in Las Vegas. She jumped on board, and Mitch obliged, recalling the events from all those years ago in Las Vegas, whispering in her ear. It didn't take long before Angela was writhing in ecstasy and enjoying her rapturous moment.

Mitch slid out of bed, jumped in the shower, and found a pair of jeans and a shirt in his wardrobe, still caringly maintained by Angela. Mitch always appreciated that about their circumstances. They were apart but always together.

"Hey, Mitch, when are you coming home?"

Mitch kissed her on the lips, "Later." He jumped into his Ford Explorer and left.

I I
JACK OF THE SEA

San Francisco, California, United
States, October 2016, Day 6

AS MITCH DROVE BACK TO his place, he recalled the night he had asked Angela to marry him. Angela had a gig in Yorkshire as a three-day event instructor at the Yorkshire Riding Center, and it was their annual Christmas party at the Yorkshire Hussars.

Mitch had just gotten back from London, a four-hour, Friday afternoon drive, in his Rhodes and Woods blue, striped suit. As he arrived at his apartment, the phone rang. It was his old mates Kipper and Jimmy. "Hey, Mitch. It's Kip. Are you coming out tonight?"

Mitch thought about a shower, a night in front of the TV, catching up with the news, and ordering takeaway and a bottle of wine. "Nah, mate. I'm knackered. I am going to stay home tonight."

Kipper responded, "Great. We'll pick you up in ten minutes! Angela will be there!"

A half an hour later, Mitch, Kipper, and Willsey walked into the Yorkshire Hussars for the Riding Center Christmas party. Within another two hours, Mitch was drinking Harvey Wallbangers with Angela at the bar, just like they had carried on from their last date after seeing *Meet the Parents*. That night, Mitch made the promise to Angela that they would marry one day.

Their first trip together was a drive north to the Highlands of Scotland to see Mitch's lifelong friend Mac. They stepped into Mitch's black Audi S8 and powered across the M62, up the M6 toward the Borders. They stopped in to see the anvil at Gretna Green before stopping off for the night at the Pine Trees Hotel. They had some Scottish fayre and whisky by the open fire before bed.

The next morning, they continued north through Aviemore, Inverness, and then on through the single-track road to take them to Mackay Country. About thirty minutes outside of Tong and the welcoming fire and Guinness of the Brass Tap Bar, a statue of a Scottish warrior adorned the side of the road, and it read, "Welcome to Mackay Territory." The message was intimidating, a warning, a statement commanding respect.

He knew that Angela never forgot that trip—the drive, the statue, and the beautiful stag they saw that day on the snow-covered hillock by the road, its beautiful antlers, its eyes staring at Mitch and Angela as they stopped to see this beautiful spectacle before them. The stag stared, motionless, confident, drilling into their eyes. This wasn't any usual wildlife sighting; this was spiritual, like two warriors staring each other down, passing their mutual respects.

The stag rattled his antlers in the air, gave one last nod, and slowly turned away and disappeared. Mitch had described the hairs on the back of his neck as he remembered the stag in the Lake District and his various sightings since. Was this real? Was it the same stag? Was it just a spirit?

"Wow!" was all Angela could say as Mitch pumped the supercharged Audi engine and they headed to the Brass Tap to meet Mac.

"Did you just see that?" asked Mitch.

Angela looked at him more than puzzled. "What? The stag back there?"

"Yes, the stag. What did you think of it?"

"Well, it was kind of magical, surreal, and special. It was like he knew you, Mitch."

Mitch flashed a smile and squeezed Angela's hand as they continued their journey.

A few months later, they were married, in a castle of course, Ripley Castle in North Yorkshire, with friends from around the world, family, and fireworks. Angela's brothers decided to have a punch-up late that night. Thankfully, Mitch and Angela had gone to bed, saving the inevitability of the groom having to clean them both up.

The next day, they headed out to Bangkok to the Emerson Hotel just outside the Royal Resort of Hua Hin. As they arrived at the Bangkok airport, the little Thai driver, Mr. Charlie, greeted them with his cardboard sign, "The Mitchells," and led them to his beat-up Toyota with three hundred thousand miles on the clock. As they traversed the slums of Bangkok, Mitch looked at Angela and realized what she must be thinking. Were they on honeymoon or on a mission?

Three hours later, as they neared the Emerson, although the density of poverty had decreased substantially, it was still very evident. It was a dark, humid night as Mr. Charlie approached the hotel and swung into the driveway to a chorus of frogs and crickets. Mitch grabbed the bags and proceeded to check in. As they walked into the complex, there were candles lit everywhere, along with the distant sound of traditional, soft Thai music and a drumbeat coming from somewhere deep inside the complex. As they walked through the grounds of waterways and lily ponds, the music got louder, although still soft and spiritual. The center of the complex opened up with tropical gardens and a large water feature in the middle, with a floating platform with three traditional Thai musicians playing their spiritual sounds.

Tea lights adorned the water, along with the lights of the squid boats and their own lanterns bobbing around on the waters of the Gulf of Thailand, attracting their catch. Angela and Mitch paused for a moment, looked around, looked at each other, and smiled. It was another magical moment they would never forget.

The next two weeks were filled with love and solitude. They played backgammon and chess together. They read in quiet moments, sunbathed, and dined at local eateries. They even took a trip into the nearby town on a *tuc tuc* to see traditional Thai boxing one evening.

Looking back on it, Mitch realized that the oasis they had stumbled upon marked the happiest two weeks of their lives, and he longed to have that time back again.

Angela, he thought, keeping his eyes on the road, *what you have gone through in this life. What we both have gone through ...*

San Francisco, California, United States, May 26, 1986

Angela would never forget the day. It was a watershed and forever changed her life. Angela's mother, Juanita, was at the stove making one of the family favorites, *lomo saltado*—sliced steak, onions, and plenty of tomatoes with braised garlic rice. It had been a family recipe passed down through the generations from her roots in Lima, Peru. Angela was in the kitchen with her siblings, Jack Junior, Audrey, and Robert. The TV was on, but it was turned down low. It was a quarter to six in the evening.

Angela's dad was away on a fishing trip, but he was supposed to be back soon. She always missed him when he was at sea. Jack Senior was born in Sferracavallo, a close-knit little fishing village just outside of Sicily's capital, Palermo. Sferracavallo was named after the horseshoe bay on the Mediterranean where it sat. This was the spiritual home of the Piscinis, rich in history over the many centuries of its existence from the ancient civilizations of North Africa, Asia, Europe. For Angela, it was a place of rich culture and history—beautiful yet severe, flavorful yet dry, full of love yet unforgiving.

The first time Mitch visited the island just off the boot of Italy, he was a child with his father. They'd driven from the north of England through Paris, the South of France, Monte Carlo, Pisa, Rome, Naples, and Reggio, and gone on the ferry to Palermo. At a restaurant in Reggio, his father met some businessmen who told them the rules of doing business in southern Italy.

This was not the first time that Mitch's father had done the grand tour. Years previously, after leaving the terrors of World War II, Walter traversed Europe in his Jaguar SS 100 with his pal Jules Constantine. On this, Mitch's first grand tour, they called into Paris on the way past, stayed the night, and went in search of his father's favorite Parisian restaurant, Le Petit Couchon, on Le Monte Marte. The Little Pig had clearly been there for decades, and so had the waiters, as Mitch recalled. The food was fantastically French, Parisian, and the atmosphere straight out of a Tintin storybook.

As they made their way out of Paris and headed south, Mitch had told her how amazed he was by the scenery and sights as they went from town to town, through the countryside and cities, across borders—the beautiful, stylish, and chic French Riviera, Monte Carlo, driving part of the Grand Prix circuit to the sophisticated Menton and on to the underwhelming pass through Pisa and its one and only interesting thing, the Leaning Tower.

Farther south, they had a stay in Rome, with hustling, bustling traffic and its beautiful grand dames, St. Peter's Basilica, the Coliseum, the Trevi Fountain, and on through Naples with its impatient drivers, beeping horns, and laundry hanging between apartment buildings over the narrow streets.

One thing Angela recalled that impressed Mitch was how there was such a significant difference in wealth as they made their journey, from the palatial palaces of Versailles to the exuberant riches of Monaco, across the border to Italy a few miles away, and farther south where the riches were less apparent, and poverty was more so.

As Mitch and his father neared Palermo on the ferry, Mitch had told her how he'd seen a collection of shanty buildings by the shore. These people were living in conditions just a couple of notches above the homeless and not dissimilar to what he would see later in life in Nairobi and Mombasa, Kenya.

They arrived in Sicily, the home of Mount Etna, the Mafia, and the Piscinis.

Jack's family house was just a block from the quay. It was tall, tiny, and narrow, with the family kitchen on the top floor.

On a later trip to the island, Mitch and Angela were seated in a restaurant overlooking the harbor of Sferracavallo, where they enjoyed a long lunch with plenty of Sicilian seafood and wine. It was a glorious Mediterranean day, with sunshine, fine food, and good company.

The resident accordionist was Aldo, and throughout the lunch, Mitch had asked him to pump out various tunes: "Moon River," "Come Fly with Me," "Strangers in the Night." Aldo told Mitch in his best Pidgin English that he was formerly a merchant seaman and he had been to Liverpool. After a couple of hours and a couple of bottles of wine, practicing Mitch's own Pidgin Italian, Mitch asked him to play *The Godfather* theme, assuming it was one of his top ten requests.

It probably was on his top ten requests, but it quickly became evident that there was no way in hell he would even try and understand what Mitch was asking, never mind play it, despite Mitch's attempt to hum the first few lines of the tune.

Aldo packed up his accordion and abruptly left. Mitch and Angela never saw him again.

Sicily was a dangerous place, especially if you were in the police or a judge trying to crack down on the Cosa Nostra. Their activities had moved far beyond olives and butchery to more profitable areas of commerce, including finance, construction, prostitution, people trafficking, and drugs.

Many Italians and Sicilians saw an opportunity in the USA to start new lives and new business interests, opportunities escaping the post-Mussolini poverty in Italy, but those who left would always remember their family, old friends, and the way of the Cosa Nostra.

On one of Mitch's trips to Sferracavallo, Mitch went to a restaurant on Father of the Sea Day, where fathers and sons would lunch together in a restaurant with a big shop window and a staircase going above. Nestled beneath the staircase and invisible to the road was the seat of preference for the chief of police, out of sight, out of visibility, and out of range. A hangover from dangerous times.

Jack of the sea needed to get out of Sicily and get out quickly. He hid in the hills above Sferracavallo for a couple of weeks until his exit was arranged. He joined a ship in the middle of the night and was on his way from Palermo to Costa Rica.

It was a long trip but a relief to be out of Palermo. Relatively safe, at home with the sea, Jack was pleased to be on his way. They had arranged for a wife to meet him, and they married, headed north, and arrived in San Francisco a couple of months later, with a divorce from this short-term chaperone quickly following.

In San Francisco, Jack quickly made friends. Important and influential friends. A senator, a judge, a mayor, and various high-profile business people. He also met Angela's mom, Juanita.

Juanita and Jack were married at Saints Peter and Paul's Church in North Beach, San Francisco.

Jack Junior was a fishing boat. Sky blue and brilliant white, Jack Piscini Senior was the captain. The boat was funded by a consortium of Jack Senior's acquaintances. *Jack Junior* was moored in Fisherman's Wharf, behind San Francisco's famous and renowned Scoma's Restaurant, where Jack Senior would deliver much of his haul.

As Jack and Juanita grew the family, Juanita's family came up from Peru, sponsored by Jack. Jack continued to send money home to the *famiglia* at home. They moved from the south side of San Francisco and bought a brand-new property that would become the family home for the Piscinis.

Jack was a fun-loving, party-loving family man. He worked as hard as a man could work, spending days at sea, applying the trade he had learned from his fishing ancestors' roots back in Sicily. The sea was in Jack's blood. He didn't need fancy technology as his guide; he knew the seas like his own hands.

He had a short fuse. Fisherman's Wharf was a rough place back then, full of other Sicilians with short fuses. Jack carried a pistol with him all the time at work, and a couple of skirmishes resulted in traded shots and traded fists.

Overall, life was good. Their Volvo station wagon would be there at the wharf to greet him upon his return from long trips, along with Juanita, Jack, Audrey, Angela, and Robert. Juanita would drive to the Buena Vista for an irish coffee with Jack while the kids would stay in the car outside.

When flying solo, Jack and his crew would head to Gino and Carlos for a quickie before heading home to see the family.

Little Jack would sometimes go down to the wharf with his dad, hang out, go out to sea on day trips, and do target practice with his dad's pistol. Those moments, alone with his dad, in the real world, would never leave little Jack.

Earlier that fatal month of May, Jack decided he wanted to cycle the Golden Gate Bridge for the very first time—suddenly, out of the blue. He did. While there were no incidents, it held lots of meaning.

And then Jack didn't come home. Angela would forever recall that fateful evening in May. At six o'clock, the piping-hot lomo saltado and rice was plated. It was Audrey's turn to say grace. When she was done, they started eating.

And then the news broke about the accident. *Jack Junior* had gone down. Eventually, a Russian freighter was implicated, and although the company tried to cover up the incident, a settlement was reached. Still, the tragic loss of her father and the subterfuge surrounding the accident made an indelible impression on Angela. Of all the men aboard, only Jack's body was recovered. Angela always wondered if the collision was an accident, or if Jack and his crew had been killed as some sort of retribution for past transgressions, possibly going back all the way to Sicily.

The words that she heard on that 6 o'clock news that night would live with her forever, "May Day, May Day….Jesus Christ, he's gonna hit us….Fuck….." Then Silence.

12
AFTER-PARTY

San Francisco, California, United
States, October 2016, Day 6

AS MITCH WALKED INTO THE Intercontinental Club Lounge, a private room on the sixth floor, he and Mac exchanged glances. They both knew there was something very wrong. They had been here before, and their telepathic senses confirmed that violence was just around the corner. This was the very same sense that his grandmother, Maggie, had described as an itchy nose, a sure indication of violent things to come.

Sam started out, having received his briefing from SAS Headquarters in Hereford earlier that morning.

"Listen, boys. Clearly, there is something not right here. Upon further investigation, they found traces of polonium-210 in Paul's blood samples. We're still waiting to get Badger's body back from Tangier City. We'll do the blood work on him ASAP. Given the added complication of Tommy Boyle's unexpected appearance last night and the shady-looking guys at the funeral yesterday, I fear we're at the start of a shit storm that we don't have the answers to. On that basis, we need to deploy and go our separate ways. I need to head back to Hereford. I'll be leaving from SFO later this morning. I would highly recommend that you stay vigilant, stay on your toes, and keep your wits about you. There's something going on here that we need to get to the bottom of.

"Thanks, Sam." Mitch exhaled loudly. "Have a good trip!"

Mac echoed the familiar phrase they used. They never knew where a fellow soldier would end up and whether they would cross paths again. "Have a good trip, Sam!"

Sam left the room with his backpack, and the balance of the room fell silent for a few moments.

Mitch took center stage. He stood and faced the group. "First of all, Sam called earlier this morning. We have confirmation that Paul had been working with international agencies, including the CIA, to understand some strange activities associated with election rigging around the world. Paul was mainly focused on the upcoming election in the USA."

The former soldiers looked around at each other.

"Paul called me the day of his heart attack and arranged to meet to discuss his latest findings on who was behind the election rigging. We were due to meet at Shanghai Kelly's in San Francisco before he apparently collapsed by his pool prior to his daily run. Now, I'm not sure how Badger figures into this or if he does but—"

Mitch was cut off by loud protests. "Oh, they're related!" "You bet your ass!" "Of course, the deaths are related! Same cause of death!" "Something clearly wasn't right!"

"Okay, okay. Guys, guys. I know what it looks like, but I'd still like more facts," Mitch stated.

"We'd all like some answers," Mac added.

"I'm going to arrange to meet with Paul's CIA contact." Mitch pulled his cell phone from his pants pocket and moved to the next room where their arguing was less noisy.

"For fuck's sake, boys," Mitch muttered under his breath.

The Dubliner, West Portal, San Francisco, California, United States, October 2016, Day 6

Wearing his Eddie Bauer puffer jacket over his Ralph Lauren shirt tucked into his Polo Jeans and Eddie Bauer boots, Brad walked into the Dubliner to meet with Mitch. Brad noted that he blended in with the late-afternoon happy hour crowd. It was a collection of contractors drinking pints with Irish whisky chasers, plucking up the courage to go home to their wives. A dozen sports fans were watching their team chase the score, a couple of business folks were catching a drink after work, and the old man at the end of the bar was drinking himself to oblivion. It was the usual midweek afternoon crowd in the Dubliner.

As Brad entered the bar, he noted that he caught the eye of a pretty redhead seated alone at a table. She smiled. Brad knew he looked good to most ladies, what with his rugged chin and athletic step. He gave the lady a quick nod to acknowledge her, and then he bellied up to the bar to wait for Mitch.

He ordered a local San Francisco gin, Junipero and Fever Tree Tonic, ice and lemon, then took his position in a quiet seating area at the back of the bar, near the only access to the bathrooms and the pool table upstairs—a quiet enough place to meet with Mitch and observe the bar.

Brad had been in the CIA for twenty years. He was an honored veteran with operations around the globe in various friendly and not so friendly states, occasionally overt but mainly covert, or black, operations—arming, funding, and training rebel fighters, extracting his own from hostile situations, extracting valuable assets with information before they got caught, bringing in intelligence, and making clandestine connections, all for the good of the United States of America. In God we trust.

He had taken the oath many years ago. He'd gone through some real shit storms in all those years, and he was relatively certain that he was in a shit storm now. Paul's death was just the beginning. And now Badger Bell was dead too. Brad and Paul had been working on an election-rigging scandal they uncovered in Thailand a couple of years previously, but the investigation had spiraled into bigger things elsewhere in the world, including more recently in the US homeland. They had made progress, and the day that Paul died, Brad was due to meet him at this very same bar because Paul had something that he had discovered, and he needed to share it quickly. Evidently, he was due to share the same with his old pal and comrade Mitch, the very same day.

Maybe as a form of insurance? he thought.

He had flown back from Washington, DC, that morning to meet with Paul, getting the news of his unexpected heart attack when he landed.

Brad had worked in many countries with many nationalities and professionals over the years, but there was something different about his relationship with Paul. No edges, no hidden agenda, just a desire to get the job done. He also liked the British sense of humor, the sarcasm; it reminded Brad of his own roots growing up as the son of a Scotsman and a New Yorker mother in Boston. It was a very different sense of humor and beat when compared with the polite political correctness of Northern Californians and San Franciscans.

Brad had also worked with Mitch some years earlier.

As a private contractor to the CIA, Mitch had been working on cracking a highly organized drug cartel backed by the Russians as an undercover operative. It seemed that, at the cusp of a major import to the US, the Russians wanted security, their own form of insurance, and as Mitch was about to make the exchange, the cartel had arranged for an aunt and uncle to collect Bella from her school. Mitch received the call and confirmed that Bella was alive and well and looked after. He immediately alerted Brad, who in turn coordinated the synchronized response. Later that evening, Mitch called to confirm the exchange, and within seconds, a Navy Seal team raided the two-bedroom hotel suite where the Russian aunt and uncle were entertaining Bella with popcorn and Popeye movies.

Bella was safe and sound, but the sheer shock of the incident was enough to unsettle Mitch and instill an almost permanent state of paranoia. He extracted himself from the operation and cursed the Russian Mafia and, in particular, one brutal, ruthless man close to the head of the organization and the Kremlin.

With Brad's bird's-eye view at the back of the bar, he could observe everything. A group of three Central American–looking men came in for one very long drink and spent as much time observing the contents of their glasses as they watched the activity in the bar. Brad spotted it but wasn't concerned. After all, this was San Francisco, and apart from the violence of the projects in Bayview, East Palo Alto, and the challenges in Oakland, the city was fairly blessed in that it was a pretty safe place to call home—certainly safer than most of the places Brad had been in his twenty-year career.

Then he saw Mitch come in. Mitch saw him and came over. As he sat down, he said, "Good to see you again, Brad. Thanks for coming."

"Sorry to hear the news about Paul. Who would have imagined? I mean, a heart attack. Based on the postmortem, it seems like there's more going on," Brad said. "Much more than meets the eye."

"There certainly is more to the story. Paul was murdered. We're thinking Badger Bell was too. Were they working together on the election tampering?"

"How do you know about that?"

"A little birdie told me. What I want to know is what you know. Come on, Brad. Let's not play games."

Brad remained silent for a long moment as he took a sip of his drink. Then he said, "We're both familiar with the Litvinenko incident in London. Similar MO but with distinct differences, including an instant effect, and secondly, barely a trace in the blood work."

"The Russians are up to their old tricks," Mitch said.

"I think so too," Brad said, "but we can't prove it."

"The fucking Russians," Mitch said.

"So, what now, Mitch?"

"I was sort of hoping the CIA could fucking tell me that!"

Brad explained that the investigation into the surprise win in Thailand unearthed corruption, bribery, payoffs, and a few eliminations. At first, they weren't surprised; those things happened all the time in many countries around the world. The difference in this case seemed to be that it wasn't driven domestically; the influences were coming from outside the country and not just exiled political activists or hackers or crazies. This was more organized, and a high level of funding was needed to pull it off—beyond the resources of the usual suspects.

Their initial investigation aimed to understand why. They came up with a list of suspects that potentially had motive—mainly developers, exploration companies, infrastructure investors, and neighbors to Thailand. Although they found plenty of and differing motives, they didn't get anything that quite made sense.

"Paul had come across this bank, based in London, that had been taking some big bets and had been winning big as a result. That was the last I heard until Paul asked me to meet with him here last week, but as we know, he never made it."

"How can we find out what he knew? Do you guys keep journals, logs, records, anything?"

Brad laughed and said, "No, Mitch, no files." Brad spotted a man walking toward them, slightly staggering, homeless looking, wearing a big gray trench coat, black pants, a black Polo, and a knitted skullcap. He stood tall and awkward before them.

"Hey, mister," said the man pointing at Mitch. "Is that your black Ford Explorer Platinum outside? The one that the SFPD are about to give a ticket?"

Mitch looked at him with a glint of recognition, but the urgency of avoiding the overzealous San Francisco Police Department giving him an expensive ticket prompted him to jump up. "Thanks," he said to the tramp.

"No worries, mate," said the tramp in a drawn-out Australian accent.

"Okay, you go sort that out, and I'll get a couple of drinks. Anchor Steam?" said Brad.

"Sure," replied Mitch as he headed out.

As Mitch walked across the street, something really bothered him. When was the last time he had heard "No worries, mate" from a tramp, a homeless man? When had he ever experienced a homeless guy caring about someone getting a ticket—never mind who? How did he know that the Ford Explorer Platinum was his?

He got to the other side of the street where he had parked the Explorer and took one final look behind him at the front of the Dubliner before skipping in front of the L-Train making its way back to the city from the zoo. With no sign of the police, he clicked the doors open, went in the driver's door, and leaned over for his cigars and lighter.

Kabbooooom!

Although the passing train shielded Mitch, he still felt the immense shockwave from the bomb blast. As the train moved on, Mitch stared in disbelief at the wreckage that once was the Dubliner. Smoke hung thick. Fire raged within the building. Bodies and body parts littered the street.

"What the fuck!"

Mitch ran across the street, but he couldn't get close to the bar, much less inside it to see if Brad survived. By the looks of it, nobody could have lived through the blast. Brad was dead. As he turned around, he caught out of the corner of his eye a Jeep Grand Cherokee and Tommy Boyle driving past the Dubliner sign in the road his furrowed face absent of his usual toothless grin, not noticing Mitch, keen to make his exit.

Farther up High Street, close to Starbucks, Mitch saw the gangly figure striding away from the scene, discarding the trench coat and the knitted skullcap in a trash can on the road before taking one last look at Mitch, then turning left and disappearing. Just a glimpse. *Who the fuck was that?* Mitch asked himself.

Mitch didn't wait for the SFPD to arrive. He jumped in the Explorer, headed down to Ocean Beach, and parked. He took a deep breath, looking out at the Pacific Ocean and the sunset, and let out a big sigh. "Fuck, fuck, fuck! Not again!" He could feel it welling up inside of him—that familiar but nowadays unwelcome feeling.

Having gotten at least some of his hearing back, and with his brain wobble starting to settle, Mitch reached for his cell phone, punched in the numbers, and held it to his ear.

"Mac, it's me. We need to get together. Where are you?"

"In Sausalito. What's up?"

"We need to pay our friend Tommy Boyle a visit tonight."

"Tonight? What's the urgency?"

"I'll tell you when we meet. Let's meet at the Mucky Duck on Ninth and Irvine. Get a cab. Leave the Rangey where you are. We'll ride together tonight. Bring the pistol I gave you when you arrived. Bring your fight boots and your boxing gloves."

"Will do. I'll be there in twenty minutes."

"Me too. See you there. Just be on the lookout, okay? The shit's hittin' the fan."

"I figured it probably would, Mitch," Mac said. "Be there in a few."

"Right," Mitch said, and ended the call.

Twenty minutes later, Mac walked into the Mucky Duck and found Mitch at the back near the bathrooms. "What happened?" Mac asked as he pulled a stool aside and sat down beside Mitch.

Mitch went through the events of the evening, the Central Americans watching their drinks, the backpack, the mysterious Australian, the explosion, Tommy Boyle speeding away.

"C'mon, Mac, let's go."

"What about the boys? Bob, Jimmy, Ryan?"

"No time. Besides, we can take care of Boyle ourselves."

Durty Nelly's, Outer Sunset District, San Francisco

Mitch parked the Ford Explorer Platinum two blocks away from Durty Nelly's and the homeland of probably one of the IRA's most dangerous and connected terrorists on the West Coast. Old habits die hard, and Mitch parked the Explorer rear end first, ready to move and not in the most obvious place to park—in the parking lot of a garden nursery business, no obstacles, no restrictions for a quick getaway yet shielded from public view.

Mitch and Mac stride the two blocks to Durty Nelly's, met by an Irish bouncer in his late twenties. "How can I help you two gentlemen?"

"We're here to see Tommy," Mitch said.

"Like fuck yer are," the bouncer said. "Besides, we don't let English fuckers of your sorts in here."

"Hey, Shamus, just fucking let us in so that you don't get fucking hurt," Mac said.

"Who the fuck you think you are, old man, coming in here calling the fucking odds?"

Mitch took the guy out in a matter of seconds. Right jab. Uppercut. Kidney punch as the bouncer whirled around, exposing his back.

"Asshole," he muttered.

"Out cold, mate," Mac said with a laugh.

"Come on," Mitch said. "Let's get on with it."

They entered the bar. Mitch saw Tommy seated in a dark corner in the back of the bar, alone but alert with a sawn-off shot gun on the table in front of him.

"Well, well, well, look what the fucking cat dragged in." Tommy aimed the shotgun at Mitch.

"What the fuck have you been tailing me for?" Mitch asked.

"I haven't been tailing you, Mitch."

"Like bloody hell you haven't," Mac said. "Look. We made a fucking deal with you many years ago. So don't fuck with us. We won't fuck with you. But it seems like it's too late now."

"Why'd you blow up the Dubliner?" Mitch asked. "I saw you there."

Tommy looked genuinely surprised. Mitch wondered what the man was thinking.

"Believe it or not, Mitch ... Mac ... I just bought the Dubliner yesterday," Tommy said. "Yeah, I was there. It's my place. Or at least it was. And I'm fuckin' pissed because some assholes just cost me a bloody fortune."

Mitch gave Tommy a hard stare. He wasn't sure, but it did seem like Tommy might be telling the truth.

"Fuck off, Tommy. Who were the four fucking thugs in the black Beemer?"

"How would I fucking know?"

"Well, I guess you'll not be needing this," Mitch said. He pulled the shotgun from Tommy's grip. At the same time, Mac grabbed Tommy's left hand and drove his horn-handled hunting knife with the thistle crest through the middle of Tommy's palm. Tommy screamed in agony.

Mitch and Mac kept an eye on the few other thugs who were in the bar, but none of them seemed interested in helping Tommy out of the situation. They just nursed their drinks and shook their heads.

"Poor Tommy," one of them said.

"Yeah. Poor fuckin' Tommy."

"I'll kill you for this!" Tommy screamed.

Mac said, "Don't be making promises you can't keep."

"Now, Tommy, what the fuck is going on? We aren't leaving until you tell us. Got it?" Mitch said.

Tommy started to whimper like a kid. "Look what you did to my hand! Just look at this mess."

"It'll get much worse if you don't start talking," Mac said as he twisted the knife in Tommy's hand. Blood poured out on the wooden table.

"Oh God! Oh my fuckin' God!" Tommy whined. "Listen, all I heard was that your Geordie mate was working with the CIA and had gotten closer to something than he perhaps should have. That's all I heard."

"Tommy, who fucking assassinated him?"

"I don't fucking know," Tommy said, grimacing in the pain from his hand.

"Who were the Central American–looking fuckers in the Beemer and in the Dubliner tonight?"

"I don't fucking know."

Mitch pointed the Browning at Tommy's knee. *Bang. Bang.* Kneecapped.

"Fuck you, Tommy. We're here to find out which of you murdering bastards killed our mates," Mitch said.

"All right, all right, you fucking crazy bastards. You need to go see

Grace and Partners to get your answers. That's who contacts us when they want a job done."

"Grace fucking who?" asked Mac as he turned the blade of the knife to inflict yet more pain.

"A pair of fucking Yorkshire sheepherders who contract for Dmitri Dankov."

"Dmitri Dankov?"

"Yes."

"What the fuck does Dmitri Dankov got to do with all of this fucking mess, Tommy?"

Mitch felt as if he'd been punched in the gut. Dmitri Dankov was one serious player. Mitch shot Mac a knowing look. They both knew that Dmitri Dankov was the mastermind behind Bella being snatched all those years ago.

Sirens were nearing. Mitch nodded to Mac. "Time to go," he said. "I think we finally got what we came for."

"Looks like it," Mac said.

"Come on, let's get the hell out of here."

With Mitch in the lead, they both ran for the back entrance. As they reached the door, they heard Tommy continuing to shriek. And then he began to laugh hysterically. An insane, hysterical laugh.

"You fuckers are in above your heads, in too deep. This time you have no fucking chance, and I'll see you both in fucking hell!"

Mitch drove in silence, turning things over in his mind. He was glad that his friend followed suit and remained quiet as well. When they got to the approach to the Golden Gate Bridge, Mac broke the silence. "What the fuck are we going to do, Mitch?"

Mitch paused for more than a few moments. "I'm not sure. I haven't worked it out yet."

"What did the CIA guy tell you before he got himself blown up?"

Mitch's mind went back to the Dubliner, seeing Brad after all those years, recalling their conversation, the bar, the after-work happy hour crew, the old man at the bar, playing it back in his mind, frame by frame. The out-of-place Central Americans, the bag he noticed on his way out. Why didn't he put the two together? *Who leaves a backpack in a bar nowadays, especially after 9/11, the Boston Marathon, and all these crazy fuckers in this world?*

The Australian. Who the fuck was the Australian? There was something vaguely familiar about him. Why did he save my life? "What the fuck?"

Tommy Boyle at the scene. *Who was in that black car behind him? Was that the Central Americans? Who detonated the bomb? Was it intended for him too?* No, no. Why would they possibly want him? Must have been Brad. They must have thought that Paul told him something. What was it that Paul had found out?

"We trace Paul's last movements. That's what we do," Mitch replied to Mac.

"We need to set up an operation. That's what we need to do, Mac."

"How the hell are we going to assemble the resources we need to do that?"

"Let's get the boys together. Get Sam on the phone and work out a plan," Mitch responded. "Let's meet at my house in the morning at eight. Angela's out tomorrow. Bella's out. Let's make a call. I have something in mind."

Mitch's phone buzzed as he received a text message, "RRR! 895 OFarrell."

Mac looked over at Mitch.

"It's a code red, red, red from Bob—extraction. Let's go."

Mitch powered the Ford to get back across the freeway and over the bridge toward the city. He recognized the address, it was the Mitchell brothers' strip joint on O'Farrell Street.

No relation to Mitch, brothers Jim and Artie created this sleazy strip, live sex, and brothel in the O'Farrell Theater, in downtown San Francisco, and it had become the place to go to see the darker arts of the flesh in action. The two brothers had links with pornography, prostitution, and other crime, with Jim shooting his brother dead after apparently threatening to throw a Molotov cocktail into the club. Jim did seven years in San Quentin, then retired to his ranch, and the club still ran on in the family, Mitch explained to Mac as they headed to the city.

It did not surprise either of them that Bob, Jimmy, and Ryan would be there. As they neared within two minutes, Mac texted on Mitch's phone, "ETA 2 Mins. Location?"

Mac got an immediate response: "OK. Outside."

As Mitch was pulling up outside, he spotted the distinctive figure of Big Bob with Jimmy at his side in a faceoff, with what seemed like a group of around ten largely Hispanic-looking men. Mitch pulled to a halt, unlocked the doors, and shouted out of his window, "Get in."

Jimmy and Bob turned to the Ford Explorer as Mac let a round off from his Browning 9 mm above their heads to keep them at bay. With the doors closed and passengers on board, Mitch swung the vehicle 180 degrees and headed out of the situation into the midnight streets of San Francisco, spotting a black BMW 750i, long wheelbase parked close by. Mitch recognized the gangly man he'd seen at Paul's funeral. He was tempted to make something of it but decided he had enough on his plate now.

Back in safety zone, Mitch looked in the mirror at Bob, Jimmy, and Ryan, all clearly worse for wear and smirking to themselves.

"The three fucking musketeers. What the fuck happened back there, boys?" Mitch asked.

"It's a long story," Bob said. "Let's go for a drink and I'll tell yer!"

"Fuck it. Why not?" Mac said. "I could do with one after today."

It was hard for Mitch to disagree. He headed back to the Chieftain and parked the car.

They bustled in with Jimmy, Bobby, and Ryan in frequent hysterics. They headed straight for the bar and ordered a bottle of scotch, then sat down in the now familiar darkest corner of the pub. The boys regaled Mitch and Mac with tales of their adventures. Mitch, who had a lot on his mind, moved on to the actual business at hand.

"So, how come the triple red and extraction request?" Mitch asked.

Jimmy's face got serious. "We ran into some muscle that wasn't local," he said.

"We got into it with them," Bob said. "Big time."

Ryan continued the story. "Well, it turns out these fuckers were from some Colombian gang from out of town. It turns out they knew our names, you two, the rest of the crew, Paul and the man from the CIA—I think they said Brad?"

"As soon as they said that, it was time to text you. What took you so fucking long, Mitch?" Jimmy laughed.

"We stopped in for a fucking pizza, Jimmy."

"We had a bit of excitement ourselves," Mac said, and he told the three about the goings-on at the Dubliner and Durty Nelly's.

As they finished up their drinks, Mitch said they should all call it a night and head back to the hotel. He noted that his friends were subdued in the car, and for good reason. It seemed clear to Mitch that all of these events were probably related, though he wasn't sure how yet.

The Russians, the Irish mob, and now Colombians? And what was up with the gangly man who seemed to be tailing them? *What was up with that?* Mitch thought.

"Nothing good," he mumbled as he turned onto Howard Street.

Mac, who was sitting in the front seat, yawned and asked, "What was that? Didn't hear you, Mitch."

"Nothing. Just thinking."

"Oh. Well, don't strain yourself."

"Very funny," Mitch said, but he didn't feel humorous. He didn't feel humorous at all.

PART III

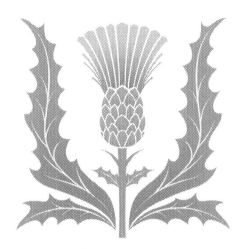

OLD HAUNTS

13
CODE ARGUS

Tiburon, California, United States, October 2016, Day 7

MITCH LEANED BACK IN HIS chair and looked at the group of old friends from across his desk, a vintage piece from the 1950s. He glanced around the room and let his mind wander to *Tintin Amerique*, *Le Lotus Bleu* and *L'Ile Noir* framed posters on the wall. A bookcase was full of places that Mitch had been—awards, memories, and three plaques, Family Crest, 22 Special Air Service Regiment, Argus. His father's maps of the Normandy invasion sat behind his desk. His various accolades and his father's medals were at the front of his desk, and his hard-earned sand beret behind.

"Well, boys," he said, "looks like we're in it real good now. No turning back, I'm afraid. We all got bull's-eyes pasted on our asses." The phone rang. Mitch saw it was Sam. He hit the button for speakerphone.

They were sat in Mitch's study in Tiburon, a cross between a museum and a homage to Tintin, the international adventurer. His grandmother's sideboard had survived the Blitz of World War II. There was a small statue of a fully laden SAS soldier, Mitch's leaving gift from the Regiment, as well as a Gilbert Rugby ball and his Army Rugby Union finalist medal when his team was defeated by the Third Parachute Regiment and he suffered a broken rib.

This was Mitch's sanctum, his museum, his lifetime collection. Every inch told a story of adventure and accomplishment, his journey.

His oak desk was full, although regimented and neat. It was busy with books, articles, papers, field binoculars, a cigar box full of trinkets like an old treasure chest, and a pewter tankard holding his pens, inscribed *The Argus Challenge Cup*, with the Argus pheasant from Greek mythology and the words of reference to Luke 14:23 below: "And the lord said unto the servant, go out into the highways and hedges, and compel them to come in, that my house may be filled."

Mitch sat at his desk. Mac and Bob pulled up in front, and Jimmy and Ryan sat on matching antique red leather chairs, listening carefully to the speakerphone on Mitch's desk.

"Good morning, Sam. How was your trip back?" asked Mitch.

"Pretty quiet. Quieter than your night, I heard!"

"News travels fast, eh?" Mitch said.

"Yes, it does. Especially when it involves the biggest IRA cell on the West Coast and the carnage left behind by apparently just two men, a bomb in a pub recently purchased by the head of that IRA cell, and a dead senior CIA agent possibly killed by a Colombian cartel."

"And now Badger has died under mysterious circumstances, just like Paul," Mac said.

Mitch said, "That's one reason why I wanted us all to sit down together to see what our next step is."

"I think that's a good idea," Sam said. "Seriously. I found out about what happened through SAS contacts with the CIA. They're pretty ramped up about the Ruskies. The DEA is ramped up about the Colombians. The FBI is pretty ramped up about Boyle's gang, the Ruskies, and the Colombians. It's all one great big shit party of three-letter agencies."

"I should think they all would be ramped up," Bob said. "Ramped up big-time. This whole thing is a web. A giant spider's web."

"Mitch. You were seen walking out of the Dubliner seconds before the blast," Sam said.

"What the fuck does that mean?" Mitch asked.

"Well, just like us, they're protective of their own, and it raised an eyebrow or two that you left, and then next thing the Dubliner was smoked."

"Come on, Sam. What the fuck?"

"Then they showed me footage of the Colombians walking in with a big-assed backpack. Looked like they were going on a two-week mission to Mount fucking Everest, never mind for a quiet drink in the local."

"How do you know they were Colombian?" asked Ryan.

"They were known to the CIA. Rastrojos operatives. The same ones that Jimmy and Bob went dancing with at the Mitchell brothers' joint."

"Why the hell would the Rastrojos want to get involved in all this fucking mess?" asked Bob.

"They had one drink and then left. Without the backpack," Sam said. "Now if I were a betting man, I would say that there is your bomb."

"No shit, Sherlock!" Ryan said.

"I know. I know. I saw them too," Mitch said, "but I didn't put two and two together until I thought it through, played it back afterward. I saw the bag as I walked out to my car. Fuckers!"

Mitch was physically shaking with anger, frustration at himself. How did he miss that? In days of old, he would not miss that, but when was the last time there was a bombing in San Francisco? It was not the environment to expect that sort of thing to go down. At least it never used to be, but he was put off, out of sorts, off guard. He recalled the old saying, "Live in California once, but leave before you become too soft."

"Who was the Australian tramp with the trench coat and the hat?" Mitch asked.

"We don't know," Sam said. "Our friends in local law enforcement caught the guy on surveillance video. Our friends at Langley ran the image through facial rec software but came up with nothing."

"Tramp, my ass," Bob said.

Mac piped in. "Sam, what happened to Badger?"

"We don't know. The local authorities turned up nothing. Of course, they're All corrupt as hell. We're having Badger's body flown back to London for a solid workup, but that's going to take a little time. Right now, Badger's case is a mystery."

"But we know Paul's death is suspicious. What would the Russians want with Paul anyway? We haven't done much with the Russians," said Ryan. "You think it's all about election tampering?"

"That's the conclusion so far," Sam said.

"You think Badger was involved in Paul's work somehow? They were both formerly from our unit, you know. That's a connection we shouldn't ignore," Mitch said. "Paul hinted about working with one of our former mates, though he never gave me details. We need to do some digging."

"Right," Mac said. "And we should do some digging as to why Colombians would resort to blowing up CIA agents in San Francisco."

"It's because Paul knew something that must have been pretty hot news," said Mitch.

"What did that piece of shit Tommy Boyle have to say?" asked Bob.

"Ah yes, Tommy Boyle. That's twice in twenty-four hours I have had to look out for you, Mitch," Sam said.

"What do you mean? Were the CIA there too?"

"No, they weren't there, but don't you think when a top operative in the Irish mob gets taken down by two unknown men with British accents, we hear about that?"

"I suppose you have a point."

"Tommy started talking about Grace and Partners and their relationship with Dmitri Dankov and that we should speak to them."

"Who the hell are Grace and Partners? And what the hell would that Russian Mafioso have to do with Tommy Boyle?" Jimmy asked.

"I have no idea, but what I do know is this thing is complicated. We need to get organized."

"Get organized? Don't you think that between the CIA, MI5, MI6, Secret Service, and the Regiment, we might have this one, Mitch?"

"Sam, this one is personal. You know that. We'll keep in touch. Get in touch yourself if anything turns up that we should know about," Mitch said.

"Will do," Sam said, and ended the call.

Mitch and his men discussed options. Ryan said he had to return to Kettering for a big rugby game but that he'd be on tap if needed after that. Bob and Jimmy said they'd head to Tangier to see what they could dig up on Badger's death. They'd leave right away.

"Mitch, we talked last night about getting a hold of Lord Beecham and Colonel Collins," Mac said.

"I think we could use their help," Mitch said.

"So do I," Mac said.

"How will we handle Sam?" said Bob.

"Sam is there for us. Although he has to tow the Regiment line, he wants us involved. We can do much more than those guys without the ties of the politician's bureaucracy. We all know how that goes, right?"

"We all have our satellite phones. Keep in touch, and I'll also handle Sam," said Mitch. "Boys, be careful and on the lookout. Keep in touch via text, code name Argus. Have a good trip."

Peggy had booked Bob's, Jimmy's, and Ryan's onward flights, accommodations, and welcome packs where needed.

Mitch sat at his desk and pondered the pewter Argus Cup that sat in front of him, a trophy he had won in honor and in memory of two former SAS soldiers and their brutal demise at the hands of the IRA.

Mitch couldn't take the events of his second week out of his mind. The outgoing communications guy was familiarizing the incoming as they were on a week's handover together. Dealing with the actual communications was the easy bit, as the equipment was standard SAS kit; the briefings were probably the biggest piece but a lot to take in. Getting up to speed and learning the lay of the land was probably the biggest task. Dave and Derek headed out to take a look around that fateful day.

Back to the Big Green Barn, Dave Howe and Derek Wood were out in Belfast on their way back from a trip to Lisburn and the 14

Intelligence Headquarters, plain clothed, in their silver Volkswagen Jetta. They decided to head through Andersontown and stumbled across an IRA funeral procession.

With many hundreds of mourners following the hearse, their car got stuck in the crowd, sticking out like a sore thumb, out of place, and—the crowd clearly thought—out of order.

"What the fuck are you doing here?" shouted one.

"Come to spy on the dead, you bastards?"

"Have you fuckers no fucking respect for the slain?"

Within seconds, the crowd turned and smashed windows, started pulling them out of the car. The black cabs were now behind them. Dave got on his feet, shot off a couple of rounds into the air. His 9 mm jammed. Derek followed suit, but after another two rounds, his oversize magazine fell out. Red rag to the bull, the raging bull of the crowd. They were manhandled into the two black taxi cabs behind them, and within a few minutes, they were gone.

There were lots of lessons to be learned from this. Mitch had sat in the briefing room for hours, watching the footage from the Helicam over and above filming the scene, unable to do anything other than hover and watch the horror before them.

He saw the reaction of absolute panic when Dave's Browning jammed and the look of terror when they saw Derek's oversize magazine fall out of the pistol grip onto the floor.

Dave and Derek were found dead. Beaten, kneecapped, and impaled up their asses on an iron-railing fence.

Since that time, the practice of oversize magazines was seen as a risk. There was more discipline around route planning and intel updates before making a trip.

Dave and Derek went through a horrific ordeal, and as the team went through the footage over and over again, despite all the learnings, the most powerful learning was not to be there in the first place.

Their demise was probably down to a string of events kicked off with Gonzo, Keith, and their team in Gibraltar eliminating the three would-be IRA bombers. A few days later, their funeral was at Milltown Cemetery, Belfast, and due to be heavily attended by the IRA elite.

Then there were the antics of one Michael Stone at that funeral. Stone, an Ulster Defence Regiment member, turned up early, long before the funeral procession arrived and many of the secret faces of the IRA.

Stone hid behind one of the headstones far enough away not to be noticed when the mourners arrived but near enough to spring a surprise attack when they did. Armed with handguns and grenades, he attacked as they gathered around one of the graves, dodging from one headstone to the next, letting off rounds, throwing his grenades, and picking off the mourners. Three dead. More than sixty wounded.

Three days later, Dave and Derek were driving back from Lisburn. They were never seen alive again apart from the haunting footage. Dead.

An incident in Gibraltar, Operation Flavius, ended up with three IRA terrorist's dead, riddled with bullets, and when Mitch asked the SAS leader, Gonzo, why he had only put thirty-eight rounds into the targets, the answer was simple. "My magazine ran out." Of course.

Mitch knew that he and the boys had been in the thick of the troubles and other dangerous ops. He knew they'd all picked up a few enemies along the way, and now it seemed that some of them may have returned to haunt them.

Nelson Harbor, Antigua, October 2016

Lord Jeffry Beecham was seated with some of his favorite people at the Royal Antigua and Barbuda Rum and Tot Club, an invitation-only honor for those who had either served in the Royal Navy or as British commanders of the oceans.

Lord Beecham was the son of a senior naval officer and the brother of a currently serving senior naval officer. He was invited to the club based on his four years of sailing the world aboard a luxury yacht, sailing from port to port with some of the world's richest and most famous passengers.

His stint at the Foreign Office and Secret Service in trouble spots around the world also made him one of Britain's eminent authorities on international affairs, criminality, and terrorist activity, with his international Rolodex including some of the most influential people on the planet, on both sides of the fence. Beecham had grown up in this fraternity. His father was a former British Intelligence officer, and his father-in-law was a former CIA operative.

Known as an affable chap, he stood five feet ten, was slim, had blond, wavy hair, and dressed in a tropical sports coat, linen shirt, linen trousers, and brogues. Lord Jeffry Beecham was a gentleman and a rare breed of times gone by.

With an Old Plymouth gin, Schweppes tonic, and lemon, not lime, Lord Beecham held the court of a small group of internationalists in the bar of the Royal Antigua and Barbuda Rum and Tot Club after one of his infamous lunches, telling tales of world travels, adventures from filming Jackie Chan on the luxury yacht, to climbing Mount Aconcagua and drinking games at the Rugby Sevens in Hong Kong. Today's ritual toast was, "There are good ships, there are wood ships, there are ships that sail the sea, but the best ships are friendships, and may they ever be."

One of Beecham's favorites.

The club steward with his starched, pressed tunic, interrupted the laughter, the fun, and the clink of glasses. "Excuse me, Lord Beecham." He passed a note. Beecham looked down at the traditional British telegram of years gone by, and his face gradually went white.

He turned to look out the window at his old friend, the ocean, where he did his best thinking. "Excuse me, boys. Terribly sorry. Something has just cropped up."

Beecham headed to the private library at the rear of this historic building, pulled out his satellite phone, and dialed the number. The phone took a moment to engage and connect, and that familiar British ring tone kicked in.

"Operations?"

"Oh yes, Operation Argus please."

"One moment, sir. I will put you through."

"Operations?"

"Sam, I just got your message. What is going on, old chap?"

"Hello, Jeffry. It's not good. We have intel that there are dark forces messing around with elections and taking out our people. It looks like they're focused on meddling with electoral systems around the world and manipulating outcomes. Mitch and the boys are up to their necks in what's going on. And, frankly, I think they're in danger. Paul and Badger are both dead," Sam said.

"Good God!" Lord Beecham paused a moment to take it all in. "I say, old chap, did you say the US elections?"

"Maybe. We don't know for sure the extent of their operations or indeed the underlying intent. All we do know is that we have three dead already, and the players so far have included Irish, Colombians, and the Russians. One of the dead was a CIA operative."

"That's an eclectic ensemble," Beecham commented. "Who is involved on our end?"

"The usual suspects, three-letter agencies from both sides of the pond, but I want you to run this as an independent. All I ask is that you keep me in the loop. We have Ryan, Bob, and Jimmy heading back to Europe from San Francisco as we speak, Mitch and Mac both in San Francisco, and with you and Collins, we should be in a good spot to work this thing out. I will act as the coordination between official operations and your independent operations. Make sense?"

"Yes, sir! Sure does. Send me over what you have on my secure portal, will you? And I can review on the way to San Francisco."

"Will do. Thanks, Beecham. Speak when you get to San Francisco."

The phone went dead, and Lord Beecham paused for a few moments to digest the content of the call. He picked up the phone again and called Peggy, the team's trusty travel consultant, who then arranged flights for him and Colonel Collins. He made another call to his team in San Francisco to get things ready. After, Lord Beecham headed to Colonel Collins, who was finishing his final tale. He leaned close and whispered, "Colonel, old boy, we are heading to San Francisco tomorrow. I had a call. Our services are needed. Sam, Mitch, Mac, and the boys."

Colonel Collins looked at the seriousness in his friend's eyes and said, "Okay, we'll be there, old boy."

Beecham responded, "Flight's booked. We leave in the morning."

Mitch had deep secrets no one knew apart from him. He sat there at the veterans' home in the Presidio, on the porch, looking out and seeing the past few days before him. Not just the past few days but the years unfolding like a multiscreen vision of his life.

He had always tried to manage stress, compartmentalize it. Keep it locked away. And the violence? The violence had been with him as long as he could remember.

He knew from an early age that he was different but always pretended he wasn't. He tried to fit in, be the normal guy, but he knew that he was not.

The last few days had been a roller coaster for Mitch. The death of one of his best friends, the coming together of his team. Good old boys, brothers. It was great to see them, although under unsavory circumstances. The night of passion with Angela. Bella potentially heading to the CIA. The incident at the Dubliner, the explosion, Brad. Mitch's return to violence and the incident at Tommy Boyle's.

It had been a while since Mitch was exposed to that level of violence, but it was shocking for him how natural it felt, as if he had never left it—or perhaps violence had never left him.

Mitch was considered a leader, and others looked up to him to keep on going, moving forward, ever onward and upward, but he knew that he was the same frightened boy who had sat on his father's knee trying to circumvent the bullies that surrounded him with his Beatles haircut and tailor-made shorts.

Mitch was a thinker. He reflected on the past and considered the future. Mitch was happy in his own company; in fact, he probably preferred his own company over the company of others. The more he had seen in his life, the less he needed or even wanted the company of other human beings, apart from maybe Bella. He loved Bella like no one else on the planet, and their connection was different, special, and almost telepathic.

He sat on the porch of his apartment in the veterans' sanctuary and reflected. The stars were out, and he could see them through the canopy of the eucalyptus trees with their distinctive and refreshing smell wafting through the evening air. A packet of cigars, a bottle of Liddlesdale whisky, and a tumbler sat on the table in front of him.

The Paludrine Club had always been a test question for Mitch as he had traversed the globe and heard the many claims of men that they were ex-Regiment. A very simple couple of questions could be asked to validate these claims or otherwise.

"What was the name of the pub at the back gate of Stirling Lines?" And "What was the name of the social club on Stirling Lines?"

For folks who had never been there, just read books like *Bravo2Zero*, these answers were considered irrelevant enough that they were never shared and therefore largely unknown, unless you had served at Stirling Lines, 22 SAS Headquarters, Hereford, UK.

Most hadn't been through what Mitch had been through, and that really, really bothered him. They really, really pissed him off. They really, really imposed upon his private world, his very private world.

Mitch was all but a kid when he first arrived at the gates of Stirling Lines. It was like a dream come true for any young soldier, the home of the 22 Special Air Service, arguably the most elite, well-respected, and feared secret military group on the planet.

As Mitch waved to his mother and father dropping him off, he passed through the rigorous security check. Mitch looked back one more time through the security fencing and saw the pride on his father's face as he mouthed, "I am proud of you, my son." This was a rare admission of love and pride and completely overdue. Why couldn't he have shared that pride earlier? It would have made Mitch's life so much easier, so much less complicated.

Mitch's father was a man of few words and praise, and yet Mitch had enormous adoration for him and all the brave things he had done in his life.

Stirling Lines, a night of entertainment at the Paludrine Club, some special evening, Regiment, families, wives. Toward the end of the evening, two Regiment guys decided to have fisticuffs and got thrown out of the club and out of the Regiment too. Internal fighting was strictly not accepted. Ever. Mitch never saw them again.

Mitch was introduced to the Game Cock that was located outside the back gate of Stirling Lines, a regular haunt for folks stationed inside the barracks and those living in married quarters close by.

This nondescript Hereford neighborhood pub reflected the largely farming economy of Hereford at that time. The civilians stayed in the front, and the back, especially on a Sunday afternoon, was full of SAS folks prior to their dispatch to various parts of the world the next morning. Some knew where they were going. Most did not or were tied to secrecy, and every Sunday was treated like their last beer together. In many cases, that would prove to be true.

Darts, pool, skittle alley, fruit machine, jukebox, and beer. It was a grand place to hang out, listen to the tunes, including the multi play of *Brothers in Arms*, and say their farewells, until next time.

Mitch poured another glass of Whisky and lit a cigar, listening to the breeze in the eucalyptus trees surrounding him and staring at the starry sky above him. All was quiet at the Presidio veterans' home that evening—the way Mitch liked it.

Mitch considered the events of the past few days—the haunting of Tommy Boyle, the reminder of the Russians and their ruthlessness. He thought about the love of his life, Bella, and he thought about the tall, homeless-looking guy in the Dubliner.

"Where will this latest journey end?" Mitch asked himself as he stubbed out his cigar and headed inside to call it a night. It had been a long few days. As he got into bed, Mitch was overcome with a strong sense of foreboding. It was a feeling he knew well, although he hadn't felt it recently, nor as strongly. He felt a cold chill sweep over him, enough so that he shivered. More people were going to die. He knew it more than he knew anything else, and he suddenly felt tired … oh, so very tired.

14
THISTLES

Bromley, London, United Kingdom, October 2016, Day 8

THE SOUND OF A CELL phone humming and buzzing broke the predawn silence in the master bedroom of the luxury apartment Nikita shared with his typically absent mother. The noise roused him from a deep sleep, a rarity for him these days. He yawned and answered the call

"This is Nikita."

"Good morning, Nikita, my man. How the hell did you call that one? Everyone was predicting a no vote for months, but not our Nikita, not our man Nikita. Months ago, you called it. We laid big, big bets, and this morning, my friend, it's confirmed, and you know that we won, and we won big! How are you feeling this morning, Mr. Big? The boss wants to see you first thing. Are you taking your usual run? In at 8:00 a.m.? Can I tell her that is okay? What do you think?"

Nikita was listening to the frantic voice on the end of the line. Simmo was a good guy, officially his line manager, but an observer to the magic that Nikita clearly had, basking in the limelight of the genius of others—in this instance, Nikita.

"Morning, Simmo. It's 5:00 a.m."

"Okay, okay already. I couldn't wait another fifteen minutes to your normal time. Nikita, I am too excited. Do you know how big this one is? Figured I'd catch you before you leave. I am on the way in now, as the boss wants to catch up with me first, then you at eight. Does that work for you?"

"Sure. See you there."

"At the city office, right? See you there, my man!"

Nikita groaned and rolled out of bed, then went to the kitchen and selected his Nespresso pod for his morning coffee. *Which one today? Brazil? Colombia? Kenya?* "I always liked Colombia," he muttered to himself in his almost perfect English accent but with a subtle and slight hint of cutting off the ends of the words, as most Russian-based speakers do. He was perfecting this, and it was much more accentuated in Nikita's mind and barely noticeable to others, even the most fine-tuned of listeners. This lack of perfection annoyed Nikita.

Coffee made, he began his usual routine—shower, shave, teeth, hair, gray pants, black shirt, shoes, gray socks, Jockeys thrown into his Nike backpack.

At 5:55 a.m., Nike running shoes, Ron Hill leggings, Nike black hoody, earplugs in, Blackphone connected. Backpack on. Coffee cup into the dishwasher, alarm on. Skip down the marble stairs, on to Bromley High Street for his 10.1-mile run to Canary Wharf and the headquarters of the First World Bank.

It was six in the morning. Today, Nikita would take it easy and give himself time to think and get his daily briefing.

At six thirty, the Blackphone rang. "Dobroye Utro." Nikita answered the call.

"Da, da."

"Ponimat."

"Da."

"Konechno."

Good morning. Yes, yes, understood, of course. This morning's call was very brief. It was best that way, today of all days. Nikita was heading back to Vilnius, Lithuania, in a couple of weeks. There would be plenty of time to catch up and download then.

This daily call was a ritual for Nikita to keep in contact with home. It gave him comfort and a sense of belonging.

At seven o'clock, Nikita commenced his workout on the grassy area to the rear of the First World Bank HQ. Since he started this ritual, others had followed, although Nikita wasn't the sort of engaging type. He just did his own thing. He did oblige shared humanity and space with a nod or a good morning. He'd say, "Later," after he finished working out. He figured people were used to the fact that he didn't talk much, that he largely kept to himself, even at the bank.

Nikita only let known quantities into his life. It was not just a precaution due to the kind of work Nikita did but a cultural necessity too. Growing up in Eastern Europe, Lithuania, his absent father, and his pain at losing Angus as a stepfather all contributed to his level of stoicism today. Nikita didn't allow himself to love freely; ultimately, people would hurt him—sometime, somewhere, someday. That was inevitable.

His Blackphone buzzed as he made his way to work. Bella. His sweet friend of many years.

"I'll always talk with you," he whispered as he answered the call.

"Hey, Bella Bella Fonterella, how are you today?"

"Nikita, you are a genius. How did you call that? You are truly magic!"

Nikita knew magic had nothing to do with his wizardly command over predicting world financial markets. He just laughed and changed the subject. "Hey, you flying over at the end of the month?" he asked. "I know you mentioned it the other day."

"I don't know," Bella said.

He could hear the hesitation in her voice, and he wasn't sure where it came from. "What's wrong? Anything wrong?"

"Things are strange at home. With Dad. A friend of his died a couple days ago."

Nikita wove around fellow pedestrians equally transfixed on their cells. "I'm so sorry! Were they close? Your dad and his friend?"

"They served in the same unit in another life," Bella said.

"Well, if you can't get away, I'll understand."

There was silence on the phone as Nikita walked. He could hear Bella breathing.

"I gotta go," Bella said.

"You'll think about coming?" Nikita asked.

"Yeah. I will."

He said goodbye. She ended the call. He fought back the disappointment, but no deal was done until the proverbial fat lady sang. He put Bella temporarily out of his mind and got on with his day, arriving at HQ at about seven thirty, where he showered and got dressed. He finished up with a little bit of his favorite scent, Diptique-Paris St. Germain, and Paul Mitchell soft hair gel. Done. Ready to meet with his boss, Sheri Brodie.

As he took the lift up to Sheri's suite, Nikita smiled. He knew he was an imposing figure at six feet four. His muscles were toned after years of playing water polo, being the lightweight boxing champion at Oxford, rowing with the crew team on the Thames, and serving two years in the Lithuanian National Guard. With his special connections with the right people, it didn't take long to work his way up the ladder in the last three years at London's prestigious First World Bank, one of the largest and most successful financial institutions on earth. His role was to assess political instability and identify risks and opportunities for investments around the globe, essentially assessing the odds-on multibillion-dollar bets. In many ways, he did the same thing that Bella did; only he had a bit of extra help.

He had nursed an interest in global affairs since he was a kid. He had studied such things as politics and economics from childhood during his conversations with his stepfather, Angus, a global Scot who had been in pretty much every war-torn territory at that time. Angus had had a profound influence on him, and Nikita loved him for it. Nikita's ability to almost see into the future won him high praise at the bank and earned him a boatload of cash in salary and bonuses.

He had predicted the annexation of Crimea and the devaluation of the renminbi, had followed the progress of Bitcoin carefully, and had predicted the Scotland say no vote, the Thailand, French, and German elections, the FIFA scandals eventually coming out, supply and demand of natural gas and trading price, Trans Pacific Partnership eventually getting completed, Greece's continued debt challenges despite bailouts, the mayor of London, and now the Brexit vote.

All were against the run of the cloth, and all in turn had made First World Bank many hundreds of millions of dollars on their many tens of billion dollars invested across the portfolio they had built— thanks to Nikita and his mercurial powers of prediction. His record was very impressive to date. At the tender age of twenty-seven, he was recognized as the rainmaker at First World Bank and was very well looked after accordingly.

The lift doors opened. Nikita said good morning to a colleague on her way down to accounting. He stepped off the lift. He was feeling elated at his latest big call, but he also was feeling a slight sense of unease, as if he didn't belong, as if he was still mired in his past. He found himself lost in thought as he strolled to Sheri's office.

Growing up in post-Communist Lithuania was hard. His mother, Viktoria, didn't have a lot but certainly more than many of the folks living in Klaipeda on the post-Soviet Baltic, and even when they later moved to Vilnius. Viktoria's new husband, Angus, worked as a contractor in war zones across the world and as a result earned good money that afforded them a reasonably swanky, three-bed apartment in the diplomatic area of the capital with his sister, Katia.

Nikita barely knew his real father, a Russian who abandoned the family when Nikita was only six. His father had sexually abused Nikita's sister and him, and Viktoria had done nothing. His father drank himself into oblivion, and he beat anyone who annoyed him, which was everyone. Although the memories were dim, Nikita would never forget what his early life was like. Viktoria was a hard, austere woman. The daughter of a Russian submariner and a Ukrainian farmhand, she grew up with no money. She moved from the Ukraine to Lithuania as a child, then to the garden of the Soviet Union, only to see it collapse and fall some years later. The newly reclaimed land went back to its original owners, who could not even afford the tractors to get the land farmable again. The once fertile soil quickly became wasteland, the produce declined and dried up, and the port of Klaipeda had nothing to export to the far-flung parts of the union. Lithuania, like the rest of Eastern Europe, was on its knees.

In those early days after his biological father took off, they had few prospects. Viktoria worked overseas to make money, and Nikita and Katia were being raised by grandparents. Life was hard, with little fun and a lot of bad memories, as it was his grandfather's turn to abuse Katia. Thank God, he left Nikita alone.

His mother met Angus overseas, in Norway, as he was passing through. She brought him home, and Nikita and he hit it off immediately, with Angus quickly becoming the light of hope that Nikita needed, that glimmer, that man, that trust in his life that he so needed. Although they were close, Angus never touched him in the way of his father, and Nikita was very pleased about that.

Nikita remembered the fishing trips, the hunting, the trips to Scotland. He recalled the trip to California to see Angus's old mate from his army days, a tough-looking bloke named Mitch. He thought about their grand tour around Europe. It was funny the things he remembered about that trip to the United States: bacon sandwiches on Malibu Beach, Disneyland, the Grand Canyon, Death Valley, Yosemite, and Lake Tahoe. Everything with Angus was an adventure, always fun and different, never a bind. Just like out of one of his comic strips.

Nikita missed Angus, as they hadn't seen each other for a while. It was a little harder nowadays. Remarried, Angus now lived in Chile, way down south near Cape Horn. Nikita despised his mother. He resented her for suffocating Angus and turning him away. He resented her for controlling everything, every single millimeter, and he hated her for many other things too.

Why couldn't Viktoria have stopped her husband from leaving them? Why couldn't she have kept Angus close? *Enough!* Nikita thought, chastising himself.

"You got a big day ahead," he mumbled as he pulled open the door to Sheri's office on the twentieth floor. He said good morning to her executive secretary.

"Ah, Mr. Saparov!" the secretary said. "Go right on in. She's expecting you."

Nikita nodded and said thanks. Then he went into Sheri's suite.

Sheri had been with the bank for fifteen years and was a veteran and recognized by most as the heir apparent to the soon-to-be retiring CEO, Sir Richard Steele. Nikita had known Sheri as an intern, and they joined her team upon his return. Even as an intern, there had been a spark between the two of them with his tall, muscular but slender frame and Sheri's tall, athletic, powerful persona. On a business trip to Paris, and after too many glasses of champagne, the bubbles got to them, and they ended up sharing a bed for the night. Sheri quickly backed off, seeing the obvious career warning sign of her sleeping with one of her interns. Nikita respected that, and they remained close friends and working colleagues. They had a liking for each other, and both knew it was beyond their healthy and highly successful working relationship. Nikita had told no one. Nikita's memory bank was neat, tidy, orderly, and compartmentalized, just like his apartment, just like his desk. Nikita held many secrets that he did not and could not talk to anyone about. He had gotten used to being able to lock things away, secret, forever. It had been like that for a long time, even while his father was still around.

Sheri looked up from some paperwork as he came in and said good morning.

"Nikita!" she said, beaming at him. "Keep this up, and you'll be making more than me."

Nikita laughed. "I doubt that."

"Wait and see! Come. Sit down."

Nikita took a seat in front of Sheri's desk, noting that even after all this time, her Texas accent remained alarmingly alluring. She was wearing a tasteful red dress that hugged her figure and set off her blonde hair and deep brown eyes.

"I'm glad you're pleased with my results thus far," Nikita said.

"Oh, honey, loosen up. We go back too far for formalities."

They were both silent for a moment. Nikita could feel something different in the room, as if Sheri was sizing him up.

The sun shone through the ceiling-to-floor windows behind Sheri, bathing the city in a warm, inviting glow that belied the October chill. The Thames meandered through it all, as timeless as it had ever been or ever would be. Global markets could rise and fall, but Nikita knew there were constants in the world that could not be denied. The power of nature was one of them. The tides were another. Volcanic explosions, hurricanes, tornados. When it all came down to it, humans were mere bugs on the face of the earth, and yet some bugs were more powerful than others. Some got eaten; others ate.

Even though it was still early in the workday, Sheri had a bottle of Dom Perignon on ice and poured three glasses. At that moment, Sir Richard Steele, the president and CEO of First World Bank knocked and walked straight in. He gave Sheri a hug and a kiss on the cheek and embraced Nikita in an awkward man hug, then grabbed his glass and raised a toast. "Here's to Brexit! Well bloody done, Nikita! Well bloody done! How the bloody hell do you do it?"

"It's a team effort, sir." Nikita maintained his modesty and his awkwardness.

"You're a bloody genius, Nikita, that's what you are! Cheers!"

They clinked their glasses and all at once said, "Cheers!"

Sir Richard ushered Sheri and Nikita to the lounge area of Sheri's office and sat down. Richard began to recount the events of the past several weeks, the ups, the downs, the shakeups, the shocks, the belief that the Remain vote would win, the cast of characters—Cameron, Johnson, Farage, Corbyn, and May. The shockwave, the fears, the potential instability, and then the opportunity that this represented for those investors who were savvy enough to take advantage of the situation.

Much of the volume of those investment dollars that betted for Brexit were either direct investments or investor investments with the First World Bank. Indeed, Steele said he had placed a rather large bet of his own, seeing his nest egg grow from the $150 million of yesterday to the nearly $200 million of today—nothing compared with the $1 trillion of investors' bets that was today worth $1.5 trillion.

"It's not every day, Nikita, you can take half a trillion dollars to the banks and investor assets, my boy. How does it feel?"

"It's good. I am sure they could use the extra money," responded Nikita coldly.

"Very cool," mirrored Sheri as she eyed Nikita with some concern.

"More than very cool, it's a bloody miracle," blurted Sir Richard. "Nikita, I came down here this morning not only to say thank you and congratulate you, but I would also like to make you our new senior vice president of Special Investment Operations."

Nikita glanced at Sheri with a look of *what's going on*, and Sheri returned the same look to Steele.

Steele continued, "And, Sheri, I would like you to join me in my office as my deputy for a few months before I make the announcement of my decision to retire at the end of the year. I would like you to commence the transition tomorrow, after I have taken you both out for a long lunch at my club today. Then take the next two months to dot the i's and cross the t's. You have both done an amazing job here at First World Bank. I am so proud of you both, and I want to spend the next three months getting you both ready to take this wonderful organization to the next level."

This wasn't a question; this was an announcement. As Steele headed for the oversize door to leave, he shouted back, "Well done, both. Congratulations! My driver will pick us up at 12:30 sharp in my garage to go for lunch. See you both then!"

Steele left the office, and Sheri and Nikita watched blank faced as Steele charmed himself through the floor, saying hello to people, shaking hands, giving hugs and kisses, going through the lift door. Sheri turned slowly and looked into Nikita's face. "Well, Nikita, seems it's turned out to be a good day for all of us!"

"Yes. It's been good day," Nikita said.

Deep down in his heart, he knew he was standing on a house of cards, or on the ramparts of a castle built from wet sand.

Tangier, Morocco, October 2016

The trip to Tangier might have been exhausting, but Bob was used to long stints in silver tubes at forty thousand feet. Long-distance air travel was nothing new to Jimmy either. Bob had slept for much of the trip. He didn't feel refreshed, but he didn't feel like the inside of a shoe.

"You get some shuteye?" Bob asked Jimmy as the plane touched down and taxied to the gate.

"Yeah. You?"

Bob nodded and stood up to grab his carry-on.

"You suppose we gonna find out anything on this little sojourn?" Jimmy asked, grabbing his carry-on as well.

Bob didn't answer. He wasn't sure. This whole thing could be a wild goose chase. After all, it already seemed that Paul's and Badger's deaths were linked. Closely linked. Still, Bob figured it couldn't hurt to poke around.

They cleared customs without a hitch and made their way to the car rental agent that Peggy had specified in their itinerary. The agent handed them the keys to a Jeep Wrangler to get them to the Hotel Farah on the eastern edge of Tangier City.

Bob parked the Jeep at the front of the hotel and jumped out. He and Jimmy walked into the lobby where the general manager, Richard Maven, was expecting them and ready to greet them. Richard was British and had been at the resort for four years now. He knew his hotel, his guests, and the local area and personalities as well. He had, in fact, met Badger on a few occasions as a regular visitor to the Farah and gotten to know him well. Richard was also ex-Royal Navy and had earned his queen's shilling. This was all in the report Peggy had put together for them.

After they checked in and stowed their bags in their rooms, they met Richard in the hotel bar for a drink. They exchanged some small talk, and then Bob got down to business.

"I hear you knew our friend, Badger. Badger Bell," Bob said.

Richard nodded. "Good chap. I must say that his heart attack was a bit of a shocker. He had been staying here for five days on one of his regular trips over here. Typical Badger, keeping himself to himself, taking his Jeep out on day trips, getting back in the evening, propping up the bar on his whisky and Cokes."

"What was he doing here?" Jimmy asked.

"Not sure, never did tell. I always assumed he was on holiday, but he didn't seem to rest too much whilst he was here. Occasionally he would spend an afternoon by the pool, but mostly he would be gone during the day, always returning with the Jeep covered in red sand, so he must have ventured inland and clocked up a few miles."

"Was he always alone?" asked Bob.

Richard thought about his answer. "Yes, mostly, however, on his arrival, there was often this guy who would turn up at the hotel to meet him. They would go for lunch at one of our restaurants, then leave."

"Do you know his name, description?" Jimmy asked.

"No, but let me check with my head of security, Mohammed. I'll get back to you."

"Fine," Bob said. "You do that. We'd appreciate it."

"No worries," Richard said. He stood up from the table. "Got to get back to it, boys. By the way, the drinks are on the house. And the pool attendant on duty right now was on duty when Badger checked out for good. Bloke's name's Raymond. He'll be glad to chat you up, if you like."

Richard walked away before Bob could thank him.

"Let's go check out the pool guy," Jimmy said. "And the infamous pool."

"Yeah, let's."

Bob and Jimmy went to the pool and looked Raymond up. Bob introduced himself and Jimmy and told the pool guy why they were there.

"Glad to help," he said. "What do you want to know?"

"Run through what happened, if you don't mind," Bob said.

"Well, sir, Mr. Badger was hanging out at the poolside, taking in the sun, a couple of cocktails. We had a group of guys, Colombians, I think, and they were playing water volleyball and enticed Mr. Badger into the game."

"Enticed?" Jimmy asked.

"Well, yes, sir, that is how it sort of played out. Mr. Badger was taking his regular laps between sunshine and cocktails, and they passed the ball to him. He passed it back, and they said they were short a player and asked him to play."

"And did he join in?" asked Jimmy.

"Yes, sir! He took one of the team's sides and they were playing. I was watching between keeping an eye on the kids in the family pool, and I could hear that the volleyball was heating up, getting competitive."

"Then what?" pushed Bob.

"There was a big play, a scramble, and then suddenly Mr. Badger launched himself out of the pool. He seemed disorientated and confused, then fell over. I was at him within thirty seconds, and he was dead."

"What did the Colombians do?" asked Bob.

" I hey fussed around him for around fifteen minutes. The doctor arrived and pronounced him dead on the scene, and then they all disappeared."

"Disappeared? Weren't they staying at the hotel?" asked Jimmy.

"Yes, I believe that they were, but they all checked out that afternoon. We all just assumed that they were in shock like the rest of us, and they went home, I assume."

"Where was home?"

"I believe they were from Bogota, Colombia, sir."

Jimmy and Bob exchanged looks.

"Oh, and I found something in a waste bin on the day Mr. Badger died," Raymond said. "It looks like a syringe or something. I didn't tell the local police about it. They're all corrupt. Don't give a shit. I figured I'd throw it away if nobody came around asking about Mr. Badger. He was a real good guy, you know?"

"We know," Bob said, getting curious. "Where is this syringe?"

"In my locker," Raymond said.

"Go get it," Jimmy said.

"Sure, Mr. Bob. Mr. Jimmy. My pleasure. Glad to help," Raymond said and hurried off to his locker. When he returned, he gave Bob a plastic bag with a syringe in it.

"Oh, fuck me!" Bob said.

In his hands was an EpiPen inscribed in Russian.

"That what I think it is?" Jimmy asked.

"Sure as shit is!"

"We got to get this back to London ASAP," Jimmy said.

"We will. We will," Bob said. "Just as soon as we poke around a bit more."

"What is it?" Raymond asked.

"Nothing you want to be involved in," Jimmy said. "Forget you ever saw it, okay?"

"Right, Mr. Jimmy. I already forget, right?" Raymond shot Jimmy a big smile.

"Thanks, mate," Bob said. "You did us real solid."

"Glad to help," Raymond said, and he walked away to the family pool where there were some kids playing.

Just then, Richard came back to them and passed a piece of paper. "Abd Al Bari. He has an office just off the Sook in downtown Tangier. He is a trader, a wheeler, a dealer, and a very colorful character, or so it seems."

Bob and Jimmy jumped into the Jeep and headed downtown to find Abd Al Bari.

They parked in the square and headed into the Sook. As they entered, the streets got narrow, and the peddlers increased their volume. There were rug shops, smoke shops, coffee shops, ivory shops, porcelain shops, and old men sitting smoking pipes and watching like stone statues, seeing nothing that had not been there for centuries.

Bob and Jimmy bustled through the crowd—the punters, the peddlers the sellers, the thieves. They came upon the address of Abd Al Bari, a solid wood red door with the inscription of AAB Enterprises positioned on a flimsy piece of cardboard below the doorbell. Jimmy pressed the bell. He waited for thirty seconds—no answer. Bob pressed it harder, as if it would ring louder, and waited sixty seconds more. They both looked around to see if the coast was relatively clear and together barged the door down. Settling the door so it looked like new, they walked into the open courtyard that led to a building at the back and what looked like some sort of office, Moroccan style. The reception was empty, no receptionist today. The place looked deserted, and in the back, there were four offices, and in the fourth one they checked, Abd Al Bari was in his office chair, rolled back, relaxing, with a bullet right in the middle of his forehead, between his eyes.

Jimmy commented, "This guy has been dead for a few days," as he noticed the purple hue of the skin, the rigor mortis, and the dried, deep purple blood on the floor. It looked like rats had started their feast, and the blowfly larvae were starting to hatch. In the humid heat, the stench had grown, and this man was dead. Proper dead.

Jimmy grabbed the corpse's laptop, his phone, and a diary that he found in his inside pocket. On the desk was a white packet with the recognizable scorpion of the Colombian Los Rastrojos cartel, a calling card, an incriminating piece of evidence or simply a gift to ensure that Abd Al Bari's death would not be investigated too hard by the local authorities.

Jimmy and Bob turned and left as unrecognized as they entered.

They drove the Jeep straight to the airport and were on a plane to London within three hours.

15
BLACKIES

Blackie's Pasture, Tiburon, California, October 2016, Day 9

AS BELLA SAT IN THE front window of the study, gazing out at the ocean, Mount Tamalpais back over the bay into San Francisco, and all its commerce and peculiarity, Mitch's black Ford Explorer Platinum rolled up the drive. She dashed out and jumped into the car next to Mitch, then leaned over and kissed him on the cheek.

"Morning."

"Morning, my Bella. Peanut."

That was Mitch's nickname for Bella. Mitch had developed a whole list of nicknames for Bella over the years—Curly, Minkle, and Bella Bella Super Duper Hula Hooper in recognition of Bella's early talent for the hula hoop.

Always comfortable with each other, neither felt the urge to talk as Mitch drove away from Bella's house.

Bella smiled to herself at how he'd taught her field craft warfare signals as a kid. Somehow, her dad's record as a soldier and his stories about his adventures had permeated her in a way that changed her outlook on life. Like those field craft lessons. He'd taught her the signal for *come here and quickly* bridging your right hand on top of your head, like a spider for *come here*, and shaking your fist up and down quickly for the latter. She had also learned from as early as a toddler the jungle call, *"Ooeer, oooer,"* mimicking the sound of a nonexistent jungle bird. Mitch and Bella over the years had used these basic skills many times at busy farmers' markets, at Giants games, and once they got separated at a rock festival and used these skills and telepathy to reunite.

As they drove out onto the highway, Bella felt that familiar sense of uneasiness, of mild discontentment. She knew she'd done spectacularly well already, at least financially. She was sitting on about a quarter-million bucks, but she yearned for something different, although she wasn't sure exactly what that was. She just had this sense that there was an important job for her to do somewhere, sometime, that there was a sense of responsibility, accountability, a sense that she could someday save the world, be looked upon just like her father, partake in important, lifesaving, nation-saving missions. Bella had a calling, and she didn't quite know what that was just yet.

"How is your mum?" her dad asked.

"She's good. She said to say hi. She told me to say that she enjoyed your night together the other night." Bella looked at Mitch with a knowing glint in her eye and a smile. Mitch gave a knowing smile back.

"Tell her I enjoyed it too when you see her."

Sensing some sort of shift in their relationship, Bella offered, "Have you been to Kokkari in the city yet? I know how you both used to love Greek food. It's fantastic. You guys would love it there. It's as good as your favorite at the Cosmopolitan, Milos."

"Milos. Now there's a blast from the past," Mitch said.

They pulled into the car park at Blackie's Pasture, Tiburon, with the monument to the faithful old horse in view, the horse that the pasture had been dedicated to all those years ago.

They started walking with the bay on their right. They passed Bella's old middle school, Saint Hilary's, and went on into town.

"How's work going, Bella?"

"I suppose it's fine. You do know I've taken the rest of the year off? Just to get my head together."

"You mentioned that the other day. You also said the CIA is interested in you. That's a pretty big deal, Bella. I'm proud of you."

"Don't be. I'm still not sure what I'm going to do yet."

"Been there," Mitch said. "We all have."

Bella sighed. "Yeah, I suppose nothing is certain."

"Nothing ever is. Except death and taxes."

"You got that right."

"There is a lot of unpredictability out there right now," Bella said. "With the world, I mean."

"Yeah, it's quite a shit storm," Mitch said. "ISIS, the Chinese building islands in the South China Sea, Iraq, Iran, Afghanistan, North Korea on the way to a viable ICBM that could hit Washington, DC, the Trump and Hillary dogfight, and, of course, there is always the Russians playing their games with the elections, both here and in Europe."

Bella liked this about Mitch. He always knew what was going on, and he always had a global perspective, thanks to the BBC, the British Broadcasting Corporation, God bless her.

"Did you see they sailed their aircraft carrier, the *Admiral Kuznetsov*, right through the English Channel the other day?" asked Bella.

"Yeah, I also have been reading about their various shows of strength, sending bombers into foreign airspace, phantom submarines off Sweden, and the Russian elections continue to be a joke."

"Speaking of elections, I wonder what's going to happen in the wake of the Brexit vote."

"You never know, but you have got to think that in this day and age, the time calls for evolution, not devolution. The UK is much better off with the EU than without, and surely politicians, businesses, and the people will see that and understand it. Especially with all the turmoil that's happening around the world today."

"Nikita predicted the Brexit vote."

"Where does he get these ideas from?"

"I don't know, but he's building a pretty good track record of getting things right. He called the whole Crimea thing two months before it started. Made First World a bucketful of money. Wish my role came with an upside like that."

"Why don't you go and work for a bank, like him?" Mitch asked.

"There's something not quite right in the whole taking bets against other people's demise. I don't like it. At least at Executive Outcomes, we protect people and businesses, instead of profiting from them."

"I've been doing that all my life. Look where that got me!"

"You're in a good spot. You've got your pension, and you made money after you finished in the army. You have the house, the place in Maui, me, Mum!"

Mitch looked into Bella's eyes fondly as they arrived at the New Morning Café.

"Yeah, I know I got you and your mum," Mitch said, patting Bella lightly on the back, "and I wouldn't trade it for all the tea in China."

"Come on, Dad," Bella said, "let's eat. I'm starved."

They went inside. Bella had been there before. It was a cute little place on the corner of Tiburon's Main Street. A beachy sort of place with a clapboard front, café seating outside, and a few seats inside. It was October, but the sun hadn't quite warmed up. They took a seat inside and were greeted with the menus. Both Mitch and Bella knew what they were having. "Two large lattes, one orange, one grapefruit juice, one Johnny Appleseed, one Original Benny." Their usual breakfast order.

"When do you think you'll be ready to move back home?"

"Bella. Let's not go there again. Let it just take its course, see where it goes."

"Follow your nose," they both said at the same time.

"Okay, okay, I get it."

"I'm sorry for the loss of Paul."

This was the first time Bella had addressed this sensitive subject, but she was surprised when instead of a look of sadness on Mitch's face, she saw something else—that immediate alertness, stepping up a gear, that instinctive demeanor that she had seen on occasion over the years.

"What's wrong?" she asked.

"All that appears before you isn't always as it seems, Bella."

"What do you mean? What's going on?"

"It's a long story. Me and the boys are looking into it."

"You and the boys … now there's something to worry about!" Bella said with a laugh, but she felt uneasy, as if there was danger lurking close by.

"Well, you guys just watch your six," she said. "I don't have a great feeling about this whole thing with Paul. He was too fit to just keel over and die from a heart attack." She took a sip of her drink. "Something's just not right. I can feel it."

"Your instincts are spot-on. Now forget about the worries of the world. Let's just have a nice breakfast, okay?"

"Sure, Dad. Whatever you say."

Breakfast arrived. Bella's latte, freshly squeezed orange juice, and her Johnny Appleseed french toast stuffed with vanilla sauce and a side of fresh fruit. Mitch's Original Benny was an english muffin, two poached eggs, canadian bacon, and Morningside's famous hollandaise sauce, Mitch's favorite, along with béarnaise, tarragon, and a side of peppercorn sauce as well.

"You know my favorite saying, Bella?"

"Which one? One sure foot in front of the other? Bravely and truly, boldly and rightly?"

"No. Andre Gide. 'One does not discover new lands without consenting to lose sight of the shore for a very long time.'"

Bella sat there looking into Mitch's eyes. Was he telepathic or were they somehow just so connected they were a part of each other? She had always had the sense that wherever she was, Mitch was always there with her. Even when she was studying in Oxford and there had been some hard, challenging times, Mitch was always on Bella's shoulder, or at least that's how she felt. That's how she completed the London Marathon, how she got through the early mornings and late nights getting top grades for her Oxford master's degree, how she landed this plum job at such an age, how she had succeeded in everything that she had turned her hand to so far. Bella, just like her father, was a 1 percenter, perhaps not in wealth or fame but certainly in terms of ability.

"Bella, you have never shied away from anything. Follow your instincts, do what you believe in, do what is right. Remember ..."

"Bravely and truly, boldly and rightly," they said together.

The rest of the breakfast passed with convivial small talk. Neither of them wanted to venture into heavy conversation. They'd touched on enough already. When they had finished and Mitch paid the check, they got into his Ford Explorer and headed back to her house.

Maybe I'll go to London after all, she thought. *The trip'll do me good.*

16
THE SALOON

San Francisco, California, October 2016, Day 10

MITCH WATCHED THE PASSENGERS EXIT through security, his eyes peeled for Lord Beecham and Colonel Collins. He was anxious to get on with business. Ryan was back in Northamptonshire. The news from there wasn't good. Ryan's mother had finally given in to the cancer, and Mitch knew his friend would take his mother's death hard. So much death. So much violence. Bob and Jimmy had returned from Tangier with staggering new information about Badger's death. All that remained was to coordinate from his end. His two colleagues from Antigua would take care of that—or at least provide invaluable assistance.

"Ah, there they are," Mitch said to Mac.

"Glad the bloody flight was on time."

"Me too."

Lord Beecham and Colonel Collins strode up to Mitch and warmly greeted him and Mac.

"Flight okay?" Mitch asked them as they headed to the vehicles. Mac had driven the Range Rover. Although it probably wasn't necessary for them to split the ride, Mitch felt better having the payload of brain trusts go in two vehicles instead of one, just in case.

"First class, old boy. Literally," Lord Beecham said.

"I'd expect nothing less," Mac said.

When they got to the parking garage and Mac gestured for Colonel Collins to get in the Range Rover, Lord Beecham laughed. "You're thinking there might be trouble?" he asked.

"You never can tell these days," Mitch said. "Come on. You're with me. We'll meet up at Cavallo Point for supper."

They all agreed and went their separate ways.

Cavallo Point was one of the many former military forts around San Francisco Bay. The bay was long considered a strategically important location that commanded a naval position for the West Coast, but it was also an obvious point for any potential invasion. As the threat decreased, so did the number of troops stationed in the area, dropping from thousands to nearly zero. As a result, the forts in the area weren't needed solely for military use anymore. Several former forts had been converted for commercial civilian use, including Alcatraz, the Presidio, and Cavallo Point.

Sitting underneath the Golden Gate Bridge on the North Shore, Cavallo Point was now a high-end hotel, with the former family quarters turned into guest rooms, the sergeants' mess now the hotel lobby, and the officers' mess now the restaurant. One road in, one road out made it a perfect location to meet with some level of seclusion. Mitch had booked a house that would sleep the four of them for the night—two adjoining suites, two pullout beds, four walls.

Lord Beecham chatted away, essentially making small talk. Mitch was preoccupied with the black BMW 750i, long wheelbase in the rearview mirror. He'd first noticed it at San Francisco International as he waited to meet the boys. He again noticed it when they headed toward the Intercontinental and again at the funeral. They were following him again. He had run a plate check already. Of course, no use. The guys in the car were all Hispanic. What with the Colombians making themselves known, he concluded the men were part of the cartel.

"We got company," Mitch said.

Lord Beecham said, "Who might that be?"

"Not sure, really," Mitch said, glancing into the rearview mirror. "It's that black Beemer behind us. Couple cars back."

Lord Beecham looked and said, "I see the blokes. Can you shake the tail?"

"Yeah, probably, but not right now. Too much traffic around the airport."

"The bane of modern life," Lord Beecham said.

"Tell me about it. It's getting worse in the city all the time."

"Price of progress."

Mitch drove on. Inexplicably, the black Beemer dropped back and then took a turn off the highway.

"Strange," he said.

"What?"

"Our company just dropped off the radar."

"Jolly good!" Lord Beecham said. "I'm getting too old for car chases."

"I'm afraid I am too," Mitch said, though he didn't really believe that. For a moment, he wondered if he should be more worried about the tail. He thought it was odd, the tail, the nonaggressive nature of it, the fact that it had dropped away on its own.

What could that mean? he wondered.

Forty minutes after leaving SFO, they walked into Murray Circle Restaurant, overlooking what was once the parade ground in front. The building hadn't changed much; it still looked and felt just like an officers' mess. Colonel Collins and Lord Beecham said they felt at home, as did Mitch and Mac. They headed to the back corner by the fire and quickly ordered drinks to raise a toast.

"There are good ships, there are wood ships, there are ships that sail the sea. But the best ships are friendships, and may they ever be," Lord Beecham said, followed the clinking of glasses and cheers. It was repetitive but an old favorite.

Over drinks, then dinner, in the quiet area at the back of the bar, Mitch explained the situation to Lord Beecham and the colonel.

"We need to set up an ops room," said Mitch.

Beecham grinned. "Perfect. That's exactly why I suggested this place. My saloon is here down by the water. I have my man stocking it and getting it open for business for first thing tomorrow."

Mitch was surprised, and Mac and Colonel Collins seemed to be too.

"Saloon? What are you talking about?" Mitch asked.

"Oh, just a little hidey-hole I've got for cases just like these. You'll see. But for now, you should eat up. Your fish is getting cold," Lord Beecham said.

Mitch shook his head and kept eating. He knew better than to push his colleague. Answers would be revealed in due time.

Mitch got his answers the next morning, just as Lord Beecham promised. While Mitch knew the man hailed from a wealthy family and had married into one of equal or more wealth, he hadn't realized the full extent of the money. When he and Mac were escorted to the saloon, his jaw dropped. Secreted away on the waterfront between a yacht club and the Coast Guard station was a simple-looking building complex and private pier. The yacht tied up to the dock was just his West Coast vessel, Lord Beecham explained.

"You can never have too many yachts, old boy," he said to Mitch with a twinkle in his eye.

Just outside the building, Mitch noted the thick concrete walls, terra-cotta tiles, and the thick, heavy lead-lined front door with the number 1101, the only marking on the building. Even to the trained eye, the cameras and the sensors were barely visibly and well concealed under the eaves of the roof.

As they neared the door to the building, a figure stepped out toward the four men.

"Good morning, sir," the man said to Lord Beecham in a fine English accent.

"Good morning, James," was Beecham's response. "Do you have the old girl all fired up?"

'Yes, sir! She's all ready to go!"

Lord Beecham got to the keypad at the door, put his right forefinger on the pad, did a retina scan, and punched in an eight-digit code. The door, assisted with hydraulic jacks, smoothly opened like the doors of a nuclear bunker. Lord Beecham ushered the three men and James inside. The big lead door shut behind them, and they faced another scan, this time the left thumb, a retina scan, and a sixteen-digit number. The next door opened up to the space behind.

"Welcome to the Saloon," Lord Beecham said with the panache of a showman unveiling his main attraction. "I also call it the Shed, but I like Saloon better because this facility houses my collection of whiskies. Some of the world's best, if I do say so myself."

"You're a piece of work," Mac said.

Mitch nodded. "Right he is."

Colonel Collins just shook his head and said nothing.

Inside the Shed, there was a warehouse-like area to the left where a couple of shiny classic cars were situated—gleaming and newly polished. Mitch recognized the curve of the wheel arches of a classic Jaguar SS100, white with red upholstery, with an F-Type Jaguar parked right next to it, British racing green, tan upholstery. Then there was a classic Porsche 550 Spyder in classic silver and black, next to a high-spec, top-of-the-range, fully loaded pursuit Range Rover.

"Crikey!" exclaimed Mac at the beauty of this car collection and the contrast of beautiful old school and stunning new.

To the right, Lord Beecham used the fingerprint and retina scans and another passcode to enter into a lead-lined fortress containing his collection of whiskies. Both Mac's and Mitch's jaws dropped as they viewed what must have been five thousand bottles. Lord Beecham pulled out a fifty-year-old Yamazaki from Japan, a fifty-five-year-old McCallan, a sixty-year-old Glenfiddich, a fifty-year-old Highland Park, and a sixty-four-year-old Dalmore Trinitas in addition to some newer malts, rising stars, and his collection of gins, including Old Plymouth Naval Strength.

"Wow!" said Mac.

"Pretty impressive," said the colonel.

"We can open a bottle later, boys," said Lord Beecham, beaming, clearly enjoying the impression he was making on his guests.

Lord Beecham loved to entertain. He loved to make those around him feel good, feel happy, and taste and delight in some of the finer things in life, not in an ostentatious way whatsoever, just proud, glad to share, and glad to delight.

In the next room, after the same security procedure, they entered the armory. There were enough weapons to feed an army to fight an army. The most modern weaponry, from small arms, assault rifles, and rocket launchers, to historic muskets, World War II relics, Russian examples, and Lord Beecham's own personal collection of mini cannons, old and new.

Lord Beecham said he liked the coexistence of old and new, the classic and state-of-the-art, technical genius. Everything about the man was this balance: the traditional tweed sports jackets with practical elbow pads, yet breathable, noniron, water-resistant pants; his old Churches brogues, yet an Apple watch and iPhone. Lord Beecham was a blend of the old traditional and shiny, bright new; this showed in every aspect of his life, including the way he tackled situations like this.

"Expecting some trouble, Beecham?" said Collins with a smile.

"You never know, Colonel. You should know that. You just never know, old boy," retorted Lord Beecham with an equally big smile.

At the end of the warehouse to the right was the boathouse containing a SC 365i Sports Coupe pursuit boat. "Perfect for hopping over to the city." Lord Beecham smiled. "And don't forget the old lady next door. She is a classic slipper, twenty-one-foot, Clinker built and beautiful."

"Bloody hell, Jeffers, you kept this one under wraps!" observed Mitch.

Using a key held on a chain around Lord Beecham's neck, he opened another door that had a simple engraved brass plaque that said, "The Saloon."

In the five walked. Like a captain's cabin, it was wood paneled with a fire ablaze, leather sofa and chairs, a big wooden planning table, a bookshelf covering one entire wall, a kitchenette, and a bedroom suite in the far back.

"Is this your bunker, Jeffers?" asked Mac.

"Where is your submarine and ground to air?" asked Mitch.

"And Winston himself?" asked Collins, referring to Winston Churchill.

Mitch could tell that the look of awe on Mac's face pleased Lord Beecham. "Welcome to the Saloon, boys."

On the middle of the reclaimed wood table was a platter of food—bacon and cheese, smoked salmon, apple and blueberry muffins, bear claws, delightful danish pastries, a large bowl of fruit salad, granola, and yogurt. There was also freshly squeezed orange and grapefruit juice.

"Sit down, gentlemen. Please help yourselves to breakfast, courtesy of Jeff and his team at the Farm Shop," said Lord Beecham. The Farm Shop was a local eating house owned by an Italian American with experience at some of the world's best restaurants—the French Laundry, Le Bouchon, Il Bulli, and now this delightful, cool, culinary experience from the Farm Shop. Mitch knew it well and remembered the night a few nights ago with Angela.

They took their seats and started to tuck in. James took their coffee and tea orders, and moments later, piping-hot delicious beverages arrived to accompany this very Californian breakfast.

"This is fantastic. Thank you, Lord Beecham," said Mitch.

"My absolute pleasure, my dear boy, absolute pleasure." Beecham smiled.

"James, screens, please."

James, at a laptop at the end of the table, made a few keystrokes, and the lights dimmed, and the panels slid back to reveal what would best be descried as a command center. Various screens with news feeds from around the world, a world map, and blank screens ready for action. One of them sparked to life with screenshots of Jimmy, Bob, Ryan, and Sam on the other end in the UK.

"Good morning, gentlemen," Beecham said. "Glad you could join us. Proceed, James."

"Right," James said.

He succinctly summed up the evolution of events, which included information about Badger, the EpiPen that the pool attendant had found in the waste bin, the mysterious presence of the Colombians in Tangier and in San Francisco, and the murder of Abd Al Bari.

"As Paul's completed postmortem indicated, traces of residues very much like those of polonium-210 were found in his blood work. This seems to be a new killing agent because the trace amounts practically disappeared in short order. An analysis of the EpiPen Bob and Jimmy found in Tangier has turned up the same agent. It seems conclusive that Badger Bell was killed with the same new radioactive substance."

"Troubling," Lord Beecham said.

"It's the Ruskies," Mac said.

"Not so fast," James said. "While the Russians are the most likely suspects, they're not the only ones at this party."

"Yeah, like the Irish—"

"No way are they involved with new killing agents," Jimmy said, interrupting Bob.

"Let James talk, please," Lord Beecham said. "Go on."

"Bob and Jimmy, like I said, it seems as though the same killing agent got Badger. This is troubling because Paul and Badger were working on the same case but for different agencies."

"The same case? Do we have confirmation on that?" Mitch asked. "You mean the Russians and the elections?"

"Let me come to that later, Mitch," James said. "We have had a lot of noise from international terrorist activity in Tangier over the past twenty-four months or so. The bad guys like Tangier. It gives them easy access to Europe. Badger was there to track down a lead. He never was able to report in."

"Let's just say Badger wasn't working for the CIA," James said.

"You're starting to annoy me, James."

Lord Beecham laughed. "Get used to it, old boy. He does that all the time."

James moved on to discuss the bomb blast at the Dubliner two nights earlier. He said the FBI, working together with MI6, cross-referenced the bomb fragments found at the bar against the UK database, and the only match was a bomb that killed twenty-two parliamentary members in Moldova back in 2010.

"We found fragments of the timer and the detonator, and they appear to be of Russian and Chinese origin, and despite the apparent political alignment of those two, Chinese and Russian parts in a bomb are very, very rare."

"What the hell was Tommy Boyle doing there—and those Colombians?" asked Mitch.

"Good question," said James. "Take a look at the video."

The grainy images showed what Mitch already knew. Still, seeing it was tough for Mitch. *And there's that bloody black Beemer again, with the three Colombians getting in,* Mitch thought.

Ten seconds later, Tommy Boyle's Jeep Grand Cherokee was shown driving by.

"He won't be driving again anytime soon," Mac said. "Bastard deserved it. He's a fucking animal."

"Boyle is disabled for a while but not out. He is a powerful broker of trouble and violence. His tail is between his legs for now, but what we do know is that he will come back, and this isn't the last we have heard from Tommy Patrick Boyle."

"What about his reference to Dmitri Dankov? What's the bloody Russian Mafia got to do with all of this?" Sam asked from Hereford.

The hairs on Mitch's neck stood on end as he recalled the loss of Angela's father, Jack, at the hands of the Russians. Was Jack just a fisherman or something else? That was always the question. How had Jack risen to fame so quickly in his new country from Sicily? How did he land so well and so quickly with the who's who of San Francisco politics? Then to be run over by the Russians and the *maskirovka* that followed, the tapestry of lies and disinformation that led to inconclusive results?

Mitch didn't like the Russians and especially Dmitri Dankov. Dmitri Dankov was the one behind the mysterious aunt and uncle who turned up at Bella's school when she was in the fourth grade. It was Dmitri Dankov's dirty money that paid for the temporary apartment, pizza, and cable TV. It was Dmitri Dankov who had crossed the line to family, and not just any family but Mitch's Bella.

He first came across Dmitri Dankov while visiting Mac in

Lithuania and the first casino to open in the country since the demise of communism. At that time, it was still considered to be a public-order offense to be in a group of three or more, and the Lithuanian agriculture economy, once the garden of the USSR, was now defunct, nonexistent. Even though democracy was the new rule to conquer corruption and some more equal than others, corruption was still rife as a national supermarket chain was granted the award from a competitive bid to build the country's first nuclear power station before Dmitri Dankov's group reversed that for his own gain.

Mac ran into Dmitri Dankov at the casino in Klaipeda on opening night. The place was empty apart from the staff and Dmitri Dankov's party. The Lithuanians didn't trust that it was suddenly okay to gamble, and frankly, they didn't have the disposable income to waste. Surrounded by his henchmen and beautiful, young women, he held court, played games, and won, of course. On a trip to the bathroom, he clocked Mitch and Mac on his way past, clearly packing a load from the bulge on his left-hand side. Dmitri Dankov looked deep into Mitch's eyes, and Mitch looked right back, scared of no man, but Dmitri Dankov was probably the single most intimidating man Mitch had ever met, and Mitch had met a few of those in his time.

James carried on with his brief. "We have found some interesting activities around Dmitri Dankov's recent activity. Dmitri Dankov has been to Tangier several times over the past six months, under the passport name of Jorgen Johnsen, a Swedish national who died in 1996. Dmitri Dankov flew into London Heathrow last night."

"So, what was Paul into?" asked Bob. "What was it that he was so close to? Surely that's the key here?"

Sam cut into the conversation. "We now know that Paul was working closely with Brad and the CIA on international election-rigging investigations. He had been on the case for nearly a year and was looking into increasingly unpredictable political outcomes across the globe and beyond some of the more obvious ones like Brexit and the upcoming presidential election in the US, also going back to issues in France, the whole Crimea thing, the Arab Spring, and the shenanigans in Russia itself."

Sam continued, "The interesting thing is that although it seems clear that the CIA was behind much of the turmoil and stirring the pot that led to the Arab Spring, and for the first time social media like Facebook and Twitter were used extensively to raise the issues and spread the word, Russia was also up to its own tricks, stimulating unrest elsewhere in what would otherwise be considered more stable nations and democracies."

James piped in, "Yes, Sam, some of the attacks over recent years, such as the various attacks in India, France, Turkey, Brussels, even the shootings in Sydney—if you look very closely at the victims list, there is an inclination that these may have been more than just acts of terror."

The screens changed to mugshots of four Indians. "Mahaj Patel, Akarsh Haneef, Divit Pradesh, and Pranay Maddasani were all high-profile, up-and-coming politicos within the Indian government." Three more mugshots. "Igor Popov, Sacha Vasiliev, and Tanya Sokolov were all victims aboard the Malaysian Airlines MH17 flight shot down over Crimea, just about to publish a book on the Putin regime, corruption, and how his cronies are more equal than others in the Russian Communist, capitalist system." Single mugshot. "Samantha Gibson, shot down in Sydney, was the chief policy maker with the Australian government, and finally ..." Four more mugshots. "Stephen Dresden, Mark Bloomingdale, Sharon Reid, and Stephan Blomberg were part of the Remain movement in the UK before they all died in a mysterious car crash on the M25 a month before the vote."

Sam's turn. "It is true that we have known for decades that the Russians have been behind several assassinations around the world, eliminating enemies of the state, but this time it's different. They appear to be using these tactics not just to defend but to destabilize; it seems they are using this as a new act of war."

Sam and James paused to let the gravity of what was just said set in to the audience.

James continued, "And they have teamed up with some pretty interesting characters outside of the traditional Kremlin soldiers and KGB. We believe that what Paul and Brad discovered were known connections between the Russian state and major criminal and terrorist organizations to achieve their aims, including ISIS, the IRA, drug cartels, and the Russian Mafia itself."

"Why would the bloody Irish get involved with Rastrojos and the Russians?" asked the colonel.

"It's a back door to their illicit dealings. Remember—the IRA is as much an organized crime syndicate as they ever were political activists. In fact, some would say that they're primarily a criminal organization," responded Sam.

Lord Beecham added, "And the Russians get the benefit of destabilizing the political world whilst using these organizations to blame on extremism and criminality if they ever get caught—the perfect malarkey, the perfect maskirovka play."

Bob added, "Lie upon lie upon lie, and then suddenly no one knows what the truth is anymore."

An alarm sounded.

Everyone in the room looked to James.

"What's going on?" Mitch asked.

"Looks like we have company," James said, his voice cool, calm, and collected. "Let's see who. Shall we?"

James zoomed the exterior surveillance cameras in on the same BMW 750i that Mitch had seen on several occasions. Its presence puzzled Mitch.

How the hell did they find us here? he wondered.

"James, can you zoom in a bit more?" Mitch asked.

James obliged.

"That's one of the guys from the Dubliner the other night," Mitch said, the anger clear in his voice.

"What the bloody hell are they doing here?" Beecham asked.

"I know the guy with the tab. That's Figo Hernandez," Mitch said.

Figo threw flicked away the cigarette rolled up the window, and then the car pulled away.

"Christ, it's as if they knew they'd been made," Mac said.

"What's going on?" Sam asked.

"Unwanted guests," Lord Beecham said.

"Who?" Jimmy asked.

"Colombians. The same assholes who blew up Brad," Mitch said.

"Oh," Bob said. "That's not good."

"You got that right," Colonel Collins said.

"James, alert our friends at SFPD and CIA to keep an eye out for that car. Observe only. Under no circumstances make any moves on them. Understood?"

"Yes, sir!"

The group broke for a stroll up to Murray Circle for lunch, keeping alert and observing the world and the people around them. There was no business talked over lunch. "Loose lips sink ships," as Beecham would describe it.

After lunch, they headed back to the Shed and the Saloon within.

James got Sam, Ryan, Bob, and Jimmy back on the line, and they spent the afternoon checking out more of James's research, the Russians, the IRA, ISIS, the Columbian cartel, the backers, the winners, and the losers.

"Okay, we have unearthed some history around the mystery bomber at the Dubliner. We ran some further checks across the CIA, British Secret Service, Interpol, and Mossad databases with the elements that we found at the scene—type of explosive, detonator, timer—and we're pretty sure it's the work of a Mr. Conrad Yee," said James with a look of certainty and as though the group would know this individual.

"Never heard of him," said Mac, along with shaking heads and puzzled looks.

"Otherwise known as 狗, Gǒu, or the Dog," said James.

"Wow, the most expensive assassin on the planet?" observed Bob.

"The reason the bomb is so hard to identify is that, first, Gǒu usually prefers to see the whites of the eyes of his prey and therefore rarely uses explosives to kill—divert yes, kill no. Second, there are only a few examples on the database; we reverse-searched and ruled out who it was not likely to be. And third, we actually found his calling card."

The men all looked at each other again and then back at James.

"Yep. Brad's wife received a FedEx earlier today with a red China zodiac dog, inscribed with the number four and a rare Chinese orchid 狗.

"The Dog was part of the Communist Secret Guard (CSG), Zodiac. Gǒu was the eleventh member of the Guard in 2006, which was also the year of the dog, and in line with the Chinese zodiac, he got the name 狗, Gǒu, or the Dog. Born in the United Kingdom, Gǒu, at the age of seven, took up martial arts and became the youngest Shodan, or First Dan, and the only one to be born outside of Asia. After five years with the CSG, he went independent and is available to the highest bidder, no matter who they are and what the target is," confirmed Bob. "This guy is the real deal."

James added, "There have been no certain sightings of the man for ten years, but in the past few years, he has been associated with thirty-six convenient endings, we believe playing to his lucky number three, three a year. He's a deeply superstitious, bloody assassin with impeccable results and is all but invisible. No one knows where he is or his movements, and the only picture on record is an old photograph from the karate club he went to in Kendal, UK, when he was just fourteen years old. Mother and father both dead, brother in a mental asylum, no records of marriage, kids, no bank account, ever, no mortgage, utilities, car purchases, no nothing, ever."

"The guy is a ghost," Lord Beecham said.

"Isn't this year the year of the dog?" asked Ryan.

Mitch looked at the grainy picture of Yee on the screen with a puzzled look and a frown, and as if a penny had just dropped in the meter, Mitch declared, "He was there that night. He was the fucking tramp who told me the SFPD were about to give me a ticket. He was the one who got me out of there that night! He said to me. 'No worries, mate.' He was out of context; this is San Francisco. An Australian tramp in San Francisco—that makes no sense. Why suffer the winter of San Francisco, especially in West Portal, when you could be living on Cottesloe or fucking Redcliffe Beach?"

The group looked at Mitch as if he had just seen a ghost, and the answer was that it sounded like he had seen a ghost, otherwise known as 狗, Gǒu, or the Dog.

"What the fuck is going on? How did I miss that? Why did he warn me? Why did he take that risk and say, 'No worries, mate'?" Mitch muttered to himself. "Did you say that he was originally from the Lake District?"

James moved on. "Another interesting twist is the big beneficiaries of some of this political uncertainty. Beyond the state-sponsored obvious winners, First World Bank based out of London just placed a trillion-dollar bet on Brexit. And although the outcome is not clear, most pundits are predicting Remain as being the much safer bet."

"That's some bet," Jimmy said.

Mitch's ears pricked when he heard the First World Bank and some of the big bets they had placed on some of these unpredictable outcomes and how they had added billions to their balance sheet in the past three years alone, never mind the money they had made for their investors. Mitch would speak to Bella tonight.

The day ended, and they agreed that Lord Beecham, Colonel Collins, and James would stay in the Saloon as operations center. Mitch and Mac would work on the Colombians and Tommy Boyle's connection. Bob, Jimmy, and Ryan would sniff around to see what else they could find out about Badger and the First World Bank. Sam would stay in Hereford, liaise closely with the Saloon operations center, and deploy resources as needed. He had already sent small teams, typically four per team, to San Francisco, London, and Tangier to follow up on any new leads that the team turned up. He would also place a team in Bangkok to support Jimmy's business and keep an eye on Bokov.

Lord Beecham came back from his cellar dusting off a bottle of Mitch's favorite, Liddlesdale whisky. He poured a dram for each, and they clinked glasses and in chorus said, "To the queen. God bless her."

17
DARK DAY

London, United Kingdom, August 31, 1997

IT WAS EARLY FOR MITCH, but he had much to do. He got up, careful not to awaken Angela, and got ready for his morning flight to London. After he finished getting dressed, he crept into the kitchen to make coffee. Angela came in a few moments later.

"God, it's too damned early to be up," she said, stretching tall and yawning.

Mitch smiled. "O-dark-thirty for sure," he said. "But you know I've got an early flight."

"Yeah. Wanted to see you off."

"You didn't have to."

"Yeah, I did. I always see my man off when he's on assignment," Angela said. She went to him, stood on her tiptoes, and kissed him lightly on the lips.

"Mmm," Mitch said. "More."

Angela kissed him again, with a bit more passion.

Mitch pushed her away. Laughing, he said, "You best stop that right now, or I'll miss my plane."

"Miss your bloody plane," Angela said, running her hands through his hair.

"Come on," Mitch said. "I mean it."

He went to the coffeepot and poured some coffee. "You want some?" he asked.

Angela nodded. He poured coffee into her favorite mug. Angela took the mug and ambled into the living room to turn on the TV. The newscast was all about the death of Princess Diana.

"Oh my God!" Angela said, setting her coffee mug down. "This can't be true!"

Mitch came up behind her, put his arms around her waist, and watched the crawl under the anchorwoman that spelled out the details of the accident in telegraphic fashion.

"Life is full of terrible things," he whispered. "Too many terrible things."

Angela began to cry. Mitch even felt some tears trying to come, though none did. He would catch a later flight that day, and instead of London being his destination, he would head to Charlie de Gaulle International Airport, Paris.

A few hours later, Mitch boarded the ninety-minute flight to Paris. He didn't know Princess Diana personally, but he did feel a deep connection to her and the royal family for many reasons. He stared out the window, lost in thought.

Serving with the Blues and Royals, Household Cavalry, Colonel Andrew Parker Bowles was Mitch's first commanding officer and Silver Stick to Queen Elizabeth II. There were many characters in this, the most prestigious and honored regiment in the British Army. Major Barclay, Captain Jacobs, Wingfield-Digby, and Captain James Hewitt to name but a few in the officer ranks. Jimmy in the other ranks.

It seemed to Mitch, in hindsight, that Jimmy wasn't the only Blues and Royal having romantic dalliances, as it turned out that the commanding officer's wife was now married to the prince of Wales, and then the royal family resemblances to one of the cast of characters was beyond uncanny.

Mitch recalled a time when Jimmy had confided in him, told him a vivid story from his past. He thought about his good friend as the plane flew over the English Channel, bound for Paris. He knew that Jimmy's romantic liaisons were many and that he was a gentleman about them, keeping a low profile. Jimmy was married once before to a girl he met in Hereford. They had a son, Beattie, and then were divorced. Jimmy was in an unusually emotional and sensitive state and found himself Down Under in Sydney. He had just lost his father, was in between girlfriends, Tonja and Helen, was resigning from his new, shiny job, and was depressed, missing home, his wife, and his son.

On the opposite coast, they were visiting friends, walking the streets of Fremantle on Christmas Eve, carols playing everywhere, families, couples, lovers, and friends enjoying the atmosphere of peace on earth and goodwill to all.

Jimmy passed a shop doorway, and in it sat a young man sitting cross-legged, with long blond hair and a kind face. He said to Jimmy, "Would you like me to read your cards?"

Jimmy looked down at the floor and realized that he meant tarot cards.

"It's five dollars for five cards, ten for three, and twenty for one."

Jimmy looked around for an excuse not to but didn't find one, so he sat down in the shop doorway with the man.

Jimmy handed over the five dollars, skeptical, awkward, almost anxious.

The young man with his slender, manicured, kind hands dealt five cards off the tarot pack.

"There is a lot of sadness in your life. A wife, a child, a home where you are no longer. A lot of loss of loved ones, friends, family, a father."

Jimmy looked at the guy with a tear in his eye.

"How do you make that up?" he asked.

"It's in the cards," was the response as the young man played with the cards in front of him. "Would you like a three-card reading?" he asked.

"What is the difference between a five-, three-, and one-card reading?" asked Jimmy.

"The cards get more specific each time, and on a one-card reading, then you get to ask one question, and I will provide you with the answer." The young man smiled at Jimmy.

Jimmy handed over the ten dollars and waited as the young man dealt the three cards.

"Your father loved you and thanks you. Your son misses you and loves you too. Your wife sits and waits and looks out of the window."

Jimmy's eyes were feeling uncomfortable, as whoever this guy was, he was touching some serious nerves in Jimmy's emotions that night, Christmas Eve.

He handed over the twenty-dollar note to the man with the blue eyes in the shop doorway, and the man turned over a single card. Even Jimmy, with his limited knowledge of things, knew this was a special card. "The Love card," the young man confirmed.

Jimmy's heart fluttered and missed a beat. Was this the sign he had been waiting for?

"What is your question?" asked the man.

"Will I ever get back together with my son and my wife?" he asked hopefully, with a distinctive tremor in his voice and a tear in his eye.

The man shook his head very slowly and said, "Although this is indeed the Love card, unfortunately, it is upside down." He went on to explain how love and hate are the same emotion but just at different ends of the spectrum, and that as the card was upside down, Jimmy would not be repatriating with his wife.

Jimmy thanked the man as he was packing up. "Are you leaving?" asked Jimmy.

"My work is done this evening." The man smiled.

"I wish you good luck, happy Christmas, and much happiness in your life to come, Jimmy."

Jimmy was puzzled that the young man knew his name; he hadn't told him. Jimmy lacked permanence in his life and had learned to thrive on the unknown. It was shocking to some that he had an apparent lack of attachment, and that life went on no matter what for Jimmy.

The plane touched down, and Mitch walked from the gate through Charlie De Gaulle where he was met by his driver to take him into the city. He had been to Paris many times. He felt comfortable there and was in awe of the beauty—the people, the smells, the food, the feel of just breathing Parisian air.

But the purpose of this trip was to find out what the hell had happened with a former soldier, a bodyguard, and one of the most protected assets in the world. Jones-Davies was a former Parachute Regiment soldier and was more than able to take care of the situation. Why did it escalate to such a level, given that there was just a handful of paparazzi to deal with? He investigated for two days, and then he called some of his close friends to join him in Paris for a debrief based on the findings of his investigation.

Some of his oldest friends at the time gathered at the Frog and Rosbif, a popular English-style pub. He was delighted to see Sam, Jimmy, and Ed. They exchanged pleasantries, took seats at a table in the back of the bar, and ordered four pints of Inseine, the establishment's own brewed best bitter. As always, they chose a position that enabled them to monitor everything in the bar at a safe distance and in close proximity to the rear exit.

"What's happening?" Sam asked.

Mitch spent five minutes going through the story, from them leaving Sardinia to the Paris Ritz and in more detail from 12:20 a.m. and the next three hours and forty minutes, to Diana's last breath at the Pitie-Salpetriere Hospital.

"It's a disaster, literally," replied Mitch. "No one really seems to know what went down. The driver was allegedly pissed, Diana and Dodi were also two sheets to the wind, and our boy was stone-cold sober."

"So why did he allow Jean Paul to even get in the car if he was pissed?" asked Sam.

"Good question. It's pretty hard to imagine that he would, and despite rumors that apparently the assets were egging Jean Paul on to go faster, if the only threat was a few paparazzi on scooters, then why would he allow the driver to have a speed chase when there was little or no risk? Doesn't make any sense."

"Yep. 'Shut the fuck up and do what I say. I am in charge, and I will get you to safety,'" piped in Jimmy with his usual finesse.

"So, what about this white Fiat Uno?" Ed asked.

"No one knows for sure if it's real or an apparition. But what we do know is the mother of the future king of England was shacked up with Dodi Al Fayed, the son of the Harrods owner who has been denied citizenship forever and no one knows the reason why!" said Sam.

"Was she up the duff?" asked Jimmy.

"That's what the rumor is, yes. Nine to ten weeks pregnant, but of course no one is accepting that as the truth," stated Sam.

Ed commented, as he stared across the room at apparently nothing, "And how that could have changed the political and religious dynamics of the world today, eh?"

"Yep, change the world forever," Sam piped in.

The four considered their own space for a few moments while trying to comprehend the potential of an Arabic bloodline being in hereditary line to the throne of England, Great Britain, the United Kingdom.

"Scary stuff," Mitch confirmed. They all nodded in agreement.

"So, if this isn't an accident, who would want her dead?" asked Jimmy. "I mean, beyond the royal family, Secret Service, Muslim Fundamentalists, Al Fayed's enemies, every right-wing organization in the UK? Apart from that, no one," retorted Jimmy to his own question.

"Yep. If this isn't an accident, then the list is very long," said Mitch.

"And given the length of the list of suspects and who is on that list, I bet you we will never find out the truth," said Ed.

"So, what's next?" asked Jimmy.

"Not sure that there's much more we can do here now. Driver. Dead. Diana. Dead. Dodi. Dead. Jones-Davies hospitalized, not talking, lost his tongue apparently, literally."

"If you ask me, this whole mess stinks," said Mitch.

"Yep, let's get back to base and see what unfolds over the coming days and weeks. What a bloody damn shame," said Ed.

"What a fucking tragedy," said Jimmy and Mitch together. Everyone shook their heads and downed their pints. Then they went their separate ways.

Next time they would see each other would be a few days later at the Game Cock, Saturday, where they would watch the funeral procession leave Kensington Palace and head to Westminster Abbey.

They would listen to Earl Spencer, Diana's brother, and his emotional speech, as well as Elton John's heart-wrenching "Candle in the Wind" before watching the procession head out of London, north to Althorp Park and the Spencers' family home to be buried.

Mitch remembered that Saturday. A whole bunch of the guys poured out the back door of Stirling Lines to head over to the Game Cock, snuggled in the back room, TV set up, beers, largely silence, and more than a tear in the eye of many of these hard men.

It was an emotional scene across the UK, the world, and even in the Game Cock that day.

After the funeral was over and Diana's body was being taken through the streets of London, northbound with millions of mourners at the side if the road, flowers marked Diana's last journey.

Mitch's thoughts turned to Bella, and he remembered a call while on his own travels. Bella was only six.

"Hello, Daddy. Did you see the beautiful singing in the church today, Daddy?" she asked.

"Yes, darling, I did. Wasn't it beautiful?" Mitch responded, once again remembering the beauty of innocence and wondering if it could ever be preserved.

"When are you coming home, Daddy? I miss you. Bunny says hello. Good night, Daddy. Have a safe trip. Bring me back something nice. Love you."

"I miss you too and love you too, my little Bella-roony."

Mitch looked out of his window, deep in Stirling Lines, at the parade square, the rugby ground, and the clock tower and thought of all his memories, his self-torture, his life of ups and downs. He saw a vision of his beautiful daughter before him, Bella. Would she ever truly understand?

Mitch hoped so with all his heart.

PART IV

WHO DARES

18
RAT TAILS

Bradford, United Kingdom, October 2016, Day 11

ANDREW HARRISON JUMPED INTO HIS black BMW 630i parked outside his home in Birkdale, Bradford, in the north of England. He was dressed in his usual work attire—off-the-peg pin-striped suit, bright gold tie, and double-cuff shirt. He fired up the engine and headed to his office, feeling old and tired, although he was only in his fifties. He'd lied and cheated his way up the ladder, and he knew he'd fallen short in many ways.

For a moment, memories of growing up as the youngest of four brothers in Bradford flashed through his mind. But then he focused on making his next phone call, one of a succession he'd already made on the short trip to work. He prided himself on his unscrupulous nature, on his ability to drive wedges to sweeten the deal at hand, not caring who he hurt along the way. His hero was Vladimir Putin. He fancied himself to be very much like the Man in the Kremlin, as Putin was sometimes called.

Although Harrison knew some people saw him as slightly effeminate, he didn't care. He didn't care that he was short, that his face was creased with wrinkles. He still had it going on with the ladies. Harrison liked women, and despite his twenty-plus-year marriage

177

and two children, he frequently strayed off the path with wives and girlfriends of friends, prostitutes, and the women who worked for him, as he took advantage of his position of power and their weaknesses. For sure, some were willing parties, but most, like all those acquainted with him, were victims at some level.

He pulled up outside his offices in Leeds, across the road from the casino, on stilts with parking below and his own dedicated parking spot. He had inherited the offices as part of one of his escapades of ripping apart a company, dispatching the previous owners, taking everything from them, and having the gall to keep some of their prized assets, in this case, their offices and the previous owner's parking space.

He jumped out of his car, bumped into the janitor, Rufus, and spent five minutes talking about family, reggae, Leeds United's performance over the weekend, Bradford City signing a new player, and the sexiest chicks in the office nowadays. Harrison liked these conversations, shooting the wind, joking with the likes of Rufus. Harrison felt comfortable in the knowledge that his intellect would not be challenged; that was how he liked it.

He trotted up the stairs to his offices, the second floor, "Grace and Partners" above the door, and breezed in. "Morning, Andrew," said Amanda with a flirtatious and knowing smile and too much cleavage on display.

Harrison smiled back and winked.

"Morning, Andrew." Kathy smiled coyly.

"Good morning, Kath. How are you?" He smiled and winked, then went into his corner office overlooking the metropolis of Leeds City Center, and in walked his latest personal assistant, Karen—tall, blonde, short skirt, long legs—with a cup of tea in her hand. Harrison gestured for her to sit. She did, crossing and uncrossing her legs, an extra button on her blouse open this morning, flirting outrageously. Clearly, she was one of the more willing victims of Harrison's ways.

Harrison had a 9:30 a.m. meeting with his business partner, Neil Grace. Harrison got along nicely with Grace, largely because his partner did business in the same ruthless fashion he did. He was from Bingley, and he was a builder, a plumber, a bully, a fighter and a trouble starter who had made more money than he deserved and used it to invest in companies. He was the founding investor in Harrison after his many escapades of ripping off innocent business owners and setting up Grace and Partners.

Grace had built a portfolio of properties in the area, hairdressers, convenience stores, and small apartments and homes, mainly rented to those trying to scrape a living. He had the upper hand and would evict at will. One of his favorite stories was about an old lady who was a tenant in a block of apartments he owned that he wanted to gut and transform into higher-premium single office spaces for young up-and-coming companies. The old lady on the top floor refused to leave. She had lived there for twenty years and had nowhere to go. Grace ripped out the staircase so she couldn't even leave her apartment. After five days of being stuck in her home, she ran out of food, gave up, packed her possessions in two suitcases, and left. She was found two weeks later, dead, stabbed in the park where she was living under the blankets from her bed, her worldly savings of $1,000 her sacrifice for her life.

Grace was not a nice man at all. He had a wife, Catherine, and two kids but wasn't much of a father either, as he treated them just like the rest of humanity—with disregard and contempt. Of course, none of that mattered to Harrison. In fact, he viewed Grace's character as an asset, not a liability.

He had first met Grace several years ago on a mission to oust one of his business partners who had found Harrison out for womanizing, stealing, sending illicit payments to his own bank accounts in Malaysia, having phantom employees on the payroll, buying company cars for his family, and generally being dishonest. Harrison's business partner at the time had worked much of this out and hired a lawyer to mediate his exit. Grace was bought in by Harrison to make sure that business partner was the one to exit with nothing and that Harrison would keep, then strip, then sell the assets of the company. That was the beginning of a beautiful friendship.

Harrison took a sip of his tea, noting just how good Karen looked. "Is Neil in yet?" he asked.

"Not yet," Karen said. "He did call in to say he was stuck in traffic. That he'd be a little late."

Harrison sighed and took another sip of tea. "Okay then. That'll be all for now. When Neil arrives, please have him come right in."

Karen smiled and said she'd take care of it. Then she left his office.

Grace parked his red Toyota pickup truck in his reserved spot next to Harrison's BMW. On entering the office, the girls feared him, as he would return the good mornings with a stroke, a touch, a fumble, and often, when no one was looking, a grope, or sometimes he just didn't care.

He knew he intimidated people because of his height, six feet five. He knew he wasn't the most handsome guy—lanky, gray haired, balding. He also didn't care. He felt no need to wear suits. Indeed, as he strolled into the office, he was dressed in construction boots, jeans, and a checked shirt. He looked like he was the same plumber he started out as thirty years ago and not the multimillionaire he was today. Grace liked it that way. He wasn't a suit-wearing type of guy. He didn't like environments where his intellect was challenged, but he was comfortable in the company of his pal Andrew, Andy Harrison. They were intellectually compatible.

He nodded at Karen.

"Oh, good morning, Mr. Grace," Karen said. "Mr. Harrison is expecting you. Go right on in."

"Fucking traffic," Grace muttered, walking into Harrison's office.

"Morning, Neil," Harrison said as Grace sat down.

"Is it?" Grace asked, already in a foul mood. "Goddamned traffic. I swear to God I'm gonna drive someone right off the bloody road one day."

Harrison laughed. "I bet you will."

"So, did you see the message from Tangier?" asked Grace.

"Yes, I did. We delivered the goods. Thank you," said Harrison.

"I gotta say we may have stepped on shit this time, partner," Grace said.

"Dealing with Dmitri Dankov on this level is just plain crazy, in my humble opinion. I mean, come on, Andrew! Murder for hire? And hitting a former sergeant major from the fucking Special Air Service?"

"You worry too much," Harrison said with a laugh. "Consider how much money we just made. That should make you smile."

"It does. I just want to be around to spend it without getting my balls fed to me."

"Well, what's done is done," Harrison said.

"I suppose so. This better not blow back on us," Grace said, getting up from his chair. He left Harrison's office in a huff.

Harrison admitted to himself that Grace had a point. He didn't like the idea of putting down a former SAS solider. But Dmitri Dankov had insisted. He needed the job done fast, and Harrison reluctantly put the hit in motion. He'd first met Dmitri Dankov in Sharm El Sheikh in 2005 while Harrison was staying at the Four Seasons on a family vacation from the illicit earnings he was reaping from his business, which he owned 50 percent of, without his partner's knowledge.

Harrison's wife, Tracey, and son and daughter were living it up thanks to Harrison's latest victimized business partner. They were using the monies he had syphoned off the business to fly the family first class and stay at one of the suites in the hotel. The resort was full of Russians and Russian money, with all their gold, brashness, big cigars, and lack of class. Harrison and his wife fit right in.

There was one Russian he met who was different from the rest. First, he was on his own in this family resort, and he and Harrison met at the bar one evening, neither men big partakers in alcohol, Dmitri Dankov with a Stolichnaya vodka and Harrison with a Budweiser. They got chatting, small talk, sharing their business interests, positioned with politeness to disguise the distaste of what they really did. They came away intrigued, wanting to learn more about each other and sensing a potential opportunity.

Over the course of that week, Harrison met Dmitri Dankov several times, and the two hit it off. Then, after the bombings, Dmitri Dankov went dark Harrison had had no contact with him for more than a year, but then the big Russian waltzed into his office out of the blue. They exchanged small talk, and then Dmitri Dankov got to the point. He said he had a business proposition but that he'd feel more comfortable talking things over at lunch. Harrison said that was fine and suggested that they have lunch at the casino across the street.

A few minutes later, they were seated at a table in the casino restaurant.

"So, what's this proposition of yours?" Harrison asked after the waiter took their drink order.

"I'll get to that in a minute." Dmitri Dankov smiled and gestured with his right arm around the room. "You see, we now own the casino."

"You're kidding," Harrison said, highly impressed.

"We have casinos over all world as part of operations. Good way to get rid of cash if you know what I mean."

Harrison nodded. Of course, he knew what Dmitri Dankov meant.

The waiter returned with the drinks, a vodka and a Budweiser, just like they had in Sharm El Sheikh, although in this shithole casino full of Chinese, pensioners, and vagrants, there was no Stolichnaya. "Fucking heathens," announced Dmitri Dankov. "You hungry?" he asked.

"You know, I'm really not. You?"

"Not really. I came to talk to you, not eat."

"About what?" Harrison asked, his curiosity building.

"Andy, I always liked you. I knew from the moment we met there was something special about you, some of the stories, conquests, victories. I checked you out, and your record is very impressive." Dmitri Dankov slowly nodded.

In the past fifteen years, Harrison had gone through four companies and six business partners, ejected multiple stakeholders, burned multiple millions of investor cash, and yet survived as the thriving party each time. The lessons he had learned about survival and maskirovka from being the youngest of four brothers had served him well. Very well.

"Well, being in business isn't easy, Dmitri Dankov. You have to take the rough with the smooth, peaks and the valleys, ups and downs," said Harrison.

"Yep, and as far as I can tell, you have always landed on the smooth, on the peak, on the up," said Dmitri Dankov with his admiring but surprisingly intimidating smile. "You are very perceptive, Andy. That is what I like about you, very perceptive, like a Siberian snow leopard. You sense things. You know how to hunt, find your prey, and make the kill. That is why I like you, Andy."

"Thanks, Dmitri Dankov. Now, can you get to the point?"

Dmitri Dankov laughed. "I have a job for you, Andy. A project that I think you might like, right up your street. A job that will be very lucrative." Dmitri Dankov rubbed his fingers together.

"Okay. What is this job you have for me?"

Dmitri Dankov went on to explain that there was a small casino group, a chain of six that he wanted Harrison to make a play for to take over as CEO. Get rid of the board, break it up, and, once it was on its knees, sell it on to Dmitri Dankov's group for a pittance. All part of Dmitri Dankov's plan, or whoever he was taking his orders from to retain cash in the motherland and, as important, get foreign currency into the motherland. It all made sense to Harrison now, and of course he took the job. He sensed that there wasn't really a choice.

They shook hands and hugged like bears, like long-lost, distant brothers in a suffocating embrace, one more dominant than the other.

From that day on, Grace and Partners, in its ordinary offices, in the ordinary town, began to thrive. Dmitri Dankov would show up every now and then. They would meet at the casino across the road, over lunch, and Harrison would receive his orders about the next project. Each one got more complex, bigger, and ever more lucrative.

This removal of Badger Bell in Tangier was the most worrisome, but Grace's men had done an excellent job with the execution of the former soldier with the tool of choice, polonium-210, or its newest derivative. This was new ground for Grace and Partners. Harrison knew that. He and Grace were uneasy about moving into murder for hire as a revenue stream, especially for a client like Dmitri Dankov. A silent client. A deadly client.

Harrison put the thoughts about Dmitri Dankov out of his mind and got on with his day. He was determined to thread the needle with the big Russian, to play him like a fiddle, if that was possible. He didn't really care about the danger. Harrison was just as smart as the Russian—and probably smarter, he thought.

19
THE DOG

San Francisco, California, United States, October 2016, Day 12

BELLA FOCUSED ON THE COMPUTER screen in front of her. Her eyes were strained, and she felt the first tinges of a headache coming on. She leaned back in her chair and took a look around the ops center in Lord Beecham's secret building. He and the colonel were both on the phone.

Her father's team certainly had been busy. Lord Beecham and Colonel Collins leveraged intelligence from the likes of the Secret Service, CIA, FBI, Interpol, Mossad, and various other intelligence agencies. The team had unearthed the file that Paul had been working on before his untimely demise. It was hidden deep in a secure storage file in the cloud, with multiple passwords and gateways, and even once they got in, it was deeply encrypted. Bella had come into the operation to help them out. "She is one very bright cookie," Lord Beecham had commented about her. "Just like her father," responded Colonel Collins.

While she was helping them crack the code, she explored the relationship between these two colorful characters and Mitch.

"So, how long have you known Mitch?"

"So, where did you first meet?"

"What is he like at work?"

"What has he done that makes him so sad?"

Lord Beecham and the colonel both had the ability to answer the question without answering the question and more than once ended with, "What we do know is that he is very proud of you, Bella."

It of course annoyed the hell out of Bella, this shroud of secrecy, the unbreakable bond between these men. What kept them so fiercely loyal to each other? They knew everything, yet no one would say anything about anything.

She had been chatting to Nikita the night before and had told him the parts of the story that she knew, not that she felt she really knew anything, just the bits she had been fed. Nikita seemed unusually preoccupied, and when Bella pressed him, he brightened up and said, "Hey, why don't you come out to London for a few days? I have a couple of weeks off. I have a big bonus in my bank. Let's go and splash out. What do you think?"

Bella said she'd love to and had booked her flight right away. She went back to work. A few hours later, she'd broken the code. They all crowded around her screen to read the file. The information was confusing, though it seemed that Paul had been connecting the dots to some seemingly unrelated yet extraordinarily connected incidents in recent history. What did Princess Diana's death have to do with shootings in Delhi and Sydney, the Arab Spring, bombings in Boston, and 9/11? Why would the Russian Mafia be working with the IRA, who was working with Colombian cartels?

"What on earth is going on here?" Lord Beecham asked no one in particular.

Brisbane, Queensland, Australia, October 2016, Day 12

Conrad Yee, also known as the Dog, sat on his deck overlooking the Brisbane River. Dressed in the traditional robes worn by masters in the martial arts, Yee was deep in his daily meditation in the early-morning sunshine. A gentle breeze stirred the wind chimes suspended above the deck under the eaves of the roof. All was at peace around him, and within him as well. Yee knew that his mental control gave him an edge as one of the world's deadliest assassins. He knew his physical stature made him appear quite ordinary, with his hazel eyes, high cheekbones, and gangly but muscular build. He was tall at over six feet, but he did not look scary. That gave him even more of an advantage over his prey, over his foes.

He had discovered karate as a boy, as an escape from the alcoholism of his father and the mental health issues of his mother. He never quite worked out which came first. Was his father an alcoholic because of his mother's mental health issues, or was it the other way around? Either way, it was still a source of pain today.

In any event, karate was his savior and his discipline. Conrad didn't drink, and his spiritual commitment kept him from insanity. Karate was his way of avoiding the demise of his parents, and it had worked so far.

He had grown up in the United Kingdom, in the north, below the Borders of Scotland, and as a child, he had found solace and escape in the beautiful mountains, the hills and the valleys. He avoided going home as much as he could, hunting, fishing, and camping with his band of merry men, or boys.

As he grew older, he became more isolated and discovered karate at eleven. One of his friend's mothers had taken the three of them to a neighboring town to discover this sport that was full of self-discipline and self-defense, hoping it would keep these three errant kids on the straight and narrow. After six weeks, Conrad was the one who persisted and continued with his studies and learning his craft, which took him at the age of seventeen to Shanghai, China, where he joined an ancient school for the brightest stars in the world of martial arts.

He lived and breathed his new culture and eventually swore his allegiance to the People's Republic of China and volunteered for the Red Army shortly thereafter. Conrad was an anomaly and one of a handful of Western-born men who had made the same step. After building up trust, he became one of the revered warriors of the Chinese Army and eventually received the honor of joining the Communist

Secret Guard, where he served for ten years under the orders of State Council, working on projects and missions around the world and quickly gaining the reputation as the Invisible Man due to his ability to blend in Western theaters but equally into Eastern and Asian theaters too. Conrad had found a niche and was a very valuable undercover, highly secret, and secretive resource for the People's Republic of China.

During that time, he gained the nickname of 狗, Gǒu, or the Dog, due to a couple of infamous operations where he had to silence the dogs in order to complete his ultimate mission. The first occasion was a raging pit bull guarding the house of a senior foreign diplomat; a slit of the throat worked immediately to silence the animal, but from that he learned to carry with him dog snacks, which were beyond temptation for even the most vicious guard animal. Laced with deathly poison, they worked instantaneously and silenced these creatures who could have easily corrupted many missions that Conrad completed.

Conrad was the number one assassin for the People's Republic of China and had completed over sixty successful missions in the past twenty years, most recently as a freelancer to the highest bidder, limit of three a year, partly due to his meticulous method of operation and partly due to superstition.

He had built up identities in eighteen different countries and in many cases multiple identities, in each taking advantage of the five different languages he spoke, not only his ability to speak but to immerse himself. He could pose as an English gentleman one day and a Chinese tycoon the next. From a German soccer supporter one day to a Japanese businessman the next. He prided himself on the skills that he had honed to become all but invisible when he wanted to be, which was most of the time.

Growing up with his father's beatings and his mother's attacks as a child made him tough. His mother would regularly turn on him and his brother with the carving knife during Sunday lunch, chasing them around the house with that crazed look in her eye. No wonder his father left and eventually drank himself to death. Conrad had no choice but to be tough and take a beating, with no flinch, with no indication of pain. His ability to ignore pain gave him still more advantages over his prey, over his foes.

He always worked alone, and he was always 100 percent successful. His success was due in part to his clinical execution of each hit. As the best hit man in the world, or one of the best, the Dog didn't come cheap. He had crafted his trade from the platform of karate, but during his time with the Communist Secret Guard, he had added an entire range of skills and techniques that he adopted and applied with extreme skill and meticulous planning. Just like a martial arts grandmaster, he would carefully select the demise of his victims and the tools that he would use to not only be the most effective but also the most appropriate, dependent upon what the person was accused of or why his masters wanted them dead.

One businessman who had been having an affair with one of the State Council's wives had his eyeballs removed so he could never look at another woman again, in this life or the next.

Another who had been molesting his own daughter had his genitals removed.

Another who had been embezzling funds, his fingers removed, slowly, one by one, before his final demise.

He also used diversionary tactics to make sure that it wasn't always obvious what or who the target was. Plane crashes, car crashes, assassinations under the guise of terror attacks. He blamed on others who were happy to take the publicity. Just like the Russians had perfected maskirovka, Conrad had perfected his own version and a perfect way to avoid scrutiny from the ordinary forces of law and order that simply didn't understand the sheer depths of his trade.

Conrad heard the familiar light ring of the handbell inside his home behind the partitions to the balcony. Without any facial expression, he completed his meditation, stood, bowed, and turned to open up the sliding doors and sit on the cushions on the floor for his daily Chayi 茶, tea, and breakfast. He went in and sat down.

In walked Mingh in traditional Chinese dress. She laid the bamboo tray and Chayi 茶 on the table in front of Conrad, taking her time to lay out the cups and pour the tea. As the tea neared the top of the cup,

Conrad tapped the table gently with his index finger as an indication to stop and to say thank you. Mingh poured a cup for herself and sat down opposite Conrad and bowed. *"Zǎoshang hǎo*, good morning," she said softly. They shared a sacred bond between them. He looked at her with a reserved affection.

Conrad had rescued Mingh from a brothel in Shanghai where she was the slave of a powerful Mafia madam, Guan Yin. Guan Yin had been hosting powerful men at her brothel for years, but her guile had increased in recent years, and her greed had demanded more and more as she blackmailed her victims until one of the State Council wanted her removed.

Conrad saw Mingh chained like a dog, a personal lapdog to Guan Yin, just fifteen years old. When he met her, she was timid, shy, scared. Even Conrad had been shocked at how bizarre it was. Mingh was dressed like an American doll, with a leash around her neck. Perfectly dressed, in expensive clothes, perfect hair, makeup, shoes, handbag, and even a perfect leash and dog collar studded with real diamonds.

As Conrad dispensed of Guan Yin's concrete coffin into the Yangtze that night, he returned to the brothel to retrieve the helpless Mingh and thereafter looked after her as a daughter. That was fifteen years ago, and Mingh was so grateful. They had cohabited since and with few words had developed a love for each other, a type of love that was unbreakable, a type of love that never used the word love, a type of love that could only exist between two lost souls who knew that they needed each other.

Conrad had been following Mitch and his activity for many years. He knew Mitch, but Mitch did not know him, or at least he didn't know that he did. Conrad and Mitch had grown up with each other as kids, a long time ago and another universe away. Conrad had always been fascinated about their parallel lives and how they had diverged—on opposite sides of the fence. Conrad's was far more lucrative. Mitch's was far safer than Conrad's. They were both warriors but in different ways. Mitch might not know Conrad's identity at the moment, but Conrad could see that he might one day. In the meantime, he would keep a watchful eye out for Mitch, his old childhood friend.

Conrad was leaving today to head to Kaliningrad, a Russian enclave on the Baltic coast where he would take his instructions for his latest assignment. Mingh and Conrad always took tea together before he left for his latest mission. This was a ritual that they had built over the years. Mingh had witnessed firsthand what Conrad did for a living that night in Shanghai, but it had never been a topic of conversation. Their code of silence was implicit and absolute.

Conrad finished his tea and light breakfast, and then he went to get changed. He put on dark gray jeans, gray boots, a gray shirt, and a dark gray trench coat. His black backpack was loaded with all he needed for his trip.

Just as he was about to leave, his son, Bingwen, ran up and hugged him.

"Dadda, Dadda."

"Good morning, my son," responded Conrad. He knelt down, looked him in the eyes, and said, "Look after your mother, my son. Do your homework, be good at school, and don't forget to do your morning meditation."

"Yes, Dadda. Of course, Dadda." He bowed to his father.

Conrad bowed back, bowed at Mingh as she did the same, then grabbed his black backpack and headed to the airport. He headed to Kaliningrad to meet Dmitri Dankov.

20
TO FRANCE

United Kingdom and France, October 2016, Day 14

THE SUN WAS ALMOST DOWN, bathing the clouds below the wing of the Boeing 787 Dreamliner in soft orange and pink. Farther out, the sky was a deep blue that faded to black. Bella continued to gaze out the window. While she was excited about her trip to see Nikita, she felt inner turmoil about her life and the lives of her immediate family.

Bella thought about her mum and her dad—how Angela had made the effort to dress at the funeral, the glint in her eye, Mitch hanging out and the fact that he was still there in the morning with Mama when Bella returned. Was that a sign?

Bella was grateful to both of them. She had a blessed childhood, and they had worked hard to get her through college and university. They had supported her, protected her, and loved her, but she always struggled with the unspoken sadness between them, their distance yet their love for each other, their respect yet conflict, the sadness in their eyes. What had they been through that made them that way?

And Bella thought about her own life. She wondered what she should do with it, what she could do.

Why am I even here? she thought. *Why do I exist?*

After a while, Bella drifted off to sleep. The plane arrived in

London, putting an end to the eleven-hour direct flight from LAX. After deplaning, she hurried with her carry-on bag down the crowded concourse to the arrivals gate, where she saw Nikita holding up a sign that read, "Bella Bella Fonterella."

She sped toward him, wrapped her arms around his neck, and said, "My Nikita." Then she kissed him on the lips.

"My beautiful, beautiful, special Bella Bella Fonterella," he said as they embraced, so happy to be in each other's arms. She recognized a familiar sadness deep in his eyes.

Nikita grabbed Bella's bag, and they headed off to the parking garage and to Nikita's waiting silver-gray, F-Type Jaguar. "Good thing I packed lightly." She smiled, referring to the lack of luggage space in the super car before her, and gave him another kiss. "So great to see you, Nikita."

They jumped into the F-Type coupe with its tan leather seats. Nikita fired up the 5.0-liter supercharged engine into life. Bella asked, "Where are you taking me, young man?"

"It's a surprise," he responded.

Forty minutes later, they were pulling into the Belmond Le Manoir aux Quat'-Saisons just outside of Oxford.

"This is where we will commence our grand tour, Bella Bella Fonterella."

Bella loved it when he called her that, the same as she also loved the nicknames her father would call her as a little girl. There was something that felt comfortable on her father's knee in his company, his clear, deep love and dedication, the feeling that in his company she was safe, loved, welcome. She felt similarly in Nikita's company as she glanced over and smiled at him with love and pride.

As they arrived on the crunchy gravel at the front door, their bags were taken care of. Nikita checked in using his First World Bank Stratus card, and they were shown to the Lavande suite, overlooking the beautiful and tended lavender beds. It was only noon, so Nikita suggested that they head into Oxford for lunch, take a look around, and go back to Le Manoir for a game of afternoon croquet on the lawn and then dinner.

"That sounds fantastic, Nikita," Bella said, though she was a bit jet lagged.

Bella hopped into the bathroom and quickly freshened up. Within ten minutes, they were back in the F-Type heading on the A4158 into Oxford, past the Mini factory in Cowley and off into the city center. "Let's call in at Magdalen College," Bella said.

"Sure thing," said Nikita.

They parked the F-Type and walked to the front archway of the college that Bella knew so well and loved.

Bella loved the history of this place. She could feel the centuries before her, the scholars, the students, as well as the memories of her wonderful time in this magical place.

As they walked through the gateway reception and stepped into the quadrangle surrounded by the beautiful, ornate building with cloisters underneath and the vast expense of grass in the middle, Bella felt a home. She had studied here, where her parents had hoped and dreamed that one day she would be, where she could reconnect with her British roots, one of the oldest colleges of one of the oldest universities in the world. She felt invigorated as she skipped across the grass, spinning around, taking in the beautiful quadrangle and the buildings steepened in history.

They had a look around the college. There were some familiar faces and some hellos, and Bella was just thrilled to be back. "Let's go to the Bear for a snack, Nikita."

"Sure. Let's go, Fonterella."

As they walked into the oldest pub in Oxford, the Bear, established in 1242, both Nikita and Bella had to duck to get into the small, dark bar with its interesting collection of dress ties on the wall. Bella ordered two pints of Old Speckled Hen and a pork pie to share. "Fantastic. It's great to be back." She smiled and kissed Nikita on the cheek.

"It's hard to imagine that this place opened its doors for business 820 years ago," Nikita commented.

"Imagine being in here back then," Bella marveled. "Can't you just imagine the old professors in the corners talking about the next big thing?"

They looked around at the display of dress ties on the walls and the ceiling, imagining the necks from which all these old ties came from. "I bet each and every one has a story to tell," said Bella with a sense of wonder.

The round, stout pork pie came out with some pickled chutney on the side. Bella took the knife and expertly sliced it into quarters. Nikita looked down at the gelatinous filling with a grimace. "What's up, Niki? It's delicious. Go on, try it."

Nikita did, and as he tasted it, he nodded with approval. "Yes. That is very good." Bella smiled at him.

They finished the pie, downed their Old Speckled Hens, and then headed for a wander around the city before Bella said, "Are you ready for that game of croquet?"

Bella's long flight was starting to catch up with her, and they jumped back into the F-Type and headed back to Le Manoir for a game of croquet and then a nap before dinner. The ride back was quick as the F-Type darted through the country roads. Nikita and Bella grabbed a croquet set and went about knocking the balls around the hoops as the chefs visited the garden for herbs and vegetables for dinner that night. Bella let out a big yawn, and Nikita invited her back to the suite to rest.

Nikita sat in the lounge area, cracked his laptop, and turned on the news as Bella went into the bathroom. She ran the roman bath, added scented salts, lit the candles, and turned on her music before climbing into the bath.

"Ah, Niki, it's so good to be with you again. It's been such a long time." She sighed as she started to relax and feel the heat and the aromas in the air.

"I'm really looking forward to the next two weeks together."

"Me too," he said from the lounge area. "It's going to be fun!"

"Just like my father always told me," said Bella, "Let's just follow our noses."

"What?"

"Just go where we want to go. No plans, no route, just follow your nose." She laughed, remembering the time all those years ago when Mitch had said that, and she had asked him, "What?" She gave the same response to Nikita today as Mitch did back then to her.

Bella finished her bath, dried herself, and snuggled into bed to sleep for an hour or so. When she awoke, she saw that Nikita was hard at work.

"Have a good sleep?" he asked, looking up from the laptop.

"Yeah. And I really needed it," she said. "I'm going to get changed for dinner."

"You do that," he said and went back to work.

A short time later, Bella was ready. She'd put on a beautiful, classic black dress with pearls and her favorite pair of Jimmy Choos, looking like a model from the catwalk—tall, slim, and elegant, with incredible warmth and confidence. He looked great in his dark gray slacks and Hugo Boss sports coat.

They were seated in the dining room a few minutes later. Bella was lost in the moment, her troubles temporarily forgotten. When the food came, she tucked in. Between bites, she said, "So, Niki, what's been happening? You said things have been going pretty well. Predicting the Brexit outcome, making billions, senior vice president of Special Investment Operations, eh?"

"It's been an interesting couple of years. That's for sure, Bella."

"It's been an amazing couple of years, Niki. You are the star. How do you manage to call it so often? What's the trick?"

"Oh, I don't know, just a lot of luck and being in the right place, I guess."

"You are always so damned modest, Niki. This is our time. Let's just have fun."

They smiled and clinked their glasses.

"I was sorry to hear about your dad's friend," Nikita said. "What was his name again?"

"Paul. My dad has put together a team to investigate his death. Looks like it might have been murder."

"Murder! Really?"

"Can't say much about it. All hush-hush, you see, but yeah. Looks like someone wanted Paul dead because of something he was working on for the CIA."

"Sounds like a James Bond movie."

Bella took a sip of her wine and dabbed her mouth with her napkin. "Sort of does, come to think of it."

"Have you made up your mind about the job at the CIA?"

Bella shook her head. "Not yet."

"Could be a great gig."

"Could be."

The dinner came and went, and neither had room for dessert. They finished off both bottles of wine between them, and then the late hour and the jet lag started to catch up with Bella. She announced that she was ready for bed. Nikita indicated that he would go to the bar for a vodka nightcap and see her in the morning.

"Night-night, my Nikita." She kissed him on the forehead, and he smiled.

"Night-night, Bella Bella Fonterella." He kissed her cheek slowly.

When Bella got back to the suite, she undressed, washed her face, and slipped into bed. She pulled out her phone and texted, "Oxford, safe and sound." Mitch texted back immediately, "That's my girl," and she sank into a deep, contented sleep.

Nikita was up as usual, ready for his morning run. It was his habit, his religion, but also his necessity. As he left the room quietly at a quarter after six, he ran around the grounds of the hotel and down to the entranceway. He started running, finding his way, discovering a new route, keeping an eye and an ear open, as always.

At six thirty, Nikita's Blackphone rang. "Dobroye Utro." Nikita answered the call. "Da." "Da." "Ponimat." "Da." "Konechno." He listened intently as the caller went through another set of updates and instructions, then hung up.

As he continued his run, he was even more conscious than usual that someone might be watching and listening, despite the fact he was surrounded by woodland, early-morning foxes, and late-night deer. No people around at this time of day in the Oxfordshire countryside, but the stakes were getting higher. First World Bank and its customers and clients had a trillion-dollar bet on the outcome of the US presidential election based on his prediction and his 100 percent past record of getting it right. Nikita was feeling the pressure.

By the time he trotted back into Le Manoir, Bella was just returning from her own morning exercise in the grounds. "Good morning, Niki. I didn't hear you get in last night or leave this morning."

"You were sound asleep, Bella. I didn't want to disturb you," responded Nikita.

"Breakfast?" Bella asked.

"Sounds good."

As he took Bella's arm, Nikita noticed the same two men he'd seen watching them in the dining room the previous evening. Now they were in a red Alfa Romeo. Seeing them again made him feel uneasy, but he put the feeling out of his mind for the moment. They went to the room and ordered a banquet breakfast, and despite the time of the year, the sun was up and the temperature crisp. It was invigorating tasting Le Manoir morning delights together. Bella went to get her map of Europe for their grand tour.

"Let's follow our noses." She smiled.

"Where to, my little Fonterella?" Nikita asked.

She looked at the map on the table and with her index finger circling, she popped it down on the map. "Let's go to Paris!"

"Paris, it is!"

"Let's stay at the Ritz and go to the Buddha Bar tonight."

By 9:00 a.m., they were in the F-Type, bags in the back, and heading to Kent and the Eurostar, driving like a bat out of hell. During Nikita's training, he had learned how to drive fast cars very fast indeed. Bella, in the passenger seat, had booked their tickets, a night in the Ritz, and a table at the Buddha Bar on Nikita's First World Bank Stratus card by the time they arrived in Ashford, Kent, at 11:20 a.m., ready to board the noon train to Paris, France.

Driving the F-Type onto the carriage, Nikita and Bella sat in comforting silence as they set off through the Chunnel underneath the English Channel.

"How is your mother?" asked Bella.

"Oh, she's okay. Hardly see her or hear from her."

"I thought you were sharing the apartment together."

"Yes, we are, but I never see her. She's looking after some oligarch's family and is always somewhere, never at home. Suits me."

"When was the last time you saw her?"

"Probably twelve months ago."

"Do you speak to her?"

Nikita looked at Bella. "Yes, every day," he responded with a tinge of paranoia. *Why is she asking me so many questions?* he wondered.

"Oh, that's good," she said. "As you know, I'm very close with both my parents. Can't imagine what it would be like not to be."

"You know my story," he said, fighting back a momentary wave of rage and sadness. "I really miss Angus. Haven't seen him in ages, what with him living in South America."

"You should fly down there, Niki," Bella said.

"Yeah, maybe I should."

They arrived in Calais on the other side of the English Channel, jumped in the Jaguar, and Nikita rode the F-Type hard to get to Paris by four thirty, just in time to check in at the Ritz for afternoon tea in the Salon Proust.

After they were seated and placed their order for tea and pastries, Bella asked, "Wasn't this where Princess Diana spent her last night alive?"

"Sure was."

"Was it an accident or was she assassinated?" asked Bella.

"Neither," responded Nikita with an air of confidence.

"What do you mean? How can you be so sure?"

"The target wasn't Princess Diana," he responded.

"Target? So, it was an assassination?"

"Put it this way. Things are never quite as they seem, Bella. If I had to guess, I would say she was just in the wrong place at the wrong time. Don't ask me how I know this. It's just gut instinct."

"Like your instincts with the bank?"

"Something like that."

"Was Dodi the target?" Bella asked.

"You have to take a look at the background of the driver to understand the real story," Nikita responded.

"Henri Paul was his name, right? What was his background?"

"Bella, these events are many years ago now and probably best left to the history books."

Nikita cut her off to avoid any further questions. He had given away too much already, let his guard down for a moment, but that was the magic of Bella; she had the ability to get through people's guards, especially Nikita's.

The waiter arrived in his starched white tunic with a selection of delicate sandwiches with the crusts cut off and a selection of dainty pastries and cakes, including the famous Parisian Madeleine cakes.

"Pretty special, eh?" Nikita commented.

"Amazing," Bella replied as she helped herself to the delicacies on the platter before her.

They concluded their afternoon tea and went to discover Paris for a couple of hours before returning to get ready for their Buddha Bar reservation at Faubourg St. Honoré, Rue Boissy d'Anglas, the coolest bar and restaurant and club in Paris and maybe even on the planet.

Thus far, Nikita thought, the trip was going well. He didn't consider Bella in a romantic way. He saw her more as a sister, though she was certainly beautiful enough to turn any man's head. Still, he sensed that she was probing him for some reason, and he wasn't sure why. The rest of the evening flew by, and they were back at the Ritz in the wee hours of the morning.

Nikita awoke at his usual time and prepared to go for his morning run. He turned on the television in the lounge area of the suite to listen to the global news. There was nothing of real importance going on, except an indication that a long-established plan, a prophecy of sorts, showed signs of coming together. He found that of interest. He thought about it as he began his run, leaving Bella sleeping soundly in the suite. As usual, his phone rang at 6:30 sharp.

"Dobroye Utro." Nikita answered the call. "Da." "Da." "Ponimat."

"Da." "Konechno." He listened for ten minutes, nodding his head occasionally, confirming certain points of the conversation, rarely sharing an opinion, just listening to the update and instructions from the caller. Finally, he said, "I saw the news this morning, and it seems the prophecy may be coming true. Are we predicting history or are we making it?" "Yes, understood. We will be back in London the day after the election." Nikita disconnected the call and headed back to the Ritz.

As he walked into the suite, breakfast was just arriving. The television news was still on, and Bella had a map laid out on the bed, "Niki, I would like to head to La Rochelle and Brem Sur Mer, Vendee." She pointed to the map and the west coast of France, the Bay of Biscay. "I would like to see where my mother and father fell in love."

"Sure, sounds good." Nikita responded. After all, they were following their noses.

After they finished eating breakfast and packing, they went downstairs to check out. The valet pulled out the F-Type on Place Vendome, outside the Ritz. Bella said to Nikita, "My turn to drive." Nikita shrugged and agreed. Bella took the wheel and expertly weaved her way through the Parisian traffic and headed to the A10 out of town, west toward Brem Sur Mer. She pressed the throttle and gunned the engine toward the west.

"I had forgotten what an all-rounder you are, Fonterella," said Nikita with pride.

"They taught me well," she responded with a wink as she expertly shifted gears.

Just four hours later, they were pulling into the little beach town. Nikita had booked them into Le Jardin des Iles overlooking the spectacular and uncrowded beach line.

"Wow, this is beautiful," said Bella as she looked out from the hotel at the Atlantic Ocean. "This is truly a place where you could fall in love, Nikita."

They took a drive to the little campsite at Brem Sur Mer where Bella's parents fell in love all those years ago.

Nikita enjoyed the afternoon and the quiet evening that followed. On the ride from Paris, he'd kept his eyes peeled for the red Alfa

Romeo. He thought he saw it behind them, but he couldn't be sure. If he saw it again, or even thought that he saw it, he would have to let his people know. If trouble was afoot, the carefully laid plans could run right off the rails, and he could end up dead.

The next morning, over freshly baked croissants and coffee overlooking the beach, Bella declared that she would like to work their way to Juan Le Pin, Antibes, in the South of France, another haunt of her parents, and the Hotel Juana. Due to the distance, she thought they should break it up, head to Biarritz and then Toulouse to watch a game of rugby and then to the French Riviera and Juan Le Pin.

"Why not? Let's go," responded Nikita.

They headed south, taking turns driving to Biarritz and on to Toulouse the next day to watch a rugby game at Stade Toulousain and see them beat rival Bayonne 22–16. Bella had to explain the rules to Nikita that she herself had learned from her father and his love of the sport. Throughout the game, they cuddled together in the cold, wet stadium, then went for dinner at Le Bibent for a proper Toulouse treat.

"Why do those people play that sport, Bella? It is so brutal," Nikita said.

"Brave men who recognize that the importance of the team is greater than them as individuals," she responded, thinking of her father as she spoke the words.

"It is so cold. It must hurt a lot."

"Not until the next day after the beer and the shepherd's pie have worn off!" She smiled.

"Didn't your father play?"

"Oh yes, he played all right. One of the originals."

Bella remembered going to the Rugby Club in Hereford as a young child and her father's lifelong love of the game even when they moved to California. He no longer played but encouraged young American kids to get off the couch and into sport. Get out of crime and into college, and, most of all, learn the key tenets of rugby—civility, discipline, and respect, the same principles that her father had abided by for most of his life.

She thought about her father's pain. At the funeral, she saw something in his eyes, a deep sadness—an element of self-doubt? No, that wasn't it. It was more like the look of a retired bull fighter getting back to work, a prize fighter jumping in the ring for his hundredth fight, a recovering alcoholic taking their first sip after many years of abstinence. Whatever it was, it was troubling Bella.

The next day, they arrived in the sleepy small town of Juan Le Pin, in the commune of Antibes in the Alpes-Maritimes, in southeastern France, on the Cote d'Azur nestled between Nice and Cannes.

Built in 1931, Hotel Juana was a popular retreat for many of the rich, famous, and eccentric, with guests including the Aga Khan, duke of Windsor, Winston Churchill, and Pablo Picasso—and Bella's mother and father before she was even a twinkle in their eyes. In the room, her mind went back to imagining her mother and father arriving here, courting, falling in love, the secretive soldier and the Sicilian siren. She giggled as she thought about them gallivanting around the French Riviera, having fun and romance.

She looked over at Nikita and felt sad as she realized that although she loved him, it was more like a brother and not like a lover. There was almost too much depth, too many closets inside, and probably too many skeletons too. She had been observing him the past couple of days, and only the expert eye of someone knowing him as long as she had could tell there was something wrong.

She knew he had big bets lined up on the US election, but at this stage, who else would win other than Hillary? She was the only candidate with the right level of experience to step into the White House. DJ, a businessman and reality TV star, certainly didn't have the right credentials, and frankly, who would bet against a former First Lady and career-long Washington politician?

Bella looked over at Nikita, and then the penny dropped. Nikita—that's who would bet against Hillary! *Oh my God, Nikita!* It took a little while to settle in the enormity of her thoughts. Who in their right mind would make that bet? Never mind a trillion dollars!

Now she understood why Nikita was acting so strangely.

They freshened up and headed down through the square to

explore the town with its restaurants and shops and cool vibe of the chic 1960s that still remained the same today. Plenty of restaurants to choose from, but they wanted to eat on the beach and chose Plage Le Colombier.

Over lunch, Bella steered the conversation back to Nikita's work. Although she was on leave, her boss had asked her to find out how Nikita was so good at predicting future outcomes. If he had a system, her boss wanted to know. Thus far, Nikita hadn't said much, and he probably never would divulge his secret, if he even had one. But she was game to try, especially since it seemed like he was betting against the favorite in the American election.

"Can I ask you something?" said Bella, trying not to sound awkward and failing.

"Sure. Fire away."

"Why are you predicting that we Americans will back the wild card and not the favorite? You know. The choice between Clinton and Trump? Many American conservatives hate Clinton, but she's still the obvious choice, isn't she?"

"Not necessarily," Nikita said.

Bella noted how serious he looked. He furrowed his brow and even began to scowl. "I didn't make a fortune by playing the favorites, and neither did my colleagues."

"Just seems counterintuitive to me," Bella said.

"Do we have to do this?" Nikita asked.

"Yes, we do. You haven't been yourself since we met at Heathrow, and I think that it's better for you to talk about it than hold it all in. It's clearly troubling you."

"There's a lot of money at stake, Bella."

"Yes, I know. But why would they put such a huge bet on such tall odds?"

"A lot of money from some very powerful, rich people. This will make them even more powerful and even richer."

"Who are these investors anyway? Who would put up a trillion dollars on such long odds? And how do they expect to make money if Trump wins? I just don't get it. Do they plan to influence markets? What's the real payoff here? What's really on the line?"

"You don't want to know these things."

Is it just my imagination, or is Nikita sounding extra Russian all of a sudden? Both in accent and sentiment, Bella thought.

"Even I don't know all the details. Don't want to know. Just let's say there are some very, very rich and powerful men pulling the levers. Dangerous men. That is enough for both of us, Bella. Let's not push it, okay? You never know who's listening."

"What's that supposed to mean?" Bella suddenly felt scared, and she wasn't sure why. Something wasn't right. Her instincts told her so.

"It means that nowhere is secure," Nikita said. "Nowhere is safe from certain people. Certain agencies. Like your CIA."

Bella decided not to take the bait about the CIA. She kept digging. "We can let the bank deal drop in a sec, okay? Just explain the rationale on the bet. It's going against what all the analysts are saying right now."

"Yes, yes, I know. Clinton is unpopular, more so than you may even know. We believe that when voters go into the voting booth, they will swing to Trump. Just look at all the question marks over Clinton's integrity. Just look at her email scandal."

"What about Trump's integrity? He's got plenty to answer for."

"Clearly, you favor Clinton over Trump," Nikita said. He folded his arms across his chest. "But you must understand that we believe Trump represents hope. He represents a move away from just appointing another politician. We believe that the people, just like with Brexit in the UK, are sick of conventional politicians. They want something different, and the new guard can give them that. That's why I have suggested to my colleagues to bet big on the election."

"What hope is there if he starts World War III?"

"We believe he has a good relationship with Putin. That's important. It will be more so as power centers shift over time. China, for example. Putin is the fulcrum of power in the East right now. The US isn't. The US is weak, feeble even, because of such tame policies from the Democrats in office right now."

Bella laughed and shook her head. "You're impossible."

"I'm a pragmatist."

"You might be sorry about the direction you're going in."

"I don't think so. Those *illegal* emails will be Clinton's downfall. After all, there are six hundred thousand of them to choose from."

"How can you be so sure?" she asked. "If Trump wins, then that would be another Brexit all over again. Surely that isn't good?"

"Pretty good if you took the bet, Bella," Nikita said curtly. "You will see, my Bella. These things have a habit of working themselves out."

"Mind my asking how big the bet is?"

Nikita took a moment to think about his answer. Finally, he said, "First World is in directly for about $500 billion."

"Wow! What the hell happens if it goes wrong, Niki?"

"I guess I go from hero to zero." He smiled nervously.

Bella saw an unfamiliar weakness in his eyes that she hadn't seen before. What were the real consequences of his employer losing its shirt? Could it be worth more than his job?

"Let's just leave it alone, Bella. I don't want to talk about this anymore, okay?"

Bella had learned many lessons from her father. He'd always been fond of saying, "Now, Bella, don't try to eat an elephant in one sitting." She'd asked him what he meant by that. He'd told her it was the same as not biting off more than you can chew, which made perfect sense. She decided to back off. For now.

21
PORTOFINO

Juan Le Pins, France, October 2016, Day 19

THE NEXT MORNING, BELLA WOKE up to the smell and sounds of the ocean lapping the shores of Juan Le Pin. Bella ordered room service for the two of them as she sat by the window soaking up the beauty of the South of France.

On the table, there was a big wad of euros that Nikita had managed to turn from 1,000 to 20,000 in the space of just two hours at the casino the previous night. Wisely, he had decided to quit while ahead. They went back to Hotel Juana and spent the rest of the night playing backgammon in the bar together. *Not bad for a boy who doesn't gamble,* Bella thought to herself as she looked at him between moves.

As breakfast arrived, so did Nikita, back from his morning run. "Bon jour!" Bella shouted out.

"Bon jour, Bella," responded Nikita as he grabbed his grapefruit juice. He took a big swig and sat down next to her and tucked into his Omelette Petit Dejeuner aux Française.

"Perfect. Thanks, Bella."

"Today, I thought we could take a trip to Portofino and the splendid Splendido Hotel."

"Sounds good to me. How far is it?

"It's about a three-hour drive."

"Cool. Let's do it," Nikita confirmed.

At nine thirty, Nikita and Bella pulled out from Hotel Juana and headed out on the coastal road to Cannes, then wound their way back through Saint Jean Cap-Ferrat, on through Monte Carlo and part of the Formula One racetrack, past the big, beautiful yachts in the harbor, through Menton, on to the Italian border and toward Genoa.

The Jaguar F-Type ate up the miles for breakfast as they traversed the Italian Riviera east, heading to Portofino, where they arrived in time for lunch.

On the veranda to the La Terrazza restaurant, Bella and Nikita took in the view before them of the houses nestled in the trees, hanging on to the sides of the hills rising from the Mediterranean below. La Terrazza was like a scene from a classic Italian film. A wedding reception of around a dozen people was taking place at the far end. Bella and Nikita went to a table at the opposite end, at the balcony's edge, touching the view before them.

"Great drive, Bella. Good time." Nikita looked at his Breitling watch.

"What did we do?" asked Bella.

"Well, I set the clock from Menton when we got past the sightseeing and 207 kilometers, or 128 miles."

"Well then, how long?"

"One hundred and nine minutes, or an average of seventy miles per hour, which isn't bad at all given some of the bends and curves along the way."

"Not too bad," said Bella.

They looked through the menu and made their selections. The waiter took their order and hurried off.

"This has been a good, relaxing break for me so far," she said, leaning back in her chair. "Thanks for taking the time with me."

Nikita laughed. "It's my pleasure. We've been friends for a long time. We don't see enough of each other, at least not in my view."

"Not in mine either," Bella said.

The waiter brought them their drinks.

"Have you ever thought about marriage?" Bella asked, her voice full of the wistfulness she felt at the moment. She laughed as she saw Nikita look at her in a mild state of panic.

"No, no, Nikita, don't worry. I don't have a ring in my pocket to pop the question. Don't panic."

He smiled uncomfortably. "Not really, no. Not sure if I ever will, seeing the pain that it can inflict."

"It doesn't have to be like that."

"What? Like your mother and father? They live apart, right?"

Bella felt less wistful now. Indeed, she was a little pissed at her friend. "My parents are separate for complicated reasons."

"Aren't the reasons for separation and divorce always complicated?" he asked.

Bella sighed. "I guess so."

"Why did you ask about marriage anyway? You have a suitor?" Nikita asked.

Bella shook her head. "No. There's nobody right now. I've been too busy with work."

"I understand. Believe me!"

"I just know I don't want to live my life alone," she said, feeling sad all of a sudden. "You know? Have someone to grow old with?"

"I'm afraid I'll always be alone. We're all alone, if you really think about it," he said.

"That's a sad thing to say."

"Well, it's true," he said.

They were silent as they sipped their drinks, munched some bread with olive oil, and appreciated the local scenery.

"Hey, Niki, I thought we could go for a swim after lunch, then head down into the town for a look around the shops. There's a cool bar down there, and I can seek revenge from the other night with a game of backgammon. What do you think?"

"I can't tonight. I have to pop into Genoa for a couple of hours this afternoon. I'll probably need to leave here by three."

Bella looked at Nikita. Nikita looked down at his food, avoiding eye contact. Bella knew that it wasn't the time to ask why, who, where, and what, so she turned her attention to the beautiful seafood salad before her. Nikita hadn't mentioned any meeting before.

When had he made the arrangements for the meeting? And who with? Bella wondered.

After lunch, Bella got changed and went to relax by the pool. Nikita came by. He bent down, kissed her forehead, and left for Genoa. "Be careful!" Bella shouted after him as she watched him stride toward the stairs and the F-Type waiting below.

The pool and terrace were quiet. In fact, Bella was the only person there that afternoon. She stayed for a couple of hours before heading to the room to shower and change. She thought of her father's question a few days ago. Why was Mitch interested all of a sudden in where Nikita worked? She looked at her watch and decided it was too early to call Mitch in California.

As she walked past reception, there was a tall, middle-aged man at the front desk. He caught her eye because he looked out of place in his cheap black suit. In fact, it looked like he'd slept in it for a week. She slowed her pace when she heard the man mention Nikita's last name.

"I'm looking for Mr. Nikita Saparov," the man said, his accent clearly American. "I know he's staying here. I need to speak to him right away. What room is he in?"

The receptionist smiled. "We aren't allowed to give out any information about our guests. I'm sorry. Company policy. But you can leave a message for him."

"Tell him that Viktoria, Mr. Saparov's mother, has an important message for him. Tell him to call her as soon as he gets in."

"And you are?" the receptionist asked.

"Who I am doesn't matter. Just give Mr. Saparov the message. Call Viktoria right away. Can you do that for me?"

The receptionist smiled. "Of course, sir."

Bella could see that the encounter with the receptionist left the man frustrated. She watched him stalk out of the lobby and get into a red Alfa Romeo. Thinking on her feet, she hurried to the glass doors of the hotel, whipped out her iPhone, and snapped a picture of the tags. "Got you," she whispered and went back to the room. She sent a text to Mitch: "In Portofino. Nikita went to Genoa unannounced. Men looking for him. Red Alfa Giulia License: BE 023 DA. Who is it registered to? Will call later."

Within five minutes, she heard back from her dad. "Will find out. Keep diligent, keep safe."

Bella had intended to walk into Portofino, but she was rattled now, so the hotel concierge organized for the hotel town car to take her down to the sister hotel, Hotel Splendido Mare, on the horseshoe harbor of Portofino. She stepped out onto the cobbles adorning the pavement that wrapped around the harbor and was home to various shops, restaurants, and bars. The tourists had mainly gone home, and no one was paying her any undue attention as she walked into the Splendido Mare and took a seat by the window, her back to the wall.

She knew Nikita well, or at least she thought that she did, but there had been something wrong with him all week. She knew he had a big job, that they were taking big bets on the election outcome, and that it felt strange that he volunteered a grand tour in the heat of the moment. She had asked Nikita, "Don't you need to be around for the big event?" Nikita's response was, "My work is done, Bella." What did he mean? *My work was done?*

She had met Viktoria a couple of times. A big, dominating matriarch type, half-Russian, half-Ukrainian, she grew up in Lithuania. She was a schoolteacher or a nanny or a politician or something. She was always vague but busy, up to something or another. She had businesses that were also pretty vague, one of which was a temporary worker agency that moved primarily women from Eastern Bloc countries to work in the Eurozone, with papers and visas. After three or six months, they would disappear, leave their waitressing jobs and staying in their country of choice. Bella had never really thought much about Viktoria, but the last week and the message the man left for Nikita about calling his mother heightened her interest.

Didn't Viktoria have Nikita's cell number? Why send a man to the hotel? How did Viktoria know where he was? They'd been randomly driving around France and Italy for several days. Bella turned all these questions over in her mind.

Bella considered her role at Executive Outcomes and how they had made algorithms to predict events around the world, and although the software was still learning, it was gaining intelligence each day and gathering data points from around the world, building its accuracy of predictability. There were outcomes that were fifty-fifty even for them, but Nikita had been the sensation in predicting outcomes with much higher odds and much, much bigger risk and reward.

Bella remembered the day she was at Lord Beecham's Shed a few days previously and saw at least some of the work they were doing on understanding the motives behind Paul's and Badger's murders, the assassination of the man from the CIA, and the incident at the Dubliner. She recalled some mention of potential election rigging on an international scale. *Oh my God. Could my Niki be connected to all this somehow?'*

Bella didn't feel like eating. She ordered a dirty martini and decided to surf on her iPad to see what was going on in the world.

After a couple of hours, Bella was even more concerned that the events as they unfolded pointed more and more to external interference in not only the world's number one democratic process but in other matters and events around the world as well.

Bella had heard of the principle of malarkey or maskirovka many times from Mitch and Angela, going as far back as her grandfather's disappearance off the coast of San Francisco all those years ago. She had heard her father's stories about the Cold War and the Russians watching the West, and the West watching the Russians. She had heard the stories about Litvinenko and others, and she had more recently witnessed the antics of Russia and Putin in Crimea, Europe, and the shooting down of MH17 with Russian weapons.

She had seen maskirovka at work firsthand as the Russians wrapped every possible theory, excuse, and lie around the MH17 incident, to such an extent it was almost impossible to understand what the real truth was. Meanwhile, the rest of the world just allowed the Man at the Kremlin to get away with what was in essence an invasion of its neighbor. No wonder the former USSR states in Europe were nervous about their sovereignty and independence and the thought of waking up one morning with Russian tanks on their streets.

It was about nine at night when Bella called the hotel town car to pick her up and take her back to the Splendido.

On her way back, on the narrow road between Portofino and the hotel, the town car slowed as a red Alfa Guilia headed the opposite way to allow it to pass. Bella noticed the license plate, BE 023 DA, and a chill went up the back of her spine. She crunched down, despite knowing that behind the blacked-out windows she was invisible and saw the man she had seen earlier in the front seat, with another big man driving.

The town car arrived back at the hotel. As Bella was getting out, Nikita pulled in behind her. He jumped out, white as a sheet, and said, "Come on, Bella. We need to get out of here. Now!"

"What's wrong?" she asked. "Hey, some guy was here about your—"

"No time. Tell me later. Let's get our stuff and bolt."

Fighting back panic, Bella said okay. They went upstairs, packed their bags, left the room keys on the nightstand, hurried to the parking lot, and jumped into the F-Type. Nikita hit the gas, and the car accelerated out of the parking lot, down the hill to the main road.

"Your mother got some guy to leave you a message at the front desk," Bella said.

Nikita shot her a startled glance. "I told you I speak to my mother almost every day. The message was fake. It wasn't from her."

"Oh God!" Bella said. "There's the car I saw!"

The red Alfa Romeo pulled up behind them, practically in the trunk.

"Shit," Nikita said. "Hang on!"

The Jaguar took off like a rocket.

"Niki! What's going on?" she screamed. "You're going to kill us!"

"Fuck those people," Nikita said, his voice more a growl. "Fuck 'em!"

"Tell me what's going on!" Bella shouted above the engine noise. She glanced in the rearview mirror. The chase was falling way behind. They were going well over one hundred miles per hour.

"I need to get back to London," Nikita said. "Right now! ASAP. Before it's too late!"

"Who were those men, Niki? Tell me!"

"I really have no idea, Bella."

"Bullshit!" she cried. "Where are we going?"

"Pisa Airport. I have the company jet waiting for me there."

"What about me?"

"I want you to take the F-Type and get it back to London."

"What? With bad guys on my ass? No fucking way. No way!"

Bella looked in the rearview mirror again and saw that the chase had disappeared.

"You'll be fine as soon as I'm on the plane."

"Tell me who those guys were right now, or I'm getting out of this damned car. And I'll never speak to you again! I know you know who they were. They certainly know you. Why would they leave a false message for you at the hotel?"

"They wanted to draw me out."

"Ah-ha! So you do know who they are!"

Bella was fighting back the anger now. She was no longer scared. She was pissed. "You can slow down now, asshole. You lost 'em," she said.

Nikita glanced over at her, slowed down, and said, "They're CIA. Just call Mitch."

"Nikita, why the hell is the CIA following you? What the hell have you done?"

"It's a very long story, and I don't have time right now. You'll be fine driving back to London in the car. They're after me, not you. Just call Mitch. Tell him what's going down. He'll know what to do."

They pulled up outside the security gate to a hangar. Nikita jumped out, got his bag, leaned in the passenger window, and kissed Bella. "You are the love of my life, Bella Bella Fonterella," Nikita said, then hurried toward the waiting jet before she could even say goodbye.

Bella choked back tears of sadness and rage. She felt betrayed, used, and more alone than she'd ever felt. She jumped into the driver's seat and sped into the night.

22
UNFOLDING THE FOLDS

San Francisco, California, United
States, October 2016, Day 19

MITCH WAS IN THE SALOON with Lord Beecham and Colonel
Collins when his phone vibrated. He looked down and saw that it was
Bella. He quickly computed that it was ten o'clock at night in London.

"Hello, Bella! How is my wandering beauty?" asked Mitch.

"Wondering what the hell is going on, Dad."

"What do you mean?"

Bella related the events of the past few hours.

"Where are you, Bella?"

"I'm heading back to Genoa then the E25 north."

"What's your plan?"

"I have no idea, just get back to London and find out what's
going on."

"I'm here in the Saloon. Let's check the best route for you. Need
to check weather too."

"Okay Dad. I'll keep on charging."

"Will do," Mitch said.

Mitch ended the call and turned to Lord Beecham. "Seems we
have some developments related to Bella's friend. A guy named Nikita

Saparov. He's big in the First World Bank. Russian ties. Seems he thinks the CIA is after him."

"Not jolly good, Mitch. If it's true." Lord Beecham glanced over at James. "You know what to do, old boy."

"On it," James said.

Mitch was anxious, but he also trusted James. Gathering preliminary information on Nikita and the mysterious Alfa Romeo took some time.

"CIA says it's not their team after Bella's friend," James said. "They don't know who it was, except it wasn't them."

"Shit," Mitch said. "That means we have a wild card."

"Looks like it," Colonel Collins said.

"I don't like wild cards," Lord Beecham said.

"Me neither," Mitch said. "You got routing and weather info for me, James?"

James gave Mitch the data, and Mitch put a call through to Bella.

"Dad? What took you so long? I was getting worried."

"All good things come to those who wait, and act while they wait," Mitch said with a smile. He could tell his daughter was scared, but she was keeping it together. He gave her the routing and weather information. He told her the chase wasn't CIA.

"I can get a flight out to London this afternoon and will text you the address to meet at. Make sure you use our special code with all communications, Bella. You remember, right?"

"Yes, Dad, of course I do."

"Okay. See you in twenty-four hours. Drive carefully. Be safe. Love you."

The phone went dead, but Bella was relieved. The person that she trusted the most and felt supremely safe with was her father, Mitch, and he was heading out to meet her. Bella was a talented driver. Mitch had taught her all the techniques that he had learned in formal training, and she had learned well.

"It's all about understanding and controlling the risks," she remembered him telling her.

"Always be aware. Beware and make calculations. Remember—if you're dead, you're no good to anyone, so only take calculated risks, Bella."

She remembered another of Mitch's sayings, "Old soldiers don't die," a reference to young, inexperienced soldiers in comparison. Bella was both young and inexperienced. She dug deep to remember all her father's teachings.

A text came through to her preceded by their code: AGA4.

Mitch and Bella had made their own code up when she was in kindergarten. Prior to that, Mitch had taught Bella their signal that sounded like a jungle bird's cry, their field craft signals including Stop, Come Here, Quickly, Follow, and the text code that he just sent Bella.

The four digits of the code covered safety, confidence, stability, and risk. G was for green, A was for amber, and R was for red, with the digit 1 to 9 for the level of risk.

GGG1 was the lowest level, and RRR9 the highest. It was a simple code but good enough for its purpose. The solemn promise to each other while using this code was to never sugarcoat the code. It had to be a real assessment of a situation.

Mitch's code was in decent shape, although there was a sense of danger, he had high confidence amber for safety and stability, and a marker on risk. It was a positive code and made Bella feel secure as she sat in the Jaguar F-Type heading back to London.

Bella texted back "GGG4."

Chelsea, London, United Kingdom, October 2016, Day 20

Mitch and his team gathered in the small briefing room in Lord Beecham's guesthouse in Chelsea. The members had come in from all over, and Mitch could see the tension was plain on their drawn and haggard faces. Bella, in particular, looked much the worse for the wear, but she also displayed her usual courage. He could see it mostly in her eyes, but he could also hear it in her voice.

"Well Ladies and Gentlemen, it seems like the shit has hit the fan," Mitch said.

"Indeed, old boy," Lord Beecham said. "The proverbial fur in the blades, as it were. I was never one for vulgarities. You know that, Mitch."

"Yeah, I know. But sometimes you just have to say it the way it is."

"Fuckin right!" Jimmy said.

Bella laughed.

Colonel Collins suppressed a smile.

Lord Beecham groaned and shook his head.

"Just get on with it," Mac said.

"Yeah," Bob said. "Let's stop pussy footin' around. We got some ass to kick."

"James," Lord Beecham said, "if you would be so kind."

"Naturally," James said. "Now, if you'll all—"

"Oh, come on, James," Bob said, "just cut to the chase, okay?"

A line buzzed. James hit a button. "Code Argus," James said.

"Code your ass."

Mitch laughed. "Hi, Sam," he said. "Sorry you couldn't join us in person."

"A bit busy right now," Sam said. "How are we all?"

Everybody laughed and said they were fine but tired. "And you, Bella? I heard you had a scare."

"I'm fine, Sam. But thanks."

"If you wouldn't mind, Sam," Lord Beecham said, "I'm simply just dying to get on with things."

"No worries," Sam said. "So, tell us what's happening, James."

Mitch was starting to get frustrated, angry, and ready to burst into the offense. He knew that letting his emotions get the best of him put him at a tactical disadvantage, and he struggled to keep himself in check.

"I intend to," James said, sounding a bit miffed.

"Go on, James. Don't let the dog bite. Toss him a biscuit," Lord Beecham said.

James grunted, sighed, and said, "We now know for sure that

Paul's death was because of contamination of the blood with a high dosage of polonium-210. The same that also killed Badger. As we've said before, the difference with this strain is that it disappears from the bloodstream quickly, but it leaves behind a signature in the blood cells that forensics has confirmed as the cause of death, in both cases.

"Thanks to all of you for sharing your reports over the past few days, Sam's help with the British Intelligence Services and cooperation by the CIA and Interpol. We have gathered up an interesting picture for sure.

"Paul and Brad from the CIA were heading up an investigation into a bizarre tri-partnership between the Colombian drug cartel known as Los Rastrojos, the Irish Republican Army, the IRA, and the Russian Mafia."

Mitch fidgeted in his seat as the screens showed photographs of Diego Perez Henao, Figo Hernandez, and Pablo Rioja from the Rastrojos.

Then the next screen showed Tommy Boyle, Patrick O'Malley, Tommy's son-in-law, and Sean Murphy of the IRA affiliation.

Then Dmitri Dankov, Yuri Bokov, and Viktoria Saparov.

James looked at his audience and reflected, "Some familiar characters to us all there."

"No, it can't be," Mac said, his voice barely above a whisper.

Mitch's stomach dropped. He recognized Viktoria. "Mac, what's going on? Isn't that—"

"Fuckin' a right, mate! That's my ex-wife! That's my Viktoria!" Mac said. "I always knew she was playing both hands from the deck. I just didn't think she could do it so easily. I thought she was better than that. An ... my son. I just can't—"

"Nikita might not be involved in her schemes," Mitch said, putting a hand on Mac's arm.

Mac buried his face in his hand. "I just cannot believe this shit. Nikita never knew my real name. Never knew my real identity. He always knew me as Angus. Lies! Lies! My life has always been all lies!"

"Keep your head, Mac. There's more to the story than this. I'm sure," Lord Beecham said. "Hear James out."

Nobody said anything. The awkward silence increased the tension in the room.

"James?" Lord Beecham asked.

James coughed and then said, "Lies are sometimes necessary, Mac. You know that. You left Viktoria because you had to ... to protect Nikita. To protect even Viktoria from herself. From you."

"That's bullshit, and you know it!" Mac screamed. He pounded the table.

Mitch could see that his friend was clearly shaken. The implications of it all came crashing in on Mitch. Then he looked over at Bella. Her face was ashen. She looked like a lorry had just run her down and left her for dead. Based on the expressions of everybody else there, the implications were crashing in on them too.

"Go on, James," Lord Beecham said, "please. If you would be so kind."

James continued. "It looks like we've got an intricate web here, one nobody could have foreseen. Let's take Los Rastrojos first. With cocaine remaining the most lucrative source of income for Colombia and the drug lords, then securing routes to market, as with any business, is essential. Los Rastrojos have taken the lead in this tri-partnership, and their rivals are looking on to observe its success. Given the amount of sheer cash these cartels generate, they were clearly of interest. Others may follow.

"The Irish Republican Army, the IRA, ran out of funding the moment 9/11 happened and the Americans realized that they weren't funding homeland struggles but cold-blooded, murdering criminals and terrorists."

"Fucking idiots," Bob, Jimmy, and Mac all mouthed, referring to the stupidity of the American funding of these killers that they had all fought against.

James continued, "To survive, they had to look elsewhere for funding, and that drove them deeper underground and to alternative sources. Given their infiltration in the USA, which was particularly attractive, but also their global footprint, they were an attractive target."

"An attractive target to who?" Lord Beecham asked.

"That's where these three come in." He brought back the screen with the pictures of Dmitri Dankov, Bokov, and Saparov. "These three have been the architects of bringing this all together. They are the architects of the preeminent branch of the Russian Mafia, long suspected as being a branch of Russian Secret Services and taking instructions directly from the Man at the Kremlin himself."

"Oh, fuck me," Mac said.

"Easy," Mitch said, feeling his friend's pain. "Just hear the man out."

Mac shook his head. Mitch could see that everyone was uncomfortable, that everyone was on edge about these latest developments. Yet a good commander always stepped up when necessary.

"We may not like what we're hearing, but we have to toe the line," Mitch said. "We're soldiers. Who Dares Wins."

Silence was followed by quiet, determined nods in agreement.

"The connections create a perfect cover to getting foreign currency into Russia, meddling with things that even the Man at the Kremlin cannot dare be directly involved in, and, if it all goes wrong, he can just blame criminals for doing criminal things. The perfect malarkey or maskirovka."

Mitch considered James's theory. Cash was a big issue for Russia as they were going through the rebuilding of the empire, and as was the case shortly after the collapse of the USSR, cash was hard to come by. International lenders and investors didn't trust the Russian government, and funding dried up. This situation created the oligarchs who were entrepreneurs who managed to secure funding to purchase up the national assets, oil fields, for a song. Buy the asset for $4 billion, and overnight that same asset is suddenly worth $8 billion.

Russia needed the cash desperately.

Then, as Putin built his power, these oligarchs surrendered the national assets back to the state, profiting handsomely, wound up in jail, or even worse in many cases.

"Dmitri Dankov is the general. Bokov runs JPAC, Japan, Pan Asia, and China."

"Yeah and is a fucking despicable animal." Jimmy added his two cents. "I know Yuri fucking Bokov."

James acknowledged Jimmy's comment and continued, "Operations are based out of Bangkok, Bokov runs Asia, and Saparov runs EMEA, Europe, Middle East, and Africa."

"What the fuck are we up against here? It sounds like fucking IBM, not a bunch of fucking gangsters. EMEA and JPAC. What the fuck?" Bob asked.

"They run the biggest gaming operations now outside of Las Vegas, focused on generating foreign currency for the homeland. They own controlling shares in utilities around the world. They even have their own bank!" Bella looked at Mitch.

"The First World Bank by any chance?" asked Mitch.

"In one," responded James, nodding to Mitch.

Seated next to Mitch, he felt Bella squeeze his hand. He could see that she was putting all the pieces together, as he was as well. Nikita was Mac's son. Viktoria was Mac's ex-wife. Viktoria was tied into Dmitri Dankov, who was tied into the Colombians and other crime partners. He knew this entire web went deep, covered a lot of distance, and would probably ensnare them all.

"Between the three of them, we think they have generated more than $1 trillion of foreign currency to pump up the Russian reserves over the past four years alone," James said.

"A sizeable chunk of change," Colonel Collins said.

"So, I get it about Paul, but what did Badger have to do with any of this?" asked Ryan.

The screen came to life again, and up popped a familiar face that Jimmy and Bob immediately recognized as the same that they had bumped into in Tangier, with a bullet through his skull.

Sam took over the briefing. "Badger had been working with Abd Al Bari in Tangier for the past two years. Abd Al Bari was Saparov's man in Africa, and he was the link to the supply route to EMEA from Colombia—a much safer route into Europe and the riches that bestowed for Los Rastrojos and of course the Russians. The more they could move, the more foreign currency they would raise. Simple business, right?"

The group looked at each other and nodded. It was hard to argue the logic.

"Badger had been working with Abd Al Bari, who was just a greedy peddler of information to the highest bidder. He didn't care about anything apart from money, even his own life, it would seem in the end."

Up popped the photograph of him in his final demise, slumped on his office chair in his little smelly office in Tangier, bullet through the head.

"Abd Al Bari was the kingpin of shipments arriving by ship to the Moroccan remote coast for splitting and entering the distribution network through Morocco, across North Africa, up into Europe through the Canary Islands, and off the coast of Morocco, up through Portugal and Spain, and through Sicily into Italy. Then across to the east coast of Africa into Somalia, Kenya, and on to the Far East. This was a major hub-and-spoke distribution operation that dwarfed any operation previously identified in Europe, or indeed anywhere in the world."

"So, we have talked about the generals, the partners. Now let's talk about the lieutenants in this web," James continued.

"We don't know how the strategy came about because the concepts of malarkey or maskirovka had almost always been used as defensive tactics during open conflicts, but somewhere along the line, it was decided that this could be used in more of an offensive tactic and during peacetime, instead of traditional weapons of war."

"Like there's more than one way to skin a cat?" asked Lord Beecham.

"Exactly," said Sam.

"Dmitri Dankov, Bakov, and Saparov took it upon themselves to build a disruptive network of resources. They have plenty of cash from the drug business and the gaming business, and they were using it to place big bets on outsider outcomes in elections and political changes in countries around the world. They were betting on the outsiders, and in many cases, the Kremlin-preferred victors."

"Nobody loves a fuckin' loser," Ryan said.

"Least of all you," Mitch said. He smiled, despite the tension. Ryan smiled back. It occurred to Mitch that he hadn't seen Ryan smile since his mother died, though her untimely passing was only just recent.

"But beyond making big bets on potential political outcomes, they got into the game of swaying and influencing, not just relying on the outcome. They were influencing the outcome and, in many cases, knew the outcome before anyone else."

"Yes, Sam is spot-on. They were no longer just betting; they were disrupting. They are not just betting on outcomes; they are changing outcomes, fiddling with the system, just like a trickster trying to swing the favor their own way in a casino—loading the dice, stacking the cards, driving the chances of winning instead of waiting to lose."

Sam added, "Leveraging resources to destabilize situations to gain the unexpected outcomes and win those big bets. They were using their henchmen in the Colombians to protect their supply chain, the Irish to boost their funds and greed, and the Russian Mafia that was intrinsically entwined with the bigger national interests of the Russian Federation."

Beecham said, "So they generate buckets of cash from illegal and questionable sources, invest the cash in unexpected outcomes, change those outcomes, and then the cash and the profits become legitimized and clean!"

"That's pretty much it," James said. "Sad but true. Ah, but the webs we weave."

"Don't gloat," Mac said. "It doesn't become your pussy ass."

"Excuse me?"

"You heard me," Mac said.

Sam continued, "The international Intelligence Services dossier goes back as far as the Sharm El Sheikh bombings, a ruse that put a stop to most Russians travelling and spending their money in Egypt and that netted the motherland something to the tune of $300 million a year. The shootings in India, Australia, and France—look more closely at the list of victims, and their backgrounds tell you that there was more to it than meets the eye. Look at the MH17 passenger list, Malaysian Airlines Flight 370, Germanwings Flight 9525, the same. There is even speculation as far back as the Princess Diana incident in Paris and who the real target was back then."

"This deadly combination of political power, an aligned underworld, greed, ruthless and hungry killers, and perverted political aspirations created a unique and potent melting pot," James added.

One of the screens flashed to life. "Abd Al Bari, the supply chain man. Two partners of a firm called Grace and Partners, Andrew Harrison and Neil Grace, based in Leeds, UK, became the undercover henchmen for hostile takeovers and growth of the Russian casino business and were most certainly the architects of the executions of both Paul and Badger, with the use of the Los Rastrojos resources in the US and Tangier with Russian polonium-210.

"Harrison and Grace do the dirty work at the direct orders of Dmitri Dankov, and they don't care what the dirty work is if it pays, and it pays well. Their original dealing with Dmitri Dankov was playing on Harrison's track record of joining companies, taking them over, getting rid of the original partners, and ripping the business apart for profit. Dmitri Dankov spotted these skills and groomed Grace and Partners to take over casinos across Europe, but more recently, they have gotten themselves into deeper and darker things, including assassinations."

Tommy Boyle's picture came up, and Sam said, "Tommy, he's old school, and although he thinks he's had a hand in controlling all of this, he has just been the puppet. The Russians and Colombians have used him and exploited him and his organization's greed and willingness to kill just about anyone for the right price, which, in the scheme of things, isn't very much at all. Tommy is small-time compared with Dmitri Dankov and Los Rastrojos. Nevertheless, he's still dangerous and a power of influence from Anchorage down to Punta Del Fuego."

James finished the briefing for that night. "It's late, 1:00 a.m., and I know that a lot of you have traveled in the past twenty-four hours." He smiled at Bella. "I suggest that you get some sleep tonight, and in the morning, Sam and I can share with you what we believe the best next steps are. Eight o'clock sharp, tomorrow morning. We have work to do."

"What about the men in the red Alfa Romeo? Who were they? Where is Nikita now?"

"We're working on that. Both of us," Sam said.

"Right," James said, nodding to Bella.

Mitch felt about as tired as he had at any time, even in the thick of combat. He could see how the news about Nikita was slowly seeping in, sapping his daughter's faith. Faith in herself. Faith in him. Faith in Nikita. Faith in everything. And it pained him.

"We have top teams out there," James said. "They may not be as good as you guys are, but they're up there. You've just got to trust us."

Bella wiped tears from her eyes.

"Bella," Mitch said, "it's going to be okay."

"You don't know that, Dad. You just don't."

"One sure foot in front of the other," Mitch said, his voice hollow and choked with emotion.

"I don't have feet anymore," Bella said. "I need some air."

Bella said she was going to head back to the hotel. Mitch felt as if he'd been stabbed.

PART V

JOURNEY TO SAMARKAND

23
CHELSEA

Hereford, United Kingdom, November 2016, Day 20

IT WAS O-DARK-THIRTY, BUT SAM didn't care. He waited outside in front of his beautiful cottage, his heart rate low, his anxiety high. The events of the last month or so had jangled his nerves. He wanted the war to be over, though he knew it probably never would be. There would always be another enemy, another kill, another killer out to get him and his mates. In the distance, he heard the familiar sound of the Rangey, and he smiled despite his foul mood.

When the armored vehicle pulled up in front of the little farmstead, he hurried down the walk and opened the door. His old mate Ed, another member of the vaunted SAS, grinned at him and handed him a Styrofoam cup of steaming coffee.

"Morning," Ed said. "Even the cocks aren't up yet, so I suppose it should be what the fuck."

Sam laughed and got in the car with his coffee. He took a hefty swig, which burned his throat. "Ah," he said, "nothing like a cuppa to get your balls loose."

"Speak for yourself," Ed said.

"You ready?" Sam asked, feeling better already because of the mere presence of his old friend.

"I was born ready, mate," Ed said.

"Well, what're you waiting for! Hit it!"

Ed pumped the gas, and they sped away. "Did you manage to catch the briefing last night?" asked Sam.

Sam glanced over at Ed and saw him shake his head.

"Nah. Couldn't be on the call. I was dealing with *the thing* in Afghanistan but caught up this morning before I left to pick you up."

"Don't you sleep, Ed?"

'You know how it rolls."

"Yeah, I do. Sometimes lately I wish I didn't."

Ed sighed. "You and me both. But you gotta stay on the horse, or the horse'll stay on you."

"Not a great image."

"Not meant to be." Ed paused and then said, "Mac's in a pickle."

"You think?"

"Yeah," Ed said. "I think."

"Me too. Never saw that freight train coming."

"Light at the end of the tunnel. Except it's comin' straight at you. Like a fuckin RPG."

"Shit," Sam said. He drank more coffee and suddenly felt tired even though he'd slept for six hours. "The whole Viktoria, Nikita thing might just be a bridge too far. They all might come after him, never mind the Ruskies."

"He'll be fine. We need to keep it that way, right? Brothers in arms?"

"As far as we can. As far as we can."

Sam thought about the meeting at Lord Beecham's place in Chelsea. The whole team would be there. At least he could take comfort in that.

Bella felt a bit uncomfortable. She hadn't quite gotten her head around all that was happening, and she was anxious about all that might happen. The team was there, including her dad, which gave her a feeling of reassurance. Lord Beecham set up a wonderful breakfast for them all, and she helped herself and made small talk with the guys. They were all so macho, all so rugged, all so silly in their apparent efforts to avoid feeling much of anything, even though they'd all lost two good friends to a bunch of ruthless criminals. Blowhards, really. People who needed to die—and die sooner than later.

She overheard her dad talking to Mac.

"What are you going to do?" Mitch asked.

"I'm not sure, probably go and see Nikita at some point. Make sure he's okay."

"You could. But you could blow things up. You heard what they said last night. This is big. This is a new strain of warfare."

"And my ex-wife and stepson are knee-deep in it. Trust me, I get it!" snapped Mac.

"Let's see what these boys have to say this morning. It can't be all bad."

"Fuck you, Mitch. It's worse than bad."

"Back at you, mate."

Bella smiled as Mac fake punched her dad on the shoulder.

"What're you smilin' at?" Mac asked, with mock anger.

"Oh, nothing, Mac," Bella said. She winked at Mitch.

At that moment, she knew she could rely on every individual in that room to give 200 percent, no matter what, and the same was expected of her. That made her nervous, not nervous because she wasn't good and couldn't perform under pressure but because she knew that was her commitment and that she would die trying whatever she was asked to do. The ultimate commitment. The ultimate responsibility.

She also thought about Nikita. His whole world would be turned upside down, and there was nothing she could do about it. Who would have imagined that coming from her humble roots, she would be one of the most powerful people on the planet right now? Overseeing billions of dollars of business as the chief operating officer for what Mitch called the dark army. She was a commander of the Europe, Middle East, and Africa branches of an octopus with arms that reached everywhere. The EMEA was just one cog in a vast machine, and her Nikita was caught up in it all. She suddenly felt sad. She also felt angry. Angry at Nikita. She wondered if he'd made a run for it, if he even knew how much danger he was in.

"Okay, everyone," Lord Beecham said. "This is my house, so I shan't herd cats. All cats come to order, please!" He clapped his hands, then clinked a silver spoon against his teacup.

Bella suppressed a laugh. The man was so pompous he could run his own ass up a flagpole and not notice people looking up his knickers. Still, he was a good guy.

"Now, now, people," James said. "Let's all have a seat. Developments are happening fast. We have to keep up, people. Focus! Focus!"

"Gimme a break," Mac said to Mitch.

"Oh, come on, mate. Sit your tight ass down."

"Yeah, Mac! You're the one whose ass is in a fuckin' sling, not ours," Jimmy said.

"Jimmy, shut the fuck up," Bob said.

Bella sat down. Sometimes it felt like she was watching a bad version of *The Three Stooges*, except there were six of them, including her dad.

Everyone sat down. Ed stood up.

"Ed has the floor, everyone," Lord Beecham said, stating the obvious.

"The next couple of days are big. We have the US presidential election taking place tomorrow and evidence that our friends have been meddling with the number one democracy in the world, the showcase of democracy."

Sam added, "Let's face it. If they can affect the outcome there, they can affect outcomes anywhere. This is an issue of upholding the value of democracy, and that is why these next couple of days are big."

"We will keep this brief and get to work." Ed continued, "We are in damage-limitation mode. Any damage that is done has probably already been done, but our job over the next few days is to make sure that, one, it doesn't get worse; two, we establish the culprits and shut the operations down; and, three, gather sufficient intelligence to ensure that it can never happen again.

"Bob, we believe that Grace and Partners and specifically Andrew Harrison and Neil Grace in Leeds are the brokers responsible for the executions of Paul and Badger. They are also the center of the web of hackers that have been messing around with emails, polls, and social media. As brokers, it is impossible to think that we can get to the actual smoking gun, but by eliminating Harrison and Grace, we can at least stop the gun from getting into the hands of the puppets who pulled the trigger. Bob, we need you to lead the team to take out these two individuals. Then we want you to take on the role at Grace and Partners as interim CEO, at least for a while, to see what we uncover over the next twelve months."

"Yes, boss. Consider it done," Bob reported.

Ed continued, "Ryan, we need you to get down to the offices of the First World Bank, Canary Wharf. Sir Richard Steele, chairman of the bank, looked like he committed suicide last night, late at night in his office at the bank, or at least that's what it looks like."

That news hit Bella hard. Steele was Nikita's boss. She wondered if Nikita and Viktoria had something to do with Steele's death, whether in fact it was a suicide.

"Are we sure Steele committed suicide?" Bella asked.

Mitch looked over at her and put his hand on her arm. "We're sure, honey. We just don't know what pushed him over the edge."

"But we're gonna find out," Ed said. "So, to get on with it. First World has some huge bets riding on the results of tomorrow's election, and we need to know what is going on. Here is the number of Simon Sterling, heading up the efforts on behalf of the British Secret Service and the interests of the US. Find out what the hell is going on."

"Yes, boss," Ryan responded.

Ed continued, "Jimmy, we want you to head out to Vilnius, Lithuania. We believe that is where Dmitri Dankov will be for the aftermath of the election, hanging out in his home casino in the city. Be careful. Dmitri Dankov is a dangerous player, as you know, but now he may be the most vulnerable, especially if his bet pays off. You need to get out to our friends at their secure facility, just outside of Vilnius. They are networked to our cyber liberation to protect them from being taken out during the blitz. Sean, Kiwi Ken, and Rusty will pick you up from the Shakespeare."

"Yes, boss. Got it."

Ed continued, "Mitch, you will head to Paris, where the head of Los Rastrojos, Paulo Mancino, is in town to meet Saparov to seal the deal on new supply routes other than Morocco that will be all but closed down after the Abd Al Bari incident. We understand that there are several options, but the favored one is through Nouakchott, Mauritania. Our links to our Irish friends managed to arrange a meeting for us under the guise of a security contractor to support the African operation and antipiracy team. We are not looking for a war with the Colombians; that's a job for the boys in blue. See what you can do, Mitch."

"I know Paulo well. We'll be fine."

Sam took over. "Lord Beecham, Colonel Collins, Mac, Bella, I want you all to get together with the cyber security branch. They have set up a worldwide intelligence agency crowdsourcing project that kicks off this afternoon, basically taking the fight to the hackers and playing them at their own game. We have assembled an army of some two thousand hackers who will target the black networks and take them down. Now you know me, boys, on technology, but their plan is to basically napalm the internet and take them out—shutting down all the dark operations, including the email hacking, social media hacking, their communications, even taking out the electricity supply if we have to. This is a form of war, and we, my friends, are on the offensive. I spoke to their head of security, and they would like the four of you to help support the cyber offensive. We are also going to have boots on the ground."

Bella looked at Mac, who was usually *the* boots on the ground, and saw his visible pain at the prospect of being stuck in some operations room somewhere. That wasn't Mac. Mac was a hands-on sort of guy. Bella felt his pain, but there was nothing she could do to help him. Indeed, she realized that there was nothing she could do to save Nikita or her own breaking heart.

24
AMBUSHED

Bromley, United Kingdom, November 2016, Day 20

NIKITA WAS EXHAUSTED AFTER HIS escape from France. He hated leaving Bella in the lurch, but he knew she'd be okay. She simply had to be. He couldn't live with himself if she wasn't. He felt a twinge of guilt about lying to her. Those men weren't CIA, or at least he didn't think they were. But what else could he have done? He couldn't involve Bella any further. In fact, he had to get out himself, no matter what Viktoria said, no matter what Dmitri Dankov might do. He poured himself a drink and offered one to his mother, who was sitting on the couch across from the wet bar.

"No, darling," she said, "I don't want to drink. We have big problem. Yes? You know about the banker by now."

Nikita swallowed hard. "I know what's going on. I'm just surprised to see you here. Why have you come?"

"Don't be foolish, darling," Viktoria said. "You know full well why I've come."

"I've done what you asked. Every morning, you call. I answer. I act. I'm like a little lapdog. Or a dancing bear. I'm fuckin' sick of it, Mama. Just sick of it."

Viktoria got up from the couch, walked over to him, and slapped him in the face. "You will learn respect. Respect your betters. Respect your mother."

"You were no mother to me."

"I was more of a mother than you'll ever know," Viktoria said, raising her right arm to hit Nikita again.

"I swear to God. If you try that again, you'll be sorry."

Nikita was gratified to see doubt flash through Viktoria's eyes, but then a hardness, a coldness clouded them over. Her face took on the grim features of stone.

"You would best not try your luck, little boy," she said. "I have killed men for much less than the disrespect you have just shown me."

"I'm sure you have," Nikita said. "Did you have anything to do with Steele's suicide?"

"Does it matter?"

Nikita sighed and shook his head. "No, I suppose it doesn't. The man is dead. And that's it."

Viktoria smiled. "Precisely. And that means there will be changes. Even for you. You will still be a chess piece for us to move around, but things will be different."

"I don't like being a pawn, Mother."

"Nobody does." Viktoria laughed. "But someone has to play the part, right?"

Nikita slowed himself down. How would he explain to everybody that he was not the genius, the prodigy they had all assumed he was, that he was just sharing information provided by his mother each morning? As the bets got bigger and bigger and their balance sheet got heavier and heavier, their hunger for information increased, while their blindness of the source grew more blurred.

"So, Mother, how much of the information you've been giving me was prediction and how much was manipulation?"

"Manipulation, Nikita, now that is big word. And anyway, what are you complaining about? Look at this place, your bank balance, your salary, the fancy car. Did you ever think this would have been possible growing up in Klaipeda with a single mother?"

Nikita thought about it for a long moment. He paced back and forth, hands clasped behind his back. "You know the answer is no. Such luxury would have been impossible."

Viktoria clapped her hands. "Ah, you see! You do know how much I've done for you, how much the Russian empire has done for you."

"Russian empire? What are you talking about?"

"I am talking about the Russian empire we have rebuilt, my colleagues and I. I'm talking about taking our power back from the West. I am talking about a new world order, the likes of which few can imagine."

"You're mad," Nikita said, genuinely shocked.

"No, Nikita. Just practical. Steele is out of the picture now. That means practical decisions must be made. We now are majority shareholders in First World Bank and—"

"You're what?" Nikita said, his voice rising.

"I said the empire is now the majority shareholder in your bank. That means, my son, that we have the power to make big changes. For instance, we have made you the new CEO and chairman of the board. Isn't that wonderful, Nikita? Isn't that just grand?"

Nikita was speechless. His mind was in a whirl. He could feel his heart rate increasing. "I, I … I don't understand."

"Of course you don't, Nikita, but you will," Viktoria said. "Trust me. It'll all become clear soon. Your colleagues no longer own the bank. We do, Nikita, and as long as I am the COO for EMEA, then this is how we are doing things around here. Now, in the morning, I want you to go to work as usual and make me an appointment for 5:35 p.m. sharp to meet with the board of directors. Ponyal?" Viktoria wanted to check his understanding. Nikita nodded, then headed off for a shower and bed.

"Spokoynoy Nochi Mat." Nikita wished his Mother good night.

"Good night, Nikita," Viktoria shouted out down the hallway. "Have a good sleep. Tomorrow is your big day."

Nikita set his alarm for 7:00 a.m. He felt enormously tired, angry, and confused. He got into bed, hoping that sleep would come, but it didn't. He merely dozed on and off all night, then climbed out of bed at five thirty. He was as tired as he was when he went to bed several hours earlier.

By the time he left his bedroom, Viktoria was up too, in the kitchen, coffee made. There were some *varenyky*, a traditional Ukrainian breakfast dumpling, for this special day. Nikita looked at his mother with disbelief. "Eat, Nikita. This is what will make you strong for today," she ordered. Nikita did what his mother ordered and remembered the familiar flavor and texture of this simple dough of flour, water, and salt. Viktoria had stuffed them with bacon and cheese. They were indeed delicious.

"Nikita, 5:35 p.m. Remember?"

"Yes, Mother, of course I remember. What should I say the meeting is about?"

"Tell your boss—Sheri?"

Nikita nodded.

"Tell Sheri to let the board of directors know that we want to discuss the Trakai investor group. She will understand the importance of that."

"Thank you for the varenyky," Nikita said.

"You are my number one son, my only son. This is your day, Nikita," Viktoria said.

"Yes, so you keep telling me. But I don't see how the change you propose, making me CEO, that is, will assist with the long-term goals you and your backers must have in mind."

Nikita glanced at his watch and stood up from the table.

"As I said, everything will be clear soon. Now go, my son. You don't want to be late for work."

Nikita left the apartment and walked over to the black Mercedes AMG S65 that was waiting outside for him, as was Viktoria's security detail, eating varenykys too. That was Nikita's mother. Nothing was ever quite how it seemed. There was Nikita thinking that his mother had gotten up to make his favorite breakfast for his big day, when all she had done was send her henchmen to go get it from the Russian quarter.

He stepped inside the AMG S65 favored by many world leaders, business leaders, and the Russian Mafia. This one, although identical to his mother's, belonged to the bank, or it did for the moment. Sleek, secure, luxury, and high performance. As he climbed into the back of the limousine, Nikita wondered why he hadn't done this more often. A coffee machine in the rear center armrest dispensed him an espresso with whipped milk for the perfect latte for his 10.1-mile journey into the office.

As they arrived at the office in Canary Wharf, Nikita found it amusing that it was quicker taking his daily run, though nowhere near as luxurious. He could get into this style of travel quite easily, but his apprehension was less about the lifestyle and more about his controlling mother. Was it he who had done remarkable things with First World Bank, or was it just, as always, his mother setting the show, calling the shots, dictating the outcomes? How could Nikita have any confidence in his own abilities? This was Nikita's dilemma, along with his relationship with Bella that was on the line, and Angus, who he hadn't seen now for some years. Those were the two he loved the most. More than the accolades, the wealth, the power, and certainly more than the greed. Angus had taught him that on their trips to Scotland.

The Mercedes S65 pulled up outside of the First World Bank headquarters. Nikita stepped out. Gray pants, gray shirt, black coat, Diptique scent, laptop bag in hand, Breitling on his wrist.

Nikita didn't feel like a CEO, a chairman, but just a guy from college who had made some winning predictions, fueled by his mother's influence and direction. It wasn't him; it was her. Always her.

Nikita walked into the front reception of the First World Bank. Everyone knew the legendary Nikita Saparov. "Good morning, Mr. Saparov," said the security guard at the door.

"Good morning, John. How are you? How is the family?" replied Nikita.

Once at his desk, he dropped off his black backpack and went in search of Sheri. Only a few days previously, Sheri had been promoted to deputy CEO in anticipation of Steele's retirement and Nikita to his own new role, replacing Sheri. Now that Steele had committed suicide, all of that would dramatically change. Especially now that the Russians were in charge.

Nikita found Sheri in her glass-doored corner suite. He strolled in and said good morning.

"May I have a word?" he asked.

"Of course," Sheri said, her Texas drawl annoying now. "Sit right down. Take a load off."

Nikita sat down and crossed his legs. He took a deep breath and said, "Sheri, we have an issue. Trakai wants to meet with the board of directors this evening at 5:35."

"And you know this how?" Sheri asked.

"One of their representatives contacted me via text. Didn't give me a name. Just a code number to verify the message's authenticity."

"Odd," Sheri said, leaning back in her chair. "What do you suppose they want?"

"Don't know," Nikita lied.

Sheri looked at Nikita, puzzled, contorting her neck, tilting her head in an almost unnatural way, trying to make sense of what was going on.

"Nikita?"

"The Trakai group requested an emergency meeting," he snapped.

Sheri blinked—and then blinked again. Nikita didn't need to explain who the Trakai group was—First World's pioneer investor, most funds on deposit with something like $10.2 billion. The investment group owned 20 percent of their stock on the Financial Times Stock Exchange (FTSE).

"Okay, Nikita," Sheri said. "I'll make the meeting happen. Still, all of this is rather unusual."

"Yes, it is. I just wanted to pass on the message. You should have a similar message in your email by now."

Sheri checked her inbox. "Well, I'll be damned. Just came in." She looked up at Nikita, and her eyes narrowed. "What's really going on, Nikita?"

"Haven't the foggiest."

"Why don't I believe you?" she said.

"Seriously. I don't have a clue," he said, getting to his feet and walking to the office door. "Got to get on with the day."

"You do that, Nikita. You do that."

Nikita left the office, said bye to the receptionist, and headed to his desk.

25
EVENING THE SCORE

Bingley, United Kingdom, November 2016, Day 22

NEIL GRACE SURVEYED THE CONSTRUCTION site in Bingley, not far from his home on the edge of town. A former mill town, Bingley was an ideal location for building anew, tearing down the old, and putting up something that would generate profits, be it a mall, an office complex, or a low-rise apartment. One problem, though, was getting good help.

"You just wasted my time," he shouted to the foreman. "I came here to see progress on this basement drainage system, not to hear excuses from you as to why you have the wrong fuckin' materials."

"I can explain. We—"

"Don't bullshit me," Grace said. He stepped forward and got in the foreman's face. "Get the fuck off the site, and don't fucking come back until you have the right fucking materials for the job!"

"Right, boss," the foreman said.

"Useless fucking bastards," Grace muttered as the contractor's white van drove out of earshot. He turned away from the half-completed building just as a black SUV pulled up. The doors flew open, and four big guys dressed in black got out.

"What the fuck do you fuckers want on my property?" Grace shouted.

The man was built like a boxer, tall with broad shoulders and a military gait. His steely blue eyes were as cold as a glacier. A stab of panic caused Grace to wince. He'd been the bully all his life, loved it, in fact, but he was scared of the man standing in front of him.

Grace, said, "Okay, gents, calm down. What's going on? Where are you boys from? I am sure we can settle this amicably."

"Don't be," said one of the men.

"Yeah, don't be sure of anything now, mate," said the leader. "You know of a guy named Badger Bell?"

Grace panicked.

Fuck, that's the guy we paid to off in Tangier! he thought.

"Never heard of him," Grace said, trying to sound confident, strong, even belligerent.

"That's not what we've heard. What we heard from a mutual friend," the leader said.

"Who would that be?" Grace asked.

"That's not important," the leader said. "Now get up the stairs. Now!"

"Up the stairs, boss," said another of the men in black.

Grace grabbed a four-by-two.

"I wouldn't if I were you, my friend. Now put that fucking lump of wood down before I shove it where the sun don't shine," said the leader of the gang of four.

Grace tossed down the piece of wood, and it rattled noisily on the concrete as Grace backed toward the stairwell and started climbing the stairs backward.

"Come on, boys. There must be some mistake. Did Dmitri Dankov send you? I can ring him now, and we can get this all cleared up in no time."

As Grace climbed the five flights of stairs, his mood swung from anger to appeal, appeal to anger, until eventually they stood on the roof of the building, five flights up, overlooking dull and dismal Bingley.

"Look, I knew that last job was a mistake. Ask Harrison. I told that bastard we shouldn't have done it. He's the one you should be after, not fucking me. It should be that bastard you should be hassling. What the fuck do you want? What the fuck are you doing?"

He realized that he was now within a foot of the edge of the building, with the menacing four still advancing. The leader put the shaft of his pickax handle into the middle of Grace's chest.

"This is for Paul and for Badger, you fucking scumbag."

"No! Oh, fuck no!" Grace said as he reeled backward toward the edge of the roof. He felt piss soak his pants.

"Well, would you look at that!" said one of the men. "The fucking scumbag has gone and pissed himself!"

The four men laughed. Grace gagged, forcing the vomit down.

"I can pay! I can give you money! Just let—"

Grace felt another hard jab in his chest, and then there was nothing. Nothing below his feet but air. He heard himself scream for a fraction of a second, and then there was nothing but blackness.

The leader used Neil Grace's cell to text Andrew Harrison. "We got Tangier trouble. Meet me right now at the site in Bingley."

The leader smiled as he read the reply. "Right. Give me twenty."

"The fish is on the line," the leader said.

"Good. How long before he gets here?"

"Bout twenty minutes. Looking down at Grace's corpse. The man had landed back first. A rusty shaft of rebar protruded from his chest. Looking like a construction site accident.

The sun went down early, it being November. And the leader was happy. The dimness of twilight suited him perfectly for the business at hand. He knew it suited his friends as well. Wet work was best conducted in the shadows, if possible. Each man was positioned out of the scope of the security lights and cameras, each merging with darkness. They were wearing ear coms, enabling them to communicate with each other.

"Got movement at five o'clock," said one of the men.

"Got it," the leader said.

"That the target?" another of the men asked.

The leader raised a small set of binoculars to his eyes and peered into the increasing darkness. "Affirmative."

The leader watched as a black BMW 630i pulled up, and Andrew Harrison got out of the driver's side in his Oasis mullet, cheap-looking suit and tie. He left the car door open. "Neil?" he called. "Hey, Neil! What the fuck?"

"Take him," the leader said.

In seconds, Harrison was surrounded. The leader noted with satisfaction that the target looked scared as he stared wide-eyed at the Brownings.

"Please don't hurt me," Harrison said. "Here. Take this," he said, reaching his hand into his jacket pocket.

"Don't move!" the leader said, his voice firm and full of fury.

"What, what do you want?" Harrison said. "What the fuck? Who are you? What do you want? Do you know Dmitri Dankov? He'll have you butchered like fucking lambs. What the fuck do you want?"

"Sit down, Andrew," the leader said.

"Where?"

"On dirt. Where you belong," one of the men said.

Harrison sat down. "Who are you and what do you want?"

"I want you to say sorry."

"What the fuck for?" Harrison hissed.

"For killing my friends," the leader said.

"Who am I supposed to have killed?"

"My friends, Badger in Tangier and Paul in San Francisco, that's who."

"That wasn't me. Wrong person. You need to speak to Neil Grace, not me."

"Neil Grace, your business partner?"

"Well, er, yes, but he's the one you need to speak to."

"You have a bit of a habit of selling out your business partners, don't you, Harrison?"

"No idea what the fuck you mean. Now let me fucking go, and no one needs to know about this, I promise. I promise I won't even tell Dmitri Dankov if you let me go."

"What did you think might happen if you start going around killing SAS men, Harrison?"

"I didn't kill anyone. It's Neil fucking Grace that you need to see, not me."

"Oh, we already have, Andrew. You don't mind if I call you Andrew?" said the leader. "I need you to say sorry for your part."

The leader held his pistol to Harrison's temple.

"Oh God!" Harrison said, his voice cracking. "Please don't kill me!"

"Now listen to me and listen to me very carefully, Andrew." The leader turned to one of the men. "Give him the pad and pen."

One of the men took a small notepad and a pen from his coat pocket and threw at Harrison.

"Pick it up."

Harrison obliged, his hands shaking.

"I want you to sit down there and right on that pad, *I am sorry for all that I have done*. Then I want you to sign it, *Andrew Harrison*. Got it?"

Harrison started to write on the pad. "There, all done. Now will you let me go and stop fucking around? I'm sure Dmitri Dankov would be very unhappy to hear that you are here right now."

"Fuck Dmitri Dankov," one of the men said.

"I have money. I can give you money."

"Money doesn't buy life, Andrew," the leader said. He stooped down and took the pad from Harrison. "Besides, you won't need money in hell. Hold his hands."

The three other men hauled Harrison to his feet and pulled his arms behind his back.

"What are you doing?"

"Taking you for the ride you deserve," the leader said and jabbed a syringe into Harrison's neck. He pushed the plunger and was pleased to see that the heroin took immediate effect. Harrison began to convulse, and then he went still. The men dropped him. The leader saw the man's lifeless eyes staring up at the cloudy sky. The night had come, even though it was before five, but the security lights were enough.

The leader sighed. "Our work is done" he said. They put Harrison back in his car with the syringe and the suicide note. "Let's get the flock out of here boys."

26
DARK FORCES

Paris, France, November 2016, Day 24

MITCH SAT IN THE BACK of the taxi as it traveled around the Arc de Triomphe, down the Champs-Élysees, onto Avenue George V and number 31, the George Cinque Hotel.

Mitch paid the driver and got out, the door having been opened by the greeting concierge. He walked into the marbled lobby and made his way to the George V wine cellar, a private room.

Paulo Mancini was the head of Los Rastrojos, a Colombian drug cartel and a paramilitary organization with over fifteen hundred soldiers and operatives worldwide.

Mitch made his way to the entrance to the underground corridor that led to the wine cellar, where he was to meet with Paulo Mancini, the head of the Los Rastrojos cartel. The security guards patted him down to make sure he wasn't armed. One of them removed Mitch's Browning from its holster.

"What have we here?" the guard said.

"I don't expect to take that in with me, but it's not safe these days to go around without some protection," Mitch said. "Keep it safe for me, will you?"

The guard laughed. "Sure thing," he said. "You can go on in."

"Gracias," Mitch said.

"De nada," the guard said.

Mitch walked down the corridor to the door of the wine cellar. He opened the door and stopped for a moment. The room was adorned with thousands of bottles of wine. The collection was incredible. He noted a table in a corner of the room and sat in one of the two chairs.

A few minutes passed, and Mitch heard the cellar door open and leather-soled shoes walking toward him. In walked Paulo Mancini— good looking, olive skinned, cream-colored suit, open necked, pink, paisley shirt, tan belt, matching shoes, and a pair of sunglasses on top of his dark brown locks, above his deep brown, smiling eyes. The Laughing Assassin, as they used to call him, was now one of the most powerful and wealthy criminal gang leaders in the world.

"Mitchell, so good to see you, my friend," said Mancini.

"Good to see you too, Paulo, although different circumstances might have been better." Mitch stood up from the table and gave Paulo a bear hug, which Paulo returned. Both men sat down.

"What is wrong, my friend?" Paulo asked. "You look troubled."

Mitch first met Paulo Mancini in Colombia when he was the commander of the Colombian anticartel forces and Mitch's team was sent in to train his team in jungle warfare. They were there for eighteen months and grew to know each other, respect each other, and become friends.

They hadn't seen each other since Paulo elected to leave the government forces and turn from gamekeeper to poacher, in light of the government's corrupt approach to the currency of cocaine in their country. In that, he witnessed how the Colombian government had colluded with the cartels and set up an ambush that killed twenty-two of his own men and friends.

Paulo crawled from that ambush to safety, escaping with a shot through the leg, and as he crawled and sheltered in the jungle, Paulo said to himself, "If you can't beat them, join them."

But the reality was that Paulo was a decent man with principles, and Los Rastrojos at least conducted business with honor, although the core business was still that of cocaine, which was compelling in terms of the wealth that it created. Now Paulo was one of the richest, most influential, and most powerful of the Colombian cartels.

"I am a little concerned at the company you are keeping nowadays, Paulo."

"Mitchell, my friend, who do you speak of?"

"Why are you getting involved in the dirty work of the Kremlin?" Mitch asked.

Paulo looked at Mitch, deep into his eyes, deep into his soul.

"We have partnerships globally now, Mitchell. You understand that? It's business."

"Since when have you started meddling in politics?"

Paulo looked confused. Mitch knew his friend had once aspired to enter the word of politics in Colombia to rid the government of corruption and make sure that the money the country made from its illicit trade would get back to the people. Paulo had realized that was impossible and that now his enterprise used the wealth he had created to build schools, hospitals, housing, and clean-water projects for the region he was from. Paulo Mancini, unlike the rest of the drug lords, was not feared but revered, not hunted but protected. Paulo had changed the meaning of the enterprise and was channeling the monies to build prosperity in his Colombian community. He wasn't ashamed but proud, and so were his people. If rich Americans wanted to abuse their bodies with drugs, then that was their prerogative, no different from the peddlers of tequila or tobacco, a legalized hybrid of the same industry.

"We work with our Russian friends to open up supply chains, not politics."

"So why are your men blowing up the CIA in San Francisco? That's not like you, Paulo."

"They were trying to shut us down, Mitchell. It's business. I told you that."

Mitch was testing his old friend's patience, which was dangerous, but Mitch new he had a lot of currency with Paulo. They trusted and respected each other despite that they were technically on opposite sides of the fence. Or were they?

"Wrong. They were investigating an international election-rigging scam."

"Aha, Mitchell, you are always making the jokes," Paulo said.

"No joke, Paulo. Brad, Paul, and Badger were tracking down election riggers, and in the US, if they are successful and get their man in power, then your business will face an even tougher time than ever before."

"Let's talk. You mention Paul and Badger. The same Paul and Badger? Our friends Paul and Badger?"

"Yes, Paulo. They were both murdered, but you knew that, right?"

"I swear on my mother's life that I knew nothing. What happened?"

Although Mitch assessed that Paulo appeared genuine on this point, he also knew that Paulo's mother was long since dead.

Mitch walked his old friend through the whole scenario, the briefings, what they had pieced together, the involvement of the Los Rastrojos, the IRA, the Russian Mafia, and the ultimate bosses above them. He shared the intelligence on the money laundering, the supply routes, the meddling, and the big bets.

"I get it, Paulo, the marriage of convenience, the route to market. I get all that, but it's not you using them, my friend—it is them using you. The supply route in Morocco is compromised now as a result of all of this. They will disappear back into the shadows as quickly as they came out, and do you think the FBI is going to be knocking on the doors of the Kremlin to seek criminal charges? No, they will be knocking on your door and the door of the other players that they have treated like puppets along the way."

"Hey, Mitchell, I am no puppet." Paulo flashed his dark brown eyes to Mitch.

"The point I am making, Paulo, is that this is modern warfare. This is why it has been set up this way, because the Kremlin, they'll just blame criminals for being criminals and deny all knowledge. I mean, who would believe that a government would work with the criminal underworld to achieve their political goals?"

Paulo smiled at Mitch. "Have you forgotten Colombia already, Mitchell?"

"So why were your men in the Dubliner that night the bomb went off? I saw them with my own eyes, Paulo."

"You were there that night?"

"Yes, I was, and if I hadn't stepped out to my car, then I wouldn't be here right now. I would be six feet under, just like Paul, Brad, and Badger!"

"Wait, wait, we didn't have anything to do with Badger—the CIA guy, yes, but you know the CIA, Mitchell. They are as corrupt as the Colombian government. You never know what they are up to. POTUS himself has no idea what they are up to, and most of what they are up to isn't good. You know that, Mitchell."

"Brad was a good guy."

Paulo shrugged his shoulders and gestured, "If you are in the game, Mitchell, you are in the game. You know that. It's the first rule of the game."

"A bomb, Paulo, seriously? That's not your play," challenged Mitch.

"That was what the Black Widow suggested," Paulo responded as he looked up to the vaulted ceiling of the wine cellar.

"The Black Widow?"

"Yes, the Baltic Black Widow, Chernaya Vdova. Viktoria Saparov."

"Paulo, what are you doing messing with her and her Kremlin puppet masters?"

Mitch explained the common link between Los Rastrojos, the IRA, and the Russian Mafia, and how they were supporting the Russian assets around the globe, funneling funds back into the motherland, the Kremlin, and Putin's regime, propping up the economy, channeling foreign currency and their adoption of maskirovka to unsettle world politics to the ultimate advantage of the ambitions of the Russian Federation and phoenix rising of the Russian empire.

"They played me as a puppet?"

"Where did the bomb come from, Paulo?"

"She provided it. Said it was from a previous campaign."

"No, Paulo, it was hand built. It had 狗, Gǒu, the Dog signature all over it."

Paulo looked at Mitch with narrowed eyes.

"He even sent his calling card to Brad's wife!"

"So, I wasn't even the puppet. I was just the delivery boy?"

"And what about Paul and Badger, Paulo?"

"I swear to God that we had nothing to do with that. I would have never sanctioned that. You know that, Mitchell; they were friends."

Mitch also knew that Paulo didn't believe in God, but his instinct and knowing Paulo as he did, Mitch believed him.

"Maybe that's why she didn't ask you, because she knew you knew them?"

"But it sounds like the bomb at the Dubliner almost got you, Mitchell."

"I wasn't the target. Brad was. Listen, Paulo, they're ready to trade you in at a drop of a hat. You're probably making great money, but let me reassure you, they're making trillions of dollars, not billions, out of this. As soon as it gets into the limelight, they will drop you like a stone, jettison anything that will compromise the path to the man at the top. Paulo, you know how their art of maskirovka works, and that's not to the benefit of Paulo Mancini, and that is an absolute fact."

Paulo listened carefully. He was powerful but not too arrogant to listen, and he also trusted Mitch. He was the one, with his team, Paul, Badger, and the other guys, who rescued him out of the jungle after the ambush. Mancini might have died if it hadn't been for them, as the infection in his wounds had taken root; it would have been only a matter of time before it killed him in the depths of the Colombian jungle.

"Mitchell, I will put this right, my friend. Thank you for opening my eyes. You were always good at that. You did that when we first met, and I came to love and trust you like a brother. Although we are on different sides today, I still know you to be true, and you also know that I am, to the things that count. I will put this right. You have my word."

Paulo scraped his chair back on the redbrick floor, stood up to meet

Mitch in a bear hug, patted Mitch's back, and gave him a quick kiss on each cheek. "Mitchell, you are my brother."

"You're mine too, Paulo, and stop calling me fucking Mitchell!" They both burst into laughter at their old joke as comrades.

"You know where I am if you need me, Mitch."

"Thanks, Paulo. You too."

Mitch collected his 9 mm Browning from the grumpy bodyguards at the door and slipped it down the back of his jeans, underneath his sports coat. He stepped out onto Avenue George V and disappeared into the busy Parisian street.

National Cyber Security Center, London, United Kingdom, November 2016, Day 23

Bella glanced over at Beecham, Collins, and Mac as they entered the austere building that housed the National Cyber Security Center. She felt both nervous and excited at the same time. "I hope we take the hackers down," she said.

Mac laughed. "With you on our side, we can't fail."

The four arrived in the lobby. The London afternoon sunshine shone through the windows, lighting the gray slate floor. They were escorted into the lift that would take them to the task force headquarters on the twentieth floor. They stepped out a few moments later, and the new chief executive officer greeted them.

"Charlie Martin! Jolly good to see you!" Lord Beecham said, his enthusiasm almost infectious. "I knew that you would need me out of retirement sooner rather than later!"

Did Lord Beecham just wink at the guy? Bella wondered. She smiled. *Sometimes these guys are like little boys.*

"Lord Beecham, how the devil are you? It's been a while. You knew we couldn't hold this party without you!"

"Forgive my manners, Charlie. Let me introduce you. I think you have spoken with Colonel Collins here, Angus Mackay, former Regiment, Bella Mitchell, daughter of a good friend and with Executive

Outcomes. I don't know what we can do, but whatever we can, we are willing and able."

"The more, the merrier," Charlie Martin responded. "We have a big task ahead of us. Welcome to the National Cyber Security Center."

Charlie Martin marched them through a first set of security doors into a reception area with further security doors to the left and to the right. "Follow me." Charlie swiped his card and tacked left through a corridor to another security door that opened into a huge space with desks, cubicles, computers, and an army feverishly tapping on keyboards with multiple screens.

"This is our main operations center. We have over seven hundred people here in London and a further thirteen hundred located around the world, including in Silicon Valley, New York, Tel Aviv, Berlin, Paris, Hong Kong, Sydney, Delhi, and another main hub in Vilnius, Lithuania. We are all preparing to go live at midnight. All-out attack."

They followed Charlie into a briefing center and operations room that put Lord Beecham's impressive private collection of the same to shame. The entire facing wall was taken up by a huge bank of digital screens, with the center taken up by a map of the world with a series of red pulses, green, yellow, and blue. Then surrounding individual screens held unfathomable data.

"Impressive." Lord Beecham nodded.

"Very impressive." Colonel Collins agreed.

They walked forward to the front of the room and a briefing platform at the front of an auditorium facing the screens.

"We have been building the footprint for years, and we have a pretty good knowledge of the dark networks across the globe. Although we have some insights as to who, we certainly know where they are and, in most cases, if and who they are controlled or influenced by—sovereign states, military, organized crime, freelance crime, and hobby hackers.

"It's only now that democracy itself is at stake that we have been allowed to wield our total power against these disrupters and take them down, or at least for now. What you are looking at here is the equivalent of launching a global missile attack on our enemies of the state. These dark forces will not know what hit them. We are going to take down every network, URL, website, and hostile posting on social media. We are going to take down power supplies, freeze bank accounts and assets, and corrupt every enemy's digital footprint out there."

"What you will witness, starting at midnight, is a total blitz that will leave those enemies disabled."

Charlie sounded like a general about to destroy the enemy. Bella wondered if he was all talk or if he really was able to do as he said.

In the operations center, there were about fifty people, and in contrast to the previous room, they all wore headsets and were in deep, urgent conversations in different languages, presumably to the allies, mobilizing resources ready for the strike.

"When we strike, some will have the wherewithal to defend and fight back, and that is where our sheer firepower comes in. We have amassed data, resources, and an army of Brightside Hackers that will inundate their systems to an extent that they will not be able to cope with the volume. You will have seen or read about this tactic before, used by hackers; we are using the same in reverse. During the strike, we will monitor the fighters and turn our technical army's attention to them to shut them down."

"As I said, Charlie, very impressive, but what is it that we can do? Sounds like you have it all tied up," said Beecham.

"Don't worry about that. I have plenty for you to do, old boy." Charlie smiled, casting a quick glance at Mac.

"Lord Beecham, I would like you and Colonel Collins to work with our boots on the ground teams across the globe. We have small units, international special forces teams out there on the ground, and where we are certain that there is a physical presence, as opposed to a virtual presence, we will be sending them out to take out, if on territory outside our jurisdiction, and arrest where we do have jurisdiction. Bella will work with the data analysis team once the attack commences and beyond the hard targets, we are pretty certain of already, with teams on the ground in standby. Some of the unknown physical sites will start to emerge as the data shows us they cannot virtualize and therefore locate the physical addresses and mobilize the strike teams.

"I will get you allocated to the team commanders right now and get you cracking."

"What would you like me to do?" asked Mac.

"Oh yes, Mac, you can sit with the international observation team. They are like the United Nations of this operation, here to make sure that we play as fair as we can possibly be. This sort of thing isn't covered by the Geneva Convention, but it's an important part of our quality control so that we can justify our actions if and when we are held to account by the Chinese, the Russians, maybe even the North Koreans and who knows who else. This is an important part of the due diligence process to make sure that this virtual war doesn't turn into a conventional one."

Bella noted that Mac looked disinterested at this back-office role.

As Bella got situated, she realized that she was on a steep learning curve, even with her advanced knowledge of code. Yet she loved the challenge. She managed to push the issues with Nikita out of her mind. He'd sent her a text to say that he'd been promoted after the tragic suicide of the former CEO. The man now ran the entire First World Bank. She understood that they might have grown apart, and that hurt, but she didn't have time for that now. She had important work to do.

27
SECRET CENTER

Vilnius, Lithuania, November 2016, Day 24

THE WHEELS OF THE KLM Flight 2845 De Havilland-Bombardier Dash-8 hit the tarmac as it landed, following its two-hour-and-forty-five-minute flight from Amsterdam Schiphol Airport. The propellers whirled as the pilot taxied the aircraft to the gate. Jimmy gazed out the window, noting that Vilnius International Airport looked gray and tired. Jimmy had taken a quick hop from London City Airport for the start of his journey to go see Dmitri Dankov. He had some unfinished business with the man. They all did.

Jimmy had been to Lithuania before, several years ago and just after the country had come out of Communist rule. He remembered the poverty and the tall, stark apartment buildings where the heat and water were controlled by the state. It came on and then turned off the same time every day, regardless of the wishes of the resident.

He recalled the empty farm fields on the road to Klaipeda and the empty port with no ships and no produce to export to Russia, as the market had simply collapsed. He remembered the men, despondent, with no work and no money, drinking neat vodka in the Baltic temperatures as if it was soda. He remembered the old women sweeping the streets. He remembered the young, beautiful Lithuanian women gladly selling their bodies to what few Westerners there were to earn some Lithuanian litas, or even better a passport and a ticket out of there as a lucky new bride.

Jimmy remembered one such encounter with Oxsana, a beautiful, tall brunette who swore love for Jimmy after his indulgence that week. She spoke decent English and was beautiful, kind, and incredibly sensitive between the sheets. She didn't seem to mind if she was the only woman between those sheets, and over the course of that week, Jimmy indulged with her friend Tanya at the same time, together but Oxsana always in control.

He had a habit of falling in love quickly, and he fell in love with Oxsana, but like so often in his life, when it came down to it, taking Oxsana home, becoming stepfather to her then eight-year-old boy, and living happily ever after, Jimmy pulled out and never saw Oxsana again.

These and other thoughts occupied his mind as he grabbed his carry-on and exited the plane. A short time later, he hailed a cab, a beat-up Mercedes, and headed into Vilnius. The place had changed a little since his last visit. Instead of Trabants plying the streets, now it seemed that every other car was a Mercedes Benz. There was, however, still a pervasive Soviet feel of austerity in the architecture, even in the air.

The cab passed by the Philip Morris cigarette factory, which was new last time Jimmy was here. At the time, he had found it ironic that tobacco companies move into places like Lithuania, down on their luck, and ply the population with addictive cigarettes that they can't afford, endangering the health of a nation. Jimmy had seen the same thing in Thailand. Getting these poor people addicted to their drugs that they couldn't afford and would probably kill them. After all, cigarette addiction was on the decline in most developed countries, and they had to dig for profits elsewhere. After all, eight billion targets and growing every day.

There were still the tall foundry towers of the factories and mills, painted in the red and white stripes, that reminded him of a marijuana-induced Pink Floyd video.

As they pulled into the city, past the cathedral and through the archway that led to the castle walls of the Shakespeare Hotel, Jimmy remembered it like it was yesterday. He booked himself in at reception and was escorted to the Oscar Wilde Suite, the room he had stayed in when visiting the city to see his good friend Angus who had lived there for several years.

Jimmy hopped into the shower, shaved, got dressed, and headed down to the courtyard to the old bar. He ordered a pint of Svyturys Lithuanian Pilsner, sat himself down at the big wooden table, and checked his phone for emails and messages. He checked out the address for the Olympic Casino on Konstitucijos and decided that he would walk the two miles and take a look around the old square and city hall before going to see Dmitri Dankov.

Jimmy headed out of the Shakespeare Arch and tracked right, then right again, up the hill on the cobbled streets that took him to the main drag and the city square. The street market was still open with local artists, gifts, Babushka dolls, old Russian military paraphernalia, books, scented candles, and musicians serenading the late-night shoppers. Jimmy noticed the difference from when he first came. There were more international tourists now, as opposed to the day he arrived and was questioned at the airport for forty-five minutes, being the only Western visitor that week. What was his business in Lithuania? they asked. They eventually pointed down their Kalashnikovs and let him through the border.

Jimmy walked past the old Russian Orthodox church, beautifully ordained with its white walls, gold, and the scent of incense as the priest went about his business anointing his evening congregation.

On up to the main square, the cafes in the center were closed for the night, with the bars remaining open and filling up. Like that first visit, the locals strolled around the square, in twos or threes, still resisting any bigger groups that in days gone by would constitute a public disturbance and arrest. On past the beautiful city hall, he went, on to the Olympic Casino, Dmitri Dankov's home casino.

Jimmy walked into the casino for a scout around, then went up the stairs and on to the main floor. Culturally, Lithuania wasn't a big gambling country, even before the Communist rule under the USSR, and tonight, as most nights, the casino wasn't particularly busy.

Jimmy headed to the bar and ordered another Systurys in a tall glass. He sat in the corner, facing the entrance to the bar and Dmitri Dankov's party.

Jimmy had met Dmitri Dankov several times at the Oasis in Bangkok with his mate Bokov. Bokov knew everything that went on in his region and who was doing it. They knew who Jimmy was, and Jimmy knew who they were too, and they both knew that they knew. Polite, cold courtesy.

"Well, well, well, you are a long way from home, Jimmy. To what do we owe the pleasure?" asked Dmitri Dankov as he strolled over with his glass of Cristal in hand. Tall, broad, white jacket concealing his handgun, a bow tie, shiny Breitling and sovereign signet ring on his little finger.

"I thought I would swing by to see how things are before your big day," Jimmy said.

"Very glad you did so. Can I get you a glass of Cristal?"

"I'm fine, thanks, Dmitry. Just having this one and heading off."

"Ah. Off to Eden to see if Oxsana is still there?"

That's one of the many reasons Jimmy detested the Russians, especially Dmitri Dankov; they made it their business to know everyone else's business, and they didn't mind using what they found against you.

"No, not Oxsana. You took care of that."

Jimmy seethed at Dmitri Dankov's arrogance. Dmitri Dankov, he was sure, had orchestrated Oxsana's overdose. She'd never been seriously into hard drugs, and yet when she threatened to leave Eden, she mysteriously died because she shot up a mix that was too strong. Oxsana, by that time, was not only the most valuable girl in terms of revenue, but she was also bed partner with the president of Lithuania.

"I brought you a present," Jimmy said as he passed the small box, the size of two packets of cigarettes, to Dmitri Dankov.

"Oh yes, Jimmy, I always like presents."

Dmitri Dankov took the box. "What is in it?" he asked.

"It's from Lord Beecham. He wanted to pass on his best regards."
Dmitri Dankov looked perplexed, even a little startled.

"I don't understand. And you still haven't told me what's in the box."

"Just open it and find out," Jimmy said.

"It's not a bomb, is it?"

Jimmy laughed. "Mate, if it was a bomb, you'd have gone boom by
now, and I wouldn't be sitting right here!"

Dmitri Dankov laughed, but Jimmy could see he was uneasy.
Dmitri Dankov opened the box. He removed a single red chess queen.

"What is this supposed to mean?" Dmitri Dankov asked.

"I am just the courier, Dmitry. Beecham sends his best regards."

"Does Beecham think he is in some sort of fucking Sherlock
Holmes movie?"

"I have no idea, but he said you would know what the red queen
symbolizes and that you would know what to do next."

"What—disappear, Jimmy? Is that what he is referring to? You tell
Beecham I will not be disappearing anytime soon. Tell him he should
stand down and let the big boys get on with the business. He has no
idea how to navigate these depths."

Jimmy was enjoying himself, winding up probably one of the most
dangerous men in the world.

Dmitri Dankov smiled as one of his big henchmen arrived.
"Everything good, sir?"

"Yes, Vladimir, no problem here. No problem here at all. Is there,
Jimmy?"

Jimmy placed both hands on the table, palms down. "No problem,"
he said, standing.

"Going so soon? Stay. Drink. If you like, I can find you some of the
sweetest company in the city," Dmitri Dankov said.

"No thanks, mate. I'm married. Happily married."

"How nice for you. Are you around for long, my friend?" asked
Dmitri Dankov.

"I haven't decided yet. Just depends what I see on my travels."

"Well, my friend, be careful of too much sightseeing. It can kill
you." Dmitri Dankov smiled.

"I'll make sure that I stick to cathedrals, castles, and crooks."

"Sounds wise," Dmitri Dankov said. "I am sure I will see you again not before too long." Dmitri Dankov smiled and turned back to his party, talking to big Vladimir on the way.

"Fucking prick," Jimmy muttered.

Jimmy stayed around for another beer. He kept an eye on the Dmitri Dankov party and played a couple of hands of blackjack, his heart not in it. He finished his beer and walked back down the stairs to head out into the Vilnius night. Vladimir stepped out of the shadows. "Hello, Vladimir. What's happening?" Jimmy challenged.

Vladimir, towering above Jimmy, just stared and said, "Take care. Have a good rest of the night." Vladimir didn't return the courtesy.

Jimmy was glad to be out of there, conscious that he had a big day ahead of him, starting at two in the morning, local time. He sent a text—"D confirmed in Vilnius. Message delivered. Pleasant encounter as always. Tosser!" Jimmy couldn't help but break the protocols.

Jimmy slept poorly. Early the next morning, he got up, dressed, and went downstairs to the lobby. He thought about his beautiful wife, Jenni. He longed to be with her back at the Oasis.

This will be my last trip, he thought. *I'm getting too old for this crap.*

Suddenly, his mind veered off to focus on his estranged son, William, at Imperial College, London. He wondered what William was doing with himself, how he was coming along, knowing full well that William was already set to follow in Jimmy's footsteps, just not as a Tom but as a fully commissioned officer. Jimmy had long since lost hope that he would get an invite to Sandhurst and his graduation parade.

He left the hotel and went to the car that was waiting for him, a Toyota Land Cruiser. There were two passengers in addition to the driver. Jimmy sat in the rear seat behind the driver.

"Good morning, boys," Jimmy said.

"Good morning, Jimmy."

Driving was Sean, one of the Kiwi SAS guys, in the passenger seat was Dusty, and in the rear passenger seat was Ken. Jimmy had known these guys for years, seeing them around the Regiment, Game Cock,

Missions, in Ireland. Jimmy was in good company with these still-serving SAS.

"Civilian life must be good, mate, staying in a fancy place like that!" said Ken as Sean pulled out of the archway from the Shakespeare onto the boulevard in front of the old cathedral.

"You know how it is, boys, when you take the queen's shilling. When you get out, you will have to learn how to earn a living." Jimmy smiled.

"Long time no see, Jimmy," said Sean from the front.

"Yep, it's been a while, Sean. Where are we heading?"

Dusty stepped in. "An underground monitoring station just out of town. Part of the global plan and network to take down the dark web and the forces at play within it. We are here to defend them for the next twenty-four hours. Should be a breeze."

"Yeah, right. I've heard that before, Dusty."

"Who are these people?" asked Jimmy.

"A disparate bunch: some government, some pseudo government, some hackers, some anti-Russian activists," replied Dusty.

"Lithuania is paranoid about Russian tanks taking their streets. There is a big movement and resistance to the Ruskies here," added Ken.

"Yep, they like their independence and the prosperity and freedom that has come their way since escaping the clutches of the USSR," said Sean.

The Toyota Land Cruiser navigated its way out of the city and then through desolate, disused farmland and country roads, about an hour out of the capital. At a junction, they turned right. There were no streetlights and no electricity out there. They went through a dense forest and turned left, over a wooden bridge spanning the river to the lake, into an opening, a huddle of buildings.

Three figures came out of the shadows as Sean flashed the Land Cruiser lights three times. They slowly approached the vehicle, Kalashnikovs at the ready, balaclavas on as much to shield the subzero temperature as to hide their identity.

"Pass?" asked a man with a deep voice and broad shoulders.

"Starry, starry night," responded Sean and with a wave of the

Kalashnikov's muzzle. The gate opened, and the Land Cruiser slipped in.

"Starry, starry night? Who came up with that one?"

They were directed into the complex to a barn structure to park the vehicle. The four got out and stretched their legs. "Antisatellite structure so they cannot see what we do or who is here," said the big man with the deep voice. "This way." He gestured.

They walked from the parking structure to one of the buildings that looked like a farmhouse, with its twinkling windows and a smoke-plumed chimney.

The big man opened the door into a cottage of wooden panels, fires, sofas, and chairs. It was candle lit and welcoming. No sight of anyone apart from the five of them. "This way," said the big man as he guided them to the back of the cottage. Just off the bedroom corridor, he popped a panel to reveal a secret, shiny lift.

They stepped in, left the big man, and headed down in the shiny steel compartment.

"Where the hell are we going?" said Ken, speaking on behalf of the other three of his team.

Seconds later, the doors slid open, making that familiar noise of well-oiled hydraulics, into a polished concrete vestibule, airlock. The doors of the lift closed automatically as the four stepped out. Five-four-three-two-one. The airlock doors opened to a bigger room. Inside were forty or fifty people tapping away at computers, heads down, some with hoodies, some without, some in smart clothes looking like civil servants, some looking homeless. No one looked up. They weren't there for keeping an eye on security. They were on a mission to break down security. The security of the Russian Federation and all its weapons of deceit.

This was the unofficial war room of Lithuania and the Baltic states, including Poland, against the evil and intimidating threat of their neighbor, Russia.

A tall, blond man with a friendly face trotted toward the four. "Welcome, welcome to our little fortress." He smiled. "You are a quarter of a mile underground, bomb proof, nuclear proof, impregnable apart from the lift you just came down on, and if we don't like the look of our visitors, they are exterminated in the airlock! That means we must like you, and therefore you must be our friends. Welcome. My name is Sven. I am your host. Come this way."

Sven guided them through the maze of people hacking away at their keyboards, totally focused and disinterested in the visitors.

They got to a meeting room with a glass sliding door and stepped in, Sven holding the door at the entrance and smiling at each of the four as he waved them in.

"Okay, gentlemen, thank you for joining us. At precisely 4:00 a.m. local time, our job begins. We have over one hundred of the most talented computer engineers and hackers in the Eastern Bloc in this bunker tonight. We have been working on pulling this together for the past two years. At 4:00 a.m., we commence an all-out onslaught on the official and black cyber operations of the Russian Federation to take them on at their own game.

"As you will appreciate, this is very dangerous work. We are less than 390 kilometers or 240 miles from Kaliningrad, 955 kilometers, five hundred and ninety miles to the Kremlin. Russians are in our towns, our villages, and our cities. We are surrounded, but this is our hour."

"What do you need us to do?" asked Jimmy.

"We need your protection. Although we have walls of concrete, steel, and lead. Although we are buried under ground with only one way in and one way out, when we start our operations, they will start the hunt for us. Until now, we have remained completely under the radar. We believe that they don't even know we exist. We have been very careful in how we built this place, and from the satellites and surveillance, we look like a farmhouse by the lake. That's it. Come 4:00 a.m., every pro-Russian force will be looking for us, and make no mistake, they will hunt us like dogs. We are just a bunch of programmers. We are not fighters, we are not warriors of the old kind; we only know how to use our code as weapons."

"What are the ways in which they will find you?" asked Sean.

"So, as you know, this is part of a bigger global operation with centers similar to this around the world—in New York, London, Tel Aviv, even Sydney and Hong Kong, but we here in Lithuania are by far the most vulnerable. We don't have the luxury of the protection of the others, and the Russians, if they so choose, could roll their tanks out of Kaliningrad and overthrow the Lithuanian military and government within a matter of days."

"But that would severely weaken the stronghold of Kaliningrad and make that vulnerable," commented Ken.

"Yes, you are right, but there has been a lot of movement of military hardware to Kaliningrad, and clusters are positioned now in the Russian border towns, indicating that a targeted effort could see Lithuania, Latvia, Estonia, even Belarus crumble at the same lightning speed. We don't have the defense capability to withstand such an attack."

"So, you want us to thwart the entire Russian army?" asked Dusty with not just a hint of sarcasm.

Sven broke his frown and let out a big smile. "No, no, of course not, my friend. We need you to help us with any potential wolves that might be sniffing around and to protect that lift shaft for the next twenty-four hours. These wolves are in sheep's clothing and not Russian uniforms but equally as dangerous."

"Yep, I know a few of them," announced Jimmy, enjoying the group's appreciation of his dry humor. "Just twenty-four hours?"

"Yes, that is all that it will take, and after that, we will go to sleep again, and once we do, we will be invisible once more."

"You mean they can't trace your footprint retrospectively?"

"They can, but once we go to sleep, we send a network of phantom signals that bounce around the globe, making it impossible to trace. During the next twenty-four hours, this phantom network is weakened as we focus our resources and launch our attack," Sven said.

"So, where are we needed? Down here or above ground?" Jimmy asked.

"We were thinking that you could work with Boris above ground."

"Big Boris we just met?" asked Dusty.

Sven smiled again. "Yes, Big Boris. He is a man of few words, but he protects us. You will find that, despite first appearances of the farmhouse, Boris has amassed some useful toys in case the wolves arrive at our doors."

Sven took them on the tour of the operations, showing them the army of hackers and the energy control room, explaining the power independence thanks to hydropower and harnessing the natural resources of the lake and its rivers and a network of backup power generators that provided four layers of backup. They went past the sleeping quarters that resembled those of a submarine, hot bedding bunks, and slimline locker storage enough to keep basics secure, to the galley where there was a buffet of pastries, breakfast meats, cheeses, orange juice, and coffee.

"Help yourself to some breakfast. We have an hour," Sven said.

Jimmy, Ken, Sean, and Dusty helped themselves to some much-appreciated breakfast and coffee and sat in the utilitarian cafeteria alone. The hackers were busy with their preparations. The big clock on the wall showing the T-minus deadline loomed above their heads.

With T-minus showing at thirty, Big Boris came through the door and invited them back to the airlock and the lift back to the farmhouse. Sven trotted over and smiled. "Thank you and good luck."

The four responded, "Good luck, Sven."

"Twenty-four hours, right?" confirmed Jimmy.

"Twenty-four hours," Sven said.

As they arrived back in the farmhouse, Boris carefully closed the door to the lift shaft, and they made their way through to the main living room where the fire was blazing. On the coffee table in front of the fire, Boris laid out a map that appeared to be of the farmhouse and the surrounding area. Clearly marked was the lake, the main road, the track that led the way down, and the farmhouse. Boris went on to describe the different sentry points around the property, the camera control room located in the farmhouse, the armory, and the firing points within the compound, manned and armed.

"Each firing point is equipped with a PKM general purpose machine gun, two thousand rounds each, twenty grenades, and a mounted MRO-A rocket launcher with twelve rounds. Here are your earpieces and radios. You will be connected to the security network. Radio silence unless critical observations. Understand?"

"Fucking hell, are you sure you're not expecting the Red Army?" Jimmy asked.

"We are well prepared."

"Damn right you are, Boris. Seriously, how many are we expecting to the party?"

"We are expecting small groups, undercover, Kremlin henchman. We are not expecting an army. If Kaliningrad doors open, then that is a different matter, and we will have NATO troops crawling all over the Baltic. This is to protect us from the wolves, but remember a pack of wolves, although even small, is very, very dangerous indeed."

The four nodded at Big Boris in agreement.

Jimmy knew how to fire all the weapons on hand, and a small part of him hoped he'd have a chance to use them. The fight was the glory. The fight ignited a rush within that was unlike any other, even sex. He picked up one of the rocket-propelled grenade launchers. "Sweet," he said, his voice quiet and full of resolve.

"You got that right," Sean said.

"Okay, Boris, where do you want us?" asked Dusty.

"I am thinking here in the farmhouse, close to the control room. There are four firing points upstairs, and you will be alerted on the radio if there is any suspicious movement. Okay?"

"Yes, sir!"

Boris took them upstairs to the four firing points, Bavarian-style balconies off each of the four main bedrooms at each corner of the farmhouse, providing 360-degree coverage to the house. Each balcony had a bulletproof screen behind the balustrades and a Kevlar hood that would come down on the push of a button, leaving just a narrow target for would-be attackers to aim at. Boris pointed at the bulletproof vests at each of the firing points, and one by one, they picked up theirs and put them on under their jackets.

"Each firing point is ready for action, PKM GPMG loaded and ready. MRO-A, one up the pipe of each. Ready to go. Only deploy the hood if it's snowing or you really need to!"

Boris continued as they looked out of the bedroom four balcony, "In the control room, there are detonators that take out the bridge across the river, four in the courtyard to the front of the house, same at the back of the house. These are for in an emergency only, if there is a significant force in the immediate vicinity of compromising the farmhouse, okay?"

"Understood," Jimmy said.

They went back down the stairs to where the map was. Jimmy noted that two more people were present, a woman and a man.

Boris introduced them. "This is Hannah and Jonah. They are both Lithuanian nationals and are the owners of the farmhouse. If we have a low-level threat, such as a postman or a neighbor or the local police stopping by, they will know what to do and send them on their way. You four will stay scarce, but if you are spotted, you are simply guests and keen fishermen for the fruits of the lake—perch, pike, roach, bream. Okay?"

Jimmy couldn't help himself and reached out to shake hands with Hannah first, then Jonah. "Very nice to meet you," said Jimmy as he looked into Hannah's eyes and remembered Oxsana.

"Very nice to meet you," she returned.

"Jimmy," he reminded her.

"Hannah," she reminded him with a smile.

The other three followed, shaking Jonah's hand first.

Hannah went into the kitchen and came back with a pot of coffee and mugs. "It's going to be long day," she said with a smile.

They poured coffee, and then Boris escorted them to the control room, a secret room with the opening under the stairs and in a vault in the center of the house, with the living rooms, kitchen, downstairs bedrooms, living area, dining room, and library surrounding it. Carefully and expertly designed, it was unnoticeable that the secret room existed.

Inside, two of Boris's team were monitoring the wall of screens in front of them, tracking alerts, and on another wall, a huge digital map of the property showed the firing stations and, through heat mapping, the operatives on the ground guarding the property.

"Occasionally we will pick up on a beaver, wild horses, or deer, but it will certainly alert us if there is anything else unwanted within a mile radius," said one of the operatives.

Boris added, "We also have Shot Stopper technology that recognizes gunfire and immediately focuses the cameras to where the shot is fired."

"Overridable in an all-out attack," one of the operatives added with a grin.

There was enough room for them to sit in the control room, and as the T-minus clock on the wall went down to zero, that was where they stayed. On the other wall was a bank of monitors playing live news feeds from around the world. One was monitoring Twitter, and another with relevant Facebook feeds.

"The weapons of modern warfare," Dusty observed.

"The weapons to fight a fucking army," Jimmy added.

28
THE BLITZ

Multiple Locations Worldwide, November 2016, Day 25

VIKTORIA WAS UP BRIGHT AND early. It was Election Day in the United States. This would be her day. It would be Russia's day. She smiled as she made herself a cup of coffee. She had been busy. Since the suicide of Sir Richard Steele and the signing over of his executive powers, Viktoria and Nikita were now in control of the First World Bank and therefore Dmitri Dankov.

The first thing that she did was increase the size of the bet on the US presidential outcome to *all in*. This would be an unprecedented move and would catch the attention of the Kremlin more so than her already high profile within those walls. Viktoria wanted to come back from the dark side and enter mainstream once more. This big bet was her route into the Kremlin and her rise through the ranks to that coveted position, the first female president of the Russian Federation. That was her ambition; ironic that on her journey, she was thwarting the opportunity for another female with the same ambition to be the first female president of the United States.

She sat in her headquarters in Knightsbridge, London, the home of the wealthy Russian family to which she was the nanny. There were no children, no Russian family, just her. This was Viktoria's headquarters and her home. That had been her cover to the outside world, including her son, and tomorrow she would no longer have to live that life of pretense. Tomorrow she would have stamped her mark. She'd be welcomed to the Kremlin, and this would just become her London residence along with the others she had amassed in Paris, France, Vilnius, and of course, Moscow, Russia.

She had an early text from Dmitry to get on an important call. This was a big day, an important day. Getting on a call at five thirty in the morning was fine with her. It was her duty, her calling, her destiny. Today was her day.

She walked from the kitchen with her plate of varenyky, through the main living room adorned with gold and art, down the corridor of the Edwardian London home, steps away from her favorite shop, Harrods. Viktoria liked to shop. She liked the best, in the greatest Russian tradition. She was the best and deserved the best, and her home in Kensington showed that clearly.

She walked down the corridor past the Monet and the Picasso. Viktoria was a keen collector of Russian art and particularly liked the portraits and still lifes of Evgenia Antipova and Ivan Argunov's portraits of women. Each with museum-grade protective glass and soft lighting, these marked her journey to her study.

Viktoria's study was her own interpretation of the Amber Room in the Catherine Palace of Tsarskoye Selo just outside of Saint Petersburg. Her chamber was done in amber panels, gold leaf, and mirrors with an Edwards and Roberts late Victorian desk in the middle of the room. No papers and no need for pictures here. No filing cabinets, no evidence. Just a phone set on the top of the leather-inlaid kidney-shaped desk. She placed her varenyky and coffee on the desk and pulled out the ornate Chippendale chair and sat down. She looked over at the fireplace, surrounded by amber, and on the white marble mantel at the Louis XVI Ormolu clock with Lepine movement—5:29 a.m. Greenwich mean time, precisely.

She picked up the secure phone and dialed the secure number.

"Dobroye Utro, moi tovarishchi." She said good morning to the group.

She heard the familiar voices on the line. Dmitri Dankov and Bokov. She despised both for different reasons—Bokov because he was a dirty, horrible, despicable man, and Dmitri Dankov because he had stood in her way for so many years. By her estimation, she could have gotten to the Kremlin two years ago if it hadn't been for him. She had delivered, made good on her promises, and made him look good, but since her First World Bank genius, things had really started to take a turn, and she had been recognized for her efforts more— and Dmitri Dankov less and less. Although today she was officially Dmitri Dankov's number two, most knew that Viktoria was the real brains behind the operation, the thinker, the one who really knew and understood the art of maskirovka, how and when to apply it, the one who was delivering the most back to the homeland.

"My comrades," Dmitri Dankov started. "We have a problem." Viktoria's ears and attention immediately went to hyper, and she turned her focus to every sentence, every word, every symbol to come.

"I received a call from our contact in Moscow, and we are under attack. Since 5:00 a.m. MSK, our international network has experienced a debilitating volume of traffic slowing our infrastructure down to almost a standstill. In addition, we have uncovered a number of sleepers in our systems that have started eating us from the inside out. This is critical. This is potentially fatal. This is war."

"Can't we just shut down the systems?" asked Viktoria.

"No, we cannot, unfortunately. Some of the bugs will continue working even if we shut down."

"What about the backup network?" asked Bokov.

"No good either. We have considered that, and the same bugs have found their way into that, and as soon as we fire it up and bring it online, we bring the bugs to life."

Viktoria stared at the Louis XVI clock in front of her. She knew that she had a lot to lose. This was her day. She had gone all in. First World was off the dark grid that she had to ensure their systems, and their money was safe. Secondly, the bet she had placed on the presidential election would still go against the odds, but without the vital last twenty-four-hour push and influence of the network, then that was at risk also. Too late to reverse the bets. She must shut the bank systems down to the outside world immediately, at least to preserve the investments.

"What does this mean for our plans on the election?" Viktoria asked.

"The way it looks right now is that our plans are disabled. We hope that the groundwork we have already put down and the work we have done already is enough. I need you to temporarily disconnect all of our businesses from outside networks, immediately, until we see this through."

"Including the casinos?" asked Bokov.

"Yes, especially the casinos, Yuri. They are most vulnerable if they also have plans to place large bets whilst we are so weak."

"Understood," responded Bokov.

"Viktoria, I need you to do the same with your operations."

"Understood." She was two steps ahead of him, as usual.

"Okay, you know what you need to do. Get to it." The phone went dead.

Viktoria heard movement in the hallway outside.

Vilnius, Lithuania

Jimmy leaned forward and stared intently at the screen in front of him. He saw two vehicles coming into range and then slowing down on the main road, stopping. Another two vehicles arrived and stopped behind them.

Jimmy and Ken stood up. "What type of vehicles are they?" Ken asked.

"They look like four-wheel drive SUVs," responded the operative.

"What are they doing?" asked Sean.

"Could be a fishing party," responded Jimmy sarcastically.

"Yeah, fishing for what is the question," said Dusty.

The two rear vehicles moved around the first two and headed down the main road as the first two turned toward the farmhouse. The occupants of the control room stayed silent as they watched the movement of the two vehicles coming down the track. They heard over the radios the comments of Big Boris's team confirming the observation.

"Two fully loaded Toyota Land Cruisers heading down the lane. Confirmed. Vehicle one, driver plus three. Vehicle two, driver plus three."

The two Land Cruisers made it to the bridge, and that was the signal for Jimmy, Ken, Sean, and Dusty to head to their bedrooms. Jimmy took up his post, which was equipped with an audio and visual monitoring system that allowed him to see and hear what was going on elsewhere.

He saw the vehicles stop just before the bridge for a few moments, and then they slowly crossed the bridge and pulled up in front of the farmhouse. The front passenger of the first car got out, stepped on the ground, and looked around before he made his way slowly to the front door of the farmhouse.

He walked up the three stone steps to the wooden porch and big wooden door. As he tapped on the door, the door opened, and Hannah, with a big smile, said, "Laukiamas." She beamed. "Come in out of the cold. How can I help you? Come to catch some fish today?" she asked the big man who was looking around the farmhouse at the open fires, the coffee and pastries on the coffee table.

Jonah came from the kitchen and said, "Laukiamas."

"We were just passing by and thought that we would check this place out," said the big man in a heavy Russian accent. *From Moscow most likely*, thought Hannah.

"Do you have any room for tonight?" the big man asked.

"Not for tonight, I'm afraid, but we do have availability next week if that would work?" Hannah said.

"Are you fully booked?"

"Yes, we have a fishing party in this week," Hannah said.

"Where are they?" asked the big man.

"They went out about an hour ago to the lakes. As you know, we have plenty of good fish here. They wanted to get an early start."

"On foot?" he asked.

"No, they took their car," Jonah said, coming up next to Hannah. "Besides, what business is it of yours?"

"I suppose you're right," the big man said. "We will be going now. Sorry to have bothered you."

"That's fine," Hannah said. "Let us know if you would like to stay next week."

"We'll do that," the big man said and turned and left.

Jimmy hurried downstairs. "That was Dmitri Dankov's bodyguard, Vladimir Vasiliev."

"Yes, we know him well," Jonah said.

"They will be back," said Hannah, stating the obvious.

Jimmy could hear the reverse progress of the two Land Cruisers to the main road through his earpiece. They headed into the control room and saw them at the main road, stopped. The other two vehicles returned.

Big Boris came through the front door. "Okay. I think this is it. They are getting ready to return, hopefully just the four of them and not more."

"What's the plan, Boris?" asked Jimmy.

"We wait for them to make their move, and if they do, then we take them out."

"Look, Boris, we know they're up to no good," Jimmy said. "We know that they're the bad guys, and we also know they're ruthless and would have all our heads on spikes if they had half the chance. The fact is if they come back down that track, they're not coming to book a family fishing trip next week, tickle some trout, or dance around the maypole. They will be coming for one thing and that will be to take this facility out, and all of us with it."

Boris looked at Jimmy, emotionless. "We don't want to give them the excuse to invade my country again. I don't want to be the one who makes that call. I remember the last time."

"If they are going to invade, they will do so regardless, Boris. This facility and the wider network, the work that they are doing now below, will over the next few hours put Putin back in his box, and tomorrow the Man at the Kremlin will not be allowed to get away with any of his antics anymore, including invading your country or anybody else's," stated Dusty.

"You asked us here for a reason. And that reason is to protect this facility and the work that is going on down below. When they return, we need to take them out and take them out decisively," said Kiwi Ken.

"This is it, Boris. The time for messing about on the periphery and playing games is done. We need to take them out. At the end of the day, we have enough munitions to take on a small army, and we have the firepower and the manpower to take them out," added Sean.

Big Boris looked at the four and nodded slowly. "Yes, you are right, of course. Let's do this."

Jimmy rushed to his post. He watched the four vehicles move in slowly down the road. They reached the bridge but then stopped. The distinct sound of choppers filled the early-morning air. Suddenly, two Mil-Mi 24, Russian-made attack helicopters rose above the trees. The two Land Cruisers, seemingly upon confirmation of the sighting, accelerated.

"Let's hope they're not the advance party from Kaliningrad," Dusty said over the coms.

Jimmy estimated the enemy strength at roughly forty. His team numbered about thirty. The odds were in favor of the enemy but not by all that much. "Take those birds out!" Jimmy cried. "Take them out now!"

Jimmy armed the rocket, lifted the launcher, and fired. A second later, the rocket blasted through the windscreen just as the pilot unleashed his weapons on the farmhouse. The chopper's missiles went wide, skirting just above the roof.

"Fucking hell, that was close!" Ken shouted to Jimmy.

On the other side, in bedroom balcony two, Sean was focusing the fire of the PKM GPMG on the four SUVs as the occupants tried to get clear and to the farmhouse. Sean had a second or two on Kiwi Ken and blasted the second Mil-Mi 24 out of the sky before anyone got a chance to exit, the ball of flames engulfing the SUVs below.

Vladimir Vasiliev and two of his team made it into the farmhouse as Boris detonated the charge in the courtyard that took out one of the Land Cruisers, tossing it in the air like a children's toy and taking out another two of the invaders. Jimmy heard firing in the house and stepped out of bedroom four toward bedroom three. Two of Dmitri Dankov's men came out of bedroom three. Jimmy used his Browning 9 mm as if it were an extension of his body, knowing where every round was going. One-two-*pop-pop*, both men down. A 9 mm each through their foreheads, just above the eyebrows.

As he rushed in, he saw the bodies of Ken and Dusty and looked up as Vasiliev was on the balcony. Jimmy turned. "Hey, Vladimir, how are you doing today, my friend?" One-two-*pop-pop*. The big Vladimir fell backward over the balcony. He tried to hang on, but Jimmy ran over, looked down, and aimed. "Bang, bang, you're dead, my son."

Jimmy quickly assessed the scene outside. All done. Wheels still spinning, fire from the helicopters and the aviation fuel still burning, the wreak of burned flesh. He turned to the bodies of Ken and Dusty, bullets to the brain. "Poor bastards." His adrenaline was on supercharge, and there wasn't time for grief yet.

Through the earpiece:

"Sector 1?"

"All clear."

"Sector 2?"

"Clear."

"Control room?"

"Clear. All good."

"Sector 3?"

Silence.

"Bridge?"

"Clear."

Jimmy ran down the stairs into the farmhouse, which was relatively unscathed, fire still burning, coffeepot on the table, Hannah on the floor, hole in the top of her head, brain exposed, crimson pool of blood growing around her like spilled ink. Into the kitchen, Jonah on the floor, still holding his Kalashnikov, riddled with bullets, having taken the double barrels from two of the intruders.

Boris walked in. "You okay?"

"Yeah," Jimmy said. "But we lost Hannah, Jonah, Dusty, and Ken."

"Three of my team are down too," Boris said.

"How's it going downstairs?" Jimmy asked.

"Good by all accounts. They're blasting them."

"Do they know we had visitors?"

"Yes, sir! They are monitoring the military channels, and all seems quiet in Kaliningrad."

"Thank fuck for that. At least for now," Jimmy said, but he knew the storm probably hadn't passed. They were just in a lull. He and Boris saw to it that all the firing points were reloaded, re-cocked, and ready to go.

Jimmy and Sean made their way to the control room, close to the monitors for any early warning signs of anything amiss. Jimmy drifted away, deep in thought.

Jimmy had learned his trade from Keith and Big Mac back in Hereford. They were both veterans of the Iranian Embassy Siege and Regiment heroes. Big Mac ran selection, and Keith was the small arms weapons instructor for undercover operations. A trip to the Killing House was a regular part of their training and ongoing professional development.

The Killing House was a mocked-up house mostly with dummy hostages and targets but occasionally with live hostages and dummy targets to make it more real. Jimmy had often wondered why anyone would volunteer to be a dummy hostage in a live firing situation, and although he never knew of anyone killed, one dummy did get shot through the shoulder and lived to tell the tale. He recalled another on an airplane siege reenactment getting a broken arm as she was manhandled in the height of the situation, the Regiment guys not knowing if she was a hostage or terrorist—*treat them both the same until you are certain.*

He thought about big Kiwi Ken and Dusty who he, Ryan, and Mitch had all played rugby with, getting to the Army Cup Semifinal against 3 Para. He thought about his colleagues, his friends, his brothers, and the incredibly stoic way in which they had become used to loss.

Special Air Service personnel were seldom lost in action, but, as Jimmy knew well, it did happen. The dead would always be remembered, like all those Pilgrims in the past. They would be revered and enshrined in the Regiment history forever. Forever proud.

"You okay?" Sean asked.

"Been better, mate," Jimmy said, rousing himself from his thoughts.

"It's always hard losing a brother, but I always told the big bastard to pay more attention!" he said with a level of dark sarcasm only known to people like this.

"Yeah, did you get his litas to spend in Vilnius tonight?" Jimmy cracked a smile.

"I just hope the Ruskies don't decide to send an army from Kaliningrad," Sean said.

"No shit, but these guys weren't military; they were Russian Mafia," said Jimmy. "Courtesy of Dmitri Dankov."

"We should pay him a visit when we get back to Vilnius tonight."

"We will, my friend, we certainly will, especially now he just lost half a mini army here today," Jimmy said, thinking that Dmitri Dankov's shit had to stop, and he'd be just the guy to make that happen.

One of the monitors cracked into a shot of Sven below.

"Good afternoon, gentlemen. I am sorry to hear the sad news of our losses, and I would like to thank you for your protection, but it is over."

"What do you mean it's over?" Jimmy asked.

Sven laughed and clapped his hands once. "Yes, we blitzed the dark army from 4:00 a.m. EET this morning and activated every bug and virus that we have planted in their system. We ramped up the volume so that they couldn't cope, froze email, social media, even bank accounts. We isolated their casino network and sources of cash, including many of their oil refineries, distribution networks, even Aeroflot. We have in effect crippled, although temporarily, the Russian Federation and all its dark tentacles."

"Wow!" Jimmy said. "Brilliant!"

"In a call from Putin to the president of the United States, twenty minutes ago, the Man at the Kremlin agreed, without admitting any accountability of course, to crack down on any Russian groups meddling with foreign interests immediately, on the understanding that we leave his national infrastructure alone."

"What? Putin surrendered?" asked Sean.

Sven smiled. "No, not quite as simple as that, I am afraid. It's basically an agreement that he will not meddle any further with the presidential election, and that is at least good for now. Today, we have taken great strides in crippling the dark army's capability and probably most importantly their element of surprise and covert existence. We have broken them, at least for now. But they will come back in a different form, a different format, another time. But for now, our work is done. Thank you, gentlemen."

Dmitri Dankov was in his control center deep in the Olympic Casino on Konstitucijos, Vilnius, the capital of Lithuania, watching the terrors of the attack on his empire as the blitz took its toll.

He had been in constant contact with Vladimir in his search for the source of the blitz until he lost contact near a farmhouse just outside of the city. He had tried to get a hold of Viktoria Saparov, no response, and his other COO, Bokov, had gone missing in Schiphol Airport on his way through Amsterdam back to Bangkok, presumably taken by Interpol, the CIA, the British Secret Service, or all the above.

At noon EET, he made the decision to suspend casino operations across the globe to protect the cash in the system and, most importantly, to avoid the hackers making big bets on corrupt systems and in effect bankrupting his operations.

He made a call to the man in Moscow. The man behind the desk let him know his decision. "I will see you in the morning, Dmitry," said the man behind the desk.

Dmitri Dankov was vulnerable. He headed to Vilnius airport and boarded his private jet to Moscow.

Dmitri Dankov figured that as a loyal and successful subject of the motherland, he would be safe there, despite the disastrous day he just had. Dmitri Dankov would be back. At least for a time. His history would one day catch up to him. That was inevitable. It was just a question of when and who.

Jimmy was pumped. He wanted to purge the adrenaline from his system. He recognized the urge, knew it came from the residue of battle, the dance between life and death. That sort of thing had always made an impression on him, as it did on most combat soldiers. He grabbed Sean and said he wanted to blow off steam.

"Suits me, mate," Sean said.

They piled into the Land Cruiser and headed into Vilnius. On the way, Jimmy said, "Let's drop by to see if we can snag Dmitri Dankov. That scum went too far this time."

Jimmy cranked up the music and drove like hell.

They pulled up outside of the Olympic Casino and valet parked. They would not be needing the vehicle again. They trotted up the stairs, Browning 9 mms in tow, and got to the top. Empty. No Dmitri Dankov, no gamblers, no gambling. Just a handful of ladies of the night trying to earn their living, scratching their heads, trying to work out what was going on.

Jimmy and Sean headed to the bar in need of a drink and ordered two beers. They asked for Dmitri Dankov—he wasn't there. Asked for big Vladimir—not there, although they knew that already.

It prompted one of Vladimir's former second-string guys, who wasn't trusted enough to go to the farmhouse, to ask the two, "What do you want?" Jimmy started the punch from his waist, moving upward, gathering momentum as he connected with the chin of the Russian, launching him. He was unconscious before he hit the floor. *Sparko.*

"That's for Ken and Dusty, you fucking prick. Come on, Sean. It's time to leave."

They walked out as quickly as they entered and stepped into the Vilnius night.

They headed to the main square and stopped in the Rotuses Aikste for a couple big steins of Svyturys and a couple shots of Jägermeister. They sat on the big wooden bench and ordered some beer snacks.

"What the fuck, Jimmy? I have had enough of this. Next time it might be us. We only have nine lives, you know."

"I think you'll find that it's a cat that has nine lives." Jimmy tried to crack a smile. They both laughed. Jimmy was tired of it too. He was already tired of it when he left the Regiment five years ago. That's why he left. Found his Oasis in Bangkok, Jenni, his life of fun and debauchery. He was ready to hang up his boots. This time for good.

"Here's to Kiwi Ken and Dusty." They crashed their steins together and drank.

They sat and talked. Two old friends. Jimmy told Sean about the Oasis, his wife, Jenni, his life. He was proud and happy. He wanted to get back to it and leave this life forever. Sean updated him with the latest on friends and brothers back in Hereford. They speculated who would replace Sam when he retired, whether he would survive retirement, how he would cope. They talked about Ryan, Mac, Mitch, and Bob. About Jimmy's son, William.

"How is Bob the bastard?" inquired Sean.

"Good. Latest episode was him Shanghaing a bunch of corrupt Africans in Malabo and sending them to Old Blighty courtesy of Her Majesty's Royal Navy, having made them pay $150 million into Bob's firm's bank account!"

"Bob, the old bastard! Never changes," Sean said.

The snacks arrived, and so do did two more Svyturys and a couple more shots of Jägermeister. "Cheers!" They clashed steins again and ate in silence.

"Let's have a couple of beers here, then head to the club," suggested Jimmy.

"Sure. Sounds good."

"Fancy a Ronson?" asked Jimmy.

"A ronson?" asked Sean.

"A Ronson lighter," confirmed Jimmy.

Sean looked doubly confused. "What?"

"An all-nighter!" Jimmy laughed, and they splashed beers again.

"You silly bugger, Jimmy. We miss you."

"Yeah, like a fucking hole in the head!"

They headed to Club Eden as much to rile Dmitri Dankov as for the Lithuanian beauties plying their trade. Jimmy and Sean settled down in a private booth with bottle of champagne and a bag of cash they had lifted off the dead guys from Dmitri Dankov's team. They enjoyed the attention of the girls. Champagne turned into a bottle of Casamigos Reposado tequila, a bottle of Stolichnaya Red Label and Red Bull—tequila, vodka, Red Bull, or TVRs. Jimmy lined up the cocaine on the glass table in front of them and took a snort.

Jimmy spent several more hours partying but eventually suggested that they finish up and head out. Jimmy looked over at the entrance and saw a cast of shadowy figures congregated. These were neither dancers nor customers; he could tell by their size, posture, and stance. He realized something was wrong and automatically switched into alert mode, 9 mm to the ready.

"Come on. Let's make like shepherds. Let's get the flock out of here," Jimmy said. "I think we got trouble, and I don't want any right now."

As they left the booth, trusty Brownings in their right hands, down by their thighs in the usual position, to avoid obvious attention that they were drawn, they stepped down from their booth on to the dance floor. The last of the girls had disappeared into the back, and the big bouncer from the Olympic Casino was there, Kalashnikov in hand, black eye from Jimmy's earlier altercation. He raised the Kalashnikov, and Jimmy fired a double tap and sent him to the floor, dead before he landed. Another three came from the back and two from the front.

Jimmy felt bullets pass close to his head as he returned fire. Bullets tore into the floor, the walls, the ceiling.

"Fuck!" he shouted, jamming his extra mag into the grip.

"Oh shit!" Sean screamed, taking the last man down. "Let's get the fuck out of here!"

Jimmy tried to run but found he couldn't move. Searing pain ripped through his chest. He looked down and saw blood. Lots of blood. He'd heard that adrenaline and battle lust can momentarily mask the pain of getting shot, and now he knew it was true. But the pain was coming on faster and faster.

"Sean! I've been hit! I'm hit!" he said, feeling dizzy and weak in the knees. He felt Sean's strong arms around him as they rushed to the door.

A black Range Rover pulled up to the curb.

"Get in, boys, and make it quick."

Jimmy recognized Mitch's voice and felt vaguely comforted by the presence of his old friend, his leader.

"Jimmy's been hit!" Sean cried, flinging the rear door open. "Come on, mate! Let's get you inside," he said to Jimmy.

Two more men rushed out of the club, guns blazing. Mitch returned fire. Bullets sparked off the doors and took out the rear window. Sean pushed Jimmy into the back seat and got in himself. The rough action brought on another wave of dizziness, then more pain.

"Shit," Jimmy said. His voice sounded far away, as if he had water in his ears.

Mitch hit the gas. "What the hell happened?" Mitch said.

"Dmitri Dankov's boys," Sean said. "What the hell are you doing here anyway?"

"I heard about the firefight. Wanted to be in on the extraction. Figured Dmitri Dankov might have some nasty plans for you guys."

"He did," Sean said.

As Jimmy listened, he faded in and out of consciousness. He struggled to stay calm, to fight the pain, hoping he might see Jenni again.

"I was sorry about the two KIA. Dusty and Ken were good men," Mitch said.

"They were. They fought bravely."

"Word has it that Dmitri Dankov was spotted in Moscow," Mitch said.

"Good riddance," Sean said. "Maybe his bosses'll take him out for us."

"Don't bet on it. How's Jimmy looking?" Mitch asked.

"Like shit," Sean said.

"Jimmy! You hang on! We got help on the plane!" Mitch said. "You just got to hold on."

"Fuck! It fuckin' hurts," Jimmy said.

Sean grabbed the first aid kit from under the passenger seat and then some dressings. Leaning over into the back seat, he tried to assess the extent of the damage and stem the flow of blood. "Hold on, mate! Just hold on!"

Everything went black.

Mitch pulled the Range Rover into the private terminal, barely slowing down as he passed the gate after the guard waved him through. He sped up to the Royal Airforce Airbus A330 and hit the brakes, the tires squealing as the car stopped. Two of the aircrew came running up.

"We got a casualty!" Mitch yelled. "We need a medic. Stat!"

Mitch got out of the car and helped Sean get Jimmy onto the stretcher the flight crew brought from the plane.

"Looks pretty bad," Mitch said as the medic wheeled Jimmy away.

Sean nodded. "We got into a real ballroom blitz back there. Took out four, maybe five of the bad guys."

"Good," Mitch said.

He let Sean climb the stairs to the jet first, then followed. Jimmy was already aboard and in the medical room on the plane.

Too much bloodshed. Too much death, Mitch thought as he pictured Dusty and Ken zipped up in black body bags in the hold. They would be packed in ice until they arrived back at base, and then they'd be readied for their families. Sighing, Mitch buckled up. The plane took off.

As soon as they were airborne and steady, Mitch unbuckled his belt and jumped up to go and see Jimmy at the back of the plane. As he got there, the medics were working hard with bandages to stop the bleeding, an intravenous drip full of a concoction to keep him alive, and a defibrillator. The ECG monitor was crazy and sporadic, making a loud, piercing insertion into the peaceful hum of the Airbus engines.

"Mitch," Jimmy called over. "Tell Jenni I love her."

"Fuck off, Jimmy. You can tell her yourself when you see her next," Mitch said, feeling a sense of panic. His instincts told him his friend had only moments to live. He'd been in that place before, crouching over a fallen comrade as battle raged all around him. It was strange how the gunfire, the screaming, and the crying all seemed to diminish in volume. Time slowed. Such moments were surreal and as fleeting as the blink of an eye.

Jimmy coughed. A trickle of blood seeped out of the left side of his mouth. Mitch wiped it clean with a spare piece of gauze on the table beside him.

"Tell William I love him too, okay?"

Mitch looked at Jimmy in the eyes. "Come on, mate. Tonight doesn't need to be your last."

"I think you might be wrong for once in your fucking life," Jimmy said, struggling to force a grin.

At that, the ECG monitor cranked into flat-line mode, and the medics cranked into emergency mode, placing the defibrillator on Jimmy's chest and letting him have it. Mitch watched the scene as the defib took the three or four seconds to regain its power and blasted Jimmy's chest again. And again, again, and again. After fifteen minutes, the Royal Airforce doctor declared Jimmy Jenkins dead. Brown Bread. Brown bread … dead.

Mitch felt numb. With Sean at his side, both men retreated back to their seats without saying a word to each other. There was no need. Everything had been said before.

29
GRUESOME DISCOVERIES

London, United Kingdom, November 2016, Day 26

LORD BEECHAM RELAXED IN HIS comfortable chair in the conference room, deep within the National Center for Cyber Security. It had been an interesting day or so. Indeed, the past several weeks had been rather spectacular in their ability to keep him and Colonel Collins on their toes, not to mention the SAS team led by Mitch and Mac.

Lord Beecham looked over at Charlie Martin to see if the gentleman was ready to update them on the situation. The election wasn't finished in the United States, though clearly it had been influenced. The dark arm was silent for now, but Lord Beecham knew the situation amounted to nothing more than a tactical withdrawal.

Live to fight another day, he thought and tapped the table with his pen.

"Quite a show so far," he said to Colonel Collins.

Colonel Collins nodded. "Indeed," he said. "A bit too much excitement for these old bones, I'm afraid. I can't wait to get back to Antigua."

"Me too," Lord Beecham said. "I know exactly how you feel. But we've done some good work here. Everyone has."

The sea of hackers, cyber engineers, analysts, and monitors

had been up all night, and with activity peaking around midnight coordinated with the various operations in Australia, Tel Aviv, Hong Kong, New York, and Lithuania, the activities had slowed down to a hum.

The coordinated international collaboration had paid off, and within just a couple of hours, the bugs that they had planted, the viruses they had weaved, and the volume of noise they had created through massive communications and noise overwhelmed the cyber weapons of the dark army and brought them to almost silence.

Charlie brought the meeting to order. "At around 1:00 a.m. GMT, it appears that an order to halt operations went out, and the dark army went dark. Very likely the high command in the Russian military realized they might be exposed to the world for what they did. The move was also to protect assets."

"Still," James said, "the damage was done even though we were able to silence the enemy hackers. For now. The results of the US presidential election, no matter what they are, will forever be in dispute. That, my friends, is a victory for Putin."

"There are dark forces in the world today that no longer use the traditional tools of war, that no longer use tanks, fighter planes, bombers, and ships. They are using something much more potent, powerful, and difficult to identify, target, and neutralize. This is the age of maskirovka. This is the age of manipulation. This is no longer about battles in the air, on the sea and the land; this is about protecting the targets of our financial systems, international trade routes, our democracy itself. And that is why I thank each one of you today for what you have done in neutralizing this threat we faced and defeated."

Charlie continued, "No matter the outcome of this election, we have thwarted their efforts, damaged their capabilities, and gotten steps closer to being able to identify the perpetrators with confidence and conviction. They do, however, live to fight another day, and as elections in France, Spain, Germany, and elsewhere around the world are under threat, the work of the national and international cyber security organizations around the world and the collaboration of the groups we have here today are critical. It is fundamental that we preserve our right to freedom and democracy and the values that we stand for—for our nations, our people, and our freedom.

"Thank you for all that you have done and continue to do in the name of freedom."

A round of applause and cheers reverberated around the room and on the satellite links around the world as Charlie wrapped up his speech.

As people got up to return to their posts or to depart the building, Lord Beecham strode up to Charlie and shook his hand. "Jolly good show, old man," he said. "We kicked Putin and his slimy friends in the balls, but we both know this isn't over. Not by a long shot."

Lord Beecham could see that Charlie was tired. He, like Charlie, knew full well that the layers and layers of deceit made it impossible to make the proven connections all the way to Moscow. The Colombians, the Irish, and the Russians could all be blamed as scapegoats in their own right, with their own motives, whether crime, control, greed, or just for the sheer sake of disruption. They weren't interested in any political gain; they were interested in the proceeds from their crimes and therefore were a perfect scapegoat for any politically motivated masters to blame their criminal partners in the shadows. Perfect—getting others to do the dirty work, but not just any others, those that would be naturally assumed to be at their worst.

Rather than using direct government forces, use those with interlinked interests that would be easy to blame and easy for the people to believe they were bad enough in the first instance to carry that blame. That is why the Rastrojos, the IRA, and the Russian Mafia were perfect partners. A bit like the CIA had done for many years.

The mood in the briefing room was certainly bittersweet that morning. Lord Beecham said, "Everyone, I would like to invite you all to my club, the Union Club on Greek Street, this afternoon for drinks and supper before we all part ways tomorrow—3:00 p.m. till whatever time we finish. I know you have planes to catch and loved ones to return home to. I hope you can make it."

Nikita didn't sleep at all the night that Viktoria made it official and took control of the First World Bank, making him CEO and chairman. He knew it was all a sham, a farce, a con job. He'd no more run operations than a chimp or a puppet with his mother and her shady Russian colleagues pulling all the strings. He got up out of bed and wandered into the kitchen. He took a tall glass from the cabinet over the microwave and got some ice water from the high-end refrigerator. The water tasted clean, cool, pure, unlike him. He felt dirty. He also felt indirectly responsible for the suicide, if it really was suicide, of Sir Richard Steele. Even if it was suicide, he knew his mother had something to do with it. Everything to do with it, in fact.

He glanced at his watch. Almost six thirty. Time for his call. He wondered if it still mattered, if he'd continue to receive those calls. Calls that had changed his life for the better and now seemed to have ruined it. The calls were no longer about suggesting courses of action or advice that led to his own decision making but had turned into instructions. The outcomes he had miraculously predicted were more than just wild guesses. These weren't just *if* bets; they were *when* investments. They were conclusions, done deals, certain wagers; the facts and outcomes had somehow been manipulated.

He looked down at his watch to see that it was 6:35 a.m. The only occasions that he could remember the call being late was due to being on a flight. He was not aware of any travel plans. He waited, relieved with the additional time to work out what to say.

Nikita wasn't ready to be the CEO of First World Bank. He sat there in the kitchen of 1B, staring at the bottle of Stolichnaya, feeling like a fraud, worthless, used, and abused.

Used, manipulated, and abused not by anyone but by his own mother. Who did she really work for? He knew she wasn't some nanny to a rich Russian family—that was for sure. Or was she telling the truth in her own twisted way? Was that rich Russian family the motherland itself?

As each five-minute increment passed, Nikita got more anxious. This was a big day for him, his mother, First World Bank, the presidency of the United States, and who knows who else. *Where the hell is she?'*

He decided to call her—not usually allowed unless in an extreme emergency, but given the weight of the moment, Nikita was compelled to do so. He punched in the number and waited the few moments for it to connect to its network and route through the encrypted network to eventually engage. The phone rang, rang, rang, and then ended. No message, no opportunity to leave any compromising messages.

Nikita tried her three more times over the next forty-five-minutes and decided he would head down to the rich Russian family's house in Knightsbridge, 5 Eaton Square, Belgravia.

He jumped in a black cab and set off on the thirteen-mile journey to Belgravia at the other side of London. His mind was made up that he would resign from First World that day. He was determined this time. This time he would not bow to his mother's pressure, no matter what. He would go and stay with Bella in California. He would head down to Chile to find Angus. He would lose himself in Central America, the Caribbean. Maybe head down to Australia.

He certainly had enough money. Some of it he'd stashed in offshore accounts. If he wanted to, he could retire and never work another day in his life. None of that financial security mattered to him at the moment, but he kept the money in the back of his mind, like a comfort blanket. He didn't know where he was heading, but what he did know was that he could no longer continue with the lies, the dishonesty, the deceit.

Thirty-five minutes later, the black cab pulled up outside 5 Eaton Square, an impressive seven-bedroom town house in one of the most prestigious neighborhoods of London, close to St. Peters, Harrods, Chelsea, Sloane Square, and many international embassies.

As Nikita hopped out of the cab, he spotted one of the Mercedes S65s sitting out front, the driver slouched as if he were sleeping. Nikita knew immediately that there was something wrong; despite the relatively early hour, his mother's personal guard never slept on the job.

He walked through the iron gate to find the back door open, slightly ajar. He walked right in—eyes open, ears open, adrenaline rushing through his veins. He instinctively headed for the amber room. This was only the third time he had even been to the property, but he recalled this was where she did most of her organizing.

The house was deathly silent apart from the ticking of the Louis XIV clock on the mantelpiece. His mother sat there at her desk, in her own amber room, a pool of thick crimson blood spilling onto the floor. Her face was pale, and her eyes were just bloody puddles where her assassin had gouged her eyeballs. Her throat was cut from ear to ear. The symbolism was not lost on Nikita—the mark of an assassination of a traitor.

"Nikita? Nikita? What the fuck have you done?"

Nikita froze. For a moment, he couldn't move or speak. He couldn't believe what he was hearing … who he was hearing.

"Tell me you didn't do this, son."

Nikita turned slowly around and stared at Angus Mackay, or Mac, as his stepfather liked to be called. Nikita said not a word. He looked at Angus and embraced him, sobbing like a child, lost in the depth of deceit that he had fallen into.

"Angus, Angus, Angus, I don't know what I have done," Nikita sobbed. "I know that it's my fault. All this mess. I should never have gone along with it. Never."

Mac gently pushed him away, looked him straight in the eye, and said, "Get yourself a cab and get home. Hang tight, and I will be there later. Got it?"

Nikita pulled himself together, swallowed hard, and nodded. "I didn't do this," he whispered.

"I know," Mac said. "You may have had reason to, but I know you better than that. You're no murderer. Come on, it's time you got the hell out of here."

Once Mac got his stepson on the way home, he returned to the town house, giving the four dead guys in the Mercedes a sidelong glance.

"I'll have to do something about you too, I suppose," he mumbled.

When he got inside the foyer, he closed the door and locked it. He called Mitch from his burner phone.

"Yeah," Mitch said.

"Mac. We got a problem."

"It's early, Mac," Mitch said. "I just got in from Lithuania. I have terrible news."

Mac began to pace. Mitch did not sound good. Not good at all. "Let's have it."

"Jimmy's dead."

"Dead? How?"

"Dmitri Dankov."

"That fucker is going down if it's the last thing I do."

"I know you already heard about Dusty and Ken," Mitch said. "I figured you didn't get the message I left about Jimmy."

"No. Been kinda busy, mate." Mac sighed, shook his head, and kept pacing. "Poor Jimmy. Fuckin' crazy old sod."

"So, what's up, Mac? Why you calling?"

"Uh, I don't want to say much on the phone, but do you know a good cleaning lady?"

Silence.

"Well … yes. I do. But I'll need to call Sam for an additional recommendation."

"You do that, mate, and hurry."

Mitch asked Mac for the address. "I'll send someone over right away."

Mac thanked him and ended the call. He then proceeded to take a closer look at the house. He'd learned of Viktoria's whereabouts from deep contacts at MI5, the domestic branch of British intelligence. From time to time, he received updates. With developments at First World Bank that involved Nikita, he wanted to confront her directly. He'd had enough of the behind the scenes, enough of playing the proverbial ostrich with its head buried in the sand.

As Mac explored, he could see the fruits of her labor all around him. She lived in incredible luxury, and he knew she'd climbed to such wealth through evildoing, mainly as Dmitri Dankov's second in command. He noticed a large travel chest, and his mind clicked, as though a lightbulb had just been turned on. He figured that he could fill the chest up with some of the prized possessions, which in turn could be used to support the widows left behind—Paul's wife, Betsy, and the family of Brad, the man from the CIA. Rusty and Kiwi Ken, who were lost in Lithuania. Jimmy. Poor old Jimmy.

As Mac was carefully but quickly making his selections, packing them into the travel chest, he spotted the Picasso and added it to his bounty. Mac would ask Lord Beecham to help him set up a trust fund for all those lost. Lord Beecham would know how to do that.

As his marriage was never finally annulled to Viktoria—she had never granted decree absolute—the property was technically his, as her husband. Mac had managed to get married to Carmen on a local license in Chile that didn't include an international check on former or existing marriages.

A short time later, Sam and Mitch showed up with the cleaners. Mac explained the situation, that he believed Dmitri Dankov had had Viktoria killed because of the attack on the dark army. "He probably thinks she had something to do with it," Mac said. "And who knows? Maybe she did."

"Or maybe the Rastrojas?" Sam added with more than a hint of insider knowledge.

Then Mac explained about the house and property, saying he probably had a legitimate claim on all of it.

"Sam, let's get this place cleaned up, lay some surveillance, and mothball it. See what happens," Mac suggested, having explained the situation and his potentially legitimate claim to keep the property.

"Why not?" Sam said. "It's better than handing it in, and some bigwig diplomat gets to live there free of charge courtesy of Her Majesty."

Sam didn't need to know about the ownership angle; Sam just needed to get rid of the mess. He knew how to do it. He had specialists. Then they would lay some bugs, sensors, and cameras and monitor it for a few months or couple of years, and if it was clean, then Mac would assume his rightful ownership. "This place must be worth a few million," he said to himself with a smile. "Why not? Fuck the proceeds of crime unit. They can go fucking whistle." He laughed.

Within ninety minutes, the cleaners were gone. No trace of the

Mercedes or its occupants—the driver and the three bodies in the trunk. Viktoria's body had been removed in a body bag, the amber room cleaned with no trace. While the cleanup team was working its magic, the tech team laid their listening devices throughout the house, along with cameras and sensors.

"Don't forget to keep the keys, Mac." Sam winked with a smile.

"Damn right." Mac patted Sam on the shoulder.

Within ten minutes, Mac was back on his way to Bromley to check up on Nikita. *Poor bastard.* Mac thought about the young boy he had met all those years ago. He had taken him under his wing, taught him English, or at least Mac's interpretation of the language, and talked to him about the world, his travels, and his adventures. He taught him how to hunt and fish and the ancient techniques that had been passed down to Mac from his ancestors.

Mac loved Nikita like the son he never had. It was unfortunate how they had drifted apart—Nikita in London, Mac's struggles with Viktoria, and now Mac living in Chile on the other side of the world. But they had managed to stay in touch, with Nikita getting more distant every time. *Must have been all the shit he was involved in here,* Mac thought as he headed out to apartment 1B, Bromley High Street.

After receiving the news about Nikita from her father, Bella made her excuses and let the cyber unit mop up operations while she headed straight to her friend's apartment on Bromley High Street. On her way, she tried to imagine what it would be like to find your mother brutally murdered. She couldn't. Her heart broke for Nikita. Even though he disliked Viktoria, she was still his mother. Couple her death with all the other pressures, and she figured Nikita was probably about to break down completely.

Bella parked in a spot near the apartment and hurried to the front door. She pressed the button for the intercom. "Nikita? Are you home? Nikita? Are you there?"

Just then, one of the other tenants came through the front door, a smart-looking man dressed for the office.

"Oh, hello," he said. "Can I help you?"

"I was trying to reach Nikita. Nikita Saparov. He lives in 1B."

"Haven't seen him today. Uh, or heard him. I usually hear him leave at the crack of dawn. Who are you?"

"I'm his girlfriend."

Bella didn't know why she said that, except that it sounded right. The man looked at her intently and then smiled. "Well, Mr. Saparov certainly has good taste. Go on in. I'm sure it'll be okay."

"Thanks," Bella said.

The man nodded and then went on his way. She hurried to the door of 1B. She knocked. No answer. She knew he left a key hidden under a plant near the hallway window. Not the most brilliant place to hide a key, but Nikita, for all his intelligence, was something of a blunderer when it came to misplacing things like keys. She went to the plant, found the key, and let herself inside the apartment. Her dad had said Mac sent him home, so she was worried that he didn't answer the intercom or the door.

As she walked into the master bedroom, she saw Nikita hanging from the chandelier, a makeshift noose made from two of his Hugo Boss belts coupled together and tied around the reinforced stem of the chandelier. Bella ran over. His body was still twitching, still warm as she grabbed his legs and lifted him up to ease the weight and the pressure on Nikita's neck. After a few moments, she was in the awful dilemma. *Do I relieve the weight, or do I get him down?* There was no way to get him down without letting his body go and releasing the belt. How long would it take her to do so? She had no idea. Could she alone lift the weight of his muscular frame and release the belt buckle at the same time? She released, sobbing, frustrated, unable to help and know what the best thing to do was. She opted for releasing the belt. She let go of his legs, jumped on the chair that Nikita himself had used what must have been only a few moments before, and struggled with the belt. She struggled with the weight and the pressure and in a huge surge of adrenaline managed to unbuckle the belt with Nikita's body dropping to the ground. A thud. No bounce, no reaction, nothing.

She managed to stay her balance on the chair and stepped down quickly, turned Nikita onto his back, and went to check his vital signs.

No breathing. No pulse. But still warm. She started immediately with the CPR, fifteen pumps to the chest followed by two breaths of air into the lungs.

She tried to keep the blood and oxygen flowing sufficiently so that he would either resuscitate or avoid brain damage or death long enough until help arrived. Between the breaths and the thirty pumps, Bella managed to call Mitch and let him know. "Mac is on his way over," Mitch said. "I'll be there as soon as I can get there."

As Mac rushed in ten minutes later, Bella was sobbing uncontrollably as she continued to pump Nikita's chest and breathe, her tears dripping onto Nikita's now purple face. "What time did you find him?" asked Mac.

"Fifteen, maybe twenty minutes ago."

Mac knelt and checked his vital signs. "Bella, it's no use. Nikita is dead."

Bella slowly withdrew, looking down at Nikita, knowing that she would never see him again in life. In that moment, she regretted not being there for him, not making more of their love for each other, not moving on from their brother-sister relationship and making it into more. They both always knew that it could be more, but neither of them wanted romance to get in the way of their deep love for each other. They were frozen by the fear of that risk and didn't want to ruin the beautiful relationship that they had.

There would be no choice now. That would never happen now.

30
HOSTILE MANEUVERS

New York, United States, November 2016, Day 27

THE DOG WAS ON THE hunt. He'd flown into John F. Kennedy International Airport and hopped a cab into Manhattan. He wasn't sure he liked the mission he was on, but he didn't question clients. If they wanted someone dead, no matter who it was, he'd oblige, just as long as the price was right.

Conrad Yee had met with Dmitri Dankov in Kaliningrad to get his orders. He was nervous at the enormity of the ask and how it would change his life. Not that Yee had an ordinary life by any stretch of the imagination, but still, this mission would change it forever. Dmitri Dankov had him cornered though, and he had no choice but to go through with it. Yee would deal with Dmitri Dankov later.

Conrad had decided to stay at the New Yorker Hotel, the venue for Hillary's concession speech if she failed to win the election, less than a mile to the Javits Center, and just four blocks from where the acceptance speech would be held if she won. The New Yorker was therefore the perfect location.

He checked into the hotel, dropped his gear in the suite he'd booked on the thirty-ninth floor, and then hired a rental car from Enterprise. He had an important errand to run. He drove across the

Hudson River to Jersey City, where he had one of many stashes for use if needed.

It had been a few years since Conrad had been to this stash. As he pulled up outside the roller-shuttered storage unit, he checked his phone and sent a text to the security system inside the unit, something he had also done before leaving Vilnius and on arrival at JFK. The third all-clear was enough for him to get out of his hire car and approach the shutter with the door and the big rusty padlock and chain. Conrad reached into his jacket pocket and pulled out the key. The padlock snapped open, releasing the chain, and the door was open.

The locker looked just like a back-street car shop. Space for three vehicles, an inspection ramp, workbench, tools, and equipment for taking cars apart and putting them together again. Conrad had bought the place from the family of the former owner who had been a small-time car repair shop by day and a serial rapist by night. Conrad's client was the father of one of his victims, a multibillionaire stockbroker who had paid him to eliminate the target in a speedier, more hideous way than would have the New York Police Department.

Conrad had met him at the car shop under the guise that he had a vehicle in need of repair. Yee found his way in and strung him up on the block and tackle inside the shop, and fingernail by fingernail, toenail by toenail, followed by fingers, followed by toes, followed by penis, dismembered him alive until he could no longer take the pain and passed out in agony. Conrad finished the job, put the pieces of his body in a suitcase, and took him down to the water, where he fed his body piece by piece to the fish in the bay.

There were two vehicles in the lockup, one of them Conrad's, the 1967 Ford Mustang that he had taken for repair those years previously. He opened the trunk, and there inside was his AS50 sniper rifle wrapped in blankets and five hundred rounds in the spare wheel compartment below.

"Hello, my baby." Conrad smiled at the AS50.

Conrad dissembled the AS50 and placed the contents carefully into the roller case that he had bought at the airport, using the blankets to pad the contents from rattling around and for stashing the rounds.

He locked up the unit with the rusty padlock and chain and reset the sensors. Then he jumped in his nondescript hire car and was there and gone within ten minutes. Conrad Yee had learned not to hang around in the same place for too long.

It was still early, only one in the afternoon by the time he got back into Manhattan. He decided to return the car, take the AS50 up to his room, and head to the rooftop of the New Yorker to check out his shooting position. Up on the forty-first floor, he climbed the service stairs to the top of the roof. He had already chosen the lower balcony area of the roof for his final position.

He got his field binoculars from his pocket and surveyed the area, taking in key vantage points and any lines of sight to his position. He carefully chose the northwest corner of the building as being his perfect position, with a clear line of sight to the main entrance of the Javits Center. He would make the shot after the acceptance speech and with the MS50's explosive rounds and the five rounds in one-point-six seconds, the result would be definitive. Satisfied, he decided that he would put on his running shoes and take a look around the city.

Back in his room, Conrad pulled on his Ron Hills and a T-shirt, put on his Nikes, and headed down to reception. He turned right, then right again onto Ninth Avenue. As he jogged down the sidewalk, he remembered the smells, the sights, the goldfish bowl of humanity that he liked and loathed about New York. The eight and a half million souls who coexisted in this city, from the billionaire bankers to the rich and the famous to the homeless and the hookers on the streets trying to make ends meet. In New York, there was as much to love as there was to hate.

He cruised the first four miles until he got to West Fifty-Eighth Street. He hung a right onto Columbus Circle and headed into Central Park, up to Strawberry Fields around past the lake on his left and back down toward the Balto statue and the zoo. Conrad stopped at the zoo and could see some of the animals inside from the path. He sat down and pondered.

It looked like Hillary was ahead by two or three points, and that wasn't a great outlook for Yee. If she did win and defeat Trump, his orders were clear. Yee wasn't politically motivated. Nor was he personally motivated. This was a dire situation. One of the few men in the world to know Yee's identity, Dmitri Dankov, had held him for ransom. He had no choice—take this job with the opportunity that Trump won as his get out, or don't take the job and Dmitri Dankov would expose him to the world. Either way, Dmitri Dankov would die. Yee would take care of that personally.

He thought of Mingh, his wife, his companion, his savior, and their son, Bingwen. He loved them both so much—or as much as his disciplined life would allow him to. Conrad wasn't good at emotion; he had never been. He had been through so much throughout his life that it was hard to make connections. He knew that everything must end, and he knew that limiting his emotional connections would make the parting easier, no matter what the circumstances.

He applied the same emotional detachment to his work. It was what made him so good at his trade, apart from the skills he had studied all his life. Conrad Yee, 狗, Gǒu, or the Dog, was also the Invisible Man, and that was exactly how he intended to stay. Invisible.

Yee had been observing two scumbags walking in his direction as he sat on the bench, hassling tourists and passersby. They were big and tall, jeans hanging around their behinds, chains apparently holding them up, wearing hoodies, smoking weed, one with a skateboard, apparently for a quick getaway.

They stopped in front of the bench where Yee was sitting. "Hey, dude. Welcome to New York City."

Yee kept his head bowed and ignored them.

"Fancy pair of Nikes there, my friend. Fancy donating them to someone in need?" the other said.

Yee ignored them again.

"What's up, brother? Can't you fucking talk?" said the first.

"Have you come in the city for a piece of ass?"

"Yeah, he sort of looks like a bit of a fairy in his running gear. Don't you know this is the wrong part of the park to be picking up a piece of ass?" said the other. Yee tightened his fists as the two got angrier that he was just ignoring them.

"Hey, brother, what's your fucking problem, heh?"

"How about you give us your fucking money, hey?" One of the two skipped his skateboard up into his hands, a weapon to strike Yee with. Yee stood up with a jolt, ducked the sweep of the skateboard to his head, deflected the knife stroke away, removed the knife, and looked them both in the eye. "I would advise you gentlemen to revise your language and get out of my face before I put you both into hospital for a very long time, and that is if I am feeling generous."

The power of his movement, the ease in which he had just disarmed them both, the cold, piercing eyes, and the deep menace in his voice made the one youth look at the other. They hurried away, occasionally looking behind them at Yee as they made their way out of sight.

The last thing Yee wanted that day was to raise the attention of a duty cop on his beat, dealing with the massacre of two thugs at the hands of an unknown, seemingly harmless tourist in Central Park. Although Yee would have loved to partake in those pleasures, today was not the day to do so. He headed down 5th Avenue to West Thirty-Sixth Street and back to the New Yorker Hotel to watch the election unfold and the fate of Hillary Clinton and Donald J. Trump. The outcome of the election would also determine his fate, his action in the next several hours.

Late in the evening, it became clear that Donald Trump was the winner and that Hillary Clinton was the loser, despite her favored status early in the US presidential election. Yee didn't want to carry through with Dmitri Dankov's orders, and now he didn't have to. At first light, he hired another rental car from Enterprise, went to his stash location in Jersey City, and dropped off the sniper rifle, depositing it in the trunk of his 1967 Ford Mustang. "Until next time, baby." He left for John F. Kennedy International Airport and boarded Aeroflot 101 to Sheremetyevo Moscow International Airport under the name Ivor Shimolin, a software engineer based in San Francisco.

That was enough. Mission aborted. A close shave.

Yee understood the enormity of the victory not only for the new president, the American people, democracy, and those who had bet big but also for him personally. This was Conrad Yee, 狗, Gǒu, or the Dog's last mission. It was time to be with his faithful wife, Mingh, and teach his son, Bingwen, the lessons of life to make him bigger, better, and, most important of all, the master and not the servant.

Conrad Yee, alias Ivor Shimolin, used the eight hours and forty-five minutes to meditate and sleep. No onboard entertainment, no food, just solitude in his business class cocoon.

He had one more loose end to tie up in Moscow on his way home, and that was Dmitri Dankov. He looked forward to it.

Leeds, Yorkshire, United Kingdom, November 2016

Bob drove up to the Grace and Partners company offices across from the Meridian Center in Leeds, across from the casino. The two parking spaces reserved for Andrew Harrison and Neil Grace, the former founders and owners of Grace and Partners, had been empty since their untimely demise in different incidents the same day a week ago—one a tragic accident, and the other an apparent heroin overdose.

Bob was there to pick up the pieces, keep the business going, and maintain the value of the current book of business. That was his story, and that what he was sticking to as he drove into Harrison's reserved spot, a space that Harrison had taken from the previous business owner. Now it was Bob's turn.

Since the demise of Harrison and Grace, the business had been closed for a week to allow those to mourn, attend funerals, bury the dead, and get their heads around the future.

On Bob's first day, he would meet with the management team in the morning, the accountants over lunch, and the bank in the afternoon. He would have a conference call with a major client late that afternoon, before dinner with the top twenty from the management team in the business. It was a busy day for Bob, but off the back of his deal in Equatorial Guinea, he was in decent shape. He had just purchased a swanky apartment overlooking the Stray in nearby well-to-do Harrogate, an Aston Martin DB9, and a new outfit from Rhodes and Woods tailors. Bob was ready to start his executive life.

He had arrived last Friday morning and booked himself into the Boars Head, Ripley. He had a hearty Yorkshire breakfast, wandered the village, and met with famed local real estate agent Jeremy Hopkinson, who would show him around. He was looking for something with three bedrooms, nothing to update, pristine shape, minimal maintenance, a garage for his DB9, and walking distance to a pub.

Bob liked Jeremy, a former rugby player, captain of the local team, and a local celebrity. Jeremy took him on a Friday-afternoon tour around Nidderdale—the Sportsman's Arms, the Bridge Inn, and Royal Oak in Pateley Bridge. The New Inn in Burnt Yates, the Station in Birstwith, then on to the Wellington Inn, Darley.

As they travelled the pubs, there were many friendly faces at each—Alan the steel merchant, John the property developer and rag trade dealer, Pete the psycho painter, Kipper the local cricket and pool champion, Tim the local art dealer, Claire the local actress and star, and her boyfriend, Paul, an old money Yorkshireman and property investor, Clive the local builder and rugby aficionado, and Helen, the local girl of international mystery, having travelled the world many times over. She was serene, beautiful, blonde, and extremely attractive both physically and mentally.

Bob was going to like his new home, and by Sunday lunchtime, Alan had organized a crew for a hearty lunch, wine, and drinks at William and Victoria's. By four o'clock that day, Bob had signed a deal on 70 Beach Road, overlooking the Stray, across the road from the Hotel Du Vin, near William and Victoria's, Betty's, and the Blues Bar. Perfect.

Helen joined the crew for lunch, and Bob was enthralled by the eclectic group of beautiful people in this beautiful part of the world, with his big bank balance and new job. He had escaped Equatorial Guinea.

Monday morning, the drive was easy. The DB9 caught the eye of most, but most importantly, it was a dream to drive.

Bob's first meeting was a bit disconcerting, as the senior management team and the management didn't seem to understand what their business did apart from arrange events, make things happen, connect people, connect organizations, and interpret between countries. It was all a bit vague. They were either lying through their teeth or they genuinely didn't know, Bob surmised.

Next meeting was with the accountants. Close to $100 million in the bank. No debt. No issues. No liabilities. No lawsuits.

Bankers. Barclays. They had sent out their senior managing director all the way from London—$100 million in funds. Investment opportunities. Offer of five times the funding if needed for acquisition or investment. *Wow!* Bob thought. *That's $600 million in access funds. If I need them!*

That night, he had dinner in the Hotel Du Vin, a classic restaurant with delectable food and ambiance. It was a great team, though clueless. Committed but not knowing to what. Glad to be rid of both Harrison and Grace.

Bob was going to like this new role, he thought, as he sipped champagne with Helen at the bar after the last of the Grace and Partners crew had gone home.

Bob was going to like his new life but was waiting for the dreaded call from Dmitri Dankov. What would he want? What would Bob be prepared to give him? He would cross that bridge when he came to it.

Bob was going to enjoy his new assignment. He just hoped the Russian affiliation didn't come back to bite him.

31
JUST DESSERTS

Multiple Locations Worldwide, November 2016, Day 30

MITCH ARRIVED AT THE UNION Club front door on Greek Street, London. It was a big red door, with no sign and just a simple doorbell. Mitch pressed the button, and within thirty seconds the door opened with a friendly smile.

"Yes, sir? How can I help?"

"I am with Lord Beecham."

"Name, sir?"

"Mitch."

"Of course, sir, right this way."

Michaela walked Mitch through the glass doors to the right and to the lounge area in the rear. Lord Beecham and Colonel Collins were already there. "What took you, old boy? We started the Bloody Marys at 1!" Lord Beecham chuckled, and Colonel Collins raised his glass.

"I was finishing up things with Bella."

"How is she?" asked Colonel Collins.

"Ah, she's been better. It's been a tough week for her, but she will get through it. She's a fighter."

"Like her father." Lord Beecham raised his glass as Mitch's pint of Old Speckled Hen arrived—cold, creamy, and smooth.

"We're flying back in the morning. She wants to get home."

"Understandable," Collins said.

"Where are the rest of the boys?" Beecham asked.

"Bob is settling in up in Leeds. Not sure how he managed to get a top spot in Grace and Partners. Could be he made a deal with the devil."

Lord Beecham stroked his chin. "Do tell. What devil might that be?"

"Dmitri Dankov," Mitch said with a sigh.

"Oh, that can't be right," Colonel Collins said.

"I'm not really sure if it is right," Mitch said. "I don't know the details. But Bob's a big boy. He knows what he's doing."

"I certainly hope so," Lord Beecham said.

"So do I," Mitch said.

"And the rest of the boys?" Colonel Collins asked.

Mitch continued, "Ryan went home to his Sally, his dad, and his rugby team. Mac is bringing Bella over in a while. Sam and Ed are just finishing up at NCSC and will be over soon. James coming?"

"What, the hired help?" Lord Beecham grinned. "He is closing up Tite Street before we head out in the morning too. What flight are you on, Mitch?"

"Ten forty a.m. American Airlines."

"How's Mac?" Colonel Collins asked.

"Ah, you know Mac. Don't come much harder than him. He's okay. Not sure he really cared for Viktoria even when he was married to her, but the boy, Nikita, they had a special bond between them."

"Poor kid," Colonel Collins said. "He was proper used and abused."

"Since childhood."

"Poor kid," Lord Beecham said.

They sipped their drinks in silence. Michaela escorted Sam and Ed into the bar. "More of your guests, Lord Beecham." Even Michaela was calling him Lord Beecham now, Mitch noticed with a smile. *It's funny how the relationship between truth and fiction can get so blurred even in this innocent case that started out as a standing joke and years later turned into a reality.*

"Sam. Ed. How's it going?"

"We have been busy sorting out the details and reports for Ken, Dusty, and Jimmy."

"There's a lot of paperwork to complete," Ed said.

"Bloody inconsiderate bastards. Dying on us," Collins said.

The group looked at each other and laughed. They were joined by two more Old Speckled Hens in the fists of Sam and Ed. "Ken, Dusty, and Jimmy." They raised their glasses, clinked, and took a swig, followed by a moment of silence.

"What's happening with the bodies?" asked Mitch.

They are flying Ken to Auckland tonight. Jimmy is heading back to his wife, Jenni, in Bangkok, and Dusty is getting buried in Hereford on Thursday.

"Poor bastards," said Collins, followed by another moment of silence between these old friends.

"What the fuck happened to Dmitri Dankov?" Mitch asked. "He still in Moscow?"

Lord Beecham nodded. "That's the latest."

"Fucking rat," muttered Collins.

The group of men went quiet as they saw Michaela escorting Mac and Bella toward them. "Lord Beecham, more guests have arrived."

Mitch went to Bella and gave her a bear hug, then Mac. Then the rest of the group hugged Mac and gave Bella a reassuring hand on her shoulder, squeeze of her hand, or kiss on her cheek.

"Ah, stop fucking mooching about, you boys, and get the fucking beers in," said Mac.

They all laughed, and Lord Beecham ordered another round of Speckled Hens.

Michaela came through to the bar and ushered them up to the private dining room on the first floor, an elegant, eclectic dining room with white linen and crystal and adorned with paintings and portraits donated to the club by members past and present. It was a perfect venue for this, their last supper together.

Lord Beecham and Colonel Collins held court, and the "Do you remember the time when" stories came out. Ed picking up Mitch, and

Tom in Coleraine having a street fight with a dozen IRA men. The two guys who thought it was a good idea to sled down the Olympic ski jump slope in Kempton. Ginge Firmer and his imaginary dog, Gripper, to Lord Beecham's escapades around the world, in Hong Kong, on the yacht, sailing in the America's Cup, to Colonel Collins's escapades, including his police chase in the metropolitan Malvern Hills of Worcestershire.

Mitch kept an eye on Bella during the proceedings and knew that despite the laughter, she was hurting inside. This was good therapy, mourning with these men who knew no other way than to mourn with humor and good memories—then to move on and fight another day.

Lord Beecham had planned the menu with the chef at the Union.

Crème Du Barry, classic beef Wellington, and crème brûlée were all washed down with Beecham's favorite selection of wines. Lord Beecham was a traditionalist, and this was the time for traditional sentiments, not the new. As always with Lord Beecham, it was thought through and executed with perfection, even down to the selection of wines that had a connection to his guests, Ramsgate Syrah from the gateway of the Napa Valley, Chateauneuf-Du-Pape and Chateau Musar from the Lebanon.

Mitch observed Mac slipping off downstairs for a smoke and went to join him.

As Mac got to the front door, Mitch was behind him. They strode onto Greek Street together, and Mac pulled out his box of Marlboro Lights.

"How are you doing, my old friend?" asked Mitch, looking Mac in the eyes.

"I'm okay, I guess."

"Good to hear it. What about Nikita?"

"Arrangements have been made," Mac said, taking a drag on his cigarette. "I thought it best to go the quiet route. No big fuss. I think he'd have liked that. Like I think he'd have liked Bella to remember the good times, not the bad times."

"I think you're right. I'll tell her."

"Good," Mac said. He thought for a moment. "The poor fucker.

Nikita had been under the finger of the Black Widow all his fucking life. What chance did he really have? I got away. Left him behind. You know what, Mitch? I'm just happy to hang up my boots, head home to my little Carmen and Sienna, back to my woodshop, my little adventures, and have a rest from all this."

"I know exactly what you mean."

"You're my best pal in the world, Mitch. You're my brother."

"Don't start getting all sloppy on me, Mac." Mitch winked, and they laughed.

"Come on, let's go see if they have any Liddlesdale and have a wee dram or two."

"Or three or four." Mac winked back, and they both laughed.

Lord Beecham and Colonel Collins had been the first men in and were the last men out just before midnight as they said their last goodbyes and planned to meet up in Antigua in the spring.

Mitch just had one more leg of his journey before heading home.

"Have a good trip," Beecham and Collins offered as they headed their separate ways from Greek Street, Mitch walking, head down, his fists thrust into the pockets in the frosty November night before he hailed a cab and headed to the airport.

Moscow, Russia

Yee handed in his Ivor Shimolin papers as he arrived at immigration at Sheremetyevo Moscow International Airport. The border guards looked him up and down a couple of times and asked him some questions. Yee responded in perfect Russian, satisfying their questions. They let him through the border, backpack in hand. He headed out to the curbside, picked up a hire car, and headed to his lockup inside the MKAD circular road around Moscow.

Forty minutes later, he arrived at 9 Гагаринский пер, an old apartment block with the former main entrance being access to Conrad's private storage. The new entrance had left this old door long forgotten. He had checked the sensors when he landed and again outside the building. He looked around—no sign of any surveillance; he was okay to go in. Just ten minutes, and he would be gone again.

On the flight, he had been contemplating his preferred method to dispatch Dmitri Dankov. That was what he was here for, an M19, US-made antitank mine, plastic-cased, minimum metal design, 10.3 kilograms of explosives, thirty-three centimeters wide, and fifteen centimeters deep. He enjoyed the irony that this US-built mine would be the last thing Dmitri Dankov ever heard.

Yee knew exactly where he would find Dmitri Dankov and headed to the Metelitsa Casino, Teatralnaya Square. Sure enough, after a couple of hours, Dmitri Dankov arrived in his black Mercedes S65, along with a driver, security guard, and fellow passenger, a big, middle-aged man in a suit that didn't fit him, with bling on his hands and wrist. Yee smiled, recognizing the companion as none other than Dmitri Dankov's right-hand man, Uri Bokov.

As they went into the casino, Yee traced the car around to the parking lot and watched the security guard and driver sneak off for vodka and a cigarette. He had fifteen minutes at the most, but it would take him less than three to attach the magnetic device to the under chassis of the car and its twenty-one-gallon fuel tank.

Yee waited for two hours. He saw Dmitri Dankov and his companion walk out, greeted by his driver and security. He got in the Mercedes S65, and they made their way to the front of the casino and main road. Yee flicked the remote-control detonator—and *boom*. The Mercedes tore into pieces as the explosion ripped and triggered the fuel tank for a secondary explosion milliseconds afterward, rendering the car destroyed and all the occupants within dead. Very dead indeed.

As the explosion settled, the car in flames, Yee instinctively felt a presence. He looked over his shoulder to a figure across the street, hands in the pockets of his coat, the familiar stature of a boxer, the shoulders of a rugby player, and the steely blue eyes of an old friend.

The figure across the road tipped a wink and slung up a quick, informal salute as they stared into each other's eyes for a moment. Slowly, Yee's hazel eyes and high cheekbones turned into a smile, and he returned the salute. Then, as though synchronized, they both turned in opposite directions and disappeared.

San Francisco, California, United States

Tommy Boyle hobbled to his bar. Under the orders of his physio, he was doing more walking to get back on track. As he walked across the crosswalk, taking his time, building up his speed and his muscles, he glanced to the left. There was something wrong. The silver Ford F150 coming at him wasn't slowing down.

To Tommy's horror, the truck was speeding up. He stared in disbelief at what he was seeing.

It can't be, he thought, raising his arms to shield his body against tons of rushing metal. *Patrick O'Malley! You fucking traitor!*

The impact threw Tommy a yard or two into the street. The pain was excruciating. He realized he couldn't breathe. In those last moments, he recalled how his son-in-law had hated him, though he'd played the game right. Played the family right by marrying his daughter.

You've been a fool, Tommy thought.

He heard the truck's engine rev. He heard the squeal of tires on the pavement, and then there was nothing but darkness.

Mitch sat in his home office and looked around at the space and memories he had created over the years—his antique 1920s desk from Chicago with his Argus Cup on top, his bookshelf adorned with travel books from around the world, noting all the interesting places he had ever been. The awards, the thank-you notes, the badges of honor that no one would see but him, and occasionally Angela and Bella if they ever entered Mitch's sanctuary. His father's maps of the Normandy invasion, Mitch's medals and his father's, the sailboat, pictures of Bella, the Tintin posters on the walls, the 22 Special Air Service Plaque behind the desk with the Bravely and Truly, Boldly and Rightly Scottish plaque, and the Argus shield. The Tanglewood guitar that he had always promised himself he'd learn to play but never did,

Angela's violin against the wall, and his trusty backpack, ready to go at a moment's notice with all the tools of his trade.

The smell of the roast beef and yorkshire pudding filled the air at the house in Tiburon. Angela was bathing, her Sunday-afternoon treat, having prepared the Sunday roast. Angela wasn't much of a cook, but while married to Mitch, she had learned the staples, or at least Mitch's favorites—coq au vin, beef bourguignonne, her mother's dish, lomas saltado, sherry trifle, fresh soups, crab salad, and of course roast beef and yorkshire pudding.

Sundays had always been special to Mitch, and not just for the religious reasons but for special moments with friends in the Game Cock and the Farm Shop. He remembered his grandfather Willy, his father, Walter, moments with Angela, and seeing Bella grow. Sundays were a time for memories, connections to the past, and getting ready to build bridges to the future. A time for reflection, a time for respect.

Mitch smiled, his emotions bittersweet. He missed Jimmy, Dusty, and Ken. He was saddened about Nikita's suicide and how it impacted Bella and Mac. Sighing, he got up from his desk and walked slowly out to the porch that overlooked the bay. He sat down and took a deep breath, admiring the view of San Francisco and the Bay Bridge in the distance. It was a bright, sharp November afternoon. Mitch had met the boys, Lord Beecham, and Colonel Collins for a couple of beers earlier. When he got home, Angela was in the bath, and before him was Bella tapping away on her Apple MacBook Air with her beautiful olive skin, her golden-brown hair, and her hazel eyes.

Mitch had spent the last twenty years observing Bella, watching her grow, learn, and make mistakes, with bumps on the way, setbacks, and celebrations. He'd seen Bella's fierce, determined, and independent personality. Mitch found it hard to believe what had happened over the past several weeks, and in that time, he had seen a change in Bella, growing from a state of innocence to a woman ready for the world, a woman who now understood cynicism, a woman who understood deceit and death, a woman who in the new year would start her career with the CIA.

Bella was the love of Mitch's life, and he would dearly miss her, but it was time for Bella to find her wings and find her own way.

He thought about his good friend Sam and could see him in his farmstead with Emily, his sheep, and his garden. He would be reading the world news, trimming his wisteria, planting his daffodils, chasing his sheep around the paddock, doing his crossword, and gazing into the Herefordshire sky and seeing his fallen friends from times long past. Sam would keep himself busy in retirement. He was built that way. His father had taught him well, and he would develop his community and civil duties in the same selfless way that he had all his life.

He remembered the team, as they were, when they were starting out, how they huddled in the back of that snow vehicle in Norway, how they were loyal, there for each other, no matter what.

He wasted no time on those enemies he had encountered, the Colombians, Tommy Boyle, Dmitri Dankov, and the rats, Harrison and Grace. He thought of Bob taking their places. *Good on Bob*, Mitch thought. *He deserves a fresh start.* And things were looking bright for him with a Yorkshire belle he had met, Helen.

He looked back at Bella and wondered about her journey, hoping that she would see no more bad, that she would avoid being further corrupted by the world at large, and that she could save a part of her beautiful innocence forever. But he feared for the worse and knew that life wasn't really like that; the longer you live, the more you get tainted from exposure to trials and tribulations.

Mitch looked down at his hands, at the wrinkles appearing. He turned his palms and saw the scars and thought about how violent his life had been and the danger he had encountered, and for a moment, in that house in Tiburon, he wondered if he was finally home.

Angela appeared at the door, scented, out of the bath, as always trying to maintain a happy tone.

"Hey, you two! Are you ready for roast beef and yorkies?"

"Damn right, Mum," Bella said, slamming down the lid of her Apple Mac.

"I'll set the table," she said and shot Mitch a big smile.

They all went into the kitchen. The trio engaged in a domestic routine, one that gave comfort to Mitch and one he knew gave comfort to the two ladies in his life.

"Mitch, can you get the beef and the yorkies out of the oven?" Angela asked as she started to mash the potatoes and dish up the carrot, swede mash, broccolini, parsnips, and gravy.

"These yorkies look pretty good," Mitch said and started to carve the beef. When he was done, he popped a bottle of his favorite Chateau Neuf Du Pape.

Within ten minutes, they were seated at the table, just the three of them, their Sunday tradition. Mitch liked traditions, as did Angela and Bella. Bella said grace, a different one each week but inevitably with some repetition. Today she was in the mood for one of her favorites, one she had recently learned but one her mother and father knew well.

"There are good ships, there are wood ships, there are ships that sail the sea, but the best ship is family, and may that ever be!"

She smiled at Angela and Mitch, and they smiled back with unutterable pride. Mitch raised a glass and a simple "Cheers."

Bella added, "Bon appetit," and winked at her father.

It was 3:00 p.m. Another tradition. The time for Mitch's Sunday ritual, a pass down from generations. Was it the queen's speech, or was it that it was when Grandad would get back from the pub on a Sunday after time was called at 2:30 p.m.? Doors closed at 2:45 p.m., and Grandad was home by 3:00 p.m. Was it coincidence that roll call was at 3:00 p.m. at the Game Cock for after-Sunday-roast drinks or, for the married boys, actual Sunday roast at 3:00 p.m.?

As they ate, they exchanged small talk about the weekend and the week to come. But Mitch knew they were all thinking about their friendships, the past several weeks, and the past extending far, far back, beyond the recent violent events that had shaken their lives and threatened their country. Mitch looked at Bella and knew she was deep in thought about Nikita. He glanced at Angela and wondered where her thoughts were at that moment. He deduced that her father was never far from her thoughts. Mitch thought about his old pal Mac in his woodwork shop in Santiago with his crazy blond mop, shirtless, in a pair of dungarees and Ronny Kray glasses. Mitch couldn't help but laugh to himself.

Then he thought about his old friend Paul—then Brad, Dusty, Ken, and Jimmy—and just shook his head. Jimmy.

After Sunday dinner, they all cleaned up together, just like they had for the past twenty years. They didn't bring up any of the dead. That was not how it worked. What was the point?

Mitch kissed Bella on the forehead and gave her a big hug.

"Take care, Dad. I love you," said Bella, barely above a whisper.

"More than the moon and the stars, the mountains and the seas," Mitch said.

Angela looked up at Mitch with a big, hopeful smile and a kiss.

"I love you, baby," Mitch said.

"I love you too, *my Mitch.*"

Mitch recognized this as a phrase she had adopted when they were courting all those years ago. It had always struck him that the phrase seemed to indicate a sense of ownership and pride back then, and it still did. After they finished cleaning up, Mitch went into his office and retrieved his backpack. He walked out onto the porch. Angela and Bella looked momentarily alarmed.

"Where are you going with that?" Angela asked.

Mitch said, "I've got one more bridge to cross. On this."

He patted the seat of his new ride, a black Enduro Pro mountain bike. "I always said I wanted to ride across the Golden Gate Bridge. There's no time like the present."

"Why put off to tomorrow what you can do today—or something like that." Bella laughed.

"You're a wise young lady," Mitch said.

Mitch got on the bike. He looked over his shoulder and saw them both waving at him. As he pushed hard on the pedal, he overheard Bella mutter under her breath, "When will you come back home?"

The question pained him, as did Angela's reply. "When he's ready."

He slowed, looked back again, and saw them both turn and go inside.

Mitch freewheeled down the hill and onto Tiburon Boulevard. He hung a right onto the cycle path and followed the water's edge onto Blackie's Pasture to pay his respects. Mitch pulled up to the statue and looked him in the eye. Blackie looked right back at him, one soldier to another.

It had been a strange few weeks. *What a strange life*, Mitch thought as he kicked off and carried on his journey through Sausalito. He anticipated riding past Pogios, where he and Angela would go on dates. Such a beautiful view of the city, up the hill, under the freeway, getting a glimpse of Cavallo Point, Lord Beecham's Shed that housed the Saloon and operations center. Then he would reach the Pacific Ocean side of the Golden Gate Bridge.

Mitch rode on. Bella was still on his mind. This would be her last Christmas at home. Then he thought about Angela, realizing that when Bella left for Langley and the East Coast, the house would be empty. Completely empty. It would be a home full of memories and ghosts. Perhaps he might change. Perhaps he might return to the marital home. Perhaps … perhaps … perhaps.

As Mitch neared the middle of the bridge, he looked to his right and saw what he thought was a blue-and-white fishing boat heading out to sea. He paused, realizing that it was Sunday. He looked down again at the sky-blue-and-white vessel. Something instinctively told him that there was something not right as he stopped the bike to take a closer look at the boat as it danced between the ocean spray, the drifts of fog that had blown in from offshore, and the fading sunlight. He could make out a man on the deck. Mitch reached into his jacket pocket, removed his compact field binoculars, and focused on the man standing alone. He had silver hair, and although the distance was too great from atop the high bridge, Mitch could have sworn that the man's eyes were bright blue. The man just stood there looking directly at Mitch.

Mitch stood aside his Enduro Pro motionless. *Who the hell is that? It can't be!*

Just as quickly as it appeared, the *Jack Junior* was gone. For the first time in Mitch's life, he was visibly shaken, as if he had just seen a ghost. He stood there motionless for ten minutes, checking the sea below him until it was dark. The sky-blue-and-white fishing boat and its captain were gone forever. Mitch knew he would never see it again.

Mitch trembled at the sight of the *Jack Junior*. It had seemed so real. And maybe it was. Who was to say that ghosts didn't roam the land and the sea, that they didn't reside in the mind and soul? He took several deep breaths. Then he turned around. He'd made up his mind. He was going home. Home to Angela. *Home.* The word was full of comfort and hope. Why should he cut himself off from either?

Mitch flicked his lights on and turned 180 degrees. He'd cross the bridge on another day ... perhaps. Now, he was going home. Home to Angela. And home to Bella.

AUTHOR BIO

Willy Mitchell

WILLY MITCHELL WAS BORN IN Glasgow, Scotland. He spent a lot of time in bars as a kid growing up, in his youth and into adulthood. He always appreciated the stories. Some true, some imagination and some delusional. But these stories are true. Willy Mitchell was there!

A shipyard worker, he headed down from Scotland to Yorkshire with his family to work in the steel mills. He retired and turned to writing some of the tales that he had listened to over all those years and focused on bringing those stories to life.

Operation ARGUS

Operation ARGUS is fast paced, thoughtful and personal. An insightful story that touches the mind, the heart and creates a sense of intrigue in the search of the truth.

While sitting in the Rhu Inn in Scotland one wintry night, Willy Mitchell stumbles across a group of men, in civilian clothes, full of adrenalin, like a group of performers coming off a stage, wherever that stage had been that night. To the watchful eye it was clear that these men were no civilians. Close knit, banter and beer, yet completely alert as each of them checked him out as they looked at his eyes and into his soul. Willy Mitchell would learn in time that this group would become referred to as call sign Bravo2Zero.

Operation ARGUS is a story of fiction based around true events as five former, and one serving, Special Air Service soldiers converge on San Francisco for a funeral of their good friend to find his apparent heart attack is not as it seems. A similar concoction of Polonium-210 was used to assassinate Litvinenko in London years previously

Bikini Bravo

Bikini Bravo continues to follow the adventures of Mitch, his daughter Bella and the team of Mac, Bob, Sam as they uncover what seems an unthinkably complex web of unlikely collaborators but for a seemingly obvious common good - power, greed and money.

Many years ago, Mitchell stumbles across a bar in Malindi, Kenya, West Africa and overhears the makings of a coup in an oil rich nation of West Africa. Could it be true that a similar plan was being hatched today?

Lord Beecham puts together the pieces of the puzzle and concludes that the Russians along with the Mexican Drug Cartels and power-hungry group of Equatorial Guineans have put together an ingenious plot to take over Africa's sixth largest oil producing nation in their attempt to win influence in Africa, the Cartels desire for turning dirty money into good and the Africans to win power and influence.

Another book of fiction by Mitchell that masterfully flirts with fiction and real-life events spanning the globe and touching on some real global political issues.

Mitch's daughter, Bella is the emerging hero in this, the second book of the Argus series.

Cold Courage

Cold Courage starts with Willy Mitchells grandfather meeting with Harry McNish in Wellington, New Zealand in 1929. In exchange for a hot meal and a pint or two, McNish told his story of the Endurance and the Imperial Trans-Antarctic Expedition of 1914.

According to legend, 1913, Sir Ernest Shackleton posted a classified advertisement in the London Times, Men Wanted: For hazardous journey, small wages, bitter cold, long months of complete darkness, constant danger, safe return doubtful. Honor and recognition in case of success. According to Shackleton, that advert attracted over 5,000 applicants, surely a sign of the times.

Following the assassination of Archduke Ferdinand earlier that year, at the beginning of August, the First World War was being declared across Europe, and with the blessing of the King, the approval to 'proceed' from the First Sea Lord, the Endurance set sail from Plymouth, England on its way to Buenos Aires, Argentina to meet with the entire 28-man crew, and sail South.

Shackleton was keen to win back the polar exploration crown for the Empire and be the first to transit across the Antarctic from one side to the other.

The Endurance and her sister ship, the Aurora both suffered defeat, resulted in thirty-seven of Shackleton's men being stranded at opposite ends of the continent, shipless, cold, hungry, and fighting mother nature herself for survival.

This is a tale of the great age of exploration and the extraordinary journey that these men endured, not only in Antarctica but upon their return to England amidst the Great War.

This is the story of the Endurance, the Imperial Trans-Antarctic Expedition of 1914, and all that was happening in those extraordinary times.

Printed in the United States
By Bookmasters